She

D0859174

EFFIN'

Hates

ME

She
EFFIN'
Hates
ME

a love story

SCARLETT SAVAGE

Skyhorse Publishing

Skyhorse Publishing books may be purchased in bulk at special discounts for sales promotion, corporate gifts, fund-raising, or educational purposes. Special editions can also be created to specifications. For details, contact the Special Sales Department, Skyhorse Publishing, 307 West 36th Street, 11th Floor, New York, NY 10018 or info@skyhorsepublishing.com.

Skyhorse® and Skyhorse Publishing® are registered trademarks of Skyhorse Publishing, Inc.®, a Delaware corporation.

Visit our website at www.skyhorsepublishing.com.

10 9 8 7 6 5 4 3 2 1

Library of Congress Cataloging-in-Publication Data

Savage, Scarlett.
She effin' hates me : a love story / Scarlett Savage.
pages cm
Summary: "Based on the award-winning play, She Effin' Hates Me is about three women relearning to love one another for who they are ... and more importantly, for who they're not"-- Provided by publisher.
ISBN 978-1-62636-556-8 (pbk.)
1. Women--Fiction. 2. Families--Fiction. 3. Female friendship--Fiction 4. Love stories. gsafd I. Title.
PS3619.A848S44 2014
813'.6--dc23
2013040783

Printed in the United States

To Daphernunu and Jessaboo, my Funny Bunny and my Baby Lady: You are the lights of my life, the pride of my soul, the treasures of my heart. Without you, I am nothing.

To Thomas Bruce Mills (*A Love for Traitors*), writer, would-be Olympian, intellect, and the best friend a girl ever had for more than a quarter of a century now: Here's to twenty-five more creative years . . . but with fewer divorces on both our ends!!

To my parents of choice, Joel and Edith Ellis. Joel, your stories about Vietnam inspired so many of the stories Buddy tells about "Jimmy." I found a way to put you onstage without putting you onstage! And Edith, at one point Buddy tells Suzanne, "Your mom was a woman, all right—wars are fought over women like that." I can't think of a better description of Joel's love for you. Thank you both for adopting me into your family and for loving me in the bad times as well as the good.

And finally, to Bruce "the Shark" Allen, who helped inspire the character of Buddy McKinley by approaching me during intermission at a fund-raising run (for Sexual Assault Support Services in New Hampshire) of my rape-awareness play "Dear Daddy, Love Cassie," and saying, "So, genius, when are you going to write a romantic lead for an old fart like me?" I knew immediately what he was saying. So many actors hit fifty or sixty and suddenly the phone stops ringing; for women, it's even worse. And why? Do we stop falling in love after age fifty? Stop learning life lessons? Stop feeling? No. Thank you for reminding me of that, Bruce. And to his two wonderful daughters, Susan and Katherine, his lovely wife, Jean, his amazing sister, Karen, and so many others in the Portsmouth theater community. I still miss you every day.

(And yes, I'll tell everyone that you were so dubbed "the Shark" because as a book reviewer you so ravaged Peter Benchley's *Jaws* in the *Boston Globe* that it prompted Steven Spielberg to name his mechanical shark after you!!!)

PART ONE

ONE

"You know, as your mother, I'd rather give myself a bikini wax with Super Glue than criticize a single thing about you. But, honey, I say this with love—when are you going to do something about your weight?"

Suzanne had been waiting for that comment to find its way into the conversation ever since she'd grabbed a third glazed donut at breakfast.

"I'm only a size eight, Ma."

Suzanne leaned back in her lawn chair, her damp tendrils framing her face as the sun streamed down on them in the front yard of Ava's house, where Suzanne was currently "hanging her hat," as her late father would have said. And it was a beautiful place to be able to do that, she thought fondly, looking through the lush, leafy yard that looked out onto the Piscataqua River. The three-bedroom, two-hundred-year-old button house was snug, but the high ceilings and smart layout gave the illusion of roominess; it had been modernized without destroying its antique value. Ava had seen to every detail of that operation personally when she'd moved in. There were several maple trees, a couple of ash, and four oak trees in the yard, between here and the riverfront, and the leaves were just beginning to hint that they'd soon burst from their deep green to their scarlet, russet, and walnut.

She hadn't travelled much in her lifetime, but every autumn she still felt blessed to live in Portsmouth, New Hampshire, right on the waterfront.

"That's four sizes smaller than the 'average' woman my age," Suzanne continued, just as though she and her mother hadn't had this same conversation a thousand times in the past ten years. "You can't force me into some ridiculous Hollywood standard just because Madison Avenue has somehow duped women into draconian methods of starvation in order to consider themselves attractive."

Suzanne tossed her braid primly, as always, priding herself for turning a fondness for cheeseburgers and fries into a political stance.

"Besides," she added, by force of habit, "it's just my baby weight."

"Your baby just turned eighteen. That's baby weight with some staying power," Ava observed; her tone of voice brooked no excuses, for this or any other matter. "Now that you're finally divorcing that bum, I would think you'd want to clean up your act altogether. You were eighteen years old the last time you were on the dating circuit. And thirty-six is a lot saggier than eighteen, if you don't mind my saying."

"Ma, I'm hardly fat, or . . ."

"And speaking of her, when is the princess coming back from freshman orientation?" Ava interrupted her. "After all, I'm not going to be around forever, so she'd better see me while I'm still here to see."

"You'll outlive us all," Suzanne said airily. "You're too tough and bitchy to die, and you damn well know it."

Ava snorted, giving her a hurt look, but she did not, Suzanne noted, deny it.

"Anyway," Suzanne informed her, "I just talked to her, and she said she had to check her schedule. Probably later this afternoon, by bus, or early tomorrow morning."

She flipped the magazine calmly, but each page snapped as she turned it.

"What she's *really* doing, of course, is checking with this new guy, Brandon, making sure that works for him. Ten to one, she's spending all her time with him these days."

"Oh, what the crap is that?" Ava scoffed. She put a yellow mum next to an orange gerber daisy; she'd been tempted to use a hollowed-out pumpkin rather than a crimson vase, but regretfully decided September 1 wasn't quite in pumpkin season. "She's way too young to 'check her schedule.' She's got her whole life to throw away on some loser, so why can't she spare a week or two for an old lady before she goes off to college? What was the last one, the one with the hair that stood straight up? A minister's son?" She shook her head grimly. "A horny teenage boy stole your last days of childhood from me, and now the sons of bitches are after Molly's. How can a mere grandmother compete with that?"

"The one before that got her forty percent off at L.L.Bean, remember?" Suzanne remembered. "I really liked that one."

"Honey, I'm more important than a silly date. And if I'm not, well, damn it, I *should* be."

Now Ava hauled out the big gun.

"I know you like to joke about it, but the fact of the matter is that I really *will* be gone in the not-too-distant future. I don't always feel as strong as I used to. In fact," she touched the back of her hand to her forehead dramatically, "I'm feeling a bit faint as we speak."

"Are you serious?" Suzanne leapt to her feet and led her mother over to the picnic bench; since her father died eight years ago, Ava's frequent jokes about her mortality didn't strike her quite so funny as they once did. "Did you take your blood pressure pills today? I knew I shouldn't have let you work out here in this sun . . ."

"*Let* me?" Ava demanded; she was getting impatient with Suzanne's overreactions to the tiniest jokes. "We've got quite a ways to go before we get to the part where you 'let' me do things. And, yes, yes, yes, of course I took the blood pressure pills. Do you think I'm crazy enough not to? And I took the vitamins. And yes, yes, yes, lots of water, and I exercise every day." She glanced at her watch. "But you're right. I should get inside and get moving. The new neighbors are moving in this week, and I want to make sure that the flower arrangement is ready. First appearances are very important, you know."

Suzanne watched her closely for another moment, to Ava's annoyance, just to be sure. Finally, she returned to her lawn chair. "How do you know they're moving in so soon, Mom? Have you met them?"

"No," Ava said breezily "But like any good neighbor, I took out my footstool and peeked in the windows."

"*Mother!*"

"Oh, I know, I know," Ava picked up the broom and started sweeping up the errant stems and petals that had fallen to the ground as she created her neighbor's welcome gift; bits of yellow mums and orange gerbera daisies decorated the ground, as though evidence of some flower-related crime. "It was a violation of my neighbors' privacy, but they weren't home. Like your father used to say, 'Cop didn't see it, I didn't do it.'"

Suzanne leaned back again in her chair, her eyes disapproving, but the corner of her mouth twitched into a smile.

"He stole that line from George Carlin. But your nosiness is getting out of hand—worse than a child's, I swear." Suzanne flipped another page to see who was wearing what to yet another unnecessary awards show. "Molly gives me less headaches than you do. Just remember, do what you have to do in this world, but if you get caught, lose my number—I'm not dipping into my cigarette money to bail you out."

"God forbid—and I *certainly* wouldn't expect you to dip into the money you've got earmarked for The American Lung Cancer Society." Ava watched

Suzanne light up the fifth cigarette she'd had in the past hour, then patted her own ample bosom. "That's why I always keep a little extra in my 'lucky pocket.'"

"You know," Suzanne warned as she exhaled loudly to annoy her mother, "your nosiness is going to get you into big trouble one day, young lady, you mark my words."

"Who the hell are you calling a *young* lady?" Ava demanded. "Look, I just needed to know if it was someone interesting, someone with stories to tell, who's not afraid to have a good time. God forbid it's some old fuddy-duddy who's going to discuss the frequency and consistency of his bowel movements the first time we say hello."

"This is the nicest retirement village on the whole Seacoast," Suzanne pointed out. "We looked at them all. You're the one who wanted to live right here in good ol' sunny, cobblestoned Portsmouth."

"If I can't see water, I don't want to live there." Ava repeated her lifelong motto firmly. "Not to mention, I have to be where I can get my fix of Molly Malone's Irish stew—it was the one thing even your father admitted they did better than our restaurant." She dumped a load of stems into the trash. "But the thing is, honey, people under fifty call it a retirement village; we call it 'A Place for Human Raisins to Turn into Mush.'"

"Give your neighbors a little credit!!" Suzanne cried indignantly. "*You're* not like that; maybe some of them aren't, either."

"Of course *I'm* not like that. *I'm* an extraordinary lady." Ava smiled to take the edge off the pompous words. "At any rate, I hope the new neighbor hates bridge and golf as much as I do, otherwise they bug you constantly. 'Just give it a try; you'll enjoy it if you give it a chance.'" She snorted. "Pushers, that's what they are, just as bad."

"I'm not sure that someone trying to get you to go golfing can be compared to a drug dealer, Mother, but A for effort."

"I mean, *golfing!*" Ava spat. "What's the point? You try to hit something into a hole. Well, if a man can't do it in the bathroom, how the hell's he gonna do it on a great big field . . . with a much smaller hole, no less?"

"Again, Mom," Suzanne grinned despite herself, "not quite the same thing."

"I'm telling you, a good neighbor is the key to *living*, and not just *existing*, in a place like this. Just someone to hang out with. As long as they like to do all the same stuff as I do, of course. If they don't, they can just go to hell, and I'll tell them so."

"I'll just bet you will, you old bat."

Ava gave her a warning look and fell silent for a moment, concentrating on her arrangement, the soothing silent harmony of the colors in the basket casting a calming spell on her. A rare quiet moment passed between the two women. The sun shone down on the tops of their heads, and a cool breeze from the shore, a hundred yards away, whirled up to take the slow burn of the strong rays away.

"What did the message say, exactly?" Ava asked innocently, snipping away at a mum head. Without being told, Suzanne knew exactly which message she was referring to.

"You were right there when I played it, Mom."

"Yes, well, my memory isn't quite what it used to be, whether I take my ginko or not."

Suzanne sighed.

"Molly said, 'I'll be home Friday afternoon, Mom. And I'd like it if you, me, and Grandma could have a talk. I've got something very important I want to tell you.' Then, you know, she said good bye, I love you, some kind of crap like that."

She hoped that would be enough to satisfy Ava and get her to shut up—at least on this particular topic—but she also knew that was wishful thinking.

"Well," Ava persisted, "what was her *tone* like? Did she sound like it was good news, or bad news?"

Suzanne paused, recalling her daughter's words, her inflection; more than anything she recalled the wall of worry that had crashed into her at Molly's words. But after repeated listenings, she had been no more the wiser as she was on the first go-round.

"She sounded like it was . . . *news*." Suzanne said at last. She continued to flip through her magazine, but she realized she was more yanking than turning the pages. *Don't take it out on the magazine,* she chided herself. *You still want to see pictures of the new Johnny Depp movie.*

"No clues at all?"

"I get the idea," Suzanne conceded, "that it's got something to do with this Brandon."

Ah, I've gone and done it, she cursed herself. *I've made him "this" Brandon. I'm officially an old bat. A thirty-six-year-old bat.*

"Well," Ava sniffed in her *I'm-not-kidding* voice, "she'd better not be engaged, or moving in with a boy, or anything ridiculous like that."

Suzanne sat perfectly still. If she froze completely, maybe time would stand still, and her mother wouldn't be able to finish this train of thought.

"Or *pregnant*, worse yet," Ava continued.

Damn it! The accursed word had been spoken aloud. Now the gods had been officially tempted.

She wondered if she should get up, turn around three times, and spit, the way her friend Thomas Mills did when he'd slipped and mentioned the name "Macbeth" in a theatre once. (Apparently, you were supposed to call it "the Scottish play.") She wondered what euphemism you were supposed to use for pregnancy you desperately hoped didn't exist.

Most women loved being told they looked young, and most of the time Suzanne was no exception. But Suzanne looked so young that whenever she introduced people to her daughter, they'd often ask both Molly's and her own age and then she could see them mentally doing the math.

Thirty-six minus eighteen equals too damn young to have a baby in this day and age.

She'd been eighteen when she pushed Molly out of her vagina and into this cold cruel world; the very same age Molly was now. The age that had seemed plenty mature at the time now seemed terrifyingly young—infantile, in fact.

Well, they say history repeats itself. Apparently they say that for a reason, damn it.

"At her age, just heading off to college," Ava continued her tirade, blithely unaware of the embolism her daughter was having. "Although, it's not like when *you* were young, sweetie. She won't have to give up college, though, not like you did. Universities are all set up for that sort of thing now—heck, even some of the high schools."

Ava snorted in disgust at this twenty-first century marvel.

"When *I* was in high school, if you got in trouble, they just shipped you off to your Aunt Sandy's in Texas," she confided, "whether you actually *had* an Aunt Sandy in Texas or not."

"Really?" Suzanne felt a bit faint, suddenly, even though she was already sitting down.

"Oh, yes, indeedy-do. But nowadays . . ." She stopped to point at Suzanne with a dahlia. "Did you know that Portsmouth High School now has day care for the *students* who have children?"

"No, I didn't know that, Mother." Now Suzanne felt downright nauseated.

Day cares in *high schools*?

It was truly a world gone insane.

There was a fine line, she felt, between making the best of a bad situation and encouraging bad behavior. She wasn't sure which side of the fence the topic of "day cares in high schools" landed on.

"Well, if she *is* pregnant, I'll just kill her." Ava pulled out two bright yellow mums in order to make way for three orange tulips a bit more violently than she'd intended, and lost a mum head in the process. "I mean it. I'll just kill her, throwing away her life like that."

She thought for a moment as she wrestled with the greenery, as Suzanne tried to keep her breathing even and calm. She flipped right past pictures of the Royal Baby—she didn't feel like seeing him just now—and found that even Johnny Depp's perfect face didn't have its usual calming effect on her.

"You were only twenty-eight when you had me," Suzanne said weakly.

"Twenty-eight is a hell of a lot more than a decade older than eighteen." Ava snipped another flower to emphasize her point. "That's a formative ten years. Especially in my day."

In my day. Suzanne wondered how often she'd heard those words in her life. Too many, she was certain, to count up just now.

"I won't kill her till after she has the baby, though," Ava decided after a moment. "Oh, I just love babies! I always wished you'd had more than one—just not with that bum."

"*You* only had one." Suzanne pointed out.

"That was different—after I had you, I couldn't have another one."

Suzanne hadn't known that; she felt a wave of sympathy for her mother.

"I didn't know that," she said softly. "You never said anything." After a moment, she pressed gently, "Why not?"

"Because," Ava said emphatically, "it hurt too damn much."

Well, I walked right into that one.

Suzanne laughed. That was one of the joys of having Ava for a mother; she was always good for a laugh or two—especially when she didn't mean to be funny.

"But to have a baby around again . . . !" Ava said wistfully. "I love their chubby little legs and their bellies. I love their smell."

"Mother . . ."

But it was too late; baby lust had already seized Ava in its mighty grip.

"Oh, a baby is a wonderful thing to have around the house!" she squealed delightedly. "Especially during the summer, waddling around its little wading pools—and on holidays!" She reached forward and grasped Suzanne's arm happily, her eyes aglow with pure grandma fever. "Remember how we used to put Molly under the Christmas tree, and she'd stare up at the twinkly lights?"

Suzanne cleared her throat loudly, hoping to drag Ava back down to planet Earth, where she could realize the actual ramifications of Molly's pregnancy, beyond the smell of baby powder and no-tears shampoo. Thankfully, Ava took the hint.

"But no, no, no, she's too young," Ava added hastily. "*Far* too young. So we'll just kill her. That's what we'll do."

She hummed for a moment, as she worked on her arrangement, before adding, "We'll kill her, and then we'll keep her baby."

Suzanne jumped to her feet and glared at her mother. "*Mother!*"

"What?" Ava asked, her eyes completely innocent.

"My daughter," Suzanne said firmly, "is *not pregnant.*"

"You're *sure*? Absolutely, completely sure? No room for doubt at all?"

"Yes, of course I'm sure." Suzanne snapped.

Her heart was pounding in her throat, and she realized she'd let herself get more worked up than she'd meant to.

"Look, I'm sorry I snapped at you, Mom. I'm just—well, as you can imagine, it's a sensitive topic for me."

"It ain't a picnic topic for me, either," Ava reminded her, arching her eyebrow.

"I know, I know, and I apologized to you for the shame of not being able to hold your head up in church a million times already."

Ava snorted a little, but gave her daughter a guilty look. The second she'd held Molly for the first time, moments after her birth, an innocent bystander would have thought the idea to have Molly in the first place had been Ava's.

"But, I'm telling you," Suzanne insisted, "I know my daughter, Mom. I got pregnant because I was more concerned with sneaking beer out of your supply than I was about getting my hands on some birth control."

"You can't imagine the amount of pride that last sentence has given birth to within me," Ava said wryly.

"My point," Suzanne willed her voice to sound calm; in reality, her heart had jumped up into her throat the moment the words *pregnant* and *Molly* had been spoken in the same sentence, "is that Molly is much smarter than to get pregnant by accident."

"Oh. You're probably right, at that." Ava looked oddly disappointed, sipping at her iced tea a bit forlornly.

Then again, once upon a time, anyone who knew me would have said the same thing about me.

Damn it!! Suzanne nearly wailed out loud. This persistent inner voice was going to drive her insane.

"Hmmm. Well, darn it all," Ava's voice was ironically tinged with sadness. "I was just starting to like the idea of four generations of Applebaum women in the world. Just think what a nice Christmas card we'd have, with the baby right in the center."

"You don't know it'd be a girl—and by the way, this is completely hypocritical of you." Suzanne looked up at her mother, fanning herself with her magazine to try to dry her sweaty face. "When I told you I was going to have Molly, you freaked—no, more than freaked, you had a total *meltdown*. Jesus, we had to get you a bucket of ice and a compress for you head."

"As well as an eight-ounce glass of vodka, straight up," Ava nodded. "The good ol' drinking days."

"But," Suzanne squeaked incredulously, "if *Molly* turns around and does the *exact same thing*, you're suddenly Granny Poppins? It's not fair!"

"Well, it's different." Ava looked at her as though this should be obvious. "You were *my* child. If Molly gets pregnant, it doesn't make *me* look completely devoid of proper parenting skills."

"Wow, you are really mean today," Suzanne marveled. "Are you sure you're taking all your meds?"

Ava heaved a deep, guilty breath and put a hand on Suzanne's shoulder. "Okay, fine. The jig is up, you caught me. I'm not taking them."

Suzanne jumped up, dropping the magazine and nearly kicking over her Diet Coke.

"*What?* Mother, are you trying to . . ."

"I'm selling them on the black market and using the proceeds to hire exotic dancers to perform on my coffee table," Ava confessed, cutting her off. "I feel so much better now that it's all out in the open."

Suzanne glared at her mother for a full minute, but she realized she'd set herself up for it.

I'll know better next time, she reassured herself, just like she always did, knowing, just like she always did, that she wouldn't.

She pulled yet another cigarette from her pack of American Spirit, hoping it would annoy her mother, and it did.

"Well," Suzanne mused, picking up her magazine and settling back down in her lawn chair, "at least I know she hasn't done anything *stupid*."

"That's good, dear," Ava replied in a voice that implied Suzanne couldn't possibly be sure of any such thing.

Suzanne diplomatically chose to ignore it. It was either that or rip off her mother's head, and what with the patrol cars coming by every few minutes . . . best not to take the chance.

"Which is not to say she's *never* done anything stupid," Suzanne conceded. "But she seems to stay stupid within, well, the reasonable sphere of stupidity, if you know what I mean. I mean, kids do stupid things. And afterwards . . . well, not *right* afterwards, usually, when the sting of embarrassment has faded a bit, she comes to me, and we talk about it. Isn't that fabulous?"

"*No!*" Ava stamped her foot, pointing her trowel at her daughter. "It is many things, but it is most certainly *not* fabulous. Your generation is all about talk, talk, talk; you kids gush about every single emotion you have every moment that you have it. In my day," she raised her chin proudly, as Suzanne groaned at the phrase, "we knew how to keep things to *ourselves*. For the love of God, there are some things that just shouldn't be discussed. And there are even more things that no one wants to damn well hear. That's what my generation knew."

"And you're allowed your opinion, no matter how misguided," Suzanne assured her. "For my part, I feel like . . . like . . . like such a *mom* during those talks with Molly. Think about it; in this day and age, my kid actually talks to me, keeps the communication going. You know how *rare* that is? And not just the little things, either—the big things. She called me from this party, once, when her girlfriend was too drunk to drive her home, so I could go get her. Or the time she got stoned behind the toolshed after school, or when she's . . ."

"Uh-uh-uh!" Ava clapped her hands firmly over her ears, spun around, and started shouting, "La-la-la! La-la-la! Too much information!"

"Did your granddaughter teach you that trick?" Suzanne asked, amused.

"I saw one of the kids on *Friends* do it—that Chandler, I think." Ava said; Suzanne should have guessed. Every time the show played—and it seemed to play at least eight or ten times a day—Ava watched each episode rabidly, as though it was the first time she'd seen it.

Now, she pulled her hands down from her ears, eyeing her child darkly.

"But, you see, that's where you and I differ as parents. There are certain things I just plain damn well *don't want* to know." She patted Suzanne on the shoulder affectionately. "Oh, I suppose I want you to feel that you can confide in me—but do you actually have to *do* it?"

"So," Suzanne grinned, "I take it that means you haven't forgiven me for telling you about the time I transcended out of maidenhood?"

"No, I have not," Ava retorted, "and neither have all twenty of my higher powers. You're going to burn everywhere from hell to Hades for making me privy to *that* information."

"Sorry."

"I doubt that."

Suzanne's phone alarm shrieked, splitting the afternoon air. "Time for your blood pressure pill, Mom."

"Who the hell made you the medication police?" Ava was not ready to have her daughter be her boss just yet, damn it, and probably never would be.

Her husband's death, eight years ago, was still fresh in her memory too, but Jimmy had been out-and-out sick for *years*. If it wasn't one thing, it was another, from arthritis to adult onset diabetes to emphysema. First glasses, then insulin, then a cane; hearing aids and a bucketful of pills followed not long after. His body, once literally glowing with health, was chipped down bit by bit over the years, until nearly every bit of him needed help to function.

But she, so far, had a perfectly clean bill of health, and she also had a doctor to tell Suzanne just that. Still, Suzanne treated her like she had one foot in the grave and was clinging desperately to the side with both hands. It made her feel old, and she hated it.

"You know, I hope your daughter doesn't start to worry like you do. Actually," she corrected herself in afterthought, "I hope she *does*. I just hope she *does* start to worry just like you do, and then she starts pestering you relentlessly, and finding ways to turn every single perfectly pleasant conversation into a health quiz."

Then Ava's cell phone, perched as always on its charger right in its place next to the landline phone, went off, singing its delicate bell-like ring.

"What's the point of owning a cell phone, Mom, if you're going to leave it in the house all the time?"

Ava stuck her tongue out at her, then strode up the stairs to the deck and into the kitchen with the same strong purpose she applied to everything.

Suzanne watched her mother go. The confidence Ava wore like an invisible cloak was comforting, it was familiar, and it was pure *Mom*. "The CEO of maternity," Jimmy had once called his wife; Ava had airily demanded a raise, but no one had denied the label after she'd gotten sober, and no one ever would.

And right now, she needed her mother in a way that she hadn't in a long, long time; and for the first time in an equally long, long time, Ava was completely there for her, in a way she hadn't been capable of during Suzanne's childhood.

Suzanne had long ago forgiven her mother for the "drinking days," as Ava now called them, but forgiving Ava didn't make up for the many years she took care of her mother instead of vice versa.

But now Ava was doing just that, happily caring for Suzanne the way Suzanne had taken care of Steve and Molly for so many years—and of Ava herself, for so long before that. It was now in her mid-thirties, instead of when she was a teenager, that Ava was making her breakfast and supper and washing her clothes. She was also washing the dishes the two of them used, paying the bills, doing the shopping, and keeping the whole house tidy.

Well, I suppose it's better to get your mothering late than never.

Ava had also insisted Suzanne quit both her waitressing jobs until she got her divorce settlement.

"You need to rest," Ava had told her when Suzanne weakly protested the idea of not working for the first time since she was thirteen years old; it was as scary as it was exhilarating. "You need to stop thinking about what Steve needs and what Molly needs and what I need, and think about what *you* need. I will hear no argument on this subject. Got me?"

All of this was a series of luxuries Suzanne couldn't quite get used to.

It had been rougher than she'd expected to leave Steve. She didn't miss The Mooch himself, not at all, but the final act of actually leaving him meant confessing that her eighteen-year-old marriage was a mistake. She was saying, in effect, that half her life had been a waste of time and energy, and frankly that was a bit hard to admit.

She wondered idly, as she sat in the sun sipping her ice-cold Diet Pepsi, if it was odd that she hadn't cried about leaving Steve yet.

Was she such a cold person that leaving a mate of almost twenty years didn't register in her feeling vault? Or simply had she, somewhere down deep, accepted this inevitability for so long that she'd finished mourning it before she'd even packed?

"A month . . . no, three weeks," he'd called after her as she loaded the last of her boxes into the back of her car. There was a note of hysteria in his voice he only used when he was pulling out all the stops. "Three weeks and you'll be hauling all this stuff back here, so don't you even think about asking me to help you bring it back in."

She closed the trunk, wiped off her hands, and turned to her soon-to-be-ex-thank-God.

"I'm leaving you everything but my clothes, the stuff I kept from Molly's childhood, photo albums, my books, and my yoga mat," she told him. "You can keep everything else; it's all yours."

"You might as well leave the yoga mat," he scoffed. "It's not like you ever use it, Pudge."

She supposed that was supposed to enrage her, but she found she didn't care if he found her pudgy; maybe she'd kept on an extra ten pounds in an attempt to keep his hands off her.

"You can keep the appliances, the furniture, and all the flatware. I've already filed the papers, so my lawyer will call yours—or rather, your mommy's—about the rest of the details, after you've gotten served." Suzanne couldn't resist the dig, and Steve's smug look turned into an almost comical snarl. "Mostly just to let you know how much you owe me for the house, if you want to keep it." Her father had been right to insist she buy a house so that she wasn't just pissing away her monthly rent, as he put it; now, it looked like she'd get it all back, and then some.

She got into the car then, backed out of the driveway, and suddenly she felt a huge whoosh, as all the air in her body escaped her. She gripped the wheel, unable to catch her breath. It felt as though, very suddenly, a two-ton boulder had been yanked off her chest, and after eighteen years of taking shallow breaths, she could now inhale and exhale freely.

"I'm free!" she said aloud, gasping, laughing, and crying all at once. Her piece-of-crap Mitsubishi Gallant, which normally took one or more tries before it grudgingly turned over, had sprung immediately to life, as if it too approved of her decision. She patted the dashboard lovingly and again shouted, *"Free!"*

"You'll be back!" he yelled, as she pulled out of the driveway, but there was real panic in his voice for the first time. She'd never mentioned lawyers before, let alone actually employed one.

Now he threw down the empty box he held in his hand; more than ever, he looked exactly like what he was—an overgrown toddler whose tantrums were no longer getting him what he wanted.

"You're just throwing good money away to show me that you're pissed!" he screamed now, stamping his foot. "You're pissed because you work and I don't! You can't *stand* it that I don't work! How sexist is that of you? Some woman-of-the-millennium you are!"

She didn't bother to respond.

Steve's idea of "woman-of-the-millennium" meant she should be more than happy to support him, clean the house, *and* raise his child, while he was holed up in his studio, getting baked and recording the same songs over and over again. Not only happy to do it but also feeling honored to do it, in his opinion.

After all, she thought tiredly, *his mother had told him so. And he always listens to his mother.*

She thought about shouting some icy response to his comment but, in the end, didn't bother. What was the point? Sooner or later, he'd realize she wasn't coming back; that he was really going to have to start taking care of himself now. Somehow, a man who had never held down a job or taken care of himself was likely to be a lot less attractive at thirty-eight than he had been at eighteen. And his mother was no longer young; she'd need care herself before long. He must be really scared now. There was no need to rub his nose in it.

He was someone else's problem altogether now.

"Thank God Almighty, I'm free at last," she sang, against Gwen Stefani's "Hollaback Girl" on the radio. Somehow, it seemed totally appropriate.

About two months into the separation, they bumped into each other at the grocery store.

He looked worn and thin, and his eyes lit up when he saw her. She looked at this man with whom she'd shared a bed for the entirety of her adult life, and tried to feel something, *anything* even slightly positive.

But for the life of her, she couldn't dig up any emotion but irritation. He'd sucked any and all good feeling toward him out of her long, long ago. She was long past forcing out feelings for this child-man that weren't there.

"You look great," he'd told her forlornly.

"Thanks," she'd said lightly, unable to return the compliment. He looked like hell. In fact, he looked like, he hadn't figured that since no one was around to make his meals and wash his clothes and charge his razor, he should to do it himself.

"I think . . ." he began, and stopped to clear his throat; her breath caught in her own.

She thought he was going to confess, at last, that he'd caused the rift in their marriage by refusing to work. By refusing to do anything but get stoned, play video games, and work in his studio on music that he never finished recording—let alone make any attempt to actually start a musical career. To apologize that it hadn't mattered how many times Suzanne had begged the management of whatever waitressing job she'd held at that moment to let him play on open mic nights. To apologize that it hadn't mattered how many times she'd broken down and told him he was going to work her to death, that she needed help, that she needed a break. To apologize for the fact that her needs and feelings simply hadn't mattered to him.

I don't do things I don't want to do, he had told her at eighteen; at eighteen, it was rebellious and badass; by age twenty-five, it was disgusting. At thirty-eight? She had no words for it.

Standing there in the grocery store, she'd held her breath anxiously; she had been waiting a long time for this apology.

"I still think," he went on, "that when you're tired of being on your own, when you feel like you've made your point, you'll be back."

She let her breath out again but found she wasn't disappointed. He'd disappointed her so many times for so long that she was immune.

Being on my own, she wanted to say, *is so much better than carrying you on my back.*

But he wouldn't understand it—he never had. It was supposed to be her joy and pleasure, remember?

Not so much, as it turned out.

"I hate to break it to you," she'd told him, and she couldn't keep the cheer out of her voice, "but I'm never, ever coming back to you. Not sooner, not later, not ever."

"My mom says," he started, and Suzanne wondered how many times she'd heard him begin a sentence that way, "that women over thirty-five have as much chance of marrying again as getting slaughtered by a serial killer."

She reached into the freezer and pulled out a gallon of two-percent milk.

"Tell her I'll take my chances with the serial killer," she'd replied, and then happily pushed her cart down the aisle, leaving him staring behind her.

One of the great things about staying with her mother was the food, of course. Ava's cooking had begun in an effort to keep herself busy after she'd quit hitting the bottle, but it soon became an addiction in and of itself. Here was a constant stream of snacks, appetizers, and entrees going at all times, not to mention several canisters waiting on the table by the door—this one was for her AA meetings, that one was for Ava's next-door neighbor's granddaughter's bridal shower, yet another was for Fritzie at the Senior Center's retirement bash. Any excuse to bust out the apron was a good excuse, it seemed.

Suzanne found herself struggling to maintain her size-eight pants, although, she consoled herself, would a size-ten thirty-six-year-old really be that bad?

After all, she reasoned, *they say the average American woman is five-foot-four, one hundred and forty-four pounds, and wears a size twelve. I'm still in the one-thirties, and I'm five seven and a half.*

But more than anything, it felt nice to take a break, for a change. A break from being the responsible one, the grown-up, the caretaker. A break, during which someone took care of *her* for awhile, while she sorted out her future.

It was wonderful . . . but after eighteen years, it was quite hard to get used to.

She kept waking up in a panic because an alarm hadn't jolted her into consciousness. She found herself leaping to her feet, sure that she'd left the stove on, that she was late for one of her two (and sometimes three) jobs, that she had to go pick Molly up somewhere, that Steve needed something fetched or dropped off or purchased, or that there was clean laundry wilting in the dryer.

And then she'd remember where she was.

At a place where her laundry was washed for her, folded and hung up neatly. Where the stove always had at least two burners going of things she hadn't had to cook and wouldn't have to clean up after.

All Suzanne had to do with her free days was to come up with a game plan for the next few decades.

Nothing in her life before this had trained her for such a task.

Her mother, such a burden once upon a time, was now a blessing. She was downright fun and energetic; she acted like Suzanne's visit was an ongoing slumber party. And, to her credit, not once had she trotted out the I-always-told-you-I-never-liked-that-boy speeches. Through a Herculean effort, Suzanne was sure, Ava was holding herself back, and that alone was a miracle, almost as big as her newfound freedom was.

Suddenly, she lifted her head off the lounge chair, hearing bits of a conversation floating to her from the sidewalk.

"Wow, I can't believe you knew my grandfather." Molly's sweet voice came floating across the yard. "That was one karmic bus ride."

My daughter, Suzanne smiled happily, getting up from her chair to greet her, *the great believer in pre-destiny, post-destiny, and all the destinies in between.*

"Oh, I more than knew him," an older man replied. His voice was strangely familiar. "He was my best . . ."

And then his eyes fell upon Suzanne, and he fell silent.

Suzanne's eyes widened in shock as she froze mid-step, completely stunned. *Oh my God. It can't be . . . Can it?*

TWO

"Hey you!" She crushed out her American Spirit hastily and searched her pocketbook for a mint. Molly hated cigarette breath, and there was nothing like a lecture from your own kid to dampen the mood.

Popping a Life Saver, she watched Molly cross the lawn. There she was, her one and only baby. Her hair was falling out of a ragged ponytail, and the mascara she'd put on that morning had run all the way down to her nose ring. Her black clothes were skin-tight and so tattered and torn that Suzanne wondered if she'd gotten them from the Goodwill dumpster.

Only Molly could look so completely disheveled and so achingly beautiful at the same time.

"Get over here!" Suzanne called. "I haven't seen you for a month; I need a hug right this minute!"

"Squishing, Mom!" Molly laughed her wind chime laugh, pushing away her mother's overeager embrace. "Hey, you're not going to believe who was on the bus with me."

Suzanne put her hand to her throat, heart suddenly pounding, and approached the handsome older man, holding out her trembling hand for a handshake.

"Excuse me, this is going to sound crazy, but you look just like . . . I mean, what I mean to say is . . ." She took a deep breath and tried again. "My name is Suzanne Lauder, but it used to be Suzanne . . ."

"Applebaum," the distinguished gentleman cut her off smoothly, "which is German, but everyone always thought you were Irish because of all that red hair . . . and because your daddy ran O'Shenanigan's, the greenest of the Irish pubs here in New Hampshire. By the way," he looked down his nose reprovingly, "after all those books you used to read by all those fuzzy-legged, braless feminists in high school, are you *seriously* telling me you took a *man's name* when you got married? Why didn't you just put on a dog collar and hand him the leash?"

It *was* him.

"Oh, Buddy! Buddy McKinley!" She hesitated for only a second, looking down at his cane, before she threw her arms around his neck (what the hell, he'd always been strong as an ox), wanting to laugh and cry all at once.

"The one and only." He hugged her back, and cane or not, his arms were just as strong as she remembered.

"I can't believe it. Just look at you. You look wonderful! Not a day older—not an *hour* older!"

"You gorgeous little liar." He let her go, and tugged on her hair just like he had when she was a little girl, and all of a sudden he was Uncle Buddy—her hero, her daddy's best friend, the man who could do no wrong, at least not in twelve-year-old Suzanne Applebaum's eyes. "I look like a retired old man, that's what I look like. But, I have a golf handicap of thirty-eight, and good enough eyesight to drive my sports car when it's not in the garage—although it seems like I ride the bus an awful lot. But enough about me. Let's look at you."

Suzanne pranced around in a circle like a proud little girl; out of the corner of her eye she saw Molly put her hand over her eyes, cringing, and laughed.

"You're not the only hot ticket in this family, Missy," she reminded Molly.

"You're the one who hasn't changed a bit in twenty years," he told her proudly, "except to get even prettier."

"Oh, listen to him." Suzanne blushed like the teenager she'd been when she last saw him. "But, go on, tell me more."

Buddy would have been more than happy to oblige, but Molly interceded.

"Hey, Mom, guess what?" She grabbed her mother's hand excitedly. "Buddy's going to be our next-door neighbor. Isn't that *great*?"

Suzanne's heart stopped, for just a second.

"Well, technically, he wouldn't be *our* next door neighbor," Molly amended, "considering that we don't live here in the retirement village permanently. But until Dad coughs up the dough for the house, and I get my dorm assignment, it's home."

"Home," Suzanne agreed. She wondered if there was some safe sort of tranquilizer to give alcoholics, because when Ava found out, she was going to shit her pants. And *not* in a good way.

Buddy glanced over at the centerpiece Ava had been working on.

"Ava's still up to her arts and crafts, I see. She used to make the most unbelievable things for the pub . . . Sometimes she'd even take a table at craft fairs and farmer's markets. I take it those are for me?" He touched the petals lightly. "Or rather, they *were*, that is, until Ava finds out who her new neighbor's going to be."

"Oh, Buddy." Suzanne laughed nervously, putting her arm around Molly. "I'm sure Mother's forgotten all about that by now."

"Grandma? My grandma, Ava Applebaum, *forget* something?" Molly roared with laughter, beating her knee. "Stop joking please, I might pee my pants." She ignored her mother's *cut-that-out* look and hauled her backpack up on her shoulder. "Anyway, I've got to take a nap and a shower, and then I'll be human again, so any lecturing can wait till later. It was nice to meet you, Buddy!" she called out, giving him one of her sweetest smiles, usually the kind she reserved for asking for a big favor involving money or a car.

Suzanne thought, *Buddy must have made his usual charming impression. Some things never change.* Suzanne found herself recalling all the times Buddy's smooth manner and earnest charm had warded off many a bar fight, or an angry employee, or an irate distributor whose product wasn't selling quite as well as it might at the Irish pub; the man was an artist with words.

"You too, Pumpkin!" Buddy called; the charm was apparently mutual. He sat down on his bench and patted the space next to him.

Suzanne skipped happily over to him, but then she remembered that while seeing him made her feel like a child, she wasn't one, and hadn't been for quite some time. As if to prove it, she lit up a Spirit, exhaling slowly.

"So, Miss Suzanne, you sit down for a minute, and tell me all about what you've been up to for the past twenty years. Are you setting the world on fire yet?"

"One needy, codependent ex-husband at a time." She giggled again, embarrassed. Last time they'd seen each other, she'd been a die-hard, college-bound women's libber, not a thirty-six-year-old divorcée with a resumé full of barely-above-minimum-wage jobs. "Actually, on the way to women's studies, I took the old marriage/children detour. You know how it goes."

She hoped fervently that he did, in fact, know how it went, so she wouldn't have to try to explain her list of life failures further.

"For shame!" he scolded, patting her hand to take the sting out of his words.

"I know, I know." Then she brightened. "But! This very winter, I am *finally* going to college. To UNH specifically, same time as my daughter goes for her undergrad at Vassar. Vassar! Can you *believe* that? Full tuition scholarship! Her entire school career, her lowest grade was one A-, and that was in gym. Considering she has Steve and me for parents, I have no idea where she gets it. I, on the other hand," she rolled her eyes ruefully, "will be paying back student loans from the grave."

Her last sentence, Suzanne thought later, could have been, *"Naked ladies are parachuting out of a helicopter!"* and Buddy wouldn't have heard a syllable of it; for at that exact moment, Ava stepped out of her house.

"Your daughter," Ava said disapprovingly as she glided down the steps, "is dressed in clothes I'd be embarrassed to have seen in my garbage cans."

"Mom!" Suzanne pasted a smile on her face, the kind usually reserved for company and job interviews. "Look who just bought the house next door."

"Well, hello there," Buddy drawled, swallowing a couple of times, his throat having suddenly gone dry. "It's you."

"Well, hello there, it's you too," Ava agreed amiably, pulling out her glasses from her jacket pocket, "but actually, I don't have my glasses on yet, so who knows, it might be someone else altogether."

Then she slid her glasses on. For a long moment she didn't move, didn't breathe, or even blink, it seemed. And neither did anyone else.

"It's . . . you," Ava said tonelessly.

"Yes, indeedy, it's me." He whispered to Suzanne, "I thought you'd said she'd forgotten all about it by now."

"You'd already unpacked," Suzanne whispered back apologetically. "What was I *supposed* to say?"

"You're . . . a . . . a . . . a *stalker*, that's what you are!" Ava sputtered. "A *stalker*!! I'm calling the police. Police!!" She stomped up and down the driveway, waving her arms frantically. "Police!! *Police!!!!!*"

"Mother, for God's sake," Suzanne shushed her before she could attract the attention of the patrol unit. There were several nosy neighbors, however, who were more than happy to watch the show. Life could get boring in a retirement village; scenes like this broke up the monotony of daily doctor reports. "You're making a complete fool of yourself!"

"Just out of curiosity," Buddy asked, genially enough for a man accused of a felony, "what am I going to be arrested for? Just, you know, so I can be sure to dress properly for the mug shot."

"I just told you, you big jerk!" Ava spat. "You *followed* me here! You're a *stalker!*"

"I did no such thing." He leaned on his cane and pulled his pipe and tobacco out of his hip pocket. "I didn't follow you; I bought a *house*. And if it took me twenty years to find you and corner you, then I'm one shitty stalker, so I'd appreciate it if you didn't tell anyone. After all, a man's got his pride."

Suzanne giggled, but a glance from Ava cut the noise off like a slash from a scalpel.

"Which is more than you deserve." She fumed. "My James didn't have much pride left after *you* got through with him."

Ava's arrow hit its mark directly, and the wounded look on Buddy's face was more than Suzanne could bear.

"Mother, that was such a long time ago." Suzanne stepped between them. "Besides, it's not good for you to get worked up like this. Dr. Maloney said so, remember?" She reached for the pitcher. "Here, let me pour you a nice glass of iced tea. You love iced tea on a hot day, right? Come on, take this, calm down, and drink up."

"After he sells his house and moves away!" Ava refused the tea. In her rage, she sounded amazingly like Molly.

"I'll do no such thing." Buddy took a moment to light his pipe, and the smell brought Suzanne back twenty-five years. It was as though the past had leaped up and put its flavor in her mouth. "Do you have any idea the amount of time it takes to pack up an entire house? Especially wrapping all the little knickknacks my mother and sister have given me over the years? No siree, Bob." He shook his head vehemently. "I spent six solid months up to my ass in Styrofoam peanuts and plastic wrap, and if you think I'm doing it again, you're nuts."

"Mother, I really think you're overreacting here." She looked pleadingly at Ava. "Buddy was such a good friend to you and Daddy for well over twenty years . . ."

"And now," Ava spat furiously, "he's a *stalker*!"

"As much as I hate to burst the bubble that your pretty little head is encased in," Buddy said, not unkindly, "I had no idea you lived here. I didn't see you once when I was unpacking, and my nephew said all he saw was a silly old lady in a funny hat peeking in the windows. Looking back, I guess I *should* have guessed it was you, but I didn't."

"And you expect me to believe *that* one?" Ava was aghast. "Look, bub. There's a set of perfectly fine brains under this funny hat. I wasn't born yesterday."

He eyed her up and down. "Clearly."

Suzanne gave him a look that said, *Was that necessary?* Buddy was too busy smiling at Ava's reaction to notice.

"I want you out of here, immediately," seethed Ava, "or, I'll, I'll . . ." She couldn't think of anything bad enough to finish the sentence, and so she stood there, sputtering, her fists clenching and unclenching.

"You'll what?" Buddy challenged her.

She spotted the half-full plastic pitcher on the table and reached for it. Suzanne could practically see her mother thinking, *This could do in a pinch.*

"Get out of the way, sweetie," she said calmly, swinging mightily. Suzanne managed to catch it just before the makeshift weapon hit its mark.

"Give me that, you crazy old lady." She wrenched it out of her mother's grasp. "I already told you I don't have bail money."

"Fine, then. If you're going to take his side, then, well, just fine." Ava smiled sweetly. "I've got more tricks than that up my sleeve. I didn't graduate college in three years and outlive all of my sorority sisters without having a where-to-dispose-the-body plan or three in my back pocket."

"So, where is this plan again?" Buddy wanted to know. "Up your sleeve, or in your back pocket?"

"You know," Suzanne whispered furiously to him, "you're supposed to be the mature one, here."

"Who the hell told you *that*?" His blue eyes were sparkling with mischief, and Suzanne had to bite down on her lip to keep the laughter back. Those dancing eyes ignited dozens of other happy memories.

Ava lost her confident Cheshire cat grin, and then she stamped her foot.

"You . . . *you*!" She cried, frustration stealing her words from her. "You are the most *frustrating* man!"

"You're not the first woman to tell me that." He leaned over to tamp his pipe a bit. "Only thing is, usually they tell me over breakfast."

Suzanne stood up and made a great show of dusting off her hands.

"Okay, that's it for me." She pointed at both of them sternly. "You're digging your own grave. If you're not going to stop pushing her buttons, then you leave me right out of it."

She walked huffily up the stairs, opened the door, poured a cup of coffee, and settled down at the kitchen table, right next to the window. It afforded a decent view of the courtyard, where she could easily spy on them.

After all, if she wasn't there, she couldn't be asked to take sides, which was a favorite trick of Ava's during arguments. *But there's no way I'm missing this conversation*, she thought with glee. Plus, there was a huge hanging plant she could hide behind if she was spotted.

She hated to admit it but some of her mother's nosiness had trickled down the family tree to her. Buddy and Ava were eyeing each other warily. Two old foes, sniffing each other out, each cautiously waiting for the other to make the first move.

"Look, Ava." Buddy was the first to break the piercing silence. "I know I'm not your favorite person in the world."

She rolled her eyes. "That's the understatement of the new millennium."

"But," he went on in that same annoyingly reasonable tone, "if we're going to be neighbors, I think we should try to be friends."

"Friends? *Friends*?" Ava shrieked. "I'd sooner befriend a snake. No, make that a *serpent*. I'd sooner eat a live puppy. I'd . . ."

A little excessive, don't you think? Suzanne winced. Moderation had never been her mother's strong point.

Buddy waved off any further declarations of vile deeds done in his honor. "Fine, fine. I get it. You're saying that it's . . . just not likely." He puffed again.

Suzanne felt a pang as the smoke wafted up from the courtyard. The smell of his Borkhum Riff, which Suzanne and Ava had both hated during Jimmy's lifetime, had been one of the things that they'd been surprised to find they missed most when her dad died. On really low nights, she and Ava would light his pipe and let it burn itself out. It was a cheap sensory trick, but it cheered them up all the same. With the wafting scent of Borkum Riff, home seemed more like home again.

"Well," Buddy was saying now, "maybe if we both really tried, we could eventually learn to tolerate each other."

"After you destroyed my James and subsequently my entire family?" Ava asked incredulously. "I'd sooner learn to tolerate arsenic."

"Frankly, I'd just bet you could, you tough old bird," he told her, shuffling back to his own side of the courtyard. "Fine, then. We'll simply ignore each other. You do your thing, I'll do mine."

"And," she hastened to add, "if we happen to come out to the courtyard at the same time, you have to leave until I've done my business and moved on."

"That's a bit extreme." He bowed to her, just slightly. "But, just to prove to you I'm a gentleman, I'll agree to that, even if you're just walking to your car. But, just out of curiosity, where do you suggest that I go? While I'm waiting for you to take your sweet time idling your days away with courtyard business, that is?"

She eyed him coolly. "Crawl back under the rock you came from, for all I care."

Give it a break, Mother! Suzanne almost shouted; she caught herself just in time. After all, she wasn't supposed to have a bird's eye view to this exchange.

"Why, Miss Ava!" he beamed. "You used the word 'care' and me in the same sentence! I think you're warming up to me. Is it my cologne?"

"Ha, ha, *ha*," Ava snorted. "You're probably the only person in the universe who still wears Old Spice. That's such an old man's cologne."

He looked down at himself incredulously and then back up at her.

"Excuse me," he pointed out, "of *course* it's an old man's cologne. Just what in the hell do I look like to you?"

"Oh," she remembered suddenly, "and I get first dibs on all the activities."

"Activities?"

"Oh, yes, there's a lot to do here at Lakeside Retirement Village," she told him with pride. Suzanne nodded. Ava would know. Her life was a series of activities and meetings. Every last one designed, Suzanne knew, to keep her from being the old woman she was so afraid of becoming. "Last month alone I won fifty dollars' worth of Tom's of Maine products in a Texas Hold 'em contest. And," she noted proudly, "last March it was standing-room-only when I played the 'Phantress of the Opera.'"

There had been only three shows, and two of them had been canceled due to health issues, but Suzanne wasn't surprised that Ava didn't mention that. "The Senior Moments Players," as they called themselves, had gone for the "no set" look, and her costume had consisted of white mask cut right down the middle and a child's black Halloween cape. Suzanne figured that Ava knew Buddy wouldn't be privy to that.

"'Phantress'?" he asked, impressed. "I'd have paid good money to see that."

"I just bet you would have," she replied haughtily, arching her eyebrows. "At any rate, I get first choice. If I don't want to pursue an activity, then by all means, it's all yours."

"You get first dibs on *everything*?" He raised an eyebrow. "That hardly seems fair, Ava." He put up a hand to ward off the searing look she was giving him.

"Fair," Ava glowered, "would be your burning in hell to make up for what you did. And I'm determined to snag the lead in *Josephine and Her Amazing Technicolor Dream Raincoat*. I don't know if you recall how much I love the theatre."

"I remember, I remember, always popping show tunes into the tape player during cleanup." He surrendered. "Fine, fine, take the damn musicals. I'm not much for singing, as you'll recall."

"I'm not surprised. Singing is an expression of the soul . . . and if your soul is made of solid crap, it's better to keep your songs to yourself."

"Listen, Miss Zippedoodah," he said firmly. "I'm trying to be patient here, but now that you bring it up, you ain't exactly Betty Buckley yourself. We could hear you all the way from the bus stop. We thought someone was torturing a cat."

Suzanne groaned again. If Buddy was going to get in on the mudslinging, they truly would be there for hours.

"These pipes are good enough to have played the three wise men in the Christmas pageant, for three years running." Ava looked down her nose haughtily at him. "The proof, after all, is in the pudding—the pudding happening to be a brilliant production. Ask anyone who attended."

"All eight of them?" he asked, smiling. "I already said you could have the theatrical events. But, just out of curiosity . . . how does one woman play three men?"

"It's quite easy—puppet heads."

"*Puppet heads?* Hmm," Buddy pretended to think. "Judge's ruling on this one is that I'm going to need more information."

Ava rolled her eyes. "God, are all men so slow, or is it just you? Puppets, you dolt, puppets. I'm in the middle, with one male head in each hand."

"That image," he replied dryly, "is going to wake me up screaming on many a night."

"I hope that won't bother your wife. Actually," she brightened. "I hope it *does* bother your wife and she divorces you over it."

Buddy took a pouch of tobacco out of his valise and tamped more into his pipe as she spoke. "Actually, I'm not married."

"Dead?" Ava inquired hopefully.

"No," Buddy answered.

"Damn," Ava sighed.

Suzanne looked down at her mother, mortified. Ava's sense of humor had always been bordering on the acerbic, especially during her drinking days. Suzanne hadn't dared bring friends home, because God knew what would come out of Ava's mouth if she didn't like their outfits, haircuts, attitudes, or all three. Now that Ava had been sober for such a long time, she seemed to have gotten hold of her runaway tongue. But making fun of someone's dead wife . . . that was going too far even for Ava. It was really lucky that Buddy hadn't been . . .

Wait a minute, Suzanne realized. *She knew that; she knew that all along. As much as she hates him, even she wouldn't cross the line of celebrate his wife's death.*

Death had become too much a part of Ava's life to not pay it its proper respect. But Ava also rarely threw a punch without throwing her full weight behind it. Suzanne looked at her mother sideways, wondering what that was about.

"If you have to know the truth, you old busybody," he said, rolling the pouch back up and tucking it into his back pocket, "I never married."

"How tragic." Feigned concern dripped from Ava's voice. "Not one woman you could dupe into spending her life with you? I find that sad."

"I just worked too hard in my younger days," Buddy said in that same easy tone, just as if Ava wasn't saying such awful things to him, just as if it were any old conversation. As Suzanne peered through the plant, her heart swelled with even more admiration for him. "Suddenly I was middle-aged, and everyone was already married, divorced, and remarried, with kids coming at them from every which way." He shrugged again, seemingly philosophical after all these years. Suzanne knew everyone had some sort of regrets, and she supposed those were Buddy's. "I never could figure out how to get in the game."

"So at least one of my prayers *has* been answered," she realized happily. "You'll die a virgin."

"I got off that train in my teens, thank you very much." He puffed on his pipe gently. "I've had my fair share of companions over the years."

"I'll just bet you have."

He grinned again. "Hey, I never heard any complaints. I just never met . . . her."

"Her? Who's *her*?"

He looked her squarely in the eyes. "Someone I could look at," he said casually, "the way that Jimmy used to look at you."

Suzanne couldn't see her mother's face, but she could tell by the way Ava sputtered that she was cursing Buddy for knocking her off her game—anything to keep the anger she insisted on hanging onto alive. "Don't try to get on my good side," she responded at last, once she'd regained her composure.

He raised an eyebrow. "*You* have a good side?"

And here we are, back at square one.

"Why am I even wasting time talking to you? I'm a busy woman." Ava sniffed and turned toward the safety of her kitchen. "I've got places to go, people to see." She started off, then looked back pointedly. "Houses to bulldoze."

"Then I'll live amongst the rubble!" he called after her. "I told you, all the activities are yours, and I'll make myself scarce when you want your privacy out here. But I'm not moving, and that's that."

"We'll just see about that!" Ava snapped with as much vehemence as she could muster. "Oh, you'd better *believe* we'll just see about that!" She turned on her heel and climbed the stairs, tossing her hair primly over her shoulders. When she reached the screen door, she slammed it as hard as she could. Almost at once, it bounced open again, but her point was nonetheless made.

Suzanne hastily picked up the paper and pretended to concentrate as her mother came in, but her efforts were wasted.

"The next time you eavesdrop, dear, try to find a place that isn't right behind a lace curtain." Ava advised. Her heels clicked all the way to the living room, where she would spend the remainder of the afternoon watching her *House* DVDs, a gift from Molly last Christmas, while taking out her aggression on a five-thousand-piece jigsaw puzzle. Those who knew her would easily recognize just how upset she was.

Suzanne snuck one more look outside. Buddy was looking somewhat forlornly at the stairs where Ava had disappeared. Then he chuckled, picked up his valise, and began sorting through the dozens of keys that had taken up permanent residence on his key chain to find the one that would let him into his new house.

"Oh, yeah," he said loudly enough for Suzanne to catch, "she fucking hates me."

THREE

$\mathcal{M}$olly grasped the railing at the bus terminal tightly as she frantically searched the face of each passenger, the knot of fear in her stomach growing bigger, darker, harder, and sicker, until she was certain she would throw up or faint.

Not that I'd particularly mind, she thought. *Either one, while gross as all hell, will at least get my mind off things.*

And then there he was, ambling up the carpet to the terminal: her gangly, bleached, baggy-pantsed knight in shining armor. All the breath came out of her with a giant *whoosh,* and she gripped the railing even harder.

Don't faint, don't puke, don't faint, don't puke, don't faint, don't puke.

They'd met in June, at her orientation at Vassar. She was an incoming freshman; he was a junior advisor who had welcomed her in front of Rockefeller Hall.

"Cool backpack," he'd remarked.

"Thanks," she'd replied, hugging the overstuffed, graffiti-scrawled, partly torn, and much-loved bag she'd carried through four years of high school—not to mention summers of art camp, autumns of model student legislature, and spring shifts at the homeless shelter where she volunteered. (The Ivy League and Seven Sisters schools, her guidance counselor had advised her, just loved volunteer work.)

"You mug a graffiti artists' homeless brother for it?"

Molly had laughed much harder than the comment warranted—and somehow the tension that had followed her from Portsmouth melted away as Brandon watched her, amused, and then slung the filthy backpack on his own shoulder.

That had been eleven weeks ago, and now when he wasn't around, after a while, she began to feel, well, panicky.

She knew *why*, of course, but it still bugged her that in so short a time, he'd become such a part of her life. It bugged her that *anyone* could get under her skin that far, let alone that fast.

Grade school, junior high, high school, it was all the same—she was everybody's buddy but nobody's best friend. Life had taught her two things: you look out for yourself, and you take care of yourself. Letting someone else do either one was like an invitation for them to wipe their muddy shoes on you. Watching her mother take care of her father had emblazoned that on her brain.

So meeting Brandon, and having him rise with meteoric speed until he was easily the closest friend—by quite a large margin—she'd ever had, was unnerving, to say the least.

"Don't think you're special, or anything," Brandon said often. "People often worship me upon first sight. It's my cross to bear."

From the time she was young, she watched her parents' marriage, which seemed different from her friends' parent's relations. The way her dad seemed to think the world owed him something. She had seen her mother work her fingers to the bone, trying to make them all into a family.

But to Molly's great relief, her mother *finally* gave up trying to fix her jalopy of a marriage, and let it die in the scrap heap. She didn't know how much she'd had to do with it, but she did remember how important the conversation had been to her, the morning after graduation, when she'd come home "disappointingly early," as her mother teased her.

Her mother had looked alarmed at the thought that her daughter hadn't had a good time at this rite of passage, alarmed that something terrible had happened, alarmed in general—and exhausted as always. If Ava was the scale by which you could measure the Applebaum women's aging chart, then Suzanne would always be a beautiful woman. But her face was so thin, her skin so taut, her eyes so weary it made Molly want to cry. It was time for it all to stop.

She'd had a whole speech prepared, but as she held her mother's worried hands in her own, across the kitchen table, she found she could only say one thing.

"Leave him, Mom," she'd whispered. Her throat was so tightly constricted she could barely breathe; she forced herself to swallow hard and repeated herself. "Leave him."

Her mother had looked stunned, but far worse than that, Molly would remember for the rest of her life, she had looked humiliated.

"Why do *you* think I should leave him?" Suzanne asked. Molly figured that her mom already knew anyone in her right mind would want to pull off a parasite that was sucking the life out of her. She just wanted to hear Molly's point-of-view, and Molly knew it.

The reasons were legion, and Molly could have listed them all backwards and in alphabetical order.

"Because I'm leaving," she said finally. "Because if there was ever a reason for you two to be together, I was it, and I'm leaving. Because it was one thing to take care of him—cook for him, clean up after him, pay his bills, do his laundry—when you were doing it coincidentally with taking care of me. But now . . ."

Molly shrugged helplessly. At that moment, music began to waft out of the room Steve used as a studio; his mother had given them a large check for the holidays that year, and rather than spend it toward bills or fixing up the house, he'd bought himself another synthesizer. The song was one Molly had heard perhaps a thousand times in her life—but it had never been played outside the house.

"You used to think he'd be a rock star, didn't you?" Molly had asked; Suzanne nodded, too exhausted to be embarrassed. "That's why you started working when you were pregnant with me, so he could record his demo and get a record deal and then take care of you for the rest of your life."

They both laughed; what had been her mother's life plan now seemed ridiculous.

"In my defense," her mom had gestured to the music, "it's really good music."

"No!" Molly had surprised herself with the force of her response. "It's not good music, Mom. It was the drug he used to dope you up with. It was the club he used to beat you with. And now . . ." She pointed angrily at the closed door behind which her father stood, most likely firing a bong, before continuing, "That music to me . . . just sounds like lies and broken dreams. *Your* dreams. I think his dreams are right here." She gestured around at the kitchen, a room that symbolized her mother's life, a life of taking care of her husband the same way she took care of her child.

Molly had left for freshman orientation three weeks later, and her mother had left the following week.

She'd been half-afraid she'd call Grandma's house and learn her mother had crawled back; after all, the host was often convinced it needed the parasite to survive. But the minute Molly had seen Suzanne's face this morning, she knew immediately that her mother would never go back. She looked ten years younger, for one thing; all of her stuff was at her own mother's, and more importantly, she was making plans for herself. For her own life.

The bridge had been burned, and if Molly had lit the match, she was nothing but proud.

She'd tried hard to muster even a little remorse for her father, but like her mom, she found there was simply none there.

There were a lot of reasons she felt nothing for her father, Molly supposed, but mostly it seemed to be that you really couldn't count on a man who called his mommy during arguments. Molly had realized long ago that her father was a complete bum, and if there had ever been a time when she had actually respected him, she couldn't remember it.

Night after night, watching her mother come home to a filthy kitchen, Molly would try to help, but her mom would shoo her away every time.

"The best help you can give me is to study hard, get a great job, and support me in a manner to which I'd dearly love to become accustomed." Suzanne had smiled, but it was hard to see the smile past the huge dark circles under her eyes. Still, the most she'd let Molly do was sit at the table and do her homework while she cleaned up.

So, if this was marriage, if this was love, she wanted no part of any of it, now or ever.

I will never let someone do this to me, Molly swore to herself time and again. *No one will ever, ever make me do this. If I work eighteen-hour days, it'll be because I want to, not because I am treading the water of life's ocean, and someone is hanging onto my ankles.*

And then, along came Brandon.

Now she needed him more than she felt she'd ever allowed herself to need anyone, and it irked her like an itch she couldn't quite reach.

Because here she was now, standing at the bus station, waiting for him like the typical pining female. For that reason, part of her was afraid he'd decide this wasn't his deal, after all.

Maybe, she'd been half-hoping all day, just maybe he'd go back on his promise to be there every step of the way, as she told her family what she knew she had to tell them. *Especially* since he was partly responsible for the fact that she was here, making the announcement; it had been his idea for them to tell both of their families and get it over with.

But facing Ava and Suzanne with this news? Why the hell *wouldn't* he blow it off?

God knows I would, if I could, she thought.

But then, there he was, all six feet, twelve tattoos, and six piercings of him, and she had never been so happy to see anyone in her life.

To her own embarrassment, she threw herself into his arms. He caught her, laughing, and swung her around.

"How's the girl?" He smoothed her hair down and kissed her forehead. He peered into her face.

"What're you looking at? Do I have a zit?"

"For any sign of breakdown," he said solemnly. "I know from personal experience that the first few hours home with the 'rents can be extremely stressful."

"I am seriously glad that you're here." She took a deep breath, the first of the day. "Did you see me when you got off the bus? Did you *see*? Geez, I almost swooned, dude, almost pulled a Scarlett Fucking O'Hara, and . . ."

"Scarlett O'Hara," he interjected, "was not exactly the swooning type. Haven't you *read* the book? Maybe in high school, like the rest of the planet?"

"No, loser." She tapped the side of his head lightly. "I was busy studying my ass off in high school to get me into Vassar—and with what few seconds I had left over, I partied and slept."

"Sounds like a photocopy of my schedule. Twenty-three hours a day of studying, one hour of sleep, and, if I was lucky, maybe an hour a week for recreation."

"This means we're officially geeks, you realize," Molly admitted. "We need to get lives."

"That's what this visit is all about, isn't it? Getting our lives out in the open?"

"Come on," she changed the subject. "Let's go. Everyone's *dying* to meet you."

It was only a mile or so to Lakeside Village from the bus terminal, and it was a hell of an evening for a walk. They chattered about light, easy things: Vassar, the friends they'd met at orientation, a recent episode of their favorite reality show.

"Sometimes," Molly said thoughtfully, when Brandon commented on the frivolity of their conversation, "when you have a lot to say, it's nice to just talk about nothing."

"God, you're smart," he marveled, squeezing her hand. "I knew there was a reason I liked you."

When they got to Ava's house on Marcy Street, they headed for the picnic table, where the fixings for Ava's flower baskets were sprawled across almost every surface.

"What's with all the decorations? Are they getting ready for some kind of party?" Brandon asked, fingering the plastic leaves. "You know, I used to hate fake plants, but in the past year I've come to realize that real plants can't survive in a dorm room. I've gained a whole new respect for them."

"You should offer to help!" Molly grabbed his hand excitedly. "You've got a great eye for that sort of thing, and it's a slam dunk to get on their good side from there."

"Uh-huh."

She frowned, looking at the perfectly manicured lawn and small garden.

"Grandma's place doesn't usually look this . . . clean. Does it?" She fingered the tall ivy and wisteria, climbing up the trellis below the second-story deck. "Are these new? I don't remember seeing these white flowers before . . . maybe they weren't in bloom yet."

"I've never been here before, remember? Hey, can I have the water I bought at the terminal? I think you put it in your backpack."

"But, the plants always look good." She mused thoughtfully. "She's a born gardener, and I was thinking, you know, that works in my favor, right? It means she's into nurture and not violence, right?"

"Sure," Brandon agreed amiably. "I think it's in your backpack. My water. Can you grab it for me?"

"What am I so afraid of? I mean, really, what in the world is there to be afraid of?" She plopped down on the grass and forced a laugh, but it sounded more like a strangled yelp. "All Grandma has ever said—ever—is that she wants me to be my own person, make choices that make me happy. And you know what? I *am* my own person, I've made my own choices, and I am happy."

"If you're happy, I'm happy." He ran his hand over her sweaty, sticky back. "But it doesn't mean I'm also not dying of thirst."

"My mother I'm not worried about," Molly mused, pulling her lipstick out of her pocket. She applied it carefully, smacked her lips, then reapplied. "After all, I can outrun her."

He clutched both hands melodramatically around his throat, whispering, "Spots dancing in front of my eyes . . . starting to hallucinate . . ."

"And it's not like they're not going to be able to tell pretty soon anyway, right?" Her voice tried for practical but landed on squeak. "I mean, this is *not* the sort of thing you can keep locked up like the moldy purple towel at the bottom of your closet." She punched her open palm with her small fist firmly. "No, this is the sort of thing you just get out into the open and, dammit, that's what I'm going to do. No matter what they say. No matter what *anyone* says."

Brandon collapsed to the ground and gave a few spastic twitches.

"Tell my mother," he croaked, his hands clutched around his throat, "that I loved her dearly . . ."

"Oh, for God's sake." Molly dug his water bottle out of her backpack. "You're such a drama princess."

Brandon sprang back to life with a single sip.

"Me? I'm a drama princess?" He pointed to her overdone lipstick. "You're about to seal your mouth shut with makeup, and *I'm* the drama princess? Prozac, sister-friend. It's all I'm saying."

Her eyes narrowed, and he groaned inwardly, cursing himself for giving her an opening.

"Oh, you'd like that, wouldn't you?" she hissed. "You and all the other head-shrinking, drug-pusher types. Did you know that antidepressants are prescribed more than twice as often to women than they are to men?" She took a ragged breath and barreled on. "Prozac is now the answer to numbing *us* out so *you* can take control. This, in addition to constantly making us feel insecure so we'll spend billions of dollars a year on beauty aids and weight loss products that you force us to focus on to distract us from . . ."

"I surrender! I surrender!" He threw himself to his knees, hands up, in a gesture of defeat. "You're better, you're superior, and for God's sake you're right, so shut up already."

"Okay, fine, you're right. Generalizing isn't a good thing. My bad." She rapped her forehead with a bejeweled knuckle. "I'm sorry. I'm sorry. It's just that, I'm nervous, and as you know, when I'm nervous I start spouting statistics and getting defensive about the laughable state of liberation today."

"Is that true? The Prozac thing, I mean?"

"Yeah, it's true. It gets prescribed to men much less often than to women. Ask any doctor."

"But only half as much?"

"Well," she wrinkled her nose, "I suppose I might use the tiniest bit of hyperbole—every now and then—when I want to really get a point across."

"I knew it!" He pumped his fist victoriously in the air. "I just knew it! Do I know you, or do I know you?"

"Ha, ha." She stuck her tongue out at him, but her heart wasn't in the banter. She grabbed her backpack and started back toward the road. "Let's go. Let's go and come back later."

Brandon caught her arm, removed the backpack from her grasp, and shook his head gently.

"Okay." She drew a deep breath. "Let's go and *not* come back."

Brandon smiled and shook his head again.

"Let's go and send a telegram!" She clapped her hands, thrilled with the idea. "Telegrams are a lost form of communication, don't you think?" She suddenly became aware of her voice, which was completely high and creaking, and put a hand on her throat, terrified. "Why does my voice sound like this? Does it always sound so high and shrill? Is there something wrong with me? Is my voice collapsing because I talk so much? Oh my God, is something happening to me? *Am I gonna die?*"

Brandon looped his long arms under her arms from behind, over her shoulders, laced his fingers on top of her head, and rocked her like he would any other psychotically babbling teenager.

"Molly," he began tenderly, "I'm not going to be upset, but you promised me that was decaf back at Breaking New Grounds."

"It was!"

"Molly . . ." He pulled her around so he could look right into her face. Her eyes were wide open and sincere.

"Bran, I swear to you," she said stridently, looking right into his eyes. "On our most sacred . . . *secret.*"

"Okay, I'll believe you. I've noticed that your head starts to implode under pressure, anyway. That's probably why you're spazzing." He'd hoped for a laugh, a smile, something, but her face remained taut and terrified. "Look," he reasoned, "we don't need to do this today."

"I'm going to throw up." She stared down at her feet.

"Okay, you win . . . come on, sweetie." The thought of vomit made the decision for him. He picked up her backpack and took her arm. "Let's just go find a motel for tonight, and then . . ."

"No!" She jerked her arm out of his grip suddenly, surprising herself more than him. "I mean, no. No. I'm here, and I'm . . . I'm an adult, so I'm gonna do this. This is the stuff that adults do. After all, this is who I am . . . right?"

He put down his water and pulled her into a hug with his long, ink-covered arms.

"What's this for?" Her grateful words were muffled in flame-colored silk.

"You said this is who you are." He smiled, stroking the back of her hair. "Well, I just wanted you to know that I really, really like who you are."

For a moment, her giggles threatened to turn into tears, but she gritted her teeth and clung tightly to him until the danger passed. "Brandon," she sighed with gratitude, "you have absolutely no idea how much I needed to hear that right now."

The kitchen door flung open, and Ava stood at the top of the stairs, peering to see who was invading her lawn. Her perfectly coordinated grandmother wore a peach-colored short set, Molly saw. Her makeup was clean, simple, and altogether too plain for her granddaughter's tastes. But there was nothing much that needed to be done to Ava's head of thick auburn, wavy hair, Molly thought with satisfaction. It was identical, if salted with grey, to her own, and her mother's . . .

In this world of change, it was good to know that at least one thing would hold up over time.

"Oh, good," Ava carried the tray of lemonade and cookies down the stairs gracefully. "You're all showered and rested. You just get over here this minute and give your old grandmother a proper hug."

"Gee, I would," Molly looked innocently all around the yard, "but I don't see any *old* grandmothers here. You must be referring to someone else," she gestured up and down Ava's body, "not this fit and fabulous young babe I see before me."

"Oh, you. Listen to you!" Ava cried delightedly. "Listen to you lie to me."

"Who's lying?"

"Suzanne! Your daughter's here!" Ava called. "Bring some napkins, a copy of my will, and a red pen. I need to cross your name off and sign it all over to Molly."

Suzanne appeared immediately, smiling at them from the door.

She popped up so fast in fact that Molly realized (with her heart jackhammering away in her chest), her mom might easily have been watching—and what's more, listening—from the kitchen window. She played back the conversation in her mind, wondering exactly how much Suzanne had heard.

Oh, God, Molly closed her eyes. *Well, that's a sign, if ever there was a sign. She might already know. So it's go time.*

No turning back now.

FOUR

"I want another hug!" Suzanne cried, seizing her daughter from Brandon's grasp. "You'll have to excuse me—this is the treasure of my heart right here, and she's about to leave me for greener pastures."

"Mom!" Molly protested, looking pleadingly at Brandon for help, but he was far too amused to throw her a lifeline.

"I had her when I was just eighteen myself," Suzanne said, rumpling her hair, "and we grew up together, year by year, didn't we, Moll?"

"Although sometimes it seems like Molly is the real grown-up in the relationship," Ava whispered, and Molly giggled gratefully.

"We were buddies!" Suzanne insisted. "She's my best friend. In fact, we shared everything but taste in fashion. Which reminds me, wasn't there enough hot water for a shower, sweetie?"

"There was plenty, Mom, why?"

"It's just," Suzanne pushed Molly's teased, overly sprayed bangs out of her face, "it's hard to tell under all that moussed hair, black makeup and, let's see—one, two, three, four piercings."

Molly sighed. "Push me a little harder, and I'll pierce my tongue."

"Don't you listen to a single thing your mother says, Molly." Ava slipped an arm around the girl's slender shoulders. "She used to leave the house looking like she'd used a magic marker for eye liner and wearing more flannel than you'd see at a lumberjack's convention . . ."

"Mother!" Suzanne pleaded.

". . . and her hair looked like she'd slept on it for days after not washing it for a week," Ava plowed on happily.

Suzanne could feel Molly and Brandon's eyes boring into her. "It was the nineties," she said wanly.

"Ugh!" Molly shuddered. "Great music, *horrible* hairstyles. Right, Brandon?"

"Right," he nodded, holding a hand out to Suzanne and then to Ava. "I'm Brandon Ellis, by the way."

"Very pleased to meet you, Brandon." Ava nudged Suzanne in the ribs. There were few things that impressed Ava like good old-fashioned manners.

He was a handsome boy, or at least, he seemed to be, from what Suzanne could see under all the accessories. His thick hair was in the process of growing out a bleach job, and he'd taken no care to soften its dark roots. He had five piercings in each ear—one way up in his cartilage, she shuddered to note—then there was one in his lip and one in his nose, like Molly's (try as she might, she could never look at a nose ring without thinking of all the boogers that must be encrusted on the inside).

His black silk shirt was painted with huge flames, and his pants were baggy black chinos. She took mild comfort in the fact that they were slung around his waist, not hanging off his rear showing off his boxers, which seemed to be the style of the day.

But . . . then there were the tattoos. His arms were gangly and long, giving him plenty of room to defile the body the good Lord had given him. There was one on his left arm, near the bicep. A dragon took up the same forearm, ending in snakes that curled themselves around his left wrist. His right arm was covered with several bands fashioned from Celtic knots, which wrapped around his bicep, near his elbow, and by his wrist. There was a date, May 15, on the inside of his right wrist, just below his palm.

His birthday, most likely, Suzanne thought. *Or the day he'd knocked over his first liquor store.*

In short, he looked like every mother's worst nightmare.

Suzanne instantly felt a pang of sympathy for her parents, way back when Steve had come roaring up the driveway on his Harley. During the intros, her dad hadn't budged from his recliner. Jimmy Applebaum, like his wife, was also a firm believer in good manners, so this was a wordless shout out to his family. His eyes didn't leave Steve, from the moment he came in the door.

Her throat closed a little, just at the memory. Her sweet, workaholic daddy . . . James went by "Jimmy" to most of his friends, even though he was well past the age when most men had graduated to just Jim. But as Ava lovingly pointed out, he was man enough to pull it off.

That night so long ago, Ava had made polite small talk, even going so far as to comment admiringly on Steve's mullet and the pink streak in his hair, but Suzanne was sure that had been reverse psychology: if the mommy don't hate him, the daughter don't date him. It had been an interesting meal, mostly consisting of Steve describing the rock-and-roll career he was going to have, but how he'd never forget "your girl here."

"You gotta know," Steve had said proudly (smugly, Jimmy later claimed), "girls dig musicians, so I, you know, I got my pick. But the minute I saw Suzanne," he stopped, reaching over dramatically to caress Suzanne's face, which, at the time, had made Suzanne's stomach roll over with passion, but now it made her stomach roll over for an entirely different reason, "I knew she was the one for me. I mean that."

Steve finished by leaning over to kiss her right at the table; even then, Suzanne knew he'd gone too far with that move. Daddy had abruptly stood up, thrown his napkin, and, casting a look of disgust, stalked away from the table. Her daddy hadn't even come out of his room to bid Steve good night; in fact, she couldn't remember her father directly addressing Steve any time after that either.

Jesus, what goes around really does come around. God had such a cruel sense of humor.

"So," she said at last, shattering the tension that lay thick in the air, "now I get to play girlfriend's scary mom to this guy, right? Mothers *live* for these moments, you know—all mothers, you'll soon find out."

Her attempt at a joke didn't do a thing to make the air any less choking.

"Well," Brandon began, but Molly was faster.

"You can grill him in a minute, Mom," she said diffidently, examining her nails. "But only after you hear that I just got another call from the admissions office at Vassar."

Suzanne stood up straight. Vassar had called again? Were they revoking the scholarship because she was pregnant?

No, they can't do that, that's discrimination, she told herself reasonably, but her stomach plummeted just the same.

"When you hear that in addition to my full tuition scholarship," she added, "they're offering me partial room and board . . . well, you might just want to hug me twice."

"Oh, honey, that's wonderful!" Ava pulled both the kids to her full grandma bosom, swinging them around in her exuberance. Suzanne wasn't sure what Brandon had done to contribute, but he patted her shoulder genially enough in return.

"Oh, my God!" Suzanne gasped. "Nearly a full scholarship? This is like winning the Parent Lottery!" A thought struck her then. A wonderful thought—no, a *miraculous* thought. "Hey, wait a minute. Was *that* your big news?" She suddenly felt light enough to fly, lighter than she had in days. In her delirium, she grabbed Brandon's large hand and squeezed it happily. "It is, isn't it?"

"Well . . ." Molly began, but Suzanne, given a ray of hope, was clinging to it for dear life.

"Did you hear that? Our girl has almost a full scholarship to Vassar! Vassar!" She gushed. "That's so much better than I ever did. Which, of course, means that I was a much better mother than you were, Mom."

Ava raised her eyebrow. "A potter's only as good as the clay, dear." Ava informed her, squeezing her daughter's shoulders; Suzanne tried to groan, but it was far too happy a sound to truly qualify.

"Watch it, old lady," Suzanne reminded her gaily, giddy from her conclusion. "Just because I'm supposed to change your diapers in a few years, doesn't mean I actually *will*."

"That's it? That's your best shot? What a disappointment you turned out to be." Ava turned to Brandon. "She thinks she's funny. Isn't that sad? Just do the polite silent laugh and head-toss thing to make her feel better."

Brandon did as he was instructed, which earned him a throaty laugh. Ava looked at the boy she'd just squeezed to her bosom appreciatively, and then her eyes narrowed. "Excuse me," she asked, "but who the hell are you?"

"Mother!" Although her tone was harsh, Suzanne was secretly relieved that Ava had asked the question of the hour. Who was this young man? Boyfriend? Fiancé? Fuck buddy? Or, what did they call them now—friends with benefits? None of the above?

Molly had always been rabidly private about her romantic life, what few dates she'd made time for during her avid pursuit of snagging the valedictorian slot. After years of arguing 'round and 'round the living room, Suzanne finally had to agree that, by age eighteen, there were certain privacy boundaries she would respect, like it or not.

And she didn't like it, but it didn't change the rules.

"Actually, he just followed me home from the bus station," Molly informed them. "He said he wanted to tell me all about his family—the Mansons, I think he said their name was?"

"Suzie," Ava was already on her feet, "you grab him and hold him here, and I'll get my stun gun."

"Mother, she's kidding." Suzanne caught Ava's elbow. "I'm assuming that this young man is probably Molly's . . . well, her boyfriend."

Oh, please let him be at least *a boyfriend,* she prayed, *and not one of those friends-with-benefits deals . . . I know it's a new millennium, but I can't be that modern.*

"Umm, I'm . . ." Brandon shifted uncomfortably, and Molly took over.

"His name is Brandon Ellis, and he's going to be a psych major. He's a fabulous student," Molly enthused, taking Brandon's hand. He smiled awkwardly at the women, offering a little wave. "He's going for his master's, and he might even go to med school."

"Actually, I just said it would be cool to be called Dr. Ellis," he acknowledged. "But I'm not sure I want to be a student till my late twenties."

Suzanne noticed not one, not two, but three bags at Brandon's feet. "So maybe your visit is Molly's big announcement, then?" Suzanne couldn't help the slight disappointment that crept into her voice. "You're the announcement—you, and all those tattoos?"

Molly glared at her, but Brandon at least had the good grace to look flustered. "Well, it's not exactly . . . I mean, I . . ." he started to say, and fumbled, looking at Molly for help.

"Oh!" Molly sighed, exasperated. "Mother, it's just that, well, you . . ."

"Don't you give these kids any trouble," Ava cut in. "The summer before your senior year, you went off camping with Steve three times with no adult chaperone, *and* you had your hair matted down in one of those baby barrettes like that Courtney Loud."

Brandon and Molly both tried not to laugh, but it was no use. Their laughter rang throughout the yard.

"Love!" Suzanne stamped her foot, even as she realized she'd laughed at her soon-to-be-ex-husband-Thank-God for doing the same thing just a few months ago. "Courtney *Love*!" Turning to Ava, she added, "You should just be grateful I didn't come home in one of those little Kinderwhore slip dresses or use my actual slips for outerwear. With combat boots."

"Oh, Mommy, I'm so embarrassed for you," gasped Molly, wiping the tears from her cheeks.

"Me too," "This Brandon" agreed.

"That was just one of the looks she tried," Ava shook her head. "For a solid year, she was trying to get two different boys to notice her. One was that fireman's son, Scott, or no, Sean? That was it, Sean Bradley. And the other was the author from Kittery. Jacob Winter. She used to write 'Suzanne Bradley' and 'Suzanne Winter' on her notebooks and then scribble it out."

"Jacob Winter, the writer?" Brandon gasped, putting his hand on his chest. "You know Jacob Winter? The guy who wrote *Bridge*? And *Berth*? And *Firewater Pond*?"

"Jacob Winter, in case you hadn't grasped," Molly told her family, "is his total hero."

"Oh, she was in all his English classes," Ava remembered.

"Look at me, Mother, because you obviously haven't noticed, I'm shooting you the shut-the-hell-up-old-woman glare of death," Suzanne chirped, through clenched teeth.

"Yes, dear, I see it, and as always, I'm ignoring it. Where was I? Oh, yes. Before she settled on your dad, let me tell you, she had such a crush on Jacob I thought for sure she'd have a heart attack if he ever did ask her out." Ava pointed to the seaman's trunk up on the deck. "You see the steamer trunk? He made that for Suzanne's dad and me. Our fortieth anniversary. Can't remember what we paid for it, but whatever it was, it was a steal. Take a look at the craftsmanship."

"Jacob was the shy, artistic type," Suzanne remembered, a warm feeling settling over her. "And Sean was, well, he was everybody's type. Everyone's buddy, easygoing. The guy who puts on a pair of new jeans, and they immediately relax."

"Jacob Winter could have been your father?" Brandon asked Molly in dismay. He shook his head sorrowfully. "Oh, Ms. Applebaum, it's not my place to judge your romantic choices, but what on earth is wrong with you?"

"I suppose you think you're the first person to ask me that," replied Suzanne. "Jacob was *exactly* my type, right up until Molly's dad. You don't know how often I wished it was Jacob instead of Steve I went to that pit party with. I spent all afternoon tracking down someone who'd buy three bottles of Boone's Farm Strawberry Hill."

"Boone's Farm Strawberry Hill? Oh, Jesus, Mom, do you have to make it worse than it was?" Molly wailed.

"Yet somehow it never occurred to me to buy the condoms." Suzanne shook her head woefully. She thought she caught Molly and Brandon exchanging a look, and hastily, she changed the subject; she realized they were right; no point in getting this intimate. Time to lighten up. "Anyway, if you'd had your way," she challenged Ava, "I'd have been wearing the Dorothy Hamill chin-length bob till I was thirty."

"It made you look adorable!" Ava squeezed Suzanne's face with one hand till her lips pooched out like a fish. "Take a look at this mug. I don't care if you're pushing forty. You're still just as cute as a button."

"Yeah," Molly interjected brightly, "but who the hell wants to fuck a button?"

"*Molly!*"

Then they were all laughing, huge great big bellows of laughter, and the tension was entirely broken. Molly had been blessed with classic timing.

"Oh, my goodness, we're low on cookies." Ava surveyed the picnic scape. "Who here needs some ice?"

"I do, Grandma."

"Great." Ava said, stepping out of her way. "It's in the ice box. You know the way."

"Mother," Suzanne protested, "she just got here. I'm sure she's still tired."

"Oh, for heaven's sake, I was just kidding, I was going to get it all along." She tapped Brandon's shoulder on the way by. "Never could take a joke, that one. You're lucky you got the daughter."

The three of them stood around the weathered picnic table, slightly uncomfortable without Ava's comedic input (intentionally funny or otherwise) to serve as conversational referee. Suzanne smiled so hard she thought she felt her face crack.

Then they heard Ava's voice, cutting through the silence like a chainsaw through butter.

"Twenty. Twenty-one. Twenty-two."

Molly and Suzanne looked at each other and erupted into giggles, while Brandon found himself on the outside of a family joke.

"What's she doing?"

"Counting the seconds," they said in unison.

"Thereby proving to us what a simple and short task getting the ice was." Suzanne lit up a cigarette; she'd held off as long as she could, but the need for nicotine momentarily outweighed her need for daughter approval.

"And since it was so simple," Molly chimed in, giving her mother a sidelong glance, "we shouldn't have made a frail old lady do it."

"Frail? *Her?*" Aghast, he jerked his thumb in the direction Ava had disappeared. "She's about as frail as Mike Tyson."

"It's not that we're not glad to meet you, Brandon. Of course we are," Suzanne said quickly, adding just as much sincerity to her voice as she was able. "It's just that . . . Well, I'm assuming you're going to need a place to stay for a few days, and as 'hip' and 'with-it' as my mother pretends to be, don't let her fool you. She's very Victorian about certain things." *That's it, blame the old lady when she's not here to defend herself.* She patted herself on the back for quick thinking.

"Ava is only Victorian," Buddy called from the door of his house, "when it comes to children or grandchildren of hers getting naked and sweaty and knocked up. Hi, Suzie."

"Hey, Buddy!" She gave him a bright smile. She saw a basket and length of hemp rope in his hand. "Whatcha got there? Arts and crafts?"

"I'm exploring my feminine side." He settled himself on his bench and held up the basket. "Macramé ropes. When I'm done with it, you can hang some of the mums and those ragweed stems inside. It'll look really festive for your party. Don't tell Ava I made them, though. God knows what she'd do with them."

"Yeah, that *will* look great." Suzanne gave him a smooch on the cheek. "You're a wonder."

"Me?" He looked at her quizzically. "How the heck do you consider an old bag of bones like me a wonder?"

"Well, my mother is plotting your death, and here you are trying to find ways to help her, even if you have to sneak around to do it. I think that's just amazing." She bent to whisper in his ear. "But please watch the talk about getting sweaty and getting knocked up in front of you-know-who," she pleaded, tilting her head toward Molly.

"Gee, I don't even have superpowers, but I can still hear what you're whispering from ten feet away," Molly marveled.

"I was just telling Molly," Suzanne smiled to show them *she* was cool, *she* was with it, *she* was all those things, but regretfully, *she* didn't own the house in which the kids planned to crash, "that springing a boyfriend as an overnight visitor on us is just the sort of thing that will rattle my mother. Really. Completely."

"She hasn't said any . . ." Molly started to say.

"Which is not to say she won't allow it, mind you," Suzanne interrupted. "She probably would. Probably. But, it's just . . . She'll be up all night listening for the slightest creak. She'll go into your bedrooms, opening the windows and insisting that the doors stay open because she needs to get a cross draft going through the house—and she has central air." She was happy to note the kids were really starting to look uncomfortable, so she pressed the advantage firmly. "In fact, she'll probably play the PTL club on every TV and radio station, all day, all night . . ."

"Look, you two," Buddy struggled to tie off the first knot. "Why don't you spare yourselves the pain and go to a hotel where you're actually going to enjoy yourselves?"

Suzanne fought off a sudden urge to slap the back of the old man's head.

"Ms. Applebaum," Brandon said politely, "really, the last thing I want is to be a burden, or to put anybody out."

"No way!" Molly said indignantly. "Do you have any idea how much hotels *cost*?"

"No, I don't, offhand, but why don't you tell us, honey?" Suzanne asked sweetly. "You sound like you're something of an expert."

"Actually, I really wouldn't know." Molly patted Brandon's arm. "My pimp here smacks me around if I ask too many questions about money."

"She's just kidding," Brandon faltered. Out of the corner of his mouth, he hissed, "Are you *trying* to get me killed?"

"So you're saying," Buddy's eyes gleamed impishly, "that it would drive Ava crazy if he stayed here? If I were a better man, I'd pass up that opportunity. Thank goodness, I'm not."

"Oh, geez," Suzanne groaned. The days ahead began to play themselves out in front of her eyes. Between finalizing her divorce, Molly's impending morning sickness, and playing ref between Buddy and her mother, it didn't look pretty at all.

"Just kidding, Suzie. Listen, Broderick . . ."

"Brandon," Molly corrected.

"Brandon, that's right. My apologies." He stopped macraméing long enough to tip an imaginary hat. "Listen, I've got a daybed in my computer room. It's not much, but it's cheaper than a hotel room, it's right next to the downstairs bathroom, and you still get to see your sweetie day and night all during your vacation. How does that sound?"

"Wow, that's awfully generous of you, Mr. . . ."

"McKinley, but call me Buddy. Everyone does. Mom named me William after her uncle, who didn't die as the doctors promised he would right after my birth, so they called me Buddy just to keep these things straight."

"Buddy, then." Brandon glanced at Molly, who was intently examining her chipped black nail polish. "But . . . I was wondering, if . . . well, maybe there's something we should all talk about, before I get settled in?"

Here it comes, thought Suzanne. *I really am gonna be a thirty-six-year-old grandmother. I kept saying it's not real 'til I hear it, and I'm about to hear it. Good God, my mother was at least forty-six. And I didn't take it seriously when she kept saying, "I'm going to be a forty-six-year-old grandmother!" because forty-six seemed really, really old at eighteen.*

Suzanne was supposed to have at least two more years before she had to worry about this.

"Hmmm," Molly thought it over, chewing her thumbnail, and finally spat it out on the ground. "Nope." She cheerfully slung one of Brandon's bags over her shoulder and headed up the stone walkway to Buddy's house, Brandon only a pace behind. "Thanks so much, Buddy!" she called back over her shoulder, her perfect button of a nose revealed sweetly in profile. "This is really cool of you!"

Suzanne drew a deep breath, surprised to find she was half-relieved at the reprieve. As long as it hadn't been spoken, maybe it wasn't true. Right? *Right.* And somewhere deep inside her, she heard her father say, *That's right, baby girl, and if you pull the other leg, it plays "Jingle Bells."*

FIVE

"You hear that?" Buddy tapped his puffed-out chest. "I'm cool."

" Don't let it go to your head. Just this side of a decade ago, she thought Barney and Santa Claus were cool," said Ava as she gathered up the empties and stacked them neatly on the tray. "Besides, we think she's pregnant, so her hormones are making her crazy and affecting her judgment."

"Mother!" Suzanne flipped her cigarette butt into her Diet Pepsi can. It made a distinct *hiss* as it hit the last sip. "My daughter *is not* pregnant. I told you, I'm sure of it."

"Okay, Cleopatra." Ava took a long, casual sip of her lemonade, adding, "Queen of De-Nile."

"You know, you've got plenty to worry about in your own life as well, Mother." Suzanne whispered under her breath.

"What's *that* supposed to mean?"

Suzanne rolled her eyes, then held up the cigarette she'd just lit.

"It's supposed to mean you watched me put out my last cigarette, and yes, I lit another one right away, but I'm going through a pretty stressful period. I'm a grown-up, and well, if I want to chain-smoke two, or three, or seven, I'd like to be able to do that without someone hovering over my shoulder watching me."

"Watching you? What do you mean, watching you? I love you, sweetie, but you're not interesting enough for me to spy on." Ava tossed her hair haughtily. "And from the looks of the past couple of weeks, my love, you could chain smoke seven standing on your head."

"See? *See?*" Suzanne shook her head, exasperated. "All you have to do is give me the 'Mommy disapproves' sidelong glance. I know that glance, Mother. I spent years perfecting it in the mirror. So, please, I'm asking just for the next week or so, cut me some slack. Take your own inventory, Mother. Isn't that what they say?"

Suzanne took one more long drag and grudgingly put it out. Ava was right: Chain-smoking was a bad—and pricey—habit to get into.

"Your grandfather, both your grandmothers, and your aunt Julianne all smoked to the day they died. Every one of them, that's all I'm saying."

"I went to their funerals with you, Mother. I know how they died."

"Does this mean you have some kind of plan to quit in the future? If I just knew that, then I'd . . ."

"*Agghhhhh!!*" Suzanne covered her ears with her hands. "Mom! My back's going to buckle if you don't climb off it once in a while!"

Buddy guffawed at that one, unable to stop himself, but Ava's icy glare sent him hastily back to his macramé.

"I'm your mother, all right? I worry. I don't care if you don't need me to worry about you. It's my right to worry about you, so I'm gonna." Ava crossed her arms and leaned back; it was the stance that meant, *conversation over.*

"Okay, okay, okay. I don't know when I'll quit, but I will look into it. And hey—I'm not the only one in this family with bad habits."

"I have never smoked a day in my life, and you know it."

"That's true. And I also know that there was a time when it wasn't even noon, and you'd be in your cups."

"Oh, sweetie," Ava scoffed. She glanced casually over at Buddy, whose fingers worked furiously but whose ears were sharply keened their way. "Believe it or not, I remember at least some of those days." Ava spoke casually but loudly enough for Buddy to hear. "I haven't so much as *looked* at a drink in fifteen years, and you darn well know it."

"Yes, I do know it," Suzanne said patiently, "but it's not what I asked you. I asked you if taking your own inventory was still the name of the game. Working the program."

Buddy didn't even glance up, but Suzanne noticed that his gnarled fingers were working even faster.

Ava sighed irritably. "Yes, my darling daughter, I still go to meetings."

"Sensing a big 'but' here, Mom."

"I do yoga—my butt is perfection," Ava sniffed haughtily, picking up the tray. "Yours, on the other hand, could use a little . . ."

"Okay, okay, fine." Suzanne covered her rear end self-consciously with her hands. Lately, it had felt a smidge fuller back there than she was used to. "I'll go with you to a couple of your kick-boxing classes. Just stop minding my business, my smokes, and my behind."

"I was not minding your business, nor was I taking your inventory. And I don't want to discuss this in front of you-know-who." She tilted her head ever so slightly in Buddy's direction.

"She means me, by the way," Buddy called helpfully.

"Thanks for clearing that up, Bud." Suzanne said wryly. "Look, Mom. I'm honestly not trying to bug you. But just tell me, have you found anyone from the village to go to meetings with since Alice passed away? I know it's a lot easier to go with a friend than all by yourself."

"Suzanne," Ava implored, "you don't know these meetings like I do. The key is finding one where the assholes haven't set up camp."

"They have camping assholes in AA?"

"You bet your chubby pink fanny they do," Ava sighed grimly. "The ones who just show up for the free coffee and to hog the spotlight—and worse yet, because they know we *have* to listen to them, they feel free to whine on for forty-five minutes or so at a clip. You think I'm kidding, don't you?"

"But," Suzanne quietly pressed, "you still go, right?"

"Honey," there was a note of finality in Ava's voice, "I read the big book every day, I go to at least three meetings a week, if not five, and I exercise every day, rain or shine."

"What does exercise have to do with it?" Suzanne wanted to know.

"Nothing." Ava put her hand on her hip, shoulder out, striking a pose for the benefit of anyone who just happened to be watching. "Just bragging."

"Okay, fine, you win." Suzanne threw her hands up, completely surrendering. "I just worry about you. I want to make sure you're okay, that's all."

"You, worry about *me*?" Ava looked at her daughter in horror. "*You* don't get to worry about *me*, sweetie. I'll tell you when it's time for you to worry about me. And at that time I'll be crapping my pants and drooling into my Jell-O." She yanked the cigarette that Suzanne had just lit out of her mouth and snapped it in two. "This is how it works, my child: I worry about you. You worry about Molly. Actually, we both worry about Molly, but it's your full-time job, okay? You don't get to worry up the food chain."

"Mother," Suzanne persisted, "I wasn't insinuating that you're not . . ."

"You're damn right you weren't," Ava stood, closing the subject for good. "Now, if anyone's interested, I've grown weary of these judgments and accusations, so I'm going inside."

"All right, Mom."

Ava stopped dramatically at the top of the stairs.

"First, I'm going to prepare something wonderfully delicious and completely fattening for myself for supper. Then, after I've eaten the whole thing, I'm going to load up your father's rifle and shoot myself." With that, she turned, put her hand daintily on the railing, and sailed regally into the house.

This type of guilt-inducing ploy had never failed to arouse sympathy—and, ultimately, an apology—from Suzanne's father, Jimmy. It had even gotten her a couple of seriously atoning presents, including the emerald on her right ring finger.

But Suzanne wasn't Jimmy.

"Can you hang yourself instead?" Suzanne called casually. "I mean, when the cops get here, I have to convince them that it was you who pulled the trigger on yourself, and, well, they might *know* you."

The screen door slammed, and the sound of Ava's indignantly clicking heels echoed down the hallway, out the door, and into the autumn air.

Suzanne looked at Buddy, who hastily buried himself in his macramé. Try as he might, he couldn't smother the broad grin Ava had brought to his lips.

"I was wondering," Suzanne asked innocently, "do you think she's still mad at you?"

SIX

Buddy's rich laughter filled the courtyard. "I always said you had a mind like a steel trap—rust optional."

Suzanne took off her sandals and rubbed her feet.

"Seriously, though." Buddy brought out a beautiful hand-carved pipe that Suzanne had seen a thousand times before, in another lifetime. "You can hardly blame her. That pub, it *wasn't* just a pub. It was her family's whole livelihood. Not to mention, it was the great love of your father's life."

"Yes, it was," Suzanne agreed. Just thinking about the pub gave her a warm feeling of familiarity, of family, of *home*. "I remember when I was really little and he was selling insurance. He'd come home and plop in front of the TV to watch to the news. He'd have this look on his face, like he was . . . *sinking*. I don't have any other word for it." A bitter chuckle slipped out. "His bosses loved him, but I guess being a depressed and frustrated asshole is an asset when you're heading the sales management team—it makes people really not want to give you bad news." She drew her legs up close to her, hugging them tightly, trying to squeeze away the bad feeling.

"That must have been right before I looked him up to go into business together," Buddy realized. "He was pretty unhappy in his job—not that I exactly loved being a district manager for Kmart, driving from Maine to Connecticut and back again, looking at the same identical stores, giving them the same old speeches about bringing up numbers. But finally, after working my tail off for ten years and saving every dime I could, I finally had enough to start my dream."

"O'Shenanigan's?"

Buddy's eyes shone just at the sound of the name.

"From the first moment I thought of it, I knew it was gonna be him and me. He was the only guy I trusted enough to open a restaurant with. We were in the army together, you know."

He held up the first two fingers of his left hand, and Suzanne suddenly remembered he was a lefty.

Weird how things like that came back to you out of nowhere.

"That's two," he went on. "Two tours of Vietnam."

"He used to say," another memory was pushing its way to the surface of her mind, "that he'd almost bought the farm for you . . ."

". . . and the farm was a fixer-upper!" they spoke together, before they laughed.

"Yeah, that's right," Buddy agreed, after a moment. "He took a bullet for me. You hear that? The man actually took a bullet for me." He shook his head, still amazed after all these years. "How many people can actually say that?"

He quickly reached up behind his glasses. Touched, Suzanne looked down, for his benefit, pretending not to see.

"Not too many. Not too many, Suzie Q, I can tell you that." The front door creaked. Buddy cleared his throat and barked, "Got to get some WD-40 on that." Brandon came bouncing down the short steps and across the yard.

It must be so damn nice to be young, and have all that energy—enough to knock up my daughter, Suzanne thought sourly.

"Where's Molly?" She produced a smile, trying to make it pleasant but not expecting any miracles.

"Oh, she took one look at the daybed and one whiff of the air conditioning and curled up into a little ball," Brandon laughed—affectionately, Suzanne was relieved to note. At the very least, he did seem to care about her. That was something. *Then again, there was a time you thought Steve cared about you.*

"So." She rocked back and forth on the bench, searching her mind for something else to say. She came up blank, which didn't happen often, so when it did, it was alarming.

"So," Brandon grinned, "I decided to come out here and start the process of making you all love me!"

He smiled broadly, his white teeth shining almost as much as the stud through his lip, but Suzanne couldn't force her lips to turn upwards in return. Her hands gripped the edge of the bench, and she bowed her head, covering her face with a sheet of auburn hair.

"Great!" She said from behind the hair curtain in a tone that aimed for friendly. "That's great, isn't it, Buddy?"

Buddy nodded, reading her discomfort and tipping her a small wink to try to console her. "Sure, honey. It's just great."

I have to get out of here, Suzanne thought. *Or I'll leap on this perfectly likable if overly pierced man and wring his tattooed neck.*

"Well," she cheerfully jumped to her feet, smiling so broadly her back teeth showed, "I'll just go fold some laundry, and the two of you start the chat without me."

She flew up the stairs before either of them could say a word to stop her. She took a few deep breaths after she got into the kitchen, catching a glimpse of Brandon's woeful stare.

She saw Brandon start to take a few uncertain steps after her, and she hoped with all her heart he wasn't going to follow, that he couldn't see her now. The Universe must have felt the weight of her plea and held him back. She wished with all her heart there was a bottle of something—anything— she could take a good long slug of.

Damn this living in an AA house!

It wasn't until she was safely in the kitchen, breathing hard, the sweat beading on her forehead and under her arms, that she realized she'd left her cigarettes and lighter downstairs. She groaned again and looked skyward.

"You couldn't have been on my side just this once, could you?" She shook her head. "That's it—no more church, period." Since she never went to church, it wasn't much of an ultimatum, but she hoped that God, in all His wisdom, would get the point.

Back in the courtyard, Brandon made a comic show of sniffing himself.

"Is it a deodorant thing?"

Buddy chuckled. "It's a mother in torment because her daughter hasn't made her big announcement thing." Buddy patted his shoulder sympathetically. "Don't take it personally."

"I tried!" Brandon exclaimed, settling himself on Buddy's bench. "You heard me try, right?"

"Yes, I did indeed, and so did Molly, Suzanne, and Ava."

"She's just not ready yet. And there's no making her do something if she's not *damn well ready*." Brandon punched his palm for emphasis. "You know Molly."

"Just barely, actually." Buddy tossed Brandon some ropes, to help the boy calm himself. "Here you go, start working. It's macramé; it's supposed to be good for my arthritis, but I'm making some ropes for Suzanne's party."

"How do you do . . . macramé?" Brandon asked, wondering what to do with the four thin ropes he'd been given.

"Watch," Buddy told him. Cross, under, flip, cross, under, flip. After a few clumsy attempts, Brandon began to get the hang of it.

Suzanne took a deep breath and emerged onto the deck.

"Don't mind me," she called merrily. "Just toss up my smokes, and then go on with your boy talk."

"You want 'em, you come get 'em," Buddy intoned solemnly, but Brandon was already mid-toss. He smiled apologetically.

"Sorry, I'm a fellow victim of the nicotine gods," he said, ashamed. "I'm in the process of quitting, but don't worry, I'm not recruiting Molly."

Suzanne smiled her thanks tightly. *If he thinks being a smoker will get him on my good side, he's got a whole new series of things coming.*

Not wanting to say this aloud just yet, she went back into the kitchen. With relief, she noticed that there was a dryer full of towels just waiting to be folded. Gripping her cigarette tightly with her lips, she began folding the laundry with a vengeance, with one ear out to the courtyard . . . but who would know that?.

"Hey." Brandon tied one end to the arm of the bench, and peered over Buddy's shoulder, doing his best to mimic his finger-work. "Is it really true, what you were saying?"

"What was it that I was saying?" Buddy's memory, much to his chagrin, wasn't quite what it once had been.

"That Molly's granddad got shot for you. Is that really true?"

"Oh, yes. Yes siree, Bob, that's true." Buddy's proud grin lit up his weathered face. "Your grandfathers, or at least one of them, must have been over there in Vietnam too, yeah?"

"Yeah, but neither of them talked much about it. I was in a production of *Hair* once, though," he was happy to offer, "and it changed my life."

"I'm sure it did," Buddy said dryly. "Good music. Made a lot of people feel like they'd been there, even the generations after. But having someone throw himself in front of you, getting himself hurt badly for you, maybe even die for you . . . There are just no words." His finger stole up into his glasses again; it didn't fool Brandon any more than it had Suzanne. "Anyway, I tried to thank Jimmy a million times. Like there was a big enough thank you for that. He saw the sniper, and he just *threw* his body at me. He didn't even stop to think about it. You get back from something like that, and you just want to forget it. Forget it, and everything that might remind you of it. But that ain't so easy. I went to work in a factory at first, and there was this guy there that thought it was funny to drop pipes just to see me hit the deck."

"Asshole," Brandon muttered, shaking his head. Suzanne couldn't help but be a little moved as she listened from the kitchen; he was maybe twenty—still young enough that the cruelty in the heart of man amazed him.

"Don't you worry about him," Buddy grinned. "He died of colon *and* testicular cancer; plus, I'm happy to report, he was allergic to morphine."

"It's things like that," Brandon sighed happily, "which make me believe that there *is* a God, and He, or She, is keeping a very accurate score."

"One day over there, on our second tour," Buddy went on, "we got our care packages from the Red Cross. We opened 'em up, and they all had a bar of Ivory soap in them."

Suzanne dropped the dishtowel, startled.

Ivory soap?

A distant memory tried but couldn't quite struggle itself free from the murkiness of her mind.

Daddy had been a storyteller, for sure; there were some stories she'd heard so many times that they felt burned onto her brain, and she could tell them verbatim, including his tone, complete with gestures.

Some of the stories had been about her, and those were the worst—the time as a baby she'd pooped so loud in the grocery store that the cashiers, all the way down the row, started laughing. And the time she gotten lost in the mall and was found dancing in the Christmas display at Wilson's leather store, or how she went through a phase of running around naked, even in front of company.

"Damned if we didn't think she'd get to kindergarten and strip down to her starkers," her dad would say, laughing until he was red in the face while Suzanne (who couldn't remember the last time she'd let someone see her naked) would stand by, wanting to die of embarrassment.

What I wouldn't give to hear one of those stories now, she thought.

Quickly, she cleared her throat and lit up a cigarette before the tears could take over.

But the Vietnam stories—she'd only heard bits and pieces of those, when she was eavesdropping or when Ava was repeating them to a friend or a relative over the phone. They were kept secret, away from her, considered either too frightening or too grown-up for her to hear.

There was something about Ivory soap and Vietnam that sent up a flare in her mind, but she couldn't quite see it. Something about a Vietnamese lady and a knife? That didn't make any sense . . . but she felt sure she was close, somehow.

"Anyway, Jimmy—Suzanne's dad—sees this little Vietnamese woman chopping vegetables with this homemade-looking machete," Buddy continued softly; in the night air, Suzanne could still see his eyes sparkle when he spoke about his best friend, and it squeezed her heart.

"A machete?" Brandon frowned. "What was she, a soldier or something?"

"No, no, no. It was actually the spoke of a wagon wheel." Buddy grinned at Brandon's befuddled expression. "See, the people there, they were serious recyclers. If something broke, they'd cannibalize it or find other uses for the various parts. So, when the wagon wheels would break, the Vietnamese women would sharpen one end of the spoke, jam a hunk of wood on the other, and they had themselves a veggie knife."

"So, rather than run from the sight of a huge knife, he just went up to this lady who was slaughtering the veggies? Wow—guy wasn't short on balls," Brandon laughed—a bit nervously, Buddy thought. From the way he was tapping his fingers—and the yellowing stains on his fingernails—Buddy wondered if he was trying to kick the cigarette habit. Jimmy used to bounce his leg like that whenever the temporary urge to quit came over him. "Then what happened?"

"So he went up to the lady and tried to buy it from her. At first, she thought he was trying to buy something else," Buddy laughed. "You should've seen it. She chased Jimmy around his Jeep with that big ugly knife while he tried to explain himself. She waved that machete around like a pro, let me tell you. But Molly's dad—despite the language barrier—somehow got his point across. He gets out his Red Cross kit and shows her his bar of Ivory soap. And then he kneels down to the little creek right next to them, and shows her how, just like magic . . ." Buddy snapped his fingers. "The soap floats!"

"*What?*"

"Oh, yeah." Buddy nodded. "You're probably way too young to remember this, but that was a huge marketing point. Ivory, the soap that floats! It was all over the place, on commercials, billboards, magazines."

Brandon considered Buddy's statement. "Just out of curiosity, why is soap better if it floats, anyway?"

"Beats the hell out of me, but it sold like hotcakes because it did. So, this lady gets a load of this soap. And she's oooh-ing and ahhh-ing . . ."

"Ah, the universal language for 'I need that.'" Brandon had paid for his first two semesters at Vassar selling cookware in the kitchen department at Sears. "I hear you."

Buddy nodded. "And Suzanne's dad was a *born* salesman. It was in his blood. Some people are born singers or math whizzes; this guy was born to separate people from their money." He chuckled to himself, thinking of Jimmy's quick way with words and quicker way with his charm. "So, before you can blink, he's got the lady trading the soap for the machete and feeling like she got the better end of the deal."

"Cool! Do you still have it? Molly'd love to get a look at that."

"Oh, he didn't bring it home," Buddy said, grinning. "No sir, he had other plans for it."

"Oh, yeah? Such as?"

"Such as," Buddy confided, "the next time we went to an officer's club for a drink, he jammed that ugly thing in the back of his pack, marched up to the highest-ranking officer in the place, sat next to him, and ordered a shot of whiskey with a beer back. That was his drink till the day he, well . . ." Buddy fell silent for a moment. Brandon continued his macramé, pretending not to notice anything unusual.

"Anyway," Buddy went on after a moment, "sooner or later, the officer would get around to asking about the big ugly knife in his knapsack."

"Yeah, Molly says he was a real storyteller." Brandon said admiringly. "The guy who sat in the corner at weddings with everyone gathering around him sooner or later. There's not really anyone like that in my family. Everyone pretty much keeps to themselves, minds their own business."

"Maybe that's why you like to hang out with chatty old men," Buddy observed. "Maybe you're hoping to hear something that will let you know about the dad who left."

Brandon was startled. "How did you know my dad left?"

Buddy smiled again. "Because you ask old men to tell you stories."

Now, *that* was perception.

Brandon hadn't met anyone that could read him that well since he'd met Molly, and he thought she'd been in a class by herself until now.

"And I'm gonna guess," Brandon mused, "that you took a psych class or two somewhere along the way."

"That I did, kiddo. Considered making it my major, for a while, before switching to business. More money, less headaches—well, it seemed that way at the time, at any rate."

"Anyway," Brandon's voice betrayed a quiver, and Suzanne, despite her best efforts, found herself beginning to like the kid. His heart seemed to be as big as his hair. "About Jimmy, it sounds like he was the life of the party."

"That he was, my young friend. That he was." Buddy stopped for a moment, his eyes wandering off to look at the river. "Jimmy wasn't just charismatic, he was a great many other things as well—too many to cover in one conversation. Anyway, back to the story. The officer would ask Jimmy, 'Hey, where'd you get that knife?' and Jimmy would say, '*This* knife?' And he'd shake his head real hard. 'Sorry, pal, this knife ain't for sale. A gook just tried to kill me with this. I buzzed him instead. This knife is coming home with me.'"

Brandon squirmed uncomfortably against the bench and tried to speak tactfully. "I gotta tell you . . . I just hate that word, Buddy."

"What word?" Buddy asked innocently. "You mean 'gook'?"

"That would be the one." Brandon held up his hand as if to physically ward it off. "Not to be a PC asshole or anything, but I don't think it's right to slur people just because they're born somewhere else and have a different look than you do."

"You make a good point, now that you mention it. But," he pointed out, "when someone of another race, or a lot of someones are trying to kill you . . . I gotta tell you, you don't care a whole lot about political correctness. It gets real, real easy to start thinking in terms of 'us' and 'them.'" He remembered the hate, the fear of seeing one of them—seeing the fear in their eyes that mirrored his own. At that moment, he knew that only one of them was going to walk away, and he would do anything in his power to ensure it would be him. Vietnam had been a good breeding ground for bigotry, that was for sure . . . But that was an awfully long time ago; he wasn't the same battle-scarred, angry boy he'd once been. "Put it this way, I wouldn't walk up to . . . to . . ." He looked at Brandon, frowning. "I'm sorry, what are we supposed to call them now?"

"Vietnamese people," Brandon answered simply.

"Thank you," Buddy said congenially. "So, please understand that I wouldn't walk up to a Vietnamese person and call him that *now*, but those were different times, and it was a different place." He knew his argument was futile, trying to make the kid really understand—how could he? Brandon had never been shipped off to war, so he didn't know—couldn't know—what it was like, and Buddy wasn't going to waste his breath trying to explain it. To coin one of Jimmy's phrases, Buddy knew when it was time to stop shoveling shit against the tide. "It was a different *planet*, believe me."

"So," Brandon was eager to get back to the pleasant conversation they were having before the PC lesson, "what happened then? To the knife, I mean. After Jimmy would tell the officer that someone tried to kill him with it and he was bound and determined to bring it home with him?"

"Right, right. As soon as Jimmy said, 'This knife ain't for sale,' the officer's eyes would start to *gleam*. Remember, a lot of these officers were seeing a lot less action and taking a lot of flack for sending boys to their deaths. There was never, *ever*, the kind of blatant disrespect—even flat-out hatred in some cases—for the military as there was in 'Nam. Before that, a veteran, and especially an enlisted man, was somebody to be respected, admired, looked up to. Someone who'd fought for his country against an outside evil. And officers, well, they were the smart guys of the bunch that were keeping our country safe. They were national heroes." Buddy shrugged. "Not this time around. And these guys were just shocked. It completely confused—no, it out-and-out *dazed* them when things changed. When officers, or anyone in a uniform, were given the entirely unpleasant name of babykiller . . . Or worse. So, something like this knife would be a good way to shut people up."

Brandon chuckled. "Little bit of fake proof. I get it."

"So the officer would say, 'I'll give you twenty bucks for it,' and Jimmy would say, 'You didn't hear me, pal. I told you, this ain't for sale. My great-grandsons will learn what this war was really like from this knife, but no hard feelings.' He'd give 'em a big pat on the shoulder and buy 'em a beer."

"Liquoring up the prospect," Brandon noted.

Suzanne finished up the folding and swept the kitchen for good measure. She cursed the fact that there were no dishes to wash, but there never were in Ava's spotless kitchen; dishes were cleaned as soon as they were dirtied, and put away as soon as they were dried. With nothing else to busy her hands, she reluctantly descended the stairs to the courtyard.

"Let me tell you, Brandon, officers just hate hearing the word no." Buddy chuckled. "All the more if it's something they can't directly or indirectly order you to do."

"I can tell you right now, I would not do well in the army," Brandon said, smiling and shaking his head a little.

Buddy laughed out loud at that one. "No offense, my young friend, but you're right, you would not. Your drill sergeant would take one look at those piercings and probably give 'em a nice little yank. Although," Buddy confided, "I gotta admit, the little diamond in your nose is starting to grow on me."

"Yeah?" Brandon was pleased. He liked going to sleep at night knowing he'd helped to open at least one mind, just a little. "So, they couldn't order him to sell the knife. That's where you left off."

"Oh, yes. Well, Jimmy and the officer would have another drink. And Jimmy would be telling the officer just how much he was going to love showing this knife to the peace freaks back home, how he was fighting to keep their asses safe and free for democracy while they screwed in the streets and got stoned. Pretty soon he'd get the officer up to a hundred, one-hundred-twenty. This was 1968, mind you. That was a lot of money in those days."

"I'm looking at forty grand-plus in student loans by the time I'm done, more if I decide to go for my doctorate," remarked Brandon.

Suzanne saw the approving look Buddy gave Brandon. Buddy had worked hard for every cent he ever had, and here was a young man putting himself through school, not relying on mommy and daddy to foot the bills. Yes, sir, if anyone asked, she was pretty sure that Buddy McKinley would tell them that This Brandon, face jewelry and all, was A-okay in his book.

"I hear you," Buddy nodded. "It truly is. So, then Jimmy would say, 'This really means that much to you?' and then he'd go on about how the wife was expecting a baby—although Suzie didn't come along till a few years later—and he'd hem and haw through the next few drinks about how much he needed the money. He'd get the guy up to one-hundred-fifty or so. And finally he'd say, in a voice just full of regret, 'Well, I guess my kid's gotta come first, so . . . Okay.' And the officer would fork over the cash before Jimmy could change his mind, and Jimmy would give him the knife and haul ass back to camp. In a day or so, there would be a money order in the sale amount on its way to Ava . . . and they weren't even married yet."

"Taking care of your loved ones ten thousand miles from home." Brandon's voice was full of admiration. "Yeah. That's just . . . That's what I want."

Me too, thought Suzanne wistfully. *Oh, you'd better believe, me too.*

"He never stopped finding ways to take care of her," Buddy said. His voice reflected something Suzanne couldn't quite put her finger on. "He pulled that one six or seven times, and then his luck ran out. One time, a guy who knew a guy who'd bought a knife off Jimmy watched him sell another to a dupe. That was the end of that little scam, but then he was on to something else."

"Something else," Suzanne said, smiling. She reached over and clasped Buddy's warm hand in the twilight. "*He* was something else, all right."

"That he was." Buddy bit the inside of his cheek to stem the flow of tears this time; he'd used the age old trick on occasion, and it hadn't failed him yet.

Suzanne heard the coffee pot burbling. "I'll be back in a second." She leapt to her feet, grateful once again for the reprieve.

If I hang out with this kid too much longer, she thought, *I'll really start to like him, and we can't have that, can we? It'll make castrating him so much more difficult.*

She was so focused on her thoughts that she nearly missed Brandon's next words.

"So," he asked, in a lowered voice that was for Buddy's ears only, "just out of curiosity, how long have you been in love with Ava?"

SEVEN

Suzanne stopped for just a millisecond, completely startled, then forced herself to keep moving up the stairs with Brandon's question ringing in her ears.

So that's the little thing I couldn't put my finger on, she thought.

But Brandon had seen it, inside of a couple of hours. Great. In addition to everything else, the kid was sharp as a tack.

For several seconds after Brandon's question, Buddy didn't make a sound. As Suzanne hastily gathered the load of towels out of the dryer, she thought of all the comebacks that would work in his favor. Knowing Buddy, it would have to be funny—*very* funny, at this point. It would have to be a wise but cutting remark that would insinuate that Brandon's observation was so off the mark, it fell into the category of the ridiculous.

Or maybe . . . maybe he'd pretend to be insulted. Ava was his best friend's widow, after all. What kind of a man was Brandon implying he was?

"Excuse me?" Buddy asked at last. Apparently he hadn't known which way to go either.

Brandon kept macraméing, not missing a beat.

"I could repeat myself," he smiled, his eyes twinkling, "but I'm pretty sure you heard me."

"Why . . . Why . . ." The sweat was really starting to trickle down Buddy's sides now. "That's just crazy. Why in the world would you think . . ."

It took only a few minutes to pour three cups of coffee. Suzanne sighed and cleared her throat loudly before coming to the top of the stairs.

"Hush up!" Buddy hissed. "Here comes Suzie."

Suzanne gave her gracious hostess smiles all around, pretending not to have heard a word.

"Hey, Buddy," she took the seat furthest from Ava's house, to keep her cigarette smoke from wafting through an open window, "I've always meant to ask, who came up with the idea of O'Shenanigan's?" She gave Brandon a casual smile. "Any word from Moll yet?"

"No. I'm thinking soon, though." Brandon said, giving her a wide smile back. He had great teeth, she was relieved to note. Hopefully it was genetic; the dentist bills from Molly's childhood had been crippling. And she'd always believed a smile bought you friends faster than anything else. "It's almost dinnertime," he allowed, "and I've never known her to sleep through a meal."

Suzanne closed her eyes briefly, but she managed to keep her mouth shut.

"What was O'Shenanigan's, anyway?" he asked.

"O'Shenanigan's was a pub, an Irish pub. And I'm proud to say, it was my idea," Buddy said modestly, "but it was Suzanne's dad who made it work on a day-to-day basis. He wasn't a full-blooded mick like me—sorry, Brandon, I can be un-PC if I'm talking about my own kind. But your dad had a real love of all things from that country. He gave us the flavor of the place, the design, the music, the decorations, the food . . ." He smacked his lips and rubbed his stomach. "I love a good rack of lamb the way Jimmy loved a good stout Irish ale. Or cognac."

"That's right. Daddy sipped, Mommy guzzled," Suzanne recalled. She opened a new pack of Spirits. Milds, these were called, and their package was bright yellow. Molly wryly asked, after seeing the package, if they were lemon-flavored.

"Oh, not in those days," Buddy corrected her. "In those days, she might have her glass or three of wine, but that was about it. I never saw her so tipsy that she had a hard time walking or speaking."

"Really?"

"Yeah, Molly said she's been in AA forever," Brandon chimed in. He unraveled his progress on the macramé and started again, watching Buddy's work more closely this time. The old man's fingers moved faster than he'd imagined.

"See, I never saw that side of her. Or, at least," Buddy admitted, "if she was drinking more than she should, she sure could hold her booze. But, then again, we were working fourteen-, fifteen-hour days sometimes. I just don't know when she'd have had the time." His mind was still back in that space on State Street, less than a mile from where they were now. It was on the other side of the river, right next to the marina. Such an ideal location. "Oh, it was such a grand bunch of ideas, let me tell you. Picking the entertainment, decorating the place, planning out the menu, familiarizing ourselves completely with all things Irish. It was the first time I'd ever enjoyed work, and the most fun I'd ever had—not counting," he winked convivially, "the graduation weekend I spent with the McShane sisters."

"Score!" Brandon offered Buddy the obligatory high five as Suzanne, the resident feminist, groaned obligingly.

"My goodness, all this testosterone," she sighed. "How very 1950s."

"The mahogany bar, the shabby furniture, the fireplaces," Buddy remembered. "Oh, Brandon, you should have seen the little tight-bodiced numbers we had the waitresses wear. We made up a whole legend around this Irish wench, Shaunessy O'Shenanigan, and printed it up on the menu in gothic script." He looked lovingly at Suzanne, who was smiling, as in-the-memory as he was. "Pretty soon, even the locals believed she'd married six times and her husbands kept disappearing in mysterious ways. And whaddya know, the bangers kept rolling in."

"And people *liked* that?" Brandon asked, aghast.

"Are you kidding?" Suzanne shouted with laughter, her cheeks flushed with the excitement of the memory. Being around Buddy reminded her so much of the old days, she couldn't help feeling like the hopeful, starry-eyed girl she'd been. "They couldn't get enough of it. On Halloween, and even on St. Patrick's Day, people came in dressed as Shaunessy. And we brought in some Irish music. At the time, it wasn't on every street corner the way it is now. You had to really hunt it down."

"Like *The Irish Rovers*?" Brandon asked. Brandon's grandmother had been hooked on the show, and its theme song haunted some of his earliest memories.

"That's right, that's right. These bands were complete with traditional Irish instruments—and that means acoustic guitars, uilleann pipes, harps, accordions, and the bodhrans—drums, to the uneducated members of the audience. Buddy ran the dining room—he never dirtied himself behind the bar. You could always see him neat as a pin, in a perfectly clean shirt, pressed tie, and jacket, while Daddy would have on a staff polo shirt covered with coffee spots and reeking of beer . . ." She caught her breath, startled by the huge wave of longing that suddenly swept over her.

She'd grown used to missing her father over the years, but every now and then she'd stumble onto something that was so Jimmy-like that the pangs would start fresh and take time to fade. Buddy looked at her kindly, reading her thoughts.

"And your dad, oh, your dad, he was—hands down—the greatest bar manager, ever. People came for miles just to listen to his fake accent and hear his jokes." He smiled proudly. "The ladies, young and old, had always loved to swarm around Jimmy. Trust me, I was plenty jealous when we first met in high school, but after a while, you just had to accept it. He was just that kind of guy. I certainly couldn't compete with Mr. Charming, so I just left him to his one-man show."

"What's the one about the house builder he used to tell?" Suzanne asked. It was hazy in her memory. "No . . . no, wait. Or was it a boatbuilder?"

"Actually, it was both." Buddy put down his macramé and raised himself onto his feet. "Let's do this properly." He drew himself up to his full six feet and paused dramatically. "A young man named Riley walks into a bar in Ireland, just as morose as could be, and the bartender asks, 'What be troubling you, laddie?' And Riley says, in complete despair, 'There is no forgiveness in this world. My mother's father was O'Malley, the shipbuilder, and in my youth I helped him build hundreds of the fine frigates that sailed to the New World. My father was McDougal, the carpenter. He hand-carved staircase railings and doorframes, and summer after summer I helped him with his work. There are houses I helped build all over Dublin. Yet, does anyone call me Young McDougal, the shipbuilder? Or Young McDougal, the carpenter? No.' Then he'd pause just long enough, lift his beer, sigh, and say . . ." And Buddy then put his arm around Suzanne's shoulder and simultaneously, they recited, "But you fuck just *one* sheep . . ."

Brandon howled with laughter, tears streaking his face.

"Wow, oh wow. That's a good one. I'm stealing that one," he said at last, wiping his face. "Well, it sounds like you guys had a good time together—one big ol' happy family."

"We sure were," Suzanne mused ironically, thinking of Ava's reaction to Buddy these days. "Those were good times. Bussing tables after school, watching the bands . . . I had my first kiss in that pub."

"Me too." Buddy confided jokingly.

"Yeah, *right*!" Suzanne thought of all the women—short, fat, tall, young, beautiful, plain—that Buddy had kept dangling in those days. Ava always nagged him to pick one, or better yet, let *her* pick one, and settle down already before it was too late and all the good ones were taken.

"You're in your prime," Ava had scolded him constantly. "Don't you want to find a woman while you're clinging to what's left of your forties?"

But Buddy, it had seemed, was content to continue the search.

"So, what happened to it?" Brandon cut in. "Is it still around? The bar, I mean?"

Suddenly all the happy memories of days past came crashing down with an almost audible thud.

"No." Suzanne sat on the bench, hugging her knees to her chest. "No, it's not."

"Oh, that's too bad." He was sorry that he'd ruined the moment. "What happened to it? If you don't mind my asking?"

"Oh, you know." Buddy shrugged. "Businesses, well, they just fold, sometimes. Recessions happen, economies go soft."

"You know," Suzanne cut him off, "I never understood that. I mean, think about it. We were open for seventeen years. Seventeen! We were mobbed every night. We even had a Sunday and a Monday night crowd. In Portsmouth. In New Hampshire. Where everyone likes to go to bed by nine o'clock in the wintertime. On the weekends there was a line around the corner. They'd even wait in the *snow* to get in. I'm not exaggerating."

Buddy studied her face for a long moment.

"I can't believe your mother never told you," he said at last.

"There's something to tell?"

Now her curiosity was really piqued. Daddy had come home one night, sat Ava and Suzanne down, and told them that the restaurant needed a new furnace, new insulation, new piping . . . In short, much more money than he and Buddy had. Shaughnessey O'Shenanigan's doors had closed that day. *And quoth the Raven, never more,* Suzanne thought sadly.

"Oh, you could say that, alright."

She looked at him questioningly. "*You* tell me."

Buddy already regretted opening his big mouth in the first place. "Suzie, it's almost dark," he protested lamely, but it sounded lame even to his own ears. "Can't this wait for another time? Anyway, why do you even want to dig up all this ancient history? It's all in the past, and it should stay there."

"Buddy," Suzanne's eyes narrowed, growing dangerously stormy, "you brought it up. Not fair to drop a bomb and run. You tell me now."

Brandon shifted uncomfortably at the intense look on her face, but Buddy laughed.

"My God, but you look just like your mother when you're mad." He tilted his head, smiling. "You really do."

"Insulting me won't distract me from the question." Suzanne tossed her hair over her shoulder, tucking it behind a shell-pink ear, but her blazing eyes belied her prim movements. "Talk now, or suffer the consequences."

"All right," he sighed, reaching for his pipe. "Where to begin . . ."

"At the beginning?" Brandon suggested helpfully. Suzanne resisted the urge to bark, *Stay off my side, you daughter-defiler.*

"Well, twenty-something years ago," Buddy began reluctantly. "The drinking age in New Hampshire used to be eighteen. And then it was twenty. And then eighteen again. And then twenty-one." He picked up the hemp strands, eager for something to look at besides Suzanne's face. "It was pretty damn confusing, let me tell you. And you gotta remember, the older you get, the prettier the young girls look, and the better they're able to wrap you around their fingers."

"*What?*" Suzanne cried. "You're telling me, you're honest-to-God telling me that the entire restaurant folded, with all its reputation and longevity, because you were serving alcohol to *minors*? Female minors, I'm guessing?"

"I thought you'd just get a big fine," Brandon mused. "I didn't know they actually closed restaurants for that."

"They did if it was the eighties, and if you served it to enough of them." Buddy bowed his head, ashamed. "I had a terrible weakness for pretty girls, and I just hated asking them questions I might get a no to. 'Can I see your ID?' 'No.' 'Will you go home with me?' 'No.'" He darted a quick look up at Suzanne, clearly hoping she hadn't lost all her hero-worship for him. She held her face perfectly still. She didn't want to alarm him, but she wasn't about to let him off the hook. Not just yet.

"Not my proudest hour, month, or year, but I'd like to think I've made up for it. That is, if carrying around ten tons of guilt on your shoulders does the trick." He gave her a little half-smile, as if mutely saying, *How can you be mad at me? I'm just a cute, little, old man.* "I couldn't help it. The ladies, I just loved them. I loved *all* of them."

"Yeah, I remember . . . Both you and Daddy—loved the ladies, that is." She chuckled a little. "Seeing your father flirt," she shuddered, "let's put it this way, it's a great diet aid. But he was just so, I don't know, suave, and charming, and I'm sure it helped the business. The girls came in to flirt with the guy with the accent, and the guys came in because that's where the girls were. He just knew how to make people—especially women—feel special. Like they were the only ones in the room."

"Yeah. Just ask me how fond your mother was of *that*. Anyway," Buddy summed up, "the judge saw how many charges there were, and he decided he was going to make an example of us."

"Got off damn light, if you ask me."

All three jumped at the sudden comment.

Ava stood at the top of the stairs. She must have come in through the back door. No one knew how long she'd been standing there, listening. She descended the stairs; each step was slow and deliberate.

"*Damn* light," she repeated. "It's pathetic—a forty-five-year-old skirt chaser, giving free drinks to young chippies in the desperate hopes they'll get drunk enough to . . . to . . . *suck face* with the likes of him!"

Buddy turned to Suzanne. "Suck face?"

"She still thinks of *On Golden Pond* as a new release," Suzanne said apologetically.

"I see." He looked back at Ava. Her face, even in this state—maybe especially in this state—was magnetic.

"I'm *so* sorry," her voice dripped with sarcasm, "that your oversized, immature libido got in the way of my Jimmy's business. Not to mention his dreams."

"Ava, look!" Brandon waved his half-finished macramé excitedly. "We're making them to help out with the harvest celebration. Buddy said . . . I mean, *Suzanne* said, it was a good idea, and we could put flowers in them, and . . ."

"Not for my party, you're not," Ava seethed. "Nothing that man has touched will be at my celebration. It's bad luck."

"Okay, Mom." Suzanne took her elbow, trying to head back into the house. "Let's get a schedule and find that yoga class you keep promising me. I want to be able to bounce a quarter off my ass by the end of the summer. Or at least two dimes and a nickel. Come on."

Ava didn't budge.

"The last twenty years of Jimmy's life," she informed Buddy furiously, "were spent stuck in a cubicle, doing the same damn job he'd always hated. He was never the same after that. You took his . . ." she clenched and unclenched her hands before her, trying to pull the word she needed out of the air, "his *joi de vivre*, dammit! His zest. You took my Jimmy's *sparkle* because you're nothing but a puppet to your pecker!"

Suzanne choked, mid-exhale, trying not to laugh. Ava glared at her.

"I'm sorry!" Suzanne ground her cigarette out. "But when one hears one's own mother say things like 'You're nothing but a puppet to your pecker,' well, allowances for giggles must be made."

"After all I've done for you, and you're taking his side?" Ava asked, aghast.

"I'm not on anyone's side! And besides, why do there have to be sides?" she protested. "Mother, please. You need to calm down. I mean it. I do *not* want to have to tell Brandon here to sling you over his shoulder and drag you into the house. But," she pointed her finger directly in her mother's face, "I am *fully* prepared to do it!"

Brandon looked at Suzanne in terror. She wrinkled her nose at him, indicating the unlikelihood of the task. Knowing that he wouldn't have to act on her threat seemed to make him feel much better.

"Yeah, I will," Brandon squeaked. "I really will."

"You broke both our hearts, when you killed our business," Ava said, ignoring Brandon and Suzanne. "And it's time you knew *that* was the reason I started drinking. What you did made me climb into a bottle for ten years!"

The silence that clapped through the yard was deafening. Brandon looked at Ava in disbelief, and, if Suzanne read it right, a little disgust as well.

But Buddy—Buddy who never got upset, never lost his composure in front of anyone, never exploded and never raised his voice except in great fun—Buddy froze stock still, gaze locked on Ava, his eyes deepening until they were dark and furious.

"I could always, always handle my liquor before that," Ava continued, her voice riding stridently, her nose high in the air. "The stress—no, the *agony* of losing the pub—ruined my Jimmy. And that, my friend, ruined *me*."

"Mother . . ."

"We had nothing when all was said and done. Nothing to show for seventeen years of working night and day. We couldn't even afford to send our daughter to college!"

"Now, hold on just one minute." Suzanne wasn't about to let herself be used as a weapon to beat Buddy with. "You know goddamn good and well that I didn't go to college because I was pregnant. Everyone knows that. Not because of lack of money, but because of lack of a Trojan."

"You ruined *all* of us," Ava raged on, ignoring her daughter's calm, rational words. "So, why don't you just be a man and once and for all own up to what you've done."

"And just what did I do, Ava?" he asked softly, his expression frozen in place.

"What do you think?" she screamed. "You turned my husband into a walking dead man, and you turned me into a drunk!"

That last word echoed endless throughout the courtyard; it seemed to Suzanne that it would never stop.

Drunk, drunk, drunk, drunk, drunk . . .

For a long moment, no one dared speak into the tense night air.

"Okay, that's it," Buddy said finally, getting his cane and struggling to his feet. "That is *it*." He took a slow step toward Ava, then another, then a third.

Ava, for her part, stuck her nose right up in the air, poised for a fight. It was the stance she took, Suzanne knew, when she knew she was wrong but was going to stand her ground anyway; in other words, it was a pose she'd seen often.

"Mother," Suzanne began hastily, "no one but you can . . ."

But Buddy would not be stopped now, and he cut her off with a softness that was chilling.

"Your drinking, lady, is *not my fault.*" He emphasized the last three words tapping his cane on the lawn. "How dare you? How *dare* you? I may have made some messes in my day, lady, but that one was all you. *All* you. As in all *Ava,* all by *herself.* You chose to pick up the booze, and you chose to pour it down your throat by the gallon, and *that* broke James's heart a helluva lot worse than anything I ever did."

It was Ava's turn to stand motionless, her expression blank, her eyes unreadable.

"Uncle Buddy . . . *Please.*" Suzanne pleaded softly.

"I'm sorry, Suzie, but some things just have to be said."

She'd only seen him this angry once before, when he'd found her crying on the steps of O'Shenanigan's after closing. The boy she'd been dating had wanted more than she'd wanted to give, and there had been a tussle before she'd been able to get out of the car. She'd hitchhiked to the pub, and Buddy had been there.

Oh, yes, he'd been this angry then—there had been rages and yelling and threats of violence, and that particular young man had never shown his face around O'Shenanigan's again. But that was the only time she'd seen his temper show itself before now.

"I loved James, Ava." Buddy's voice was choked with thick emotion. "Like a *brother,* I loved that man. Do you hear me? Like a *brother!*" He pounded his cane again. "And where I come from, lady, that means more than any damn restaurant." He took a moment to calm himself, trying to force his voice back down to its normal register.

Suzanne closed her eyes, remembering other fights, long ago, fights about Daddy's flirting, fights about Mom's drinking. She remembered clapping her hands over her ears, just wishing this would stop, wishing she were somewhere else. This, strangely, felt an awful lot like that.

"I will take a lot of crap in the name of that love," he said evenly, "but there is a *limit,* and as usual, you just kept pushing and pushing until you found it. You *found* it, lady. Believe me, if you wanted to hear, there are things I could fill you in on. There are plenty of things I could tell you. I could . . ."

He stumbled and shot a panicked look at Suzanne. She raised her head and listened keenly, waiting to hear what he could tell them. Buddy's mouth worked, he swallowed hard a couple of times, but nothing came.

"You could tell me *what*, Mr. McKinley?" Ava asked icily.

When he spoke, it was in a gentle voice full of regret. "How just plain rotten and nasty it is for you to keep rubbing my face in this," he said at last. "Those mistakes cost me the business I loved too, you know. I lost too. I lost *plenty*. But I guess you never thought about my losses, did you? You never thought about anyone but Ava, and what Ava wanted, and who to bulldoze over in order to get what Ava wanted, and who to punish," he tapped his chest, "once things didn't turn out the way Ava hoped."

His voice was rising again, so he stopped then. It was enough. Time to go. He bent over, gingerly, to pick up his cane. Brandon leapt to his feet to try to help him, but Buddy waved him off impatiently. Once he had it firmly in hand, he stalked angrily up the stairs into his house.

"Uncle Buddy, please," called Suzanne, knowing it would be futile, but needing to try. "Come on, come back here. You know she didn't mean it." She turned to her mother and savagely hissed, "Tell him. Tell him you didn't mean that."

Ava remained silent, but it didn't matter anyway; the door to his house slammed shut so loudly that Suzanne was amazed the glass didn't shatter. She slowly turned to look at Ava, still unable to process the fact that her mother, her very own, normally intelligent and rational mother, had made such a patently ridiculous accusation.

"Alcoholics aren't made," she'd told Suzanne a thousand times or more. "They're born. Just like people are born deaf or with a clubfoot. We have a medical condition that we have to be treated for."

So to hear her allege that anything Buddy had done, no matter how awful, had caused her condition . . .

Well, she knew Ava couldn't possibly believe that was true. The way her mother was staring after Buddy, fidgeting just ever so slightly, confirmed it.

"Why don't you go into our house," Suzanne suggested to Brandon. For the moment, she'd completely forgotten that he was This Brandon, the enemy. "He probably needs a little space."

"Thanks." Brandon cast one last disappointed look at Ava, then hopped up the stairs to the deck, into the kitchen, and out of sight.

It was just the two of them now, and for the first time in a long, long time, Suzanne couldn't make her mother meet her gaze.

"Well," Suzanne said finally. "Well, well, well."

"Well? That's a very deep subject." Ava forced a bright smile. "Get it?"

"Mother." Suzanne's voice was full of meaning.

Ava sighed heavily and turned to her daughter. Their identical deep brown eyes locked, and Suzanne could literally feel what her mother was thinking.

What Ava had done was wrong, and she wanted her to apologize; moreover, she wanted her to apologize right now.

But from the look in Ava's eyes, she might as well have wished for the moon in a Mason jar, to quote her father. There seemed to be a lot of Jimmy's quotes floating around all of a sudden.

The streetlight came on just then, though it wasn't quite dark yet, and the buzz startled them both.

"After we lost the pub, the stress was . . . overwhelming." Ava said colorlessly, reaching up to fix her perfectly secure chignon. "No, more than that, it was *smothering*. The money worries were a nightmare, and your father had to find work, and we didn't know how long it would be until he got back on his feet." She shuddered. "Picking up a new career in your late forties—I wouldn't wish that on my worst enemy. After a few years, we got Grandpa Joe's money, and things got a lot easier, let me tell you. You remember that?"

Suzanne did remember. The inheritance had left her parents so giddy with relief it was hard to recall that someone had recently died. Debts were paid, money was put away for retirement, and their house was paid off. Brand-new cars replaced the old ones for the first time in Ava and Jimmy's marriage.

Once, on a class trip to Boston right after they'd lost O'Shenanigan's, Suzanne had seen something she didn't know existed: an entire homeless family. Two parents and a son who appeared to be nearly thirty walking along the cobblestone sidewalks, looking for cans, for money, for food people dropped. The mother had been nagging the son.

"Flatten this up, and put it inside your shirt, for God's sake," she'd scolded, handing him a newspaper she'd picked up from the gutter. "Or you'll catch your death of cold."

For months afterwards, Suzanne wondered if someday that wouldn't be her family. She could almost imagine Ava's raspy voice saying, "Don't smoke that cigarette out of the gutter, dear. God knows what you'll catch."

But then grouchy Grandpa Joe had died from a stroke in his sleep at the ripe old age of ninety-three. In life, he'd never hugged his son or given him compliments or even showed up for his basketball games in high school. But in death, he'd given Jimmy every penny he'd ever pinched, nearly three hundred thousand dollars of it. Hardly a fortune, especially after Uncle Sam took his share, but enough to buy an awful lot of reconciliation, Daddy used to say. Pay off the mortgage and lots of other pressing bills. Buy a car that wasn't a hazard to drive. Put a little aside for the future. Invest.

In short, it did all the things that O'Shenanigan's was supposed to do for them . . . except paying the fines incurred when O'Shenanigan's was closed.

"Come on, Suze," Ava held out her hand, breaking the terrible tension. "Let's go find you that yoga class."

After a moment, Suzanne took her mother's hand, and together they climbed the stairs to the warmth of the kitchen to look for the brochure. But she couldn't resist a quick glance back at Buddy's house when she was sure Ava couldn't see. She and Ava wouldn't discuss what Ava had said to Buddy, Suzanne knew. They would gloss over it, as though it never happened. Trademark of alcoholic dysfunction, she recognized. Anything to cover up Mommy's missteps . . . She knew the drill well.

"Believe me, if you wanted to hear, there are things I could fill you in on," Buddy had said to her mother. "There are plenty of things I could tell you. I could . . ." And then he'd looked right at her, ended the conversation, and marched back into his house just as quickly as a man with arthritis and a cane can march.

What in the world had he meant? Just what was it that he could he tell Ava? Suzanne had no idea . . . but she damn well intended to find out.

EIGHT

"Why are we out and about so early?" Suzanne complained the next morning as she followed her mother through the farmer's market. She hadn't had her coffee, her shower had been cut short by Ava's nagging, and worrying about Molly had robbed her of sleep. All in all, a totally crappy way to start the day. "I'm not usually awake yet, let alone walking anywhere."

"It's Wednesday," Ava told her, as though this should be obvious. "I do all my marketing on Wednesday mornings."

The outdoor farmers market, during the summer, was held in the old Citizen's Bank parking lot. From there it spilled onto Prescott Park, right on the waterfront, about a quarter of a mile from home.

It was easier to go on foot than to try to find parking, Suzanne agreed, but it didn't make walking along the Market Street extension, where cars came whipping around from Woodbury Avenue, any more fun or less life-threatening.

Retail therapy, Ava decided, would be good for Suzanne. There was nothing for the soul like spending money, as far as Ava was concerned.

"Fine, you hate shopping—come with me, so I don't have to do it alone, and you can consider it rent," she said, when Suzanne tried to protest that she was one of the few females who really didn't enjoy shopping. (Ava correctly assumed that it was all the years of penny-pinching on a small salary that supported three people that had turned Suzanne off the idea of spending money on things that weren't absolutely necessary).

Though Suzanne would never admit it to her mother, she always found herself enjoying elbowing tourists out of her way and haggling over the price of a wooden spoon that had cost a twentieth of the sticker-price to make.

The summer people had already left, but the leaf-peepers had just begun to trickle in, even though the colors were just barely beginning to shift.

"Why do we have to call it 'marketing,' Mom?" Suzanne grumbled. "It doesn't make it sound any more fun than just plain, old grocery shopping."

Ava waved the complaint away, carefully looking over the carrots. "Do you see a grocery store here, anywhere?" She gestured around. "No? Me neither. I see a good, old-fashioned outdoor market. So, it's *marketing*."

Suzanne sipped the coffee she had picked up at her favorite coffee shop, Breaking New Grounds (or, BNG, as Molly called it), and waited patiently while Ava found the perfect okra and cabbage. She refused to think of what dish her mother might have in mind for those two particular ingredients. Ava had spent a great deal of time and energy all summer trying to find some way to cook two of her favorite dishes that Suzanne would eat.

"Oh, I'm so sorry," Ava's voice dripped mock sincerity. "You're right. It's *much* better to go inside with the cement floors that give you shin splints, and the fluorescent lights that wreck your eyes, and arm wrestle old Mr. Petrovski from down the block for the last unbroken pushcart. And then, you get stuck with the one with the crazy left wheel anyway. Then you have to make sure you've got your discount cards, and those young kids, they don't help you out with your groceries anymore the way they used to . . ."

"All right, all right, all right!" Suzanne held up her hands, officially surrendering. "I'm wrong. You're right. You're always right. You're superior to me in all ways. Why do I ever question you? Happy now, you wicked old witch?"

"*Ecstatic.*" Ava reached out to pinch her daughter's peach-colored cheek. "Hearing those words is every mother's dream, my darling."

"Yes," Suzanne admitted, "but knowing Molly, I doubt I'll be getting hit with them any time soon."

"You might be right, at that."

Suzanne took a good look around at the sea of booths. The sun was hot, even at this time of day, but the trees provided a canopy, granting a break from the relentless glare. She breathed deeply, tasting the clean air by the water—which was really why she secretly enjoyed the outdoor market. She had always loved being around the milling shoppers; she loved the ambitious retailers and their inventive products. But her token resistance was a preventative measure so that Ava wouldn't get in the habit of having her on call for any and all social outings.

One perk about shopping here was not having to fork over her hard-earned cash to the Corporate Monster, in the form of any "superstore." She remembered once, over a decade ago, Molly had asked her to explain the difference between a store and a superstore. Suzanne had thought about it for a moment.

"Maybe superstores can fly," she'd finally suggested. Molly had dissolved into giggles. From then on, every time they passed by a self-proclaimed superstore, Molly would swear she could see it readying itself for takeoff.

Where did those days go? We used to have our own language. We laughed at things no one else got. We were closer than two peas in a pod . . . Where did that go? Suzanne ruminated but then shook the thoughts away.

Melancholia was no way to start the day.

"Hey, Mom?" She picked up a wedge of cheese that was made in Milton. "How did you feel when I told you I was pregnant?"

She was as startled to ask the question as Ava obviously was to hear it.

Where the hell did that come from? she wondered.

Ava put down the zucchini she'd been squeezing; she clearly wondered the same thing. "You've never asked me that before," Ava said softly.

"Well, it's like . . . it's just, it's the one topic we never touch," Suzanne stammered. "We've tiptoed around it for years like it's a land mine that might go off."

"Well, it was such a long time ago," Ava began. "And I never wanted you to feel as though I was judging you. Motherhood is hard enough without that."

"I know, Mom."

Ava was in the last throes of her embarrassingly pickled days when she learned she was going to be a grandmother at age forty-six. It had probably been hard for her to judge anyone else when she was drinking vanilla extract and Scope.

The first year of Ava's sobriety had been the first year of Molly's life. Suzanne never knew if it was the impending baby that did the trick, but Ava had put down the bottle, and this time it had stayed down. AA meetings, which previously had been "for whiners and losers" in her book, were suddenly part of her daily routine.

Slowly, during that last trimester, Suzanne began to see bits and pieces of the mother she remembered from her earliest years.

Understandably, they had been wary around each other—Ava out of humility, as she had a lot to make up for; Suzanne out of caution, as she didn't want to get bitten again.

But when the baby came, that pink little bundle of smells with her long eyelashes and tons of hair, with the big dark eyes that seemed to seek out her own and find comfort there, Suzanne had been terrified.

How on earth am I supposed to take care of this child? she wondered. *I couldn't even pass advanced physiology junior year. This is the real thing. What if I accidentally kill her? Maim her? Sing her the wrong lullaby and emotionally scar her for life?*

Despite herself, Suzanne desperately craved her mother's nearness. Not drunk, drooling, smelly, rambling Mom; the sober, sweet, nice mother that she once was. It was an ache so deep that it felt like a physical longing.

Ava, for her part, didn't push herself too hard toward her daughter. Instead, she called twice a week, religiously, to ask if there was anything Suzanne needed, and once a week she'd stop by to help with the housework. (Steve, even then, spent most of his time out with his friends or locked in his studio.)

The first few times she'd done that, Suzanne had been furious; she was perfectly capable of keeping a house, even if the "house" was a tiny one-bedroom on Rockingham Street. After all, she reasoned, she'd been taking care of Ava's since Ava decided that drunkenness was more important than cleanliness.

But as the months went by, and she got bigger and bigger (after her seventh month, she had them weigh her backwards on the scale—she knew she was officially a whale, but there was no need to rub it in), Ava's assistance with the vacuuming, dusting, and folding the laundry became a welcome event. To her horror, she found herself looking forward to seeing her mother's car pull into the driveway each week as she brought along a snack (she'd begun cooking as a way to keep her hands busy) and usually just one more thing she'd seen for the baby that she couldn't resist.

Grimly, Suzanne staved off the feelings of gratitude, of pleasure in her mother's company. After all, it could, and probably would, end at any moment. She knew alcoholism was a disease, and she knew it would be difficult for anyone to conquer.

It's not like I don't have compassion for her, she reasoned darkly. *I'd also have compassion for a rabid dog caught in a bear trap . . . But I'm sure as hell not going to get so close that it can bite me.*

It was during one of these visits, when Ava came to take Suzanne to her high school graduation where Steve was performing with the band, that Ava had noticed Suzanne wincing and touching her stomach. "What's the matter, dear?"

"Nothing," Suzanne replied, her teeth clenched. "I'm just nervous about graduation tonight . . . I think I'm constipated again. I've been having the most awful cramps all . . ."

As soon as the words came out of her mouth, Suzanne realized what the pains really were; from the look on Ava's face, she did too. She expected Mommy Dearest to fall to pieces, as she always did in time of crisis, but if necessary she'd walk right over Mommy, call a taxi, and get to the hospital herself.

But Ava didn't fall to pieces. Instead, a calm that Suzanne had never seen before seemed to settle over her features.

"Let's just time these stomach cramps," she suggested, "and see if there's a pattern to how far apart they are."

Suzanne, suddenly terrified, realized they'd begun around noontime. It was now almost five, almost time to leave for the school. What if she had waited too long? What if she was going to give birth any second now? And worst of all, what if it was too late for the doctor to give her the epidural she'd been promised, and she'd actually have to feel it?

"Ten minutes apart," Ava said calmly. "Plenty of time. Do you have your suitcase all packed?"

Suzanne shook her head miserably. Her due date was two weeks away, and the doctor had told her—had practically *promised* her, dammit—that first babies were always late.

"Well, then, let's get that settled."

Ava strode into the bedroom, found the backpack Suzanne used for textbooks, and emptied it. Within minutes, it was filled with Suzanne's favorite pajamas, her toothbrush, makeup kit, and a loose jogging suit that would be among the few clothes of her own that she'd fit in after the baby came.

Ava also took it upon herself to throw into the bag a couple of books off the nightstand, plus Suzanne's Walkman with the three tapes lying next to it: Nirvana's *Nevermind*, Hole's *Live through This*, and the best of Guns 'N Roses. A graduate of the nineties, she would always be an nineties girl at heart, in regards to both music and fashion.

She also remembered to pack the white cotton gown and matching booties one of her AA pals had knitted to bring the baby home in.

"That's sorted out." Ava came out, smiling. "Now, let's get you off to graduate."

"Graduate?" She stared at her mother, in horror. Was she *serious*? She really is crazy, even stone cold sober. "But Mom, you just said . . ."

"I said they're ten minutes apart," Ava told her, reaching for her hand. "If I took you to the hospital right now, they'd send you right back home 'til they were five minutes apart, and that could be hours from now. Isn't that what your doctor told you?" She didn't wait for Suzanne's answer. "There's no reason we can't get you graduated, and then take you."

Graduation suddenly didn't seem so important. "But *Mom* . . ."

"But, nothing," her mother told her. "Maybe you're not valedictorian, but you're in the top ten, and that's something that I wish I could brag about. It'll only take a couple of hours, and by then, maybe it'll be time to get you to Portsmouth Regional."

Maybe? Suzanne felt like she had little choice as Ava marched her to the car and strapped her in. She even insisted on coming into the back rooms with her at the school to help her with her hair and makeup—and to struggle with the zipper on the gown that would barely close.

Oddly, Suzanne was grateful for her presence; no one dared snicker or giggle with a mom around.

"I have to find Steve and tell him," she said, drinking her third pink lemonade from the newly-installed soda machine in the cafeteria. She seemed terribly thirsty all of a sudden, and no matter how much she drank, she couldn't quite quench it.

"I'll go find him. You just stay here and rest until it's time to take your place in line." She kissed Suzanne firmly on the cheek, then wiped off the coral lipstick smudge.

She strode out before Suzanne could say another word; in a way, Suzanne was glad that Ava would be the one to tell him. Although she was sure (at that time) that Steve was the love of her life, and soon he'd be rolling in record deal offers and money, suddenly she felt, as she breathed carefully through another contraction, slightly angry and very annoyed with him.

Finally, the band had begun to play the ever-familiar tune of "Pomp and Circumstance," and Suzanne and her classmates marched slowly down the hallway of the auditorium. The speeches, the songs by the chorus, the scholarship announcements, and finally, the handing out of the diplomas—all of it seemed to take forever.

She barely heard any of it; she was too busy watching the clock. It seemed to her that the contractions were getting closer together, but it was harder to tell with all this noise, all these people distracting her.

Finally she heard her name, and when she stood up, something happened. For a horrible moment she thought she'd wet her pants, because her gown was sopping wet from the waist down. She looked up at the principal, who was waiting with her diploma.

She didn't know what to do. The girls on either side of her were scooting away from her on the bench, so as not to get any on their gowns, which were still a pristine white.

Ava was already up and on her feet, striding down the aisle while the crowd began murmuring. She gestured to the principal, who stood at the podium, looking back and forth from Suzanne to her mother, completely perplexed.

"Give me that, you idiot," Ava hissed, snatching the diploma from the red-faced principal, and then proceeded to go to her daughter, putting her arm around her as if it were the most normal thing in the world to have your water break at graduation. "Come on, honey, this means it's time to go the hospital."

She marched her daughter down the aisle. Suzanne gasped; the contractions were much more painful now. Ava motioned to Steve, and the three of them made their way to the car.

At the hospital, Steve insisted that he and Suzanne be alone when the baby was born, and Suzanne felt a pang of regret watching her mother wave to her as she was pushed directly into the delivery room. Looking up at Steve's handsome, nervous face, suddenly she wanted her mother more than she ever had before.

Two hours later, Molly was there, with her little toes and little fingers and curly hair. They had told her that her eyes wouldn't open for several days, but Molly's eyes were already open, dark blue eyes gazing up at her. As she touched her little face, Molly's tiny fingers had wrapped around her pinky, and Suzanne was so touched, she almost stopped breathing.

Is this how my mother felt when she had me? she wondered. *Is it?*

With each month that Ava miraculously didn't fall off the wagon with an audible thud, Suzanne found something returning that she hadn't ever expected to see again: her trust in her mother. When Molly was one, Suzanne forced herself to test this trust, to ease herself out on the ice, to see if it held strong or if it broke and threw her and Molly into the freezing dark currents.

She began asking her mother for rides to the dentist when she knew he was going to give her gas, bring over the occasional cup of special coffee just to talk, or help her plan out a dinner menu for her first dinner party.

Then came the first truly terrifying test. After screwing up her courage by chain-smoking half a pack of cigarettes, she had called her mother, hands trembling.

"Hey, Mom," she said, as casually as she could. "There's an office management class and a computer class over at UNH I'd like to take. It's three nights a week, for ten weeks. Do you think," she had to stop and clear her throat, "do you think you could watch Molly for me?"

There was a long pause, and Suzanne thought that maybe, just maybe, Ava wasn't prepared to look after an active toddler so often.

"Of course I'll watch Molly for you," Ava replied lightly, sniffling back her tears. Suzanne could practically hear her smile through the phone wires. "You know that I'd just love it."

"Great, great," Suzanne said. Working days at the Pic 'n' Pay on Islington and three nights a week at the Blue Mermaid left little to put away for Molly's schooling. Their budget was stretched as thin as a tightrope, and Suzanne was sick to death of struggling so hard to make ends meet.

Night school seemed like a step in the right direction. More education meant a better job.

She remembered every detail of that first computer class, every time the professor scratched his head (he had dandruff), and every tick of the second hand on the clock. She tried to take notes, but she couldn't focus on anything the professor was saying.

How could she have left that helpless little baby alone with her mother? Ava had only been sober for three years; anything could set her off, and Molly would be defenseless without a responsible adult there to stop it.

Suzanne began biting her nails, and during the class break, she resisted the urge to call home just to "check" by sheer willpower alone . . . That and the Rastafarian guy who smelled like patchouli and pot had beat her to the pay phone.

Fifteen minutes before the class ended, she couldn't take it anymore.

She sprinted to her car and proceeded to break every speed limit on the way home. Her heartbeat was deafening as she fumbled for her keys to the front door. She burst in, fearing the worst, that she'd come home to a passed out mother and a dead child.

"Mom!" she shouted, bursting through the front door. There was no answer. Her heart threatened to pound right out of her chest. *Mom! Where are you?*

"In here, dear," Ava had called, and Suzanne followed her voice to the bathroom.

She opened the door to find Molly playing happily in the bathtub with suds up to her chest and her hair in soapy horns. The front of Ava's shirt was soaked, Molly had placed a crown of suds on her head, and they were both laughing hysterically as a Barney tape whined cheerily in the background.

Suzanne stood there in the bathroom door, feeling ashamed, as her heart rate slowly returned to something approaching normal.

"You're back early," Ava observed, but her eyes were soft and kind.

"Yeah," Suzanne nodded, trying to breathe evenly. "First class, they let us out early."

Ava looked up at her; their eyes met for just a moment. And after a decade of Suzanne taking care of her mother, the mother-daughter relationship finally rearranged itself to the proper order.

And now that my kid might be following in my steps, I guess might be a good time to finally ask The Question About Which We Do Not Speak, Suzanne realized, taking a sip of her cooling coffee.

"Well," Ava began, haltingly, "truth be told, I was a little disappointed. No, no, make that *very* disappointed. Not in your behavior," she said hastily, "because teenagers will do what teenagers will do, and Lord knows I'm not one to judge anyone. Your father and I . . ."

"I can and will vomit in the middle of this open market if you talk about sex and Daddy, Mom. Just you watch me," Suzanne warned.

"Oh, all right, fine." Ava picked up several McIntosh apples, tossing them into her sack; that meant apple pie tonight, Suzanne knew. Yummy. Suzanne wouldn't think about what it would do to her waistline. Everyone knew that the autumn, which was right before the holidays, was a crappy time to start a diet. Plus, she wouldn't be living with Ava the uber-chef forever.

"Where was I?" asked Ava.

"You were disappointed in me," Suzanne said breezily, trying to keep the tone light. This was, after all, a lifetime ago—Molly's lifetime ago.

"Oh, no, sweetie!" Ava poked her finger at her to make the point. "I said I was disappointed, not disappointed in *you.* You were a kid, and kids make mistakes."

She stopped, debating over a plate of homemade peanut butter fudge, wondering if she could safely fall off the diet wagon this week and still fit into her pants the next. Deciding against it, she continued on.

"But the reason I was disappointed was . . . well, as you found out pretty darn quickly," she linked her arm through Suzanne's as they walked, "that once you have a child, you have to stop *being* a child, and awfully darn fast. And I didn't want you to have to stop being a child. I wanted you to . . . Oh, I wanted you to go to football games and frat parties. I wanted you to spend your junior year abroad in France and come home a bilingual person. I've always wanted to speak two languages myself, you know."

It was perhaps the three hundredth time her mother had shared this particular confidence.

"I know, Mom. It's still not too late, you realize."

"Oh, you." Ava waved her off, moving on to the stand that sold homemade raspberry jam, Molly's favorite, as well as her own. For reasons Ava could never understand, Suzanne preferred apple jelly from the store above all else. "You have to learn that stuff when your brain is young and fresh. My brain spent a lifetime getting stuffed with all kinds of data and then about fifteen years being pickled."

"Mother!" Suzanne giggled, a little shocked, looking around to see if she'd been overheard. Mom didn't often joke about her disease, and she certainly did not while in public.

"Well, it's true." She paid for the two Mason jars of jam and stuffed them into Suzanne's tote.

"So, was that it, then? Disappointed because I lost out on my childhood?" Suzanne ventured.

"Well . . ." Ava fingered a homemade friendship bracelet, wondering if it would be too corny to buy matching ones for herself and her two girls. "That was most of it. And Steve wasn't my idea of the kind of man for you. I knew he'd suck you dry—that refusal to work, or contribute, that sense of entitlement he always had. So sure that the world was going to just walk in and hand him what he wanted."

"I think—I'm not sure," Suzanne said slowly, "but I think Daddy wanted me to get an abortion." It was another question she'd never dared to ask, certainly not while Jimmy was alive.

"Oh, yes, he certainly did." Ava nodded rapidly. "He didn't want to pressure you about it, because, well, he was brought up in a strict Catholic household and he didn't want your soul to be damned for all of eternity." Ava rolled her eyes all the way back in her head and snorted. Many an argument they'd had was about how Ava's nondenominational God was a lot nicer than Jimmy's Baptist one. "So, on the one hand, he was hoping that you'd have one, and on the other, he didn't want you to burn for it."

"We almost did, you know," Suzanne admitted, then drew a deep breath of salt air, throwing her hair back to let her face be cleansed in the breeze. To this day, it was hard to talk about. "Don't get me wrong, I'm still pro-choice and all that, and I don't think anyone who doesn't truly want a baby should be forced to have one, but . . ."

"But, what happened?" Ava prodded gently.

"Well . . ." Her breath caught again, just a tug this time. "We had the appointment. Steve drove me there, and he was going to pay for half of it . . ."

"What a gentleman," Ava remarked sarcastically. "A true prince among men. Tell me, is that what passes for manners in the new millennium?"

"Yeah, well, I thought I was in love, you know? And for a while, I guess I was." Those times had gotten harder and harder to remember in the past ten or so years. In fact, she had trouble remembering what even *liking* Steve had felt like at all.

"So." Ava moved swiftly past the dandelion wine stand. Suzanne shuddered to think that even such a disgusting concoction could tempt her mother. "So, what happened?"

"Well, we were there, we were actually at the clinic, and I was in one of those Johnny gowns, you know, where the back swings open for all the world to see your butt. They showed us this cheesy little film on abortion, how it's difficult but it's a necessary evil in this world . . ."

Ava frowned, fingering a green sea-glass necklace. It would look so pretty with Molly's hazel eyes, but she wasn't sure if it was appropriate for a former drunk to give her granddaughter jewelry that had once been a beer bottle. "They actually used the term necessary evil?"

"No, no." Suzanne bought a homemade cookie from a sprightly elderly woman, split it in half, and handed the bigger half to her mother. Ava pretended not to want it, but in the end, she gave in. "So, after the little film festival, they tell Steve to wait in the waiting room . . ."

"They don't let them stay in there with you?" Ava asked in dismay. "That seems awfully cruel."

"I asked about that," Suzanne agreed. "Apparently, if someone's holding your hand or something, and you're tensing in any way, it can completely screw the procedure up. Don't ask me how. They're probably more afraid of the emotional scenes causing problems than anything else."

"You're very likely right."

"Anyway," Suzanne plowed on, knowing that if she ever stopped, she'd never start again, "they told me to lie down and put my feet up in the stirrups, and . . ."

"And?" Ava asked softly.

"Well," Suzanne began, "and here's the big part, the part that might very well convince you once and for all that your daughter was certifiably insane." Suzanne swallowed, hardly believing she was about to reveal her deep dark secret. *I must be more vulnerable than I thought.* "As soon as I lay back, and my feet were in those ice-cold stirrups, I heard, literally *heard* a voice in my head that seemed to come from every part of my body say, '*Don't!*'"

Her stomach still fluttered thinking about it, and she knew she wasn't going to be able to finish the cookie. She handed the rest of it to her mother, who wrapped it in a napkin and put it in her purse.

"Really?" Ava turned to her in astonishment. A man in a Boston Red Sox shirt bumped into her, but she waved away his apology, completely fixated on Suzanne. "A voice *said* that to you? You actually heard a voice?"

Suzanne nodded. She'd always been nervous about telling anyone this, but she found herself tingling with relief more than burning with embarrassment.

"That was it. That was the reason I decided I had to have Steve's baby. And then everyone was talking to me about my options and how I was throwing away my precious last days of childhood . . . But from that single word, I understood that I was supposed to keep her and raise her. It seemed to come from inside of me."

She had never told anyone this story before, because once you tell people you've heard voices, she knew, people started prescribing drugs like Haldol and telling you that you couldn't go outside without an attendant. But finally speaking the words after all these years was such a relief that it spread from her toes to her head, making her almost giddy.

"The voice," she went on, "was so . . . comforting, so loving, so strong, and completely firm. It was like, I didn't even *think* to question it."

"Was the voice male or female?"

"Hmmmm?"

"The voice," Ava wanted to know, "was it male, or female?"

Suzanne looked at her mother and burst out laughing. Leave it to Mom to come up with the one question that, after eighteen years, she hadn't even thought to ask herself.

"Well, to tell you the truth, it wasn't really . . ." She thought for a moment, trying to put her finger on it. "It wasn't really one or the other. Or maybe it was both." She shook her head, frustrated with her inability to describe it. "But it seemed to come almost from inside me, inside my head, inside my heart. Like I could feel its vibrations through my whole body."

Ava was smiling at her in an almost awed fashion. "What did you do then?"

Suzanne shrugged again, popping a cigarette into her mouth and lighting up. That was another benefit of an outdoor market; they couldn't tell you not to smoke.

"There wasn't much *to* do. I got up, pushed the nurse away, told her I'd changed my mind, and ripped off that damn ugly Johnny."

"Did she try to talk you back into it?"

Another question that no one but Ava would consider asking, Suzanne thought, amused.

"No, not really. She spoke very calmly, telling me that it was my choice and if 'another option' was better for me, then I should follow that option. But I could tell she was trying to keep me in the room as long as possible, in case it was just a momentary lapse."

"I bet they get a lot of those." Ava plucked the cigarette from Suzanne's lips and flung it to the ground, smushing it out with her foot. "I'm sorry, dear. I know we're outside, but a little consideration for others, hmm?" Without giving Suzanne a chance to react—let alone respond—she plowed on with the conversation. "So, what did young Mr. Lauder have to say about all this when you came out of the room? Was he upset? Angry? Did he try to talk you out of it?"

"Well," Suzanne replied, looking longingly at the crushed butt beneath Ava's heel, "he was sitting there in the waiting room, flipping through *Highlights* magazine, and I came barreling out. He just looked up at me, not like he was surprised or anything, but like he was wondering what the heck I was doing out there so quickly. I think I said something lame like, 'I changed my mind, let's get out of here,' and just walked out. He followed me, of course, and we just sat there in the clinic's parking lot in his brother's cruddy truck, staring off into space for a couple of hours. Then he drove me home."

"So, he didn't try to make you feel better? Comfort you? Like it was all going to work out beautifully, and everything was going to be okay?"

"Nope."

"Well, you gotta give the little booger that," Ava conceded. "At least he didn't pull out those crappy clichés on you."

Ava stared out into the marina for a moment. She loved the water, and she couldn't understand how people in landlocked states managed to avoid becoming completely claustrophobic. Some of the boats were being put up for the season as they spoke, while braver members of the yacht club would leave theirs in the water for another couple of weeks, hoping for just one or two more blissful outings before the harsh cold reality of winter struck.

Suzanne gazed right along with her mother, loving the way the waves gently lapped up on the rocks, below the decks. She'd spent many a childhood hour watching the boats go by, while escaping Ava's drunkenness.

One day, I'll get one, she told herself, as she did every year. One day. Of course, now that all that money she'd had earmarked for Molly's education wasn't needed, maybe someday could be now.

But after years of pinching pennies, spending thousands of dollars on a boat . . . She didn't know if she could do it.

"Well," Suzanne spoke suddenly, shaking off the seriousness of the conversation, "the voice was *right*. So the next day, Steve and I went to find the cheapest wedding rings we could, and nine months later, I gave birth to the prettiest, purplest, gooiest, eight-pound, eleven-ounce baby that this world has ever seen. I remember being shocked at her hair. She had a full head of curly hair, even though every baby I'd ever seen before that had been bald. She looked like a monkey. That's what we called her, remember? Till she was about two, she wasn't Molly, she was Monkey."

"I remember." Ava fell quiet for a moment, taking everything in. Suzanne used the opportunity to stealthily light another Spirit, surreptitiously blowing the smoke as far away from Ava, and every other patron of the market, as she could. "Has anything like that ever happened to you before?" Ava asked. "The voice thing, I mean?"

Suzanne opened her mouth to say no, when a memory came rushing back to her. She'd been about eight years old, climbing the big oak trees with the McHenry brothers from down the block a ways. They were prodding each other: "You go higher," "No, *you* go higher," "No, you go first," and suddenly, there was a big black electrical cable within reach.

"I *dare* you to touch it," the oldest one, Rick (or was it Todd?) challenged her. He had only mustered up the nerve to climb to the top branches after she did, and he had to save face somehow.

"Why would I want to touch a stupid wire?" she had said.

"Yeah, I wouldn't do it," John sniveled, wiping his nose on his arm.

Rick/Todd pulled a package of unopened gum out of his pocket. Grape Bubblicious. Her very favorite.

"It's all yours if you're not chicken," he sang, waving the purple foil package back and forth. "Come on, it's totally safe, you big wimp."

"If it's so safe," John shot back, "why don't *you* do it?"

"Because I already have a pack of gum," Rick/Todd replied confidently. He looked up at Suzanne. The look said, *are you tough, or a sissy girl like all the rest of them after all?* "Well?"

Suzanne, knowing nothing about electricity, started to reach for the wire, wanting the gum, but most of all not wanting to be seen as a wimp by the McHenry brothers. Then suddenly, that voice, that same voice that later saved Molly's potential life, spoke right in her head.

Don't! The voice screamed. *If there's even a chance you'll get a shock, you shouldn't do it. Don't!*

She pulled back, gasping, as though she had just escaped a great danger (and she found out years later that she had—touching the wire would likely have fried her to a crisp right in the tree).

She was suddenly sure she had done the right thing. She also just as suddenly didn't give a darn what Rick/Todd thought about it.

"What's the point of grabbing a big old wire?" she sniffed haughtily, as she climbed down the tree. "You just go ahead and keep your stupid gum."

Dangling by her arms, she dropped the remaining foot and a half. As she hit the ground, she landed on one ankle funny, and it rolled a bit. She felt a small crunch that would later turn her whole foot an explosion of various shades of purple, but at that moment, she didn't so much as utter an "ouch."

Standing, she daintily wagged her red-mittened hand at him and flounced home. He stared after her, a stupid look on his face, wondering how she had managed to avoid the dare but still get the best of him, and it made her feel strong. For the first time in her life, she felt *empowered*—even though she didn't yet possess the word in her vocabulary. She didn't feel the pain of her injured ankle until she was safely home.

"Now that you mention it," Suzanne said to her mother, "I did hear that voice, just one other time." She filled her mom in on the Rick/Todd adventure. "It's just like . . . there is something, or someone, up there rooting for me."

"I bet there is, sweetie." Ava stopped at a table full of candles, and Suzanne picked up what looked like a small bamboo tube with a crystal glued to its end. The owner of the booth, who seemed to sell primarily Halloween items, had the audacity to ask twenty-two dollars for it.

"Well, look who's here!" a voice said brightly from behind the booth. "Hey there, Suzanne." Suzanne looked up into the face of someone she never expected to see again—and someone who she never expected to greet her with such cheer.

NINE

"Wow. Oh my goodness . . . This is a surprise." Suzanne put a hand to her throat, composing herself. "What a surprise." She felt like a dope.

"It sure is," Laura Caldwell replied in her smooth, deep, perfect voice. There was very little about Laura Caldwell that wasn't perfect way back in the years between ages five and eighteen.

Every school had a Laura Caldwell, Suzanne supposed, but that didn't make it any easier to deal with. She was drop-dead gorgeous, but it was the kind of beauty that required only the smallest amount of makeup. Her golden hair bounced to her shoulders in perfect curls, and her blue eyes always seemed to glow with amusement at life in general. She didn't take herself, or anything, so seriously she couldn't laugh at it. At five-foot-two, she was a little on the short side, but she possessed one of those figures that wasn't thin, wasn't fat. Just perfect. Curvy where men liked the curves, and slender where women liked to be slender.

She'd been one of the soloists in chorus for all four years in high school, not to mention head of Student Council, captain of the cheerleading squad, cocaptain of the dance squad . . . The list went on and on.

Worst of all, her personality was sweet, funny, effervescent, and gracious. Which was likely why she hadn't exchanged more than two words with Suzanne during her entire high school career; Laura wasn't exactly the smoking area type. Laura was also the girl who had given the Soap Opera Queen of the Year award (for mastering the fine art of bursting into tears at the library) to Suzanne during Senior Assembly—when the top ten students gave out appropriately made-up awards to the rest of the class. (Suzanne had been told that, when Laura found out *why* she was so emotional that year, she had had the good grace to blush.)

Laura didn't exactly *pick* on her, per se, but there were enough instances to make Suzanne think of Laura with a sour taste in her mouth. Freshman year,

Suzanne and Laura had been neck and neck for grades, for accomplishments, for attracting boys and ringleading the girls.

But by senior year, Suzanne had been the drama queen (on and off the stage) who got knocked up; Laura had been salutatorian and Most Likely to Succeed. The sting had never really worn off.

And now here Laura was, right in front of her, just in time to witness her divorce and most likely hear about her daughter's Monkey-See-Monkey-Do senior year pregnancy through the local grapevine.

To make matters even worse, Laura seemed to have barely aged a day. Her figure was still perfect, her skin still flawless without makeup. And she'd let her gorgeous hair grow so it hung like a sheet of gold to the middle of her back.

Suzanne reminded herself to have a quick word with God later on the topic of fair play.

"It's been a while," Suzanne smiled broadly, not knowing what else to say.

"Yes, it has," Laura agreed with a musical laugh. "In fact, last time I saw you, your water broke."

Suzanne smiled thinly, unable to come up with the polite obligatory laugh that she'd given a thousand times before.

"You look terrific! Even better than in high school, you lucky thing." Laura sounded absolutely sincere, Suzanne noted warily.

"Well, I recently lost two hundred pounds of dead weight—you went to school with Steve, so you know what I mean," she cracked, running her fingers through her hair, wishing she hadn't decided to put off doing her roots again last night. Maybe this was what Ava meant when she said you always wanted to put your best face forward. Laura's roots, of course, were perfectly blonde, as they had always been.

Laura laughed; again, the sound was remarkably genuine.

"Still, eighteen years for a teenage marriage. It's amazing you managed to hang in there as long as you did. I mean," she added hastily, "because, well, the odds of teenaged marriages aren't good."

"Right." It struck Suzanne that Laura seemed nervous that she might have been offensive, and wondered why. People like Laura didn't generally give a good crap if they offended people like Suzanne or not. She looked around at the melee for her mother, who'd been swallowed by the crowd just at the moment when she needed a rescue. Laura smiled at her happily, easily, and Suzanne again tried to force a smile, feeling wildly uncomfortable.

"So," she said, trying to sound pleasant, "what are you up to these days?"

Laura spread her arms, indicating the table that was stocked full of new-age and ancient religious paraphernalia: crystals, wands, bracelets, necklaces, books, bumper stickers, and Halloween decorations of all kinds.

"This is it." She handed Suzanne a card from a stack at the corner of the table, which was covered with a blood-red velvet cloth.

"*Goddess Treasures*," Suzanne read the antique script aloud.

"It's a small store over on Market Street. We sell all sorts of Goddess relics."

"Goddess? What do you mean?"

Laura's eyes lit up, and Suzanne cursed to herself, realizing she had just asked the million-dollar question. Now she was trapped, with no Ava in sight.

"In the Wiccan religion, we believe in the Goddess as well as the God—two sides of the same coin. In fact, many Wiccans believe only in the Goddess and not the God. But I find that a bit close-minded."

Laura picked up a small statue that showcased three women, all perched on the branches of a solid, ancient tree. On the uppermost branch sat a withered, wizened old lady. Near the middle of the tree was a woman cradling a newborn, and the branch nearest the ground held a very young girl.

"It's the triple Goddess, see? Maiden, mother, and crone. We sell crystals, magical tools, books, candles, chimes, glassware, incense. Some clothing, but those are generally for the teenaged wannabes." She rolled her unadorned light blue eyes, still smiling patiently. "Still, if they've got money to spend, they're welcome in my store, and they get as much respect as Laurie Cabot would—and she's known as the official witch of Salem, Mass."

"What do you mean, 'wannabe'?"

"Wannabes—as in, people who *want* to be Wiccans, witches, or pagans. Or, more accurately, who want to dress like witches and pagans, and get the attention that witches do, but don't want to commit to the work it takes to protect the earth or do the religious worship." Laura paused just long enough to take a breath. "Although Wicca is the accurate term of our religion, many of us choose to call it witchcraft to honor those before us who were killed for practicing their beliefs."

Just then, Suzanne saw the star within the circle dangling from a thin leather strap around Laura's neck. It was very old, and it looked to be made of brass. She'd seen them before, mostly on Goth teenagers, their skin white as sheets, their eyes lifeless. (Molly, who often dressed semi-Goth, at least managed to retain her rosy glow, and her eyes were always bright with love, laughter, and life. Suzanne supposed that made Molly a wannabe, and that pleased her to no end.)

"Also, we do our part to celebrate the accomplishments of women of the world today," Laura continued enthusiastically. "We have weekly readings of women writers. Not just women of our faith but women who write poetry, fiction, spiritual books, or even women who are just entertainers. Whatever springs to our amazingly creative minds, we celebrate."

"So you're . . ." Suzanne swallowed; she wasn't sure she could bring herself to say the word. After all, maybe Laura was putting her on, and this was just an effect for the business. If she fell for it, she would surely be the butt of many jokes later on, as she had been senior year.

"A professional witch, yes," Laura said comfortably. No one turned around in shock or looked particularly surprised when she said it out loud; apparently the downtown crowd was quite used to her.

"Wow." Suzanne didn't know how to reply. She still wasn't convinced this wasn't some kind of elaborate marketing ploy. "Wow, that's just . . . great. Good for you. I'm just . . . well, last I heard, that is, you . . ."

"I, what?"

"Well, weren't you off to Columbia law school, after college?" Suzanne was starting to get the idea that this earthy, relaxed woman before her might be a whole different person from the feverish go-getter she'd known twenty years ago. "Last I heard, you were in New York making tons of corporate cash."

"The dark days." Laura closed her eyes, shivering, as if the memories were too terrible to think of. She leaned forward, speaking softly. "I try to never think of them, but I'll spend the rest of my life atoning for them."

This woman just proudly announced that she's a witch, but she needs to whisper the fact that she was once a corporate attorney? Will the real Laura Caldwell please stand up?

"I worked for one of those big, big corporate firms that were killing small businesses all across the country," Laura went on. "I was helping the big guy beat up the little guy." She covered her face, still mortified after all this time. "Each day, the knot in my stomach grew bigger and bigger, until one day I just snapped—snap, crackle, *pop*. I quit my job, came back home, and then, just by chance, a month later I went to this amazing reading at a Goddess bookstore in Boston. It truly opened my eyes to the wonder that we females are. Nothing stops us: we're givers of life, we're nurturers, we're gutsy and fearless and creative . . ." She lowered her voice again, adding slyly, "And it's my experience that we take on more than any three men in our lifetimes."

"You're right about that," Suzanne agreed, thinking of how unfairly balanced the workload was in her marriage. She hadn't realized it was an epidemic.

An adorable blond girl of about nine popped up and took Laura's hand; something about her was very familiar.

"Mommy, can I have money for a piece of fudge?" she asked.

"Honey, you know how bad refined sugar is for you. Why don't you go buy a nice pear instead?" Laura reached into her pocketbook even as the girl began pleading her case. "Oh, all right, but just this *once*. First, introduce yourself to my friend."

Wow, thought Suzanne, *the most popular girl in school just referred to me as her friend. Is it weird that makes me want to call my old frenemies from high school and brag?*

"How do you do?" The little girl curtsied, pulling her very long skirt up perfectly as she dipped, which charmed Suzanne instantly. She seemed very feminine and sweet, and there was an air of almost disturbing maturity about her. "I'm Hermione."

Suzanne smiled at the girl and held out her hand.

"I'm Suzanne, and I'm just fine, thank you. And how do *you* do?"

"Fine, thank you," answered the girl.

Suzanne had to resist the urge to pick her up and put her in her pocket.

"Hermione," Suzanne tried to remember, "is that one of the Roman or Greek goddesses?"

"Nope, it's the all-consuming influence of Harry Potter in my life." Laura pulled her hair back from her face, chuckling at herself; it made her seem even lovelier. "But you know, it could have been worse, I tell her. Remember that girl in our class named Earth? Who moved away in eighth grade?"

"Oh my God!" Suzanne did, and shuddered. "I'd forgotten all about Earth 'til this very second. She was anything but earthy."

"She was the first girl to get sent home for wearing a tube top in junior high," Laura nodded. "My husband wanted to name her Picabo, after Picabo Street, the skier from New Hampshire."

"I can honestly say she'll be thrilled one day that you won that round." Suzanne grinned. She marveled again at the fact she was actually enjoying spending time with Laura Caldwell. Who would've thought?

Hermione let go of her hand, snatched up the dollar, and skipped off, presumably in search of fudge. Laura watched her, smiling; it was clear she was in awe of her child.

"You'll never guess who I wound up with—who Hermione's father is." Laura held out her hand to show off a silver claddagh with a heart-shaped emerald at its center. "Billy Wentworth."

"*Billy Wentworth?*"

Now *that* was news.

While Laura was busy perfecting popularity to a science, and Suzanne was busy eschewing birth control, Billy had little or no time for such frivolities.

"The guy who spent all of his time welding metal chairs from cubicles to railroad tracks and labeling it 'Corporate America'?" Suzanne replied.

"He sold that piece to a collector before he even graduated," Laura noted proudly. "Made five thousand bucks."

Billy hadn't been popular or unpopular, just one of those odd kids who skirt along the outside of the class. Handsome, interesting, sort of admired from afar but never really fitting in, living in his own artistic world, doing the work required for his classes and no more.

That's why the girl had looked so familiar, Suzanne realized. She was the spitting image of her rebel father.

"Yep, good old Billy and me, the artist and the litigator," Laura laughed happily. "When I came back here to get a real life, he came into the store one day to buy some dragon's blood . . ."

"*Dragon's blood?*"

"Throws you for a loop, doesn't it?" Laura rolled her pretty eyes. "It's just a red ink that you make by soaking a chunk of red stone in water. In our business, pretentious names for products equal Shit Sells Faster."

Suzanne laughed again, amazed that she didn't have to force it. Whoever High School Laura was, it seemed that Wicca Laura had a terrific sense of humor and liked to tell it like it was—two qualities that appealed to Suzanne enormously.

"Anyhoo, we got to talking, and when the store closed six hours later, we were still talking." She gave that laugh again, that rich, seductive sound that somehow pulled Suzanne in, made her feel included. "And ten years later, we still haven't stopped. I'm so in love." She sighed, twirling a strand of hair around and around her finger. Even though the trappings were completely different, at that moment, Suzanne saw the girl she'd once known.

"Well, that's just great." Maybe that was the trick to Laura's incredible complexion: love. Maybe her husband had a friend for Suzanne. She'd give love another whirl if it gave her skin like that. "It certainly looks good on you."

"Suzanne, come on!" Ava yelled from several booths down, shaking a Mason jar of salsa at her. "I've got to get back in time to go to my . . . I mean . . . you know."

"Coming, Mom." Suzanne turned to Laura. "I guess I've gotta jet. I'm in charge of carting the old bag around today."

"Don't you talk about Ava like that," scolded Laura. "She's a champ."

Really? Laura thought Ava was a champ? How would she know? Was Ava hanging out at the Witch bookstore between casseroles and AA meetings?

She couldn't quite picture her impeccably dressed mother pawing through the poet's shirts, floor-length tie-dyed skirts, and crystal jewelry that made up most of those stores Suzanne had ever seen.

How many of my other classmates is my mother chumming with? Suzanne wondered. Since the moment she came back to her mother's house, every moment was a surprise.

"Listen, the readings are every Monday night." Laura handed her a schedule, which was printed on the back of her card. "This coming Monday is Susan Poulin; she's a terrific Maine humorist. And then the Monday after that, there's this wonderful woman, Jennie Woods. She's reading from the book she published about surviving divorce, especially after years of convincing everyone you've got the perfect marriage."

Suzanne found herself nodding. It was a topic she knew something about.

"Please promise me you'll come; it'll be so great to sit down and have a real catch-up."

"Suzanne!" Ava's voice was nearing glass-shattering capacity. "I'm going to be late!"

"Sorry she's being so . . ."

"Not to worry," Laura waved off Suzanne's concern, "I know what it's like to be behind schedule . . . Actually," Laura leaned forward, those amazing eyes twinkling, "now that you mention it, I'm extremely offended that your mom is rushing you, so the only way you can make it up to me is by attending the reading on Monday, okay?"

Suzanne burst into laughter this time.

Blackmail? she thought. *Maybe Miss Goody-Two-Shoes and I have changed enough to be friends after all.*

"Why the heck not?" she agreed. She talked over her shoulder as she hurried after her mother, trying to let Laura know she had to go, not that she wanted to. "I haven't done anything social since I broke up with what's-his-name; maybe it would be good for me."

"Damn straight it'll be good for you—get you back on that merry-go-round," Laura nodded.

"Should I bring anything? Snacks, or maybe drinks? Juice?"

"You just make sure you bring yourself. The store provides the snacks," Laura called as Suzanne hurried to catch up with her mother. "House rules."

Laura turned her smile to another customer, and the weirdest reunion of Suzanne's life was over.

"Really, dear, have another cigarette," Ava remarked, when Suzanne caught up to her, choking and spewing and drawing deep breaths to make up for the short, oxygen-depriving run. "You're right, those American Spirits with no chemicals are really not that bad for you. I can still hear some air getting through between coughs."

"Okay, Mother, ha, ha, very funny, I get it." Suzanne's breath finally eased back to normal, and she threw a dark glance at her mother. She'd quit when she was damn well ready, and not one minute before. Ava should know all about that philosophy.

"I didn't know you were friendly with Laura Caldwell," Ava said.

"Well, I sure wasn't back in high school, but she seems all gung-ho to be buddies now." Suzanne cast a backward glance at the market. "Did you tell her I won the lottery, or something?"

"You know," Ava returned to their previous conversation as though they'd never been interrupted, "I remembered while you were talking to your friend, I heard the little voice too, just once in my lifetime."

"Really?" That was odd—this was the sort of thing her mother would normally have told her about and then repeated until mere mention of the story made Suzanne feel like screaming. "When?"

"Back in my drinking days." Ava looked both ways, then both ways again, and one more time before dragging her daughter by the elbow across Daniel Street. "I would start first thing in the morning with little airplane bottles that I'd hide around the house. I'd gotten to thinking that if your father didn't see me drinking, he wouldn't be able to tell. Drunks will believe whatever they want to, believe you me."

"So I've heard," Suzanne said dryly.

"Anyway, one day I was making chicken salad for lunch. I remember that clearly. Then, the next thing I knew, I was sitting on the couch, reading a book, wearing a completely different outfit. Oprah was talking about her book club and recommending *East of Eden*, by John Steinbeck."

"I don't get it."

"I'd had a blackout. A *two-day* blackout." She shook her head a little as she opened the door to her ten-year-old Taurus, which still looked new because of frequent waxings and the dust buster and Windex she kept ready in the glove box. "Disgusts me to even think about it now. I'd had them before, of course, but for a half hour here, an hour there . . . But to lose two whole days?" She clucked her tongue and eased out of the parking spot. "That's when I heard my little voice."

"Yeah?" Suzanne wanted to know. "What'd it say?"

"It said, 'This is the last wake up call you'll get, you dumb old broad.'" Ava slipped her arm around her daughter's shoulders. "And you want to know the really funny thing?"

"Tell me."

"My little voice," smiled Ava, "sounded an awful lot like you."

TEN

On the two days Molly and Brandon had been visiting, each afternoon Buddy and Brandon had settled into the habit of drifting outside and taking their seats on the bench. Sometimes they'd work on Buddy's macramé, sometimes they'd play chess. Brandon was a quick study, and Buddy had never been particularly adept at the game.

"There is nothing, *nothing* like New England air in the autumn." Buddy would say, lustily breathing the air and tasting it as it passed into his lungs.

He loved the autumn air ferociously, but the real reason, of course, was so that Buddy would be outside to catch sight of Ava, and Brandon could be outside if and when Molly ever decided to drop their bomb. But together, they were strong in their denial, and there was strength in numbers.

Sooner or later Suzanne would join the boys, because her mother wouldn't let her smoke in the house. It also gave her an excuse to spend time alone with Brandon. Much as she resented Brandon's overly pierced presence, there was always the chance the boy accidentally might spill the beans.

Molly's lips, unfortunately, had remained firmly shut.

On Friday, Buddy headed outside after their rice and beans dinner earlier than usual. When Brandon wondered why, Buddy remarked, "That was a great casserole, as far as those super healthy, good for your colon, light on your taste buds dishes go." Buddy eased himself onto his bench and lit his pipe. "But we ate a lot, we're big guys, it's a small house, and, well, do the math."

Suzanne followed just a few minutes later, with her ever-present pack of cigarettes and ashtray. Brandon looked longingly at the smoke Suzanne lustily blew out into the cooling night air. Molly came next, carrying a frosty glass of lemonade. She sat on the ground, near Brandon's feet. Suzanne ground her teeth so hard she thought she heard one of them crack.

She's always been a floor sitter, you know that, she scolded herself. *Last night she sat down in front of Mom. It doesn't mean anything, and you know it.*

". . . not dust bunnies, dust *rhinos*—dust *dinosaurs*," Brandon was telling Molly. His voice came from far, far away. "Some of them were so big, I've housebroken them and taught them how to speak."

"It's a basement, for Lord's sake." Buddy looked pleadingly for support. "Jeez, Molly, your guy is a regular Martha Stewart."

"You don't like the way he smells either?" Ava came down the stairs carefully with a tray of cookies and ice tea. "Perfectly understandable." Ava went on, "You can come over and stay right here with us. I'll give you my bed, and I'll bunk in with Molly."

"I still wet the bed sometimes, Grandma." Molly teased as she cast a despairing look at Brandon. The idea of sharing a bed with her grandmother, much as she loved her, was about as appealing as a bikini wax with super glue.

"Actually, I'm really enjoying myself in Buddy's guest room." Brandon tipped his imaginary hat at his host. "I alphabetized his leather book collection in the living room, not to mention his vinyl record collection. I didn't think anyone had those anymore."

"They're burying my Elvis, my Byrds, and my Beatles with me when I go," Buddy tossed right back at him. "Those CDs, they got no heart."

"You're crazy, Buddy, I'm telling you." Brandon held up his glass as Suzanne walked by with the pitcher. "Can I have some iced tea, please?"

"So how are you feeling?" Ava stroked Molly's hair, which was just flowing plainly over her shoulders for once. Molly leaned back happily, lapping up the affection. "I heard you took a three hour nap this afternoon."

Suzanne almost snapped at that, but restrained herself at the last second.

"Yeah, I had a hell of a headache," Molly agreed. "I can't swallow pills, so sleep is the only thing that gets rid of it."

"She's been really wiped out lately." Brandon reached out and began rubbing Molly's feet. Suzanne shot him a withering look.

"You know what?" She placed the pitcher carefully on the picnic table. "I think we've talked about Molly enough. Brandon's short visit *has* to be the big news she was talking about, because it's not possible for it to be anything else."

"You see?" Molly whispered miserably to Brandon. "She's already getting that aneurysm crease in her face, and I haven't even *hinted*."

"Definitely talked way too much about Molly," she repeated, as Brandon patted Molly's knee. Her eyes fell on Buddy. "Buddy, let's talk about you." She walked closer to the white-haired gentleman. "Let's talk about things like Irish bars, liquor licenses, and lies . . . Not necessarily in that order."

"Hmm?" Buddy looked up from his work, startled. "What?"

"You'll have to tell me what you think of my cookies, Brandon. I made them myself, from scratch." Ava pushed her way in front of Suzanne, pressing a crumbly cookie directly in his hand. "I don't believe in those cookie-in-a-roll-up things, where you just unwrap the dough and slice off a hunk and pop it in the oven. Any moron could cook those. Where's the love in that?"

"Great." Brandon bit off half the cookie in his first bite with ferocious enthusiasm. "These are fabulous! I love oatmeal raisin."

Everyone agreed with Brandon, though not quite so violently, and then they were quiet for a moment. Everyone was waiting for someone else to speak, and no one wanted to go first.

"Hey, listen." Brandon stood up, trying to get the group's attention. "I've only known all of you a few days, but I like to think that I've begun to get to know all of you. And just as importantly, to let you all know the kind of guy I am."

Suzanne froze, mid-inhale, and smoke burned her lungs.

Here it is, she realized as she closed her eyes. *Whatever it is, there's no going back now.*

Ava reached out to take her hand, and she clutched at it.

"And since we're all getting to know each other," he continued, "when something important has happened, I think that it's equally as important to get it out into the open. As soon as possible. Don't you, Molly?"

"Bite me, Brandon," Molly replied with mock sweetness.

"Go be honest with *your* own family then, sweetheart," Ava said, just as sweetly. "We'll just keep standing here with our heads in the sand and our asses proudly in the air."

"Hey, Suzanne," Buddy leaned forward, "what were you saying before? You know, about . . . liquor licenses and lies, or some other such thing?"

He let his voice trail off; no need to give her any more ammo than she already might have accumulated on her own.

"Well, just what I said. While Mom was at her meeting, I went to the county clerk's office, and they found the records I was looking for in record time. It's all been computerized, back to 1975, all matters of public record. But there wasn't that much to see, other than the things you told me, and the actual facts of the matter."

"Such as?"

"For one, such as the name on the complaint against . . ." Suzanne began, when her iced tea was slammed back into her hand by her mother, who was suddenly very busy dusting away cookie crumbs from the linen tablecloth.

"Move your drink for just a second, sweetie. Thanks," Ava told her, humming while she worked.

On the ground, sprawled in the grass, Brandon and Molly seemed to be involved in some sort of whispered debate.

"I just got home!" Suzanne heard Molly hiss. "Can't I have a couple of days? Or a couple of decades?"

Brandon raised an eyebrow. "Oh, you don't think they're gonna guess before a couple of decades?"

"More cookies, kids?" Ava sang, stepping between them, handing them more even though they hadn't finished the first round. "I'm glad you like them so well, Brandon. Maybe I'll teach you the recipe. The cooking gene in this family seems to have stopped with me."

It was a slick attempt to change the subject, but Buddy wasn't having any.

"It just doesn't make any sense to me," Buddy said, "why you'd want to go digging up all that ancient history. Everyone knows what happened. I'm the asshole who ruined everything." He turned to Ava for support. "Right, Ava?"

"Right, Buddy," she agreed, shoving a cookie in his face. "You're the asshole . . . have a cookie."

He looked bewildered for a moment and then took the baked good gingerly, as if a sudden movement might trigger a hidden booby-trap.

"Thanks, but . . . you fuh . . . *hate* me." Buddy knew that Ava hated the f-word like slugs hate salt. "This morning you called me a bottom-feeding scum sucker." He grinned at her. "I think you're warming up to me!"

"In your dreams, dirty old man," Ava sniffed haughtily. "It's just that, well, if these cookies don't get eaten, they wind up on my hips." She rubbed her linen pants self-consciously. "Better to ruin your arteries than my figure."

"As I was saying," Suzanne tried to cut her way back into the conversation, "it seems that there were certain errors made over who was . . ."

"This is just crazy!!" Brandon exclaimed suddenly, jumping to his feet and looking down at Molly with exasperation. "Enough is enough."

"This is just crazy. I agree with Bentley," Buddy said, standing up. "He's staying with me, and that's final. C'mon, Barney, let's go regrout some tiles, or do something else equally masculine."

"It's *Brandon*."

"Whatever. Get a move on."

Brandon collapsed back onto the ground, sinking his head into his arms.

"We just got back from my family's house," he pleaded. "I'm sort of burned out on regrouting. Or garage cleaning. Or tarring the roof . . .'"

"Okay, Buddy, the kid already cleaned your entire house, top to bottom. I'm not going to let you work him into the . . ." Suzanne began, when suddenly Brandon's words hit her like a bucket of ice water. She put her glass down on the table carefully, almost in slow motion, as she turned to look at her only daughter.

"His house?" she managed. "*His* family's house?"

"Thank you for that," Molly whispered to Brandon. Brandon smiled weakly, not sure how he'd set the bomb off.

"You went to his parents' house with this news . . . first." Suzanne tried to process the news; any way she looked at it, it felt like an enormous betrayal. "Before you came *here*, you went *there*."

"It's not that big a deal, Mom," Molly said earnestly. "It was on the way back from orientation, so we thought . . ."

"Oh, no. It's okay. I get it. Well, isn't that a fine kick in the butt." She laughed bitterly, taking a nice long sip of her iced tea. "At the very least, I would have liked to have been among the first to find out, and now I find out that I'm . . . I'm . . . what, just some name on the newsletter?"

"I've been trying to get a word in edgewise, Mother," Molly protested. "But you were too busy busting Buddy's balls."

"She can't really help that. She's been a ball-buster since the day she was born." Buddy interjected, pointing to Ava, who glared frostily back in return. "Just look at her genetic blueprint, for God's sake."

"I'm getting a glass of milk." Molly jumped up, apparently looking for an escape—any escape—from the choking tension that was surrounding her on all sides. "Anybody need anything from the kitchen?" Molly started to get up, but Ava stopped her.

"No, sweetie, don't you move. I'll get it for you. You just stay put." She sounded downright happy as she jumped up. Normally she waited on people with sighs and heavy groans, as if the effort was a huge imposition.

This new enthusiasm was frightening; Brandon and Molly exchanged a confused look.

Milk. Of course she wants milk. Pregnant women crave milk, Suzanne thought as she stared forlornly at her daughter. She wished this was a nightmare; she wished someone would wake her up.

"It goes well with cookies," Molly said, puzzled at the look on her mother's face.

"Sure," Suzanne said sadly. "It sure does."

"Milk is actually just cow sweat, you know," Buddy told them, working his fingers around yet another macramé knot.

"Cow sweat?" Molly's face froze; she looked as if she might throw up. "Cancel the milk, Grandma." She sighed and picked a dandelion, twirling it in her fingers. "And now we're talking about cow sweat. At least at your parents' house, we could get a word in."

Suzanne slammed her glass down on the table so hard Ava was sure she heard a crack. It was the final straw on the poor camel's back—she simply could take no more.

"And just how did they take it, Brandon?" she spat out furiously, advancing on him. "Just so I have an idea, you know, of the protocol."

Molly slowly sat up straight, looking at her mother almost fearfully.

"What are you saying?" Molly stammered. "Are you saying . . . you already *know?*"

"Maybe I didn't get SAT scores as high as yours, Moll." Suzanne seethed. "Or grades nearly as good. But yes, miraculously, I have been able to put together the incredibly obvious signs that you've put out here." She stopped herself, drew in a deep breath, and forced herself to calm down. "So, Brandon? How did they take it?"

"Well," Brandon answered slowly, glancing over at Molly nervously, "my stepdad felt kind of funny about it, I think, because he didn't say much. But then again, he never really says all that much, so that's cool. He just went out and did whatever he does out in the garage, with all his tools." He smiled then, thinking of his mother. "I think my mom . . . Actually, I'm sure Mom was mostly relieved."

"Relieved?" Suzanne was aghast.

"Yeah, relieved," he answered. "Because, well, she'd already guessed. And it's one of those things that you don't want to have to come out and ask. So, when I told her, she was relieved. You get the idea."

"Yeah, I can relate," Suzanne said vaguely. Maybe she'd call his mother later, and they could have a long-distance cry together. "And the rest of the family?"

"Then, both my brothers said, 'Who cares? Let's go play some football.' And my aunt, my favorite Aunt Jennie, she just wanted to take me shopping."

"That's just how I feel." Suzanne felt suddenly dizzy. She sat down on Buddy's bench and lit up a Spirit with a hand that trembled so badly Buddy had to steady it before she could get the flame to touch the tobacco. Once lit, she did her Lamaze breathing around the smoke until the courtyard righted itself. "That's just how I feel. Like all four of those reactions. Wow. Oh, wow."

But inside, she was screaming. *Didn't I teach her to think ahead, to be careful, that every action has a consequence?! Didn't I at least teach her she had to have a* childhood *before she could have a* child*?! Oh, dear God, didn't I teach her* not *to be like me?!*

She closed her eyes and tried to tell herself that Ava was right, things *were* different now. And, she supposed, a thin light of pride shining through the despair, that if anyone could make Vassar combined with new parenthood work, it was Molly.

It just . . . It's not what I wanted for her, she thought sadly. *It's not what I wanted for her at all. I wanted her to have a complete childhood . . . I wanted her to have the childhood that I didn't.*

Ava came to her and began stroking her shoulders soothingly. She took a napkin and dipped it in the ice water pitcher.

"Now, honey." She gently put the cold cloth on her forehead. "Don't get yourself all worked up. We knew this was it."

"You *knew?*" Molly leaped to her feet, looking at Brandon accusingly. His equally surprised face cleared him instantly of guilt. "How? *How* did you know? My God, is it that obvious?"

"No, we didn't!" Suzanne retorted. "For a week now, ever since she told us she had an announcement, we've been very, very happy, *not* knowing!" She drew a deep, ragged drag on her cigarette. Ava winced at the smell but didn't pull away. "But now . . . Now we know we know, you know, and there's no way to *un*-know . . ."

"I know," Ava whispered soothingly.

Molly came to her and knelt nervously by the bench. "Mom?" She cleared her throat. "Mommy?"

"What?"

"Well, I just . . ." Molly swallowed hard and started again. "I just wanted to know if you . . . I mean, do you . . . Do you still love me, Mommy?"

Suzanne peeled back the napkin and looked at Molly in disbelief.

How could Molly possibly think that this—or *anything*—would make her not love her anymore?

It would be physically impossible to stop loving her only child. She couldn't imagine circumstances under which she'd want to stop loving her, but even if for some reason she did, it would be no more possible than sprouting a second head would be. If Molly walked into Market Square and decried her undying allegiance to Osama Bin Laden's grave, Suzanne would still love her and stand by her. If Molly ever went to jail, she'd probably commit a crime herself, so they could at least be together in jail, if nowhere else. And Molly, she was sure, knew this down to her bones.

And yet, there was a foggy, distant memory nagging at the back of her mind.

Her parents, great as they had been, hadn't they let her sweat for a few days, just the same, wondering if she would ever be their little girl again?

Hadn't she been terrified that her own mother would kick her out, disown her, and sit shivah for her, just like Rachel Lebowitz's parents did when they found out she was in the same condition Suzanne was? Her parents weren't Jewish, but still, the image of sheets draped over the bathroom mirror had haunted her just the same.

She dropped the Spirit now and grabbed Molly, dragging her up from the ground. She held her as close as humanly possible. Molly clung back, her shoulders heaving with . . . fear? Relief?

"As you're going to find out," she whispered fiercely into the girl's hair, "your child is your child *forever*. If we get mad, it's because we want you to do it all better, not to have to work as hard, or struggle as much, but things are different now. I love you, I adore you, I'm crazy about you, but I want to *strangle* you right at this particular moment." She pressed her hot forehead against Molly's cool one to take the sting from her words. "But the other things I said . . . Well, *more*. I feel those things much, much more. You get me, Missy?"

Molly nodded, tears choking her throat, not trusting herself to speak.

"Oh, my. Oh, dear." Ava could contain herself no longer, and let the happy tears spew forth as they would. "It's just, it's just . . . Oh, honey, I'm so happy for you!!"

"You are?" Molly stared at her. This scene wasn't playing out at all like she'd imagined.

"Oh, yes." She plucked her lace hankie out of her bosom and carefully began dabbing her elaborate makeup job. It would not do to have her mascara run into clown face right in front of all these people. "I would certainly have never said it before you were ready to tell us, but this . . . this is what I've *always* wanted for you."

"It *is*?" Molly's astonished expression was almost comical; she kept looking at Ava as if waiting for the punch line.

"Well, of course, what did you expect?" Ava smiled through her tears, reaching out to stroke Molly's cheek. "Maybe now wasn't quite the time, of course," she conceded, "but what's done is done, and I'm just thrilled. I'm so excited. We'll have to go shopping first thing in the morning. And, oh, then to the bank to set up a savings account."

"Wow." Brandon finally found his voice. "You guys are just . . . my family took it well, but they sure didn't react like that."

"Well, of course. Just a little something for the future, everyone can use that." Then she grabbed Molly by the shoulders and shook her finger at her warningly. "This is a big change, I know, but there is no reason, you know, not one reason in this world why this should interfere with your studies."

"Oh, well, my folks *did* say that." Brandon nodded.

"Can I ask a question?" Buddy asked.

"What the hell," Suzanne sighed.

"What in the heck is going on?" He could make neither hide nor hair of the pieces of the rapid-fire conversation he'd been able to pick up.

"Is it possible that you are really and truly this clueless, man? Those bimbos really did suck every last brain cell out of your head, didn't they?" But Ava's banter couldn't conceal the joy in her voice, and she took a deep breath, thrilled to be able to say it out loud for the first time, blurting, "Brandon and Molly are having a baby!"

But at the same moment, Molly replied, "I'm gay! Finally, I've been trying to work up the guts to say it out loud, for months now, so here it is, once and for all . . . I'm here, I'm queer, get used to it!"

She was so relieved she laughed, but then Ava's words registered in her ears, just as Ava heard her own.

They both stopped speaking at the same time and stared at each other.

"What?" Ava asked, befuddled. "You're what? What did you say?"

"I'm *gay*." Molly looked around at the now bemused faces of the group around her. "What the hell have we just been talking about?"

Not pregnant. Gay. Not pregnant. Not pregnant. Not pregnant.

Although it was what she'd prayed for, Suzanne couldn't quite wrap itself around the concept, for a minute.

This wasn't a repeat of pattern? She wasn't going to be a thirty-six-year-old grandmother? Nope, she was the mother, apparently, of an eighteen-year-old lesbian. "*What*?" Suzanne asked again, stupidly.

For a moment no one moved, as they all looked at each other . . . but Ava could always be counted upon to break a silence.

She grabbed a napkin, wrapped one end around her hand, and with the other end, began viciously whacking Brandon.

"What the *hell*?" Molly cried.

Brandon tried to shield himself, bewildered. For a defenseless old lady, she was really kicking his ass. He fell to the ground like he did when the gay bashers came calling, and wrapped himself into a ball.

"Mother!" Suzanne pushed herself between Ava and her victim. Brandon hid behind her as Molly got the napkin away from Ava for good. "Mother, what on earth are you *doing*?"

"Didn't you hear?" Ava furiously pointed at Brandon. "Not only did the little bastard knock her up—he turned her gay!"

PART TWO

ELEVEN

$\mathcal{T}$he air had started to take on the golden tone that Suzanne had long associated with the coming of autumn, where the days got shorter and the nights cozier. When it was time to put away the shorts and start taking out a few light jackets and sweaters. It had always felt to her like a new beginning, just like the start of each school year when she was a child.

Well, if ever I was in need of a new beginning, she thought, walking down Daniel Street, looking in the windows of the antique bookstore and stopping to read the schedules at Molly Malone's, *it's now. A new beginning, and a new friend.*

It wasn't Monday yet, but somehow Suzanne found herself slowly winding toward the Goddess Treasures shop all the same. When she had walked around enough to allow herself the illusion that she had just happened across it, she pulled open the heavy oak door.

The shop had large bay windows in front, but somehow most of the corners seemed dark and mysterious—not by accident, she was sure. The walls had been done up in dark maple and deep red accessories, and there were high arched doorways, both in the front entrance and between sections of the store. Long, heavy silver candlesticks were lit on several carefully placed pillars, and an ancient chandelier hung from the middle of the store. The front door had been covered in some material that made it appear to be carved out of stone; a little showy, a little too Dracula for her particular taste, but still very effective, she had to admit. It certainly set a tone.

Suzanne had expected that someone who worked in a shop like this would be fully decked out in a flowing, lace-up dress—maybe some kind of cape, with extra-thick eyeliner, flowers in her hair, and perfectly applied red, *red* lipstick.

But there was Laura behind the cash register in a perfectly respectable red cashmere sweater, her simple pentagram necklace, and hip-hugger jeans with a long rose winding up one leg.

A little too "hip" for a lady our age, maybe, but that's not her problem. Suzanne had an almost paralyzing fear of dressing in such a way that people would think she still considered herself a teenager.

But Laura certainly had the figure for it, so why the hell not.

Laura looked up, and for a second, Suzanne almost fled, wondering if the head cheerleader was going to take a jab at her pregnant belly, before remembering Laura wasn't a cheerleader and she wasn't a knocked-up senior. Instead, a smile of real pleasure crossed Laura's face when she saw Suzanne.

"Well, hello, you!" she greeted her. "Or rather, 'Blessed be,' as we say in the business." She gave Suzanne a huge, warm hug, not just the polite, obligatory embrace she'd expected. It was a bit startling at first, but then she hugged back. "So, what brings you here on a Saturday morning?"

She might have said, *Well, I'm not going to be a grandmother after all. Maybe I never will be, because my daughter came out of the closet, where I had absolutely no idea she was lurking.*

But what Suzanne said instead was, "Oh, just taking a walk downtown before the really cold weather sets in. Plus, we're having a bit of a family reunion this week, and it's been so wonderful that . . . Well, frankly I could use a little break from all the reuniting."

Laura grinned. "I hear you. Most of my family is in Southie now. My dad got transferred when I was in school."

Southie—what the locals called South Boston—was a place Suzanne knew well; it was where Steve's people were from. She'd be spending a lot less time in Southie, she realized with a jolt, still holding the pumpkin candle she'd been meaning to sniff midair. Hell, she might never go there again, come to think of it. There were members of his family—his Irish grandmother, who cooked in pinches and dashes, and his brother-in-law with the incessant knock-knock jokes—whom she had grown really fond of over the years. She'd likely never see them again now.

And there was that sudden, sharp pang, the pang that hit her every time another delightful repercussion to splitting with her groom appeared.

Consider the trade-off, she reminded herself. *You might not get to see Grandma any more, but you don't have to endure visits with Steve's mother either.*

"Yeah, Southie's just far enough away, but still close enough." Laura gestured to one of her clerks, who took her place behind the counter. "Come on, let me show you around my world."

The objects that were lovingly placed around the shop weren't just for decoration. All had a purpose, or a use, either practical or religious. There was something almost hypnotic about the crystal display. The knives—or athames, pronounced *ath-UH-mays* as Laura pointed out—came in all sizes and shapes. Some had elaborate, bejeweled handles and fancy sheaths; others were plain and wooden, encased in only a leather envelope. But without exception, all of the blades were dull.

"I don't sell bladed weapons," Laura stated firmly. From the way she said it, Suzanne could tell she'd said this a thousand times or more. She ran a hand through her pretty blond hair, the two small brass pentagrams in her ears swinging with the movement. "They can take them to a bladesmith or sharpen them on their own if they want. I only sell knives intended for spiritual use."

"What sort of knife would be needed for a spiritual use?" Suzanne was completely baffled now.

"Athames," Laura answered cheerfully. "Look it up, you'll find the explanation enchanting. I did."

The other items, like the baggy, colorful skirts, the lace-up shirts, the scarves, the dangling jewelry, while just a tad flamboyant for Suzanne's own tastes, were kind of fun. There were definitely a few cute tops in the collection, and the fountains, made of crystals and stones, were downright soothing.

"What's this?" She picked up something that looked like a yellow, opaque lump, but it smelled like gardenias in full bloom. The stamp on the label read "Hermione's Herbals."

"Soaps, with a foot scrub," Laura told her. "I do the soaps with my own two hands, but all the scrubs, foot, body, and facial, in the shop here are Hermione's."

"*Really?*" Suzanne had been right, Laura's daughter *was* more mature than she looked; ten years old and already an entrepreneur.

"Oh, yeah," Laura nodded rapidly. "That kid was born with a thousand-year-old soul and the mind of an accountant. She studied the books on herbs and oils and incenses, and then, last year, she made her first batch. All the money goes into her college fund—and let's just say it's well past four figures."

"Wow," Suzanne marveled. "And she's smart enough to save it by hitting her mom up for fudge money." Both women laughed.

"Yeah, well, I don't want her buying cars she can't drive or houses she can't move into—although last year she was talking to her dad about 'investing in real estate,' and I have to say, that's a damn good idea, considering it's the only thing that always appreciates."

"And these?"

Suzanne picked up something called a "Spell in a Bottle." It was a small glass jar with all the ingredients, apparently, for the spell in question, written down on a small scroll of parchment. There were spells for money, there were spells for happiness, there were spells for health . . . But most of all, there were spells for love. *Wouldn't that be nice,* Suzanne thought wistfully.

"They're just what they say they are—spells. You follow the directions, and they work," insisted Laura.

"Oh, come on," Suzanne blurted, and then looked hastily around. Putting the glass bottle down, she asked, "I'm sorry, Laura, but you really can't believe that, can you?"

"I most certainly do," Laura said serenely. She picked up a small bottle, which held, according to the label, a spell for prosperity. "Listen, I have no idea why soaking a bit of apple tree branch in cinnamon for three weeks, then burning it on the night of a full moon makes you prosper. But I also don't know why mixing chocolate, butter, and flour and applying heat makes a cake." She smiled. "I just know it does."

"Wow," Suzanne said, shaking her head a little. "Either the crazy is rubbing off, or I totally understood what you just said."

They crossed to the back of the store then, and Suzanne sucked her breath in, completely blown away. "Oh, wow," she whispered, and Laura grinned again, that happy-go-lucky grin Suzanne would forever associate with high school.

"I had a feeling you'd think that."

It was a bookstore, built right into the back of the store, away from everything else. A huge, hand-carved maple sign proclaimed it "The Book Nook." It had its own back entrance and a coffee, cocoa, and tea bar. Plush leather chairs that looked like they'd lovingly held a thousand readers or more were tucked away in various corners, and an ancient emerald green velvet sofa stood proudly in front of a fireplace. Matching loveseats, equally time-worn, sat on either side. The sturdy coffee table looked hand-carved rather than produced in some factory.

"Is this a Jacob Winter piece?" Suzanne asked, running her hand along its even seams. Something about it reminded her of the steamer trunk he'd made for her parents.

"You bet it is—one of about seven he made. Just before *Bridge* hit the bestseller list. It's a collector's item. I've had more offers for this than half the pieces in the store, I swear." Laura ran her fingers along the scars and scratches, which enhanced the piece even more. "But some things just aren't for sale. He made the shelves too."

The shelves showed the skill of Jacob's craftsman's hands just as well. They were the kind of shelves you would expect to see in the homes of dukes, of families with old money—in general, in the homes of people who had libraries. Also dark maple, they rose almost seven feet tall. The appropriate old-fashioned stepladder obligingly rested on the end of every third aisle or so.

"Paganism, Wicca, Goddess Worship," Suzanne read the sections aloud. "Celtic legends, candle magick, herbalism, yoga, color-charting . . ."

"There are also nine different kinds of bibles on my last count," Laura told her. "As well as the Koran and the Torah. And on the back of that shelf you're looking at, there are a bunch of works on ghost sightings, UFOs, the Tarot, divining, past life-regression . . ."

"Will there be a quiz on this later?" Suzanne pleaded. "Don't get me wrong, a lot of this stuff really interests me—more so now that I've seen it up close and personal—but geez, there's so much of it. I feel like I don't know where to begin."

"Here." Laura handed her Silver Ravenwolf's *To Ride a Silver Broomstick* and Scott Cunningham's *The Truth about Witchcraft Today.* "These two will answer all your questions about our religion, and if they inspire any other interests, like candle magick, well, we'll just go from there."

Suzanne took the books, flipping through them as Laura got them a couple of honey teas with vanilla creamer. "Soon enough it'll be time for indoor fires." Laura took off her knee-high suede boots and propped her stockinged feet on the coffee table with a satisfied sigh. "Still too damn hot outside."

They spent a few minutes catching up, the way old acquaintances do. Who from their graduating class was married, who had divorced, who was successful, who was caught buying scrip drugs down in Lawrence. It was fun, but Suzanne would remember every so often that she was gossiping with the most popular girl in school, and her head would spin a little.

"So, what's up?"

Suzanne glanced up to see Laura's crystal blue eyes trained on her like a cool, friendly homing signal. Not much got by those eyes, she supposed; likely a holdover from the Horrible Lawyer days.

"What's up with you specifically, I mean," Laura added. "You've already filled me in on Molly's schooling—congratulations, by the way, that's terrific—and your mom's issues with her neighbor. How are *you* doing?"

"Oh, you know." Suzanne casually sipped her coffee. "My only kid's going off to college, my divorce isn't final yet because my ex is dragging his feet on the financial settlement . . ."

"Divorce, divorce, divorce." Laura sang the word, taking some of the sting out of it. "It's a real bitch."

"You've been divorced?" Suzanne was surprised. That juicy tidbit hadn't made it to the Portsmouth grapevine.

"Oh, yes indeedy-do." Laura placed her tea carefully on a coaster on the coffee table, smiling ironically. "For the longest time, there I was, living the life I'd always set out for, and I was just miserable. Absolutely miserable. Prozac didn't help, booze didn't help, spending huge amounts of money on art I didn't understand didn't help, working eighty hours a week didn't help . . ."

"What did help?"

"Well," Laura flashed that ironic smile again, "I had myself all convinced for a while that the reason I was so suicidally unhappy with my job was that I just needed a good man to come back to at night. To cook for on the holidays and weekends, rub his feet by the fire, bear his overachieving young . . . You get the picture."

Suzanne looked around the woman-empowering surroundings and then back at Laura. "I'm sorry, I just can't imagine that color on you."

"Oh, I wore it, let me tell you." Laura nodded rapidly. "I went out and found myself an investment banker, Joe Collins, and we bought ourselves a perfect little third-floor apartment on Park Avenue. He was gorgeous— probably still is—and made ten times what I did. It was the fairy-tale wedding with five hundred people I'd never met, and I wore a dress that cost more than my first car. We went on vacations to England and France; Aruba, I can't count the times; toured the Orient, Australia." She ticked off the locations on her fingers like items on a grocery list, and with the same amount of enthusiasm.

"You should have *seen* our apartment on Park Avenue. It was like Bombay Company and Shabby Chic exploded in there. I had clothes from every name designer from Chanel on down—my closet was so big, it had its own bathroom." She shook her head, embarrassed by the blatant materialism.

Suzanne wondered what it would be like to live like that, with unlimited funds in the alleged coolest city on earth. "I hope you get to the bad part soon. So far, it sounds like a shopping addict's dream."

"*Exactly.* But that's *all* it was," Laura emphasized. "Lots of *stuff.* One day, I woke up, and my husband had left a note on his pillow, saying, 'Let's have lunch, I have a late squash game, and oh, by the way, I think it's time for us have a baby. My boss was making comments the other day that I'm the only partner in the firm that doesn't have any kids.'" She shook her head; it seemed the audacity of the note still hadn't quite sunk in. "Think of it. The same four-line note that included my lunch plans also planned my reproductive ones—all for how his bosses saw him at work. It was like getting hit in the face with a hammer. I told him I wasn't happy, I wanted out of the marriage, and I moved out later that week. We were divorced within the season, and I let him keep the apartment."

"How did he take it?"

"He beat the ever-loving shit out of me." Laura calmly sipped her tea. "Broke one arm, cracked a rib, bruised a kidney, and this," she pointed to her upper left bicuspid, "is a crown."

Suzanne's jaw dropped. "What?" she stammered. This was the kind of thing that happened in the news or to trailer trash, not educated, employed people of means. "*What?*"

Laura placed a cool hand over Suzanne's suddenly inflamed one. "Sweetie, it's okay, it really is."

"It'll be okay," Suzanne said furiously, "when we get a baseball bat and meet the son of a bitch in a dark alley. Then I'll feel *very* okay."

"Violence doesn't solve violence," Laura admonished, but she leaned forward to kiss Suzanne on the cheek. "But I feel better with people like you and Billy on my side. Thank you for the offer; I'd be lying if I said it didn't make me feel better."

"But, was he . . ." Suzanne stuttered, forced herself to calm, and started again. "Was he like that before?"

"No," Laura emphasized. "Not once, not ever. And that's the fascinating thing."

"There's something fascinating about this?"

"Oh, absolutely." Laura leaned forward. "Think about it. It was enough for him. This cold, hard, shallow life full of aesthetics—that was his dream. He *wanted* it. And when I told him that I wouldn't play the game anymore, and why, he was . . ." Laura frowned, trying to remember exactly how he'd been before the rage, trying to separate feeling from fact in order to make an accurate observation. Suzanne was overwhelmed with admiration that Laura would still seek to be so objective. "Well, I think—I'm sure, that is—that it would have been enough for him. To be Mr. and Mrs. Corporate Couple who hardly knew each other, who worked fourteen-hour days, who had two-point-five kids raised by boarding schools and the help, who had pieces of art by every hip new artist, and for whom every designer-of-the-moment came in to redo the walls . . . He didn't want me getting closer, because clearly there were some ugly things there."

"Like his disgusting excuse for a soul?" The depth of Suzanne's fury surprised her.

"Wow, you are a loyal bird, aren't you?" Laura hooted again. "I really *am* over it. But, even before he went nuts on me like that, I was . . . I was drowning in loneliness, but he was filling up on *things.*" She shrugged, philosophical after all this time. "But hey, if that's the way he wants to live his life, that's his life. I just realized it couldn't be mine. And believe it or not, it helped me. Not the *beating,* of course, but living like that, with all those beautiful things and being so alone. It was suffocating. I was drowning in so many material things. It really forced me to realize what I wanted, what would make me happy, as opposed to what I thought *should* make me happy. And killing him would only shorten the life that is clearly making him miserable. I let the fact that he has to be him every day of his life be its own punishment."

"Wow," Suzanne said enviously, "you are so . . . *together.* Some things never change."

"Oh, don't let me kid you." Laura ran her hands through her hair, shaking her head. "That's just my veneer. I've been doing it since high school. Before, even. That's who I am: the girl who's got her game so straight she doesn't need any help."

Suzanne wanted to shake her head and tap one side firmly. Was she really hearing these words? These gut-wrenchingly honest, soul-baring words from someone whom, until last week, she had written off as a Miss Phony-Baloney Sunshine, Portsmouth class of '94?

"Well, let me tell you," Laura went on, "I needed just as much help as anyone, maybe more, and I was so damn proud I couldn't even let anyone close to me to really *see* me. That's what I need to work on, asking for help. Letting people see I'm not perfect."

"Yeah, because it would make the rest of us feel a whole lot better about our lots in life," Suzanne agreed. "What happened to Joe? You reported it, right?"

"Yes, I did. I did all the right things, pressed all the right charges, but in the end I just hit him where it would really hurt him—in his wallet. I knew I could use the money to finance my own dreams," she spread her arms, "and the amount he had to pay hurt him a hell of a lot more than jail time would have. You think I'm together? It's the secret of life: You *act* like you've dealt with all your shit, and people will actually think that you *have.* I'm trying to find a more honest way to deal with my craziness, of which, believe me, there's plenty."

Suzanne laughed, amazed. "You are the single most self-aware person . . . No, I'm going to stop because you'll just find a way to self-deprecatingly cut yourself down on that one." She raised her empty mug. "But I better see some of this craziness damn quick, or my self-esteem will severely plummet."

"What's this?" Billy Wentworth suddenly leaped into the room with a broad grin on his handsome features. Suzanne would have recognized him instantly. His face was a bit older, and there were some grey strands in his curls, which were spattered with paint flecks. He was wearing clothes that had seen many creative afternoons, judging by the many stains and holes in them, but he looked no less adorable than he had twenty years before.

He bent down to kiss Laura, who lit up as soon as her eyes found him. "Hey, baby," she said happily.

"Oh, Lordy, Lordy, don't tell me," he backed up, hand on his chest. "Don't even *try* to tell me that the class of 1994's head cheerleader," he pumped his fists in a cheer and gave a fine rendition of a jumping kick, "and the star of the drama club, on- and offstage are actually hanging out together?" He covered his eyes with one paint-scarred hand. "They'll be gossiping about this one for weeks!"

"Sadly, that's probably not too far from the truth," Suzanne retorted. "We're part of the New England grapevine. There are practically hourly updates. And my mom's the worst of all—my dad used to call her the Town Crier."

"Good old Ava." Laura affectionately plucked paint flecks out of her husband's hair. "She comes in here looking to see if I've got new books on angels every month or so. I'm supposed to call her the minute they come off the truck."

Suzanne blinked. "Books on angels? *Really? My* mom?"

"It helps her with her sobriety," Laura added, which startled Suzanne in her seat. She would have spilled her tea if there had been enough left. "She usually comes in right after the lunchtime meeting at St. James, on Mondays, Wednesdays, and Fridays."

"Hey, we're not discriminatory here at Goddess Treasures," Billy drawled. "We'll take anyone's money, even those darn drunks'. Sell those tourists books on how to spot a UFO using only a penlight and a stick of gum."

"Billy!" Laura admonished, and Suzanne laughed, feeling a little queasy. Her mom was one of those drunks, after all.

Billy and Laura kissed again, and this time he shook some paint flecks onto her nice outfit. She shrieked a little in complaint, but it was the kind of shriek that was made mostly of pleasure.

Suzanne smiled and politely turned her eyes away from the moment, but she was thinking of the fact that Laura, and who knew who else, casually knew about Ava's jaunts to the hallowed halls of sobriety at AA.

Alcoholics Anonymous? she wondered. Maybe they should change it to *Alcoholics, Once Anonymous, and Now . . . Not So Much.*

"Laura?" The young clerk with short, sparkly black hair poked her head back into the bookshop. She was chewing her lip and kept throwing nervous looks back at the cash register. "I'm having a problem with the computer, and the customer is getting . . . Well, he's getting a little impatient."

Laura put her arm maternally around the girl's shoulders.

"Customers," she whispered, "can be real assholes, but they are especially assholes with money. Surviving that is the first rule of retail." The girl smiled, hesitantly, while Laura pulled her into the main room. "C'mon, let's go see if we can find out what crawled up his butt and died."

Billy watched her go, admiringly. "She's really something, my wife. Isn't she?"

"She sure is," Suzanne admitted, an unexpected wave of warmth flowing over her.

"So, anyway." He hopped up on the arm of the couch and asked a bit more formally. "How've you been? How have the years treated you?"

"Oh, you know," she replied casually. "Been kicked around a little, did some kicking back. You?"

"Been eking out a living as a singer-slash-actor-slash-artist in New Hampshire." He smiled proudly, running his hands through his sweaty, paint-flecked hair. "Not many can brag that."

"Oh, no, they can't. You've sure got that straight."

"Hey, look." He glanced out to the front to make sure Laura was still occupied at the front register. "I've always meant to ask you . . . You were something in high school, you know? A real firecracker."

"Well, thanks." Suzanne wondered if it was odd that that particular word followed her around and if it was odder still that she'd always liked it.

"And I was just wondering why, you know, you never gave me the time of day."

The question caught her completely off guard. Billy was looking at her earnestly, almost an expression of pleading in his eyes. Had she meant something to him, something much more than he had to her? A crush, maybe? A crush so strong that, unrequited, still haunted him after all these years?

Ah, Christ. What better way to ruin a budding friendship.

"I'm not sure what you mean," she asked, putting down her empty tea cup, trying to keep her voice light, even.

"I'm sorry," he said softly, "but I really, really need to know."

Oh, Lord. She looked around, desperately hoping to find an ashtray, even though business establishments didn't allow smoking in New Hampshire.

"Well, you know, you were kind of like this off-by-yourself-guy, you know? It wasn't because I didn't like you," she added hastily, "but you just gave off this, you know, this vibe of . . . I thought you were a great guy, Billy, but—"

And then Billy was doubled over, laughing so hard, tears were streaming down his cheeks. Suzanne watched him, bewildered, as Laura came back to the Book Nook, shaking her head.

"Is he messing with your head?" She rubbed Suzanne's back consolingly. "Don't worry—he only does it to people he likes."

Billy sat up and wiped his eyes.

"Sorry, Mommy," he said sweetly. "She was just sitting there, looking all nervous. She brought it on herself."

It was beginning to dawn on Suzanne that she'd been made sport of, and suddenly she felt much less nervous and much more comfortable. She reached out to swat at Billy with one of her new books.

"If you must know, I didn't pay attention to you because my geek-dar went off whenever you got within fifty feet of me," she retorted, and Laura howled.

Before Suzanne knew it, a perfectly lovely afternoon had passed reminiscing about those days long ago and about those people who had long fallen out of her life.

"My Goddess," Laura looked at her watch; Suzanne wondered if she'd ever get used to that phrase. "Is it time to do the lock up already? I can't believe we've chatted this long."

"What's not to believe?" Billy put on a Jewish accent. That was another thing Suzanne had forgotten, the way Billy always made jokes in different accents. Funny how you could forget such a unique trait about a person. "A couple of broads, some coffee, a couch . . . That's gonna add up to endless hours of talk, talk, talk."

Laura swatted him again, and he grabbed her. For the thirtieth time that afternoon, the ten-year married couple kissed.

Suzanne pretended to smile and looked away. She and Steve hadn't been like that since Molly was born. It was the kind of easy, un-self-conscious love that books and movies were written about.

Will I ever have that? Or has my boat sailed? I'm thirty-six, and I haven't been out on a date since I was seventeen. I wouldn't have the slightest idea how to flirt with a guy, to put those vibes out there, she thought in despair. *I'm going to die alone. No, worse, I'm going to die after living the rest of my life alone in a house . . . with my mother.*

She had to get out of here right now before this totally pleasant day ended in a knot of jealousy.

"Well, I've got to run, before my mother thinks I've decided to hurl myself off the docks, since Molly came out of the closet last night."

Laura's eyes widened. "Your daughter's gay? And she just told you?"

"Yeah, we thought she was pregnant. Turns out, she's just gay. Didn't I mention that?" Suzanne grinned and stood up, trying to hand Laura a couple of bills for the books, but Billy waved it away.

"Your money's no good here, Applebaum," he drawled. "But if you don't come back Monday, the wife'll hunt you down and skin ya alive."

Applebaum, she thought. *Yeah, I guess I am Suzanne Applebaum again, after all these years. Well, what the hell do you know about that.*

Outside, she lit up a cigarette and dragged in the smoke desperately. It had been nearly four hours since her last smoke, she suddenly realized. It had been quite a while since she'd let that happen. Holding the cigarette with one hand, she fished around in the paper bag Laura had handed her with the other, wanting to flip through one of her new witchy books as she smoked.

But her hand closed upon something else. Curious, she pulled it out.

Inside the package was the love potion she'd seen on display at the store. Suzanne stared at it for a moment, then laughed into the crisp air. This was Laura's way of telling her that just when she'd given up on love, she'd found Billy, so it could happen for Suzanne too.

Suzanne shook her head, putting the potion back in the bag, knowing that it was silly and knowing that she'd probably try it, out of sheer curiosity if nothing else. She gave the matter one last laugh as she climbed the steps to Ava's house.

Subtle, Laura. Real subtle.

TWELVE

"Mom?" Molly called hesitantly. She took another step into the bright yellow afternoon light of the courtyard. "Hey, Mom?"

"Hmmmm?" It had occurred to Suzanne that she would be much less worried about her daughter's life, and envious of Laura's, if she went out and got one of her own. She'd checked the junk drawer, and yep, the forms to Southern New Hampshire University were right where she'd left them three months ago. She stared at them for ten full minutes before taking them out, then closed the drawer.

Watching her in the courtyard, Molly tried to remember how proud she'd been of herself the moment she decided to come out to her family. But what she felt, more than anything, was lonely, even in front of her mother—her best friend, really.

"I was . . . I thought . . . Well, here's a cup of coffee," Molly said at last.

"Oh, thank you, sweetie. Could you put it down for me?" Suzanne replied, shuffling through one stack of papers, finally locating the one she needed.

"I've always liked cloudy days," Molly ventured. "You know, better than the hot, hot sunny days."

"Yeah, ever since you were a little girl, they were your favorite," Suzanne remarked absently.

"Listen, Mom." Molly put both hands on the table. "Isn't there anything you want to ask me?"

Suzanne forced herself to look up from her work.

"I'm sorry, honey," she faltered, "what did you say?"

Molly stared at her. She looked so exasperated Suzanne wondered if she was going to get brained with her own napkin. Then Molly regained her composure.

"I was just wondering," she asked softly, "if there was anything you wanted to ask me. Anything you might want to talk to me about. Anything at all."

"Oh," Suzanne suddenly realized what her daughter was saying. "You mean, how long have you known, was it something I did, that sort of thing?"

"I guess so. Well, yeah."

"Listen, sweetie," she reached across the table to pat Molly's hand briefly, "I've got to wade through all these financial aid forms if I'm going to get my own transcripts in order. I'm not going to be offered scholarships like *some* people I know." She squeezed Molly's hand extra tight and then let go, picking up the pencil again. "Sweetie, I know what you're after, and I agree. We certainly have, well, things to talk about, don't we? And we will. We'll do it soon, I promise." She tapped on her stack of forms. "But I have a deadline on these forms . . ."

"Oh, no, hey, sure, I get it." Molly stood up hastily. "I just went through this myself, remember? I know how hard it is. I didn't mean to bug you."

"You're *not* bugging me." Suzanne stood up quickly, grabbing Molly's hand. "Please, baby, don't ever think that, it's just . . . It's just I hate forms, that's all. Serves me right for dropping out in the first place. I hope you're learning from this."

"Okay, I've got some stuff I want to do in town, so . . ." She looked at her mother and cleared her throat. "I just want you to know, I'm really proud of you, Mom."

"Really?" Suzanne was genuinely surprised. "I mean, well, for what?"

"For *this*." Molly tapped the stack of forms. "For deciding to go back to school and then actually doing it. Do you have any idea how many of my friends' mothers decide to go back to school, and they just talk and talk about it and talk some more, but they never actually get around to doing it?"

"All talk no action—reminds me of your father." Suzanne instantly regretted saying this; no matter what else the whiney little Mommy's boy was, he was also Molly's dad.

"I know, I know, your credo's always been 'Shit, or get off the pot,'" Molly nodded. "I can't count the number of times I heard you tell Daddy that. Anyway, *you* didn't do that—blow stuff off like he does, I mean. You said it, and now you're really doing it, and I just . . . Well, I just think that's great."

"Well, thank you, sweetie." Suzanne wasn't quite sure what to say. She cleared her throat, reaching for a joke. "And if you ever think of dropping out, just imagine my sitting here on this stoop, throwing pencils at the ground, and cursing my eighteen-year-old self. And if you ever give it up for a man . . ." She stopped herself, "I mean, a . . . a person, or, that is, a partner—well, I'll just kill you. No! Worse, I'll kill myself and *then* haunt you."

Brandon came out of Buddy's house with a pitcher of lemonade, and Suzanne was surprised at the measure of relief she felt. Why was she suddenly so uncomfortable around Molly, anyway?

"Hi there, Bobby." She cheerfully misused his name the way Buddy had been doing; Brandon looked every bit as impressed by it as he had when it had happened earlier. "How're you sleeping on that rusty old daybed?"

"As long as you're not sleeping on her daughter," Ava interjected, as she came down the stairs, "she hopes you're resting comfortably."

"Classy, Mother." Suzanne shot her a look that went completely ignored.

"The daybed is great. It's complete heaven compared to the beds in the dorms."

"Brandon spent the first two months of summer vacation up at the college getting some of the core classes for his degree," Molly informed them proudly. "Mr. Ambitious."

"That's *Dr.* Ambitious to you." He loftily straightened an imaginary tie.

"Hey, Grandma, are you ready?" asked Molly.

"Sure, just let me make sure I've got my stun gun." Ava opened her purse to check.

"*Stun gun?*" Buddy let the door slam behind him, a worried crease on his brow. "Where the heck are you going that you'd need a stun gun?"

"Don't you read the papers?" Ava turned to him, incredulously. "Every day, older people such as ourselves get attacked by people looking for our prescriptions and our money. It's not a safe world out there."

"I always thought your screeching voice would ward off any would-be predator." Buddy puffed his pipe until he got it going nice and strong.

"Anyway," she glowered in his direction, using one of New England's most oft-repeated quotes, "you just never know what you'll see when you don't have a weapon."

"Grandma, there's nothing to be ashamed of. Honesty is always the best policy," Molly said firmly. Turning to Buddy, she said proudly, "We're taking Grandma to an AA meeting." She smiled at her grandmother. "See how easy that was?"

"Actually," Ava put a soothing hand on top of her granddaughter's head, "the meetings are for Molly. She's a recovering crack whore. You're right, sweetie," Ava told Molly. "I feel so much better now that's it's all out in the open."

"Ha!" Brandon laughed, and lemonade came out his nose. He later claimed he could taste lemonade for three days afterwards, but it was well worth it.

"Mother, really," Suzanne responded perfunctorily, but her mind wasn't really on the banter.

"Come on, we're going to be late," Brandon said to Molly, "and I didn't wax my back yesterday for nothing. Any redness?"

Molly ran a hand over his shoulders. "Smooth as a baby's ass."

Watching them, Suzanne wondered how she could have misread the true nature of their relationship. Brandon wasn't as overt as some of the gays she knew, but if you looked closely, there was a softness, a hint of a feminine quality present in some of his mannerisms. Molly didn't seem at all masculine or butch to her, but maybe that was because she was used to her . . .

Or maybe, she thought, shamefaced, not all the stereotypes always applied. And, facing facts, she'd been told—more than once—that she had an awful lot of testosterone herself. Over the past few days, being around Molly had been difficult. It had made her feel, in fact, like a failure. She tried to shake the feeling off, but it kept bobbing up, and it was worse when Molly was right there in front of her.

"What is that thing," Ava went over to Brandon, and pushed his hair up, "this thing you've got tattooed right here, on the back of your neck?"

"It's a Chinese symbol of sobriety." He put an arm around her shoulder and whispered in her ear, "I'm a friend of Bill W.'s too."

"Friend of *whose*?" Buddy looked at them over his macramé, as Ava appraised Brandon with a whole new respect. There was now an instant camaraderie between the older lady and the college man in each one's recognition of a fellow traveler.

"It means," Ava said, taking Brandon's arm, "that he likes free coffee and donuts too. Hey, wait a minute . . ." She stopped for a moment to ask him seriously, "If I go with you, won't people think I'm one of those fag hags?"

"Only if we stop and get you some new shoes on the way. And sister," he pointed at her neat but somewhat vanilla ensemble, "while we're on the subject, extreme makeover, grandma edition, coming your way."

"Oh, really? Do you think so?" Ava's hands reached up and found her small pearl earrings and her perfectly knotted scarf. "I know this look is a little tired, and I have been meaning to have someone help me out with my colors for the longest time."

"Grandma, you could have asked me." Molly considered herself the fashion guru of the Applebaum clan. "You know how much I love to go shopping with you."

Ava turned to her, confused. "But, I thought you were gay now?"

"Oh, yeah, I forgot," she deadpanned. "The second I turned lesbo, I had to turn in my mall card and start buying all my clothes at Home Depot."

"They don't sell clothes at Home Depot!" Brandon corrected her.

She looked at him in disbelief. "So now I gotta explain sarcasm to a gay guy?" She looked imploringly to the sky. "What *has* this world come to?"

Ava, Molly, and Brandon headed to the AA meeting, their chatter trailing off in the cooling air.

Buddy put down the macramé and opened up a crossword puzzle. He had once told Suzanne crosswords were the real love of his life, and meant it. "She's a pip, that one."

Suzanne snorted. "*Which* one?"

Buddy shrugged, acquiescing. "Both of them, really. But I was talking about your daughter. Her grandfather would be so proud."

"Yes, he would." Suzanne watched the back of Molly as she walked down the road. "That girl was the apple of his eye. No matter how sick he got, she could always get a laugh out of him."

"If I'd had a granddaughter like that," Buddy told her, "I'd have bragged about her just as much as Jimmy did."

"He sure did." Suzanne's voice trailed off then, inevitably thinking about how her father would have reacted to this most recent turn of events. Jimmy hadn't had anything against gays, he often said. He just wanted them to stay away from him, and he'd stay away from them. Maybe it was just as well he hadn't been around for this. Molly had enough on her shoulders as it was, with school coming up. Suzanne didn't have anything against gay people— the pharmacist down at Market Basket and her dental hygienist were both as gay as the day is long, and since they were comfortable with it, so was she. But neither one of them was her kid. She remembered Daddy's awful prejudices— words like "fags," "gooks," and "niggers" that he only used behind closed doors, but used nonetheless. Ava had always snapped his head off when he said any of these in front of Suzanne. Then sometime later, Ava would take her aside and tell her that people were people, no matter the color of their skin or who they chose to love. The only thing that mattered about a person, Ava told her, only slightly slurring her speech (she tried to stay as sober as possible when she had important information to impart), was the things he or she did. You could only judge people by what they contributed to this world.

And Molly, well, just look at her . . . Eighteen years old, and her brains were practically paying her way through school. Not just any school, but *Vassar. I must have done something right,* Suzanne decided, feeling warm as she remembered Molly going up in her cap and gown, getting her sheepskin, valedictorian of her class. Her speech was all about how life would be what you made of it. Molly had listed off the people who had faced much harder challenges than the average bear yet had still made something of themselves. She attacked the laziness and apathy that had settled on today's youth, but in such a way that the other students in her class didn't feel chastised, only gently reminded of the real world. Then, she had said out loud, in public, that her mother was the hardest worker she knew and that she intended to follow in her footsteps, using her mind and strength just as much as she could. Suzanne, who hadn't seen that coming, had burst into tears.

Buddy attacked his puzzle for a while, then put his pen down and stretched out his arthritis-ridden hand.

"So," he said, by way of openers, "how did you take the news?"

Suzanne looked up. Her mind was so wrapped up in the numbers she'd just jotted down on her financial aid form that she had no idea what he was talking about.

"The news," she repeated, blankly. Then she remembered. "Oh, the Great Family Outing, as Brandon calls it?" She shrugged and leaned in confidentially. "Truth be told, I'm just so thrilled she's not pregnant—she can sleep with animals if she wants. As long as she's happy and she uses a condom. Or, you know. Whatever it is gay ladies use."

"I thought they liked to be called lesbians. But when I asked Brandon what to call her, he said, 'Molly.' I asked her what I should call her, she said, 'Fabulous.'"

She chuckled. "That's my girl, all right."

Buddy smiled and went back to his crossword.

"So, how's it going with him living over there, anyway?"

"You're not implying I'm uncomfortable with the gays, are you?" Buddy raised an eyebrow. "Besides, I knew he was gay since the moment he moved in."

"You did?" Suzanne's eyes widened in dismay; Buddy had more gay-dar that she did? This was terribly disconcerting. "How?"

"He organized my spices and seemed overly concerned with the crease in my pants," Buddy puffed. "He paints his nails. And in the shower he sings 'I Could Have Danced All Night.' Sorry, darling, but they're stereotypes for a reason."

"Why didn't you tell me?"

"Not my place to say anything," Buddy said in a calm, easy manner. Suzanne realized he was right. "Although, I have to admit, I didn't know about Molly. I guess it's harder to tell with the ladies. Is that un-PC of me to say?"

"Hell if I know." She bent over her work then. "So, it doesn't bother you having him there?"

"No, it's fine. Great." Buddy nodded. "He makes all kinds of teas, and we have the same taste in movies, from the black and whites to the Star Wars trilogy. But, well, there is the one thing . . ." He seemed to hesitate, looking guiltily at Suzanne.

"C'mon, Buddy, spill it. You can't throw something like that out and leave me hanging." Suzanne realized she wasn't going to be able to focus with Buddy there to talk to, so she put the cap on her pen and took out her Spirits.

"Well," he divulged finally, "the guy cleaned the place. I mean, he *cleaned* the place. Top to bottom, back to front, windows, closets, floors, you name it."

"Geez, send him over to our house. Mom might never let him leave."

"I just moved in!" Buddy protested. "I haven't had time to accumulate any good dirt yet!"

"You're a guy," Suzanne informed him. "Guys come with built-in dirt. It magically appears on all your stuff, behind your couch, under every shelf, where somehow, no matter if you're an engineer, a doctor, or a very successful businessman, you just can't ever seem to remember to look for, let alone clean it up." She puffed on her cigarette, satisfied that she had made her point. "Built-in dirt, I'm telling you. You all come with it. It's in your DNA."

Buddy gave that some thought. "We do," he agreed. "I guess we do."

"See?" She smiled. "It's not such a bad thing."

"So, listen," Buddy said casually. "The other night, before all the confusion . . . You were mentioning that you had come across some *information.*"

"Oh, I haven't forgotten." Suzanne lit a fresh cig off the one that was nearly dead, and looked directly into his eyes, smiling. "I was just waiting for you to sweat a little before bringing it up again. So, are you sweating?"

THIRTEEN

Buddy stared at her for a moment and then finally broke into a huge grin.

"Boy, you really are your mother's daughter, aren't you?"

"I shudder to admit it," Suzanne grimaced, "but there it is."

"So, why don't you tell me what you know?" Buddy said amiably. "And, just out of curiosity, *why* you know it, so I can set about denying it."

"It just struck me," she began slowly, tapping her fingers on the arm of her chair, "as, well, awfully out of character for someone like you to get caught serving booze to little girls."

"Why?" Buddy asked, sincerely surprised. "Your mother has told you any number of times how many skirts I chased, what an absolute pig I am . . . Sometimes I'd get me some action in the backseat of my Jeep in the alleyway of the restaurant, between shifts. That's how much of a horny bastard I was. I . . ."

"Okay, okay, we all know that if it moved, you tried to mount it." She held up her hands, fending off the details. "Go on, be proud of it, be a guy if you have to. Just don't make me have to hear about it—that's practically incest. But, that's not why I thought it was weird."

"Well, then," he repeated, "why?"

"Because, as you said, Daddy loved the ale, and the cognac, and he ran the dining room, and therefore the bar. Most of the time, you were in the kitchen or in the office."

Just talking about it brought back memories so dear a fine mist appeared in his eyes. He bit his lip until they subsided. Ever since they'd lost the pub, he'd tried as hard as he could not to think of O'Shenanigan's. But how, he often asked himself, do you not think of the happiest time of your life? "Yeah . . . *most* of the time . . ." Buddy kept his voice casual, wondering where she was going with this.

"Sometimes when it was slow," Suzanne went on, "you'd take your paperwork out into that circular table in the corner, remember?" She stopped for a moment, looking at him, smiling, remembering. "That was Buddy territory, when there were no customers. You'd sit there, with a big ol' rack of lamb and a Guinness. Or the pub-pub platter and a Guinness."

"Pub-pub platter." The memory flooded back to him so fully he could smell it. "Let me see, that was mushroom caps, potato skins, curly fries, and a cup of Irish stew. Chef Fred, he was a genius. Best working suppers of my life."

"You weren't behind the bar often." Suzanne crushed out her butt, stood up, and began to pace around a little, in full-on Nancy Drew mode. "In fact . . . actually, no, I'm sure. I'm absolutely sure that I can't recall seeing you there at all. You used to joke you were nervous about all those hanging glasses; something about being a bull in a china shop, I think."

"Well, sure I was nervous." Buddy admitted. "Those were some expensive frosted glasses, and there were hundreds of them, all hanging from the ceiling." He shrugged, pulling his gold Zippo out of his front pocket, and lit his pipe. "I'll admit I stayed out of the bar as much as I could, but with a place like that, everyone pitches in with everything. I used to catch your mother, who was the hostess, running the dishwasher. Your dad would shovel the walkway in the wintertime, when he couldn't pawn that chore off on you, that is."

"Like you said," she continued, not giving him the smile he was after, "I wasn't old enough to work at the pub, but sometimes they'd let me do my homework at the bar. Daddy and that guy, Terry, would be behind the bar serving drinks, but Terry was only there Thursdays through Saturdays. Sometimes, if it was busy, Mom helped if it was just wine, or beer, or something simple. But not you. *Never* you." Buddy started to protest again, and she held up her hand, and took a deep breath, exhaling carefully. "And then," she said finally, "there's the simple matter of the TEAM test."

"What the hell," asked Buddy innocently, "is a TEAM test?"

And with those seven words he completely hung himself.

She squatted down next to Buddy's chair to look him directly in the eye.

"The TEAM test," she told him softly, "is a safety course required of each and every bartender in the state of New Hampshire. The politicians cooked this one up special for us back in the sixties when reefer started actually making its way up from the big bad city. Anyway, it's a tough test. Really tough. So tough, I'd really expect you to remember preparing for it and taking it. That is," she reached out and tapped him on the chest to emphasize each word, "*if you'd ever taken it.*"

"Oh, that." Buddy said hastily. "Well, that was a pretty damn expensive test, you know. When you're running a business, you cut a corner or two."

"Two minutes ago, you didn't know what the hell it was, and now you remember how much it cost?" Suzanne stood up and went back to her chair. "And if you cut that corner, it was the only one. Those books are as clean as a whistle. I could eat off those books."

"This hinting is giving me a freakin' headache, Suzie-Q," Buddy grumbled. "So if you have something to say, do us both a favor and just say it."

She crossed her arms and looked at him for a long moment with a mixture of admiration, confusion, and love.

"You weren't the one," she said at last. "You were not the one who was caught serving alcohol to pretty young things."

Buddy was shaking his head back and forth before the words were out of her mouth.

"See, you've got it all wrong." He struggled to stand, reaching for his cane. "Wrong, wrong, wrong, *wrong*. You see . . ."

"And you took the fall for Daddy," she overrode his words, "because of what he did for you in Vietnam. Because you loved him like a brother. And because you knew my mother would castrate him with a rusty grapefruit spoon if she knew."

Buddy held up a weathered hand to stop her.

"I love you, sweetie, but you just don't know what you're talking about, and I don't want to discuss this anymore. I'm going inside." Having gotten a firm grasp on his cane, he planted it hard and stood, managing a few firm steps toward his own house until Suzanne's voice stopped him.

"People make mistakes, Buddy," she said gently. "All the time. They fuck up. I'm pissed as hell at Daddy—it's weird being pissed at someone who's dead. You can imagine the guilt. People do stupid things, but you don't stop loving them for it. So there it is. I can see forgiving him for something like that." She took a few steps closer, tilting her head, looking at him in wonder. "But you *taking* those charges for him? I don't understand—that's too much, Buddy! You didn't owe him your life. No matter what you might think, you didn't."

Buddy spun around and walked to her faster than she thought him capable of.

"Didn't I?" he asked fiercely. "*Didn't* I owe him my life? I wouldn't have come back if it weren't for him. Understand? My life would have been over. *Over*. You should have seen the way his whole body jerked back when that bullet hit him. The way his eyes rolled back in his head, all that blood . . . That bullet he took would have got me right in the throat," he tapped just the spot, "and I'd be lying there still. I'd have rotted in some jungle while the enemy cut off my nuts and wore them for cuff links." He took a deep breath; the doc was always telling him that getting too strung up about anything wasn't worth it these days. "So that's where I think you're wrong, Suzie-Q. Because what I do think is maybe I *do* owe him my life."

"You're right," she admitted softly. "I *don't* understand, because I've never been there. I've never had anyone do anything like that for me, and I've never been in a position that I'd do that for anyone, except, of course, my kid. But no matter how it's sliced, diced, or cuisinarted, I *do* know it's stupid to ruin your future for your past—all over someone else's screwup. Daddy fucked up, Buddy. Not you. *Daddy* did. So, his fuck up, his punishment. He should have been the one to pay for it." She looked down at the ground, tears blurring her vision, and wiped them away discreetly before she looked up at him again. "Look, don't lie to me, Uncle Buddy. Please? It's insulting, it's infuriating, and I already know the truth. So please do me the honor of not lying *directly* to my face."

He stared at her for a long moment, and then he sank back into his chair. "Yeah. Okay. You happy? Yeah. It was Jimmy." He took a deep breath, surprised how good it felt to say it out loud, to tell the truth out loud, even if it also felt like besmirching his dead best friend's name. "I didn't like having my name in the newspaper, and I didn't like paying the fine, and I sure as hell didn't like having a record that kept me from ever getting a liquor license again, thereby killing any future plans I had for another restaurant. That squashed what little soul I had left. I *loved* that business, you know? I always imagined . . . You know how I loved going to the theatre; I always thought the restaurant biz was a lot like Broadway."

"Broadway?" Suzanne smiled at the analogy. "How do you figure?"

"Oh, the preparation, the costumes, the lighting, the crazy hustle-bustle feeling of the 'meal must go on,' the fake accents, even." He relished the flavor it all brought back. "Those were the days, kiddo."

"So," Suzanne asked hesitantly, "if you knew that all that would happen if you took the blame, then . . . *why?*"

"Because," he shrugged weakly, "love will make you do funny things. Far more than booze or drugs ever could."

"Love is a dangerous drug—right up there with crack," Suzanne agreed. "But still, throwing your life away because of your best friend, it's just ridiculous. Even if the man is just like a brother to you."

"I wasn't talking about Jimmy," Buddy said softly.

"Well, if you're not talking about Daddy," she demanded, "then who the hell *are* you . . . ?" It all fell on her then, like a piano falling out of the sky and landing on her with a musical grunt. "Oh. My. God," she said faintly.

He looked at her for a long, hard moment. "If she'd have known it was Jimmy, it would have killed her," he said. Suzanne wondered how many times he'd said that phrase to himself over the years, to reassure himself he'd done the right thing. "And that would have killed *me*. Okay? You get it now?"

FOURTEEN

There was a clump of smokers in front of the AA meeting place, which was held in the top floor of a Salvation Army store on Congress Street.

"At least they make them smoke outside now," Ava acknowledged as they scooted in the door, hopefully before any of the disgusting smell stuck to their clothing.

Molly wrinkled her nose in distaste. She'd read that once smokers quit, even after a couple of weeks, the smell would become repellent to them. If only she could somehow strap her mother down and slap a NicoDerm patch on her.

"You think this is bad?" Ava asked as they climbed the stairs to the meeting. "You should have seen it in the old days; the place had a huge cloud over it. The reasoning was, if you tried to make someone quit drinking *and* smoking, they'd cave on one, then figure they might as well do both again. Sort of a joint disease," she snorted. "It was hell on the few of us nonsmokers. I'd have to shower and change my clothes in the hallway before I'd go into my house. Jimmy used to say, 'Baby doll, you gave up drinking so you go to AA and get lung cancer.'" A smile usually rose on her lips at the sound of her husband's name, followed by a quick catch of her breath. Then, she'd raise her hand to her mouth and, clearing her throat, change the subject with a vengeance. This time was no different. "Yes, we've got us a big bunch of randoms today," she commented.

The meeting room was already half-filled with AAs walking around, easily chatting with each other. Some of them looked like they'd spent the night in the gutter, some of them looked like they'd just gone shopping at Neiman Marcus, and there was a whole host of other types in between.

Brandon muscled his way to the coffee line as Molly and Ava tried to find three seats together.

"Will they mind that I'm not an alcoholic?" whispered Molly.

"Just don't mention it, because then they'll think you're in denial," Ava informed her. "Then, this whole room will turn into an angry mob of people trying to make you see the light."

"Got it. Don't deny my problem." Molly winked, giving her a thumb's up.

"Feel free to tell me if it's none of my business, dear," Ava dug through her pocketbook in search of a mint, "but how often do you drink?"

"Please, Grandma." Molly glanced around, then remembered where she was.

"Look, I'm just asking. I asked your mother the same question." Ava popped a butter rum Life Saver into her mouth thoughtfully. "She doesn't seem to drink much."

"For a long time, she didn't drink at all." Even in such accepting surroundings, Molly still found herself wanting to fall off the wooden fold-up chair and right through the floor. "Not even champagne on New Year's Eve when I was little. And when I got old enough to bring home all the Just Say No stuff from Officer Smiley at school, she sat me down and told me that you had a special disease called alcoholism." She glanced apologetically at Ava, hoping she hadn't offended her, but Ava didn't bat an eye. "She also told me it was hereditary, so she might have it, and I might have it. And what alcoholism did was, well, when you drank alcohol, it made you crazy. You'd start drinking, and you couldn't stop, and you'd do all kinds of nutty stuff that you'd be embarrassed by later."

"Like getting on a bus bound for Boston in the dead of winter with no shoes, no jacket, and no money, save bus fare?" Ava said lightly, crossing her legs. "When I came out of that blackout, it took me half an hour to figure out where I was, how I'd gotten there. Some helpful soul had seen me wandering around and got me to a soup kitchen. By the time I called your grandfather, he was frantic; he'd already put out a missing person's report." She shuddered again, thinking of that awful day. She'd been physically unable to make herself look her husband in the eye when he came by to pick her up. "The scary thing is, that wasn't even my bottom. It took a couple more adventures like that to set me straight."

Brandon caught the end of that story as he was passing out the drinks: two cups of black coffee and one cup with enough milk and sugar to make it almost a milk shake.

"I hear you." He pulled up his shirt. On his chest was a picture of a lion tearing through his flesh. "On my back, I've got his rear end. I came to about an hour after this ugly thing was finished." He woefully pulled his shirt back down. "That was my bottom."

"It's not bad, as far as tattoos go." Ava tried to console him. "It's actually quite well drawn. It's just, well, it's . . ."

"It's sooooo not you," Molly declared firmly.

"That's it exactly," Brandon concurred. "Sitting in a tattoo parlor getting a tattoo that I think will make me more 'butch' while loaded out of my mind—definitely not me."

The chattering and squeaking of wooden chairs suddenly ceased as a man in his late fifties ambled over to the podium. He wore a plaid shirt, worn jeans, and a cell phone peeking out of his front shirt pocket, the plastic-coated kind that you could take outside in all kinds of weather. He looked vaguely familiar to Ava.

"Hello, everyone, I'm Sean." His dark hair was sprinkled with grey, and he had the easy speaking quality of someone who'd been around awhile, who'd earned a dogged respect—and who had the battle scars to show how he'd found his way to the doorstep.

"Hello, Sean." Ava and Brandon greeted him along with the rest of the group, and Molly chimed in at the end, feeling a bit embarrassed. Brandon squeezed her shoulders. "It's always tough for virgins," he whispered, and she bit back a giggle.

"Well, they tell me it's my turn to get up and say something since I didn't bring the doughnuts this time," Sean continued, and everyone laughed.

Ava whispered, "He's got a landscaping business. He's also divorced. Three-time loser, as he says—four kids, all grown and gone."

"I never met a beer that I wasn't best friends with . . . But I was in love with the one I was gonna have after it," Sean said with conviction, and a wave of been-there laughter ran through the room. "Most of my waking hours, I was walking around in a booze-soaked fog, but I got away with it for years. I was in control of it because I was the king of the 'yets' for a long time. I never got a DUI. Never spent a night in jail. Never cheated on a woman. Never missed work because of my drinking and my drugging. Never let a good friend down, never told a lie, never stole any money. Then the nevers . . . Well, any drunk knows 'never' means 'not yet.'" He counted off on his fingers. "A few years rolling around in the gutter, and then I got a call from my ex-wife Margie. I don't even know how the hell she'd managed to track me down, but track me down she did. She'd been to the doctor, and he'd told her that her breast cancer had spread to her lymph nodes. In other words, she was gonna die. I didn't even know she'd been sick." He stopped again, clenching both sides of the podium so hard his knuckles turned white.

The room fell completely silent. Some people bowed their heads, some nodded, but *all* understood.

"She didn't have any family, and my folks she didn't trust a damn. So, when she died, that meant our boys would grow up in foster care. Now, I'm sure it's come a long way since I was growing up, but, well . . ." He rocked in his boots a bit, trying to think of an inoffensive way to put it, in case any social workers were in the group. "Lord, it's such a bitch being so PC all the time!" he groaned, getting another huge laugh. "Sorry to generalize, but let's just say, in my day, nothing very good happened to boys in foster care. If you didn't get worked to the bone, you got molested, or worse. Pretty much the best you could hope for was some little old lady that would ignore you and pocket your check every month."

The thought of two little boys with no homes still made tears well up in Molly's eyes. Brandon put his arm around her comfortingly, draping it over the back of the wooden folding chair.

"Margie told me that her boys were *not*, repeat, *not* going to end up on the State," Sean went on, "and, unfortunately—that's just the word she used—I was the only chance of keeping them together and making sure they were cared for. So," he said, smiling, "she laid it all out for me. I was going to get sober. I was going to reinstate my business. I was going to fix my credit and make sure my boys had enough money to get to college. I was going to be a good and attentive father, and if I couldn't figure out how, then I'd have to marry someone desperate enough to marry me who could do it in my stead."

Another wave of laughter rippled through the room, but Molly understood it better now. Laugh at all the jokes, even the little ones, because the tension here builds so fast that any release at all is needed.

"She told me flat-out that this was going to be the way it was, and from her tone, I gotta tell you, I didn't even think about saying no." He drew a deep breath, gave a broad, easy grin, and shrugged, as if to say, *What are you gonna do?* "She got me to rehab and got me all detoxed, and also got me my twenty-eight days, you know, the full month that we used to get before the HMOs fucked it up for us the way they have everything else."

There was a lot of mutual groaning about that one.

"Now rehabs generally last four or five hours a day," Brandon whispered. "They'll cover it, as it's preventative, but this way they don't have to feed you or give you a bed. A lot less people make it than with the twenty-eight full days."

"Cheap-assed bastards," Ava chimed in, and the room agreed. Molly giggled. She always got a kick out of it when Grandma swore.

"Then I was back home," Sean continued. "Back home, and going to four, maybe five meetings a day. Not a week," he stressed to their disbelieving faces, "a *day*. And for the first two months I was home, on weekends we just drove from one meeting to another. I'd go inside, and she'd find a playground for the boys to play at while I was in the halls. It was a crazy schedule, but it *worked*. She watched me like a hawk; she'd even follow me into the bathroom for a time, and let me tell you, no one wants to be close to me for that." All the men in the hall whooped at that, while the women made faces. "After three months, she let me down to three a day, then after three months of that, two a day. All the while, she was getting skinnier and skinnier." He paused to take his handkerchief out of his jeans pocket. "But she stayed tough as nails on me, no matter how frail she looked on the outside. I called up a couple of my clients, told them I was sober now and trying to stay on the straight and narrow. Mostly, I called to apologize, especially to Dolby—that's the guy I hit. But, you'll never believe it." He looked openly around the room, still surprised by their reaction. "Once they'd heard I was in the program and had been sober for four months, you know what they did? Some of them, they, well, they immediately offered me some work. I didn't have my equipment anymore, but I asked around and borrowed a riding lawn mower, a weed whacker, and Margie went right out and bought new hedge clippers and pruning shears with what little credit she had left on her Visa. Word about me spread, and my phone started ringing." He reached up and unashamedly wiped his eyes. "Before I knew what hit me, I'd been sober a whole year. Not only had I made a down payment on a new truck and some new equipment, I'd read every book on parenting that Margie could carry home from the library, every single word Dr. Spock, Joyce Brothers, and Dr. Phil ever wrote down, and after a bit, my boys actually lit up when they came home from school and saw me there. They'd look over at me in the stands at their Little League games, like they couldn't quite believe I was there . . . And then they'd look anxiously back, like they were sure I'd take off any second. After two, three years, they stopped looking surprised that I was there and started complaining I was in their faces too much." He smiled right through the tears now.

"By then, Margie was near the end, and no matter how long I'd been sober, no matter how well I was doing, every night she would make me promise her that I wouldn't become *that guy* again. *That guy* ruined her credit, ignored our sons, broke her heart. And every day I'd promise. I'd say, 'No, honey, *that guy* is gone, and he's gone for good.' One day, right after she made me promise, she closed her eyes, and then . . ." He pinched the bridge of his nose, pushing back the sobs. "Then she just . . . She just wasn't there anymore. I could see it happening." He bent his head again for a moment, then looked up and smiled, this time a little weakly. "Part of me thinks she hung on as long as she did just to make sure I was really gonna do it, that I was gonna take my life back, the one that she'd forced me to resuscitate from the dead. And I gotta tell you," he admitted, "I didn't want any part of sobering up, at first. Especially when the shakes set in, or I couldn't stop throwing up, or I couldn't sleep. But I did it for Margie. Because she told me I had to, and because, even through the haze, I still knew I loved her more than I'd ever loved anything, and what's more, I was stunned that she'd take on the not-small task of sobering up a slobbering drunk like me, just to protect our boys. But she saw that as the only option. So when she set out to do it, nothing was gonna stop her." He was quiet for a minute.

Molly could hear the traffic outside on Congress Street, crossing onto Islington. Then Sean continued, "They say you can't get sober for someone else. It won't work. It's gotta be for you. Well, I'm here to tell you, that's not true. I got sober for Margie and my boys, all those years ago, and it *did* work, because in the end, it was all for me anyway. No matter what I was able to give Margie toward the end, or to my boys, it all meant I got my *life* back. And when I got my life back, and realized it was a damn tough thing to do, well, I started doing something I hadn't done since I could remember." He paused just long enough to make sure that he had everyone's full attention. "I started to respect myself. And as long as I, as we all," he gestured to all of them in the small, dusty, room, "respect ourselves for all we've done, it makes it a hell of a lot harder to even consider picking up again. One drink," he intoned darkly, "and for me, it's all over. I respect myself too much to go back to being *that guy*. But I did lie to her about one thing; *that guy* could come back at any moment. If I stop working the program, *that guy* is right here. And I never want to see *that guy* again . . . so I hope you all don't mind seeing me as often as I can get here."

There was a round of applause as he finished up, and he waved it off, then took a small, jovial bow. People stood, wiped their eyes, stretched, reached for their cigarettes and empty cups, and began mingling.

"Break time." Ava yawned and stretched a little. "My, my, some of the speakers do run on a little."

Glancing at her watch, Molly was surprised to see that Sean had spoken for half an hour. She could have listened to his hypnotic voice all day.

"You were never that bad, Grandma," she felt compelled to say.

"Look for the similarities, not the differences." Brandon and Ava spoke in unison and then looked at each other, laughing.

"Jinx," said Brandon affectionately, "you owe me a Coke."

"You two rehearsed that," Molly accused, as they stood to refill their Styrofoam cups with more weak coffee.

"You'll learn the lingo if you're around it enough. Through osmosis," Ava told her. "It's our mantra. And when we need it, it helps."

Molly'd had a few drunken nights in her life, but they were few and far between. It had taken a lot of hard work, after all, to get that scholarship to Vassar. But it was a hereditary thing, everyone said. Did that mean that there was a real possibility that one day she'd be here, right next to these people, saying these words? She shook her head. *That's tomorrow's problem*, as her grandfather would have said. *Best spend today looking out for today.*

Sean walked by them then, looking for a place to sit in the crowd. He smiled briefly at Ava, a bright, engaging smile that closed off quickly once it had done its job. Ava suddenly realized where she knew him from.

"My goodness, that's Sean . . . oh, what was his last name again? Williams, that's it."

Molly suddenly turned to Ava. "He's got a landscaping business," Molly intoned. "He's also divorced, three-time loser—and yes, Brandon, I know that means he's been to rehab three times, see how in the loop I am?—and, as he says, four kids, all grown and gone." She leaned forward and whispered, "Are you thinking what I'm thinking?"

"I can't imagine what you're thinking," Ava said breezily, "but I'm going to go invite our new friend Sean for a cookout next Monday night."

FIFTEEN

"Oh . . . my . . . *God!!*" Suzanne repeated about five or six times until the realization began to sink in. So many little details . . . So many comments . . . So many *years*. It all started to snap into place with almost audible clicks.

"Will you keep your voice down?" Buddy threw a worried glance down the block. "Even if they're on the bus by now, that woman still has ears like a bat."

"Okay, okay, okay." Suzanne grabbed for her trusty Spirits and tried to compose herself, her hand shaking as she touched the lighter's flame to the tip of the cigarette. "Okay, Buddy, you sit. Oh . . . you're already sitting. Okay, I'll sit. Now that I'm sitting, *you* talk."

"It's a long story, sweetie, maybe we can just leave it at . . ." he began weakly, but one look from Suzanne's face convinced him of the futility of the argument. "Okay. Fine." He drew a deep breath and started again. "Your mom must have told you how she and your dad met."

"Probably," she shrugged. "But I gotta tell you, any story that had to do with her and sex with Daddy . . . Frankly, I just tune her out like a radio."

"It was after our tour of duty," Buddy began. "We were home on leave. It felt good to be home, but scary too. Everything had changed, everyone had changed, and who knew if we'd see anyone ever again? You tried not to think that way, but you did."

Suzanne nodded. She couldn't imagine having to go through that herself and knocked on wood that her only child was a girl so she'd never get drafted either—although that might change by the time she had grandchildren. If she ever had grandchildren. Come to think of it, she wasn't quite sure how that worked.

"There was this big USO Christmas dance at the Rochester Recreation Center," Buddy was saying. "One minute, we're facedown in the mud, covered all the time in blood, brains, and guts, killing men and screwing every whore we could find." He laughed ironically. "But you put us in a rec hall that we'd been in a thousand times, with a basketball hoop, some colored lights, and a bunch of clean-cut American girls in skirts and sweater sets—all of a sudden, you'd think we didn't know how to talk. We'd stare down at our feet, kicking at our shoes, drinking cup after cup of soda." He reached underneath the chair and pulled out his macramé basket. In addition to helping with his arthritis, he noticed, it did wonders for calming the nerves. "Your dad was worse off than I was."

"Daddy was *shy*?" Suzanne's mouth dropped open, letting herself fall back against the iron bench; that didn't fit with any picture of her dad she had in her mind. "Mr. Giggles and Gin, *shy*?"

"After half an hour or so, I look up, and there's this girl." Buddy spoke the word softly, tenderly, almost as though it were a kiss. He was really warming up to the story now—his eyes were starting to gleam, and there was more color in his face than she'd seen in a long time, since all those years back on State Street in the pub. "This tall, auburn-haired girl with big dark eyes and hair done up all fancy; her headband matched her sweater." He met her eyes and touched his hand to his chest. "I was just a *sucker* for that. She was wearing a strand of pearls her father had gotten her for graduating high school."

"A strand of *pearls*?" She shot a betrayed look at her mother's house. "All I got was a stinkin' typewriter."

"I think the balance of your graduation present was spent on baby clothes," Buddy reminded her, and Suzanne ducked her head, properly chastised. "So, I couldn't take my eyes off this girl. She was a *knockout*. Neither could Jimmy. And not just her face, her body, but she had this, this energy that radiated from her in waves. You couldn't be in a room with this woman and not notice her. Anyway, we're both standing there like a couple of dorks, downing cup after cup of soda, trying to egg each other into making the first move, when," he held up a finger to draw out the suspense, "what do you think? The girl comes over herself and starts talking away."

"Yeah, so?" It was something Suzanne had done a hundred times or more at dances in high school. Well, until senior year, at least, when her belly started sticking out.

"You gotta understand," Buddy smiled a little, "this was before the women's lib movement. And Portsmouth was always a little behind the times anyway. Some would have called her a floozy just for doing that. But not me. Frankly, it turned me on to no end. Since she was so brave, it was easy for me to be brave, so pretty soon I asked her to dance, and she said yes. Now, Jimmy never worked up the nerve, and he'd had his chance, so I didn't feel too badly, at first . . . If Jimmy really wanted something, he went for it. I figured this was his way of throwing me a signal. Boy, did I misread *that* one. Anyway, for the rest of the night, I danced with her. She smelled like . . . like lilies of the valley." He closed his eyes and inhaled; sometimes that was enough to bring the scent back.

"Let me guess," Suzanne said, closing her eyes. "That brave, tall, auburn-haired, dark-eyed, mystery woman was my mother."

"That's right," he nodded, his eyes soft and dreamy. "That, indeed, was your mother."

Suzanne was silenced. She drew her knees up to her chest, thinking. Mom had always been, well, Mom. When Suzanne was very little, Ava had been pretty much the average Mom, making sure she wore sweaters if she was cold, putting a piece of fruit in her lunch box every day. But then, Mom became the drunk Suzanne avoided or helped Daddy take care of for *years*—until it was hard to remember the lunch-making, sweater-bearing, fruit-giving Mom she'd once been. Then, just as suddenly, Mom was the clear-headed, AA-going, constantly cooking woman who tried—but not too hard—to get to know her daughter. The daughter who'd had grown up considerably since she'd taken a dive into the bottle. And now, it was Mom, who she was counting on, depending on, for the first time in her life to take care of her, the way she'd taken care of Molly all of Molly's life. The way she'd taken care of Ava, before she'd gotten sober.

But this was a whole new Mom altogether. Hearing someone talk about Mom like she was . . . A woman? A *hot babe*, no less? No, she was quite sure no one had ever spoken about Mom like that in front of her before.

"So," he went on, "during these furloughs, courtships moved pretty fast. It gave new meaning to the word whirlwind. It wasn't at all unusual for a couple to get married in a matter of a month or a couple of weeks."

Suzanne turned her face away. "If you're about to tell me that you danced naked with the woman who gave me life," she said sternly, "well, good for you and all, but if you make me listen to it, I'll scratch your eyes right out."

"In those days," Buddy told her, "you had two categories. Girls you 'danced naked' with and girls you gave rings to. Ava . . . Ava was definitely in the second category." He stopped for a moment, considering this. "Actually, she was the kind of girl who told you when to give her a ring and exactly what kind she'd like. And I liked that. You always knew where you stood with her. No guessing games."

"I can see where that would be attractive." Suzanne nodded sympathetically. "You had no way of knowing that same determination to get what she wanted was going to extend to the kind of toilet paper she preferred."

"So," Buddy went on as if Suzanne hadn't spoken at all, "we had about two more weeks of leave before we shipped back. I saw Ava three times the first week, five times the second—each date was better than the last. And she made me laugh. Lordy, did she make me laugh! But, then, she wasn't just . . . She had *plans*. She had *thoughts*. Just about everything. When she talked, it was fascinating. And her silences were more interesting than most people's conversations." He shook his head, full of admiration that had never truly waned. "And I knew, I knew with all my soul by the end of the first night that I wanted to marry her. I even went to my mom and asked her if I could have my nanna's ring, the antique, emerald-cut diamond that had been in our family for generations, because I'd met the girl that was going to be my wife."

Suzanne exhaled slowly and stubbed out her cigarette, trying hard to picture it all. "It's just," she said at last, "she's said such terrible things about you for so long. To find out that all this time, you loved her, it's just really weird."

"So, on the day I was supposed to ask her, I take her to this really romantic restaurant—it even had cloth napkins." He sat up straight, making a hoity-toity face. "The Army wasn't paying us PFCs much, so this was a big deal. I had the waiter light the candles, bring the wine . . . I even sniffed the cork just like my dad taught me to, and let it breathe. When the waiter came, I didn't look at the prices, and I ordered for both of us."

She wrinkled her nose. "That's so chauvinistic, Buddy."

"Hey," he raised an eyebrow, "it was considered the height of romance in those days. Anyway, the evening went well. So well, in fact . . . Well, I suppose there's no getting around telling you this: we're not quite sure whose daughter you are—mine, or Jimmy's."

For a second, silence thundered through Suzanne.

"What?" She cleared the brick out of her throat long enough to ask. "*What?*"

Then Buddy looked up at her, impishly grinning. "Jesus, I can't believe you fell for that one. That one's older than the hills."

"*Buddy!*" she gasped, standing up; she was horrified, she was furious, she was humiliated.

And then they were both laughing, doubled over, tears streaming out of both of their eyes.

"Well, do a little arithmetic, kiddo," he wheezed, wiping a tear from his eye. "Geez, if you'd been conceived in our first TDY, then you'd be, what, forty one, forty two?" He took off his glasses and wiped them clean, his hands still trembling with the force of the laughter. "Your bullshit detector must be on the fritz is all I can say."

She took aim with her pen and tossed it at him, being careful to miss widely. "You're just lucky I'm not a better shot," she told him menacingly. "Okay, back to the story. You were in the fancy restaurant."

"Oh, yeah," he said, picking up the hemp ropes and bringing himself back to the story. "Your mom is a sharp one, and she saw me coming, I think, because before I could pop the question, she put her hand on my wrist and told me she had something important to discuss with me."

"Ouch!" She winced. "That's never good."

"Rarely," he agreed. "So, she went on to say she liked me very much. She liked me very, very much, in fact, and she thought she could probably even fall in love with me. But," he stopped for just a millisecond—even now, he had to close his eyes to say it, "that she couldn't seriously commit to a guy who was going off to war. She knew a few girls who were waiting for their men to come home . . . And then their men . . . Well, their men didn't. She said she'd pray for me and all that, and to please look her up when I got home, if I wasn't engaged or married to someone else." He stopped talking then, stopped macraméing, stopped moving, his eyes locked on the ground.

"Wow, that must have been awful," Suzanne ventured. "Were you sad?"

"Sad?" he repeated. "Sad would have been a day at the beach. I was *crushed.*" He clenched his hand, demonstrating just how crushing it had been. "More than that even—devastated. I was so sure she was the *one* . . . Never in my life had anything knocked me on my ass like that, unless maybe it was getting drafted. Yeah, it was about on par with that. It took me four days before I could take a deep breath, like I had a broken rib or pneumonia. After I got out of the restaurant and went home, I was almost glad to be going back; it was good to be crawling through the mud and trying to kill something right about then."

Suzanne thoughtfully lit another cigarette. It had been a full five minutes since her last, she noticed with satisfaction. "So, how did Daddy get involved in all this?"

"Now, let me just . . . Oh, yes." He had to think a minute before he put his finger on it. "On our third date, I'd given her a book of poetry that my grandmother had handed down to my mom, and my mom, to me. Emily Dickinson. She liked the story of how none of Emily's poems were published till after she died; she said it made her feel like there's always hope." Suzanne laughed—and her laugh sounded like Ava's too, to Buddy's ears. "Anyhoo, Jimmy wanted to get it back for me, it being a family heirloom and all. Or, at least, that's the excuse he used to write to her—I certainly couldn't do it. It was one thing to give out my family's Dickinson to a woman who was 'the one,' but just some girl who dumped me after two weeks—well, let's just say it wasn't something I was going to hear the end of any time soon. And every time I heard about it, I was going to think of Ava, and I wanted to get her out of my mind as soon as I could."

"So, Daddy wrote to her to get the book back?"

"In a word, yes, but he really wanted to rip her a new one. Your dad could use language pretty creatively when he wanted to."

"You mean he had special talent for making people feel like shit." Suzanne leaned forward a little, smiling. "You should have seen him on prom night when I came home at four in the morning with my dress on backwards."

"Well, rather than crumble under his harsh words—like everyone else did—your mom immediately wrote him back." Buddy sighed. "She told him that she was terribly sorry if she'd led me on or hurt my feelings, and told him why, and no matter how you slice it . . . At least, she was being *honest*." He shrugged again. "You had to respect that, anyway."

"The thing about not being able to handle getting that telegram?" Suzanne shook her head, wildly disappointed in her mother. Somehow, she temporarily forgot that if her mother hadn't made that particular choice, she wouldn't be here. "She could have thought of that before she started dating you."

Buddy puffed out his chest a bit, and patted his hair. "I like to think," he said smugly, "that she found herself completely unable to resist my animal magnetism."

He looked so cute he made Suzanne momentarily forget her cigarette worries. "You know, I've seen pictures of you as a younger man, my friend." She winked at him, approvingly. "You were the total package—a real looker."

"I was, wasn't I? If I do say so myself." He reached down for his abandoned macramé. "Anyway, he wrote back, apologizing for being so harsh; she wrote back, forgiving him. Pretty soon letters were making the nine thousand mile journey pretty regularly."

"Uh-oh." Suzanne wrinkled her nose. She knew how the story turned out. "But, what about all that stuff about not wanting to date a soldier?"

"They weren't *dating*." He held up a finger, carefully differentiating the semantic. "They were *writing*. I guess, somehow, that didn't bother her quite so much. With each letter, things get just a bit friendlier. And with each letter,

Jimmy comes running to me. Sort of, checking in, to see if it's all right. To see, I suppose, if at any time, I'll get mad and demand he stop writing to her, and, up to a point, I'm sure, he would have done that." He lit the pipe and puffed gently until the ember glowed. "And then, after a point, I'm thinking, nineteen or twenty letters later, they had a whole other connection with each other, totally separate from me. Next thing you know, it's fifty-seven letters later, we're both back home, both of us in one piece. Exactly two months to the day after *that,* they were standing in front of a preacher on his parents' front lawn. Jimmy took me aside the day before he proposed and asked me if I minded." He choked out a short, bitter laugh. "Did I mind? Did I *mind?*"

From the strident sound of his voice, forty-plus years later, Suzanne guessed that, in fact, he had minded. Quite an awful lot, if you got right down to it.

"I minded like I'd mind a hot coal burning inside my chest. But what was I supposed to say?" He shrugged again, sadly. "I saw the way she was looking at him."

"So," Suzanne asked softly, "what *did* you say?"

Buddy stared off into the cool afternoon air for a long time before answering. "First and only time in my life," he said at last, "that I ever lied to that man."

"Oh, Buddy . . ."

He waved off her empathy; he'd lived too long in Jimmy's shadow to be jealous now. "Your dad, he was the character. I was the straight man, the one standing next to him to set up the joke, or the one there to tell of the adventures he'd had. You couldn't really be jealous of it, you just . . ." He tried to describe the magnetism of the man's personality. "He was just Jimmy. Everyone, *everyone* loved Jimmy. Trust me, she wasn't the first gal to walk right by me on her way to Jimmy."

"So, is that why you did it, because you felt guilty because you'd been in love with his wife?"

Buddy shrugged, suddenly shifting in his seat, looking away. Suzanne frowned and edged closer, trying to see his face.

"Oh, I get it, because even at the time, you still resented him, and felt guilty about that?" Yet another idea struck her. "Plus the guilt you probably still had, of him getting shot for you? Or, maybe, I don't know, maybe you still weren't over his wife, even then?"

Buddy turned his face away even further, and then the light bulb finally exploded in Suzanne's head.

"Because you're *still* not over his . . . Oh, my God." Suzanne's breath came out in one big whoosh. "Oh, my *God . . .*"

"Now, listen, you," Buddy said hastily, tamping out the pipe. "I didn't say that. Did you hear those words come out of my mouth? No, *sir*," he shook his head firmly. "I didn't say that."

"You didn't *not* say it," Suzanne retorted, "and very loudly."

Buddy sighed, irritably. "You know," he said, "I liked you a whole lot better when I could distract you with a candy bar and a quarter." He dug around in his pocket and came up with a coin. Holding it up before her, he cooed, "See, honey? Look how *shiny*!"

She stuck out her tongue at him, then snagged the quarter. "It's just," she said, flipping the coin between her fingers, "there must have been so many other women since then."

He nodded, conceding. "I didn't let my bed grow too cold or cobwebby over the years. Comparing them to Ava, though, there was just no comparison. None that gave it to me straight and still got my blood up like she did. Pardon me, but it's true."

"It must have been hell working with them, seeing them together all day, every day, day after day." She suddenly clapped her hand over her mouth. "Oh, my God, it must have been so awful when she blamed you for losing O'Shenanigan's; you must have felt . . ." She gestured wildly, trying to pick the word out of the air.

"Like a perverted asshole?" Buddy finished for her. "Yeah, I did. But, it beat the alternative."

"And working with them?"

"That was actually okay, at first." He sounded surprised himself. "Working with them, at least I got to see her. I thought that would make me immune after a while. But then she was always trying to fix me up—she felt *sorry* for me. That was when I found out that there are things worse than fearing death."

Suzanne looked at him, questioningly.

"There's *pity*," he told her. "Pity from the woman you love. It's definitely worse than fearing death. When she hated me, at least she was *passionate* about the hate, instead of looking at me like some big dumb lump of . . ." He gestured with his hand, trying to grab a word out of the word, but failed.

Suzanne walked over, her heart aching for him, and put her arms around his shoulders, giving him a kiss on the top of his head.

"Now, how come I can't find a man who's gonna love me like that?"

"He probably got run over by the Harley of that teenaged bum you married."

SIXTEEN

From every sitcom that had dominated the airwaves in her youth—*Sex in the City, Friends, Will & Grace*—Molly had pretty much convinced herself that she belonged in Manhattan. Everyone said it was cultural and intellectual center of the known universe, and every visit there had seemed more like coming home. Even Poughkeepsie wasn't close enough, although with the package they were offering her, it would have to do. At least for the next four years, unless she managed to get an equally good deal from Columbia or New York University, which didn't seem terribly likely at the moment.

But when autumn rolled around, she always reconsidered this plan.

When the air turned suddenly crisp, and the leaves turned from green to gold or russet, she could sit for hours, coffee in hand, sketchbook in the other, and just absorb the atmosphere. She could literally feel the Pilgrims who'd first docked at Portsmouth harbor, seeking a new life of religious freedom or a more prosperous place to begin again.

Or, for a great many others, she supposed, it had been "America or jail." She could feel the hope, the worry, the fear, the determination, the history in every storefront. Legend even had it that the small theatre, the Player's Ring, on Marcy Street had been a nineteenth century brothel.

It was at times like this when Molly thought, maybe she truly was a New England girl, maybe she'd come back here after she finished her studies. Right now, she was planning on becoming a broadcast journalist but was fully aware that four years was a long time for plans to change. She didn't mind not knowing what the future held; she planned to take each new experience as it came her way.

"I feel the same way you do, Moll," Suzanne said, even though Molly hadn't spoken aloud, as they sat in Prescott Park with cups of coffee from Breaking New Ground. She took in a deep lungful of the autumn air. Sometimes she and Molly could take one look at the other and tell just what the other was thinking.

"I always thought I'd be off in some big city somewhere, but when you come right down to it—this just always felt like home. Like I belonged here."

"Is this lipstick too bright in the sunlight?" Ava snuck another peek in her compact. She still wasn't used to "the look" Molly and Brandon had created for her yesterday after their AA meeting. She had always put her best face forward, but it had been years since she had been this worried about her appearance. The makeup, the accessories, the brand-new golden highlights in her auburn hair, the semicasual blazer and jeans with two-inch pumps . . . It was all quite startling to take in at the age of sixty-something years (she'd stopped counting at fifty-two and refused to do the math now).

On the walk downtown, Brandon had pushed Ava to stop at the shoe store and go for three-inch heels, but Ava had absolutely balked.

"Listen to me, you. At my age, I'm lucky I'm not pushing a walker along," she'd protested firmly, putting back the spiked heels. "I'm sure there's a broken hip or three in my future. I'm just in no rush to get them."

It seemed to take Ava a day or so to get used to it, but once it sank in that Molly was gay, it just didn't seem to matter that much. Maybe years ago it would have, when the gays were so shunned in New Hampshire, and everywhere else. But now they were out and about, and everyone loved them. They were even on the television, almost on every show. She watched *Friends* and *Will & Grace* every night reverently, to the point of scheduling her meetings around them (not that anyone had to know that).

"I still want her to find a nice ma—*person*," Ava had corrected herself; she didn't kick herself as badly as Suzanne did when Suzanne did it; after all, it was going to take some time to readjust to an eighteen-year-old assumption of her granddaughter's straightness, and there was no shame in it that she could see, as long as she kept making the effort. "To take care of her and spend her life with, but she's got all the time in the world for that. College is for playing the field."

Wow, she's good, Suzanne thought now, letting the sun shine down on her face. *She can accept Molly's lifestyle and slam my life choices, all in one short sentence.*

"Now, show Mom the walk we taught you," Molly instructed. "Come on, lady, don't be shy. You can do it."

Ava pulled herself up with Brandon's assistance and began walking, taking careful note to shake her butt lazily to each side as she took slow, long strides. She wobbled quite a bit more than she did in her regular shoes on the way to the gate, but on the way back, she felt as though she was starting to get the hang of it.

"How did I do?"

"This must be how momma ducks feel when baby ducks get pushed out of the nest." Brandon smiled tearfully, pretending to blot each eye.

"You really don't think the eyeliner's too much?"

"It just takes a little getting used to, Grandma." Molly handed her a napkin. "But you're right about the sun and the lipstick: it *is* a little bright for outdoors. Blot." Ava complied obligingly, and Molly sang out, "There she is! My grandmother, the new face of Maybelline!"

"Oh, you," Ava flapped the lipstick-smeared napkin playfully at her granddaughter. "You're right, maybe I'm just not used to it. But the look I'm going for is 'Elegant, Independent Lady about Town,' not 'Sixty-Something for Sale.'" She clicked her compact shut and slid it into her Kate Spade knockoff purse that Brandon had insisted she needed. "Now that my looks are conveying a message, I want to make sure they're saying the right thing."

"Trust me, lady," Brandon chimed in, "no one on the Seacoast could afford you."

"I gotta tell you, I'm jealous, Grandma." Molly took a bite out of her muffin. "When I'm your age, I'll probably be a raisin. With varicose veins, like Aunt Harriet. No, wait, make that a raisin with varicose veins and no hair, like Nanna Wilkie, Daddy's mother. Damn, it's an unfortunate genetic bunch of possibilities I've got tumbling around inside of me."

"That's not true," Ava scolded. "I like to think I've held onto a vestige of my looks, and so has your mother—she looks very young."

"Anyway, raisins don't have hair, sweetie," Suzanne corrected, holding up her Intro to Psychology book to ward off the glare of the sunlight.

Ava rolled her eyes. "Ever since your mother decided to go back to college this January, Molly, she's become the Figure of Speech Police."

"I'd be going now if I'd gotten my applications and financial aid forms in on time," Suzanne lamented. But she'd been busy recovering from eighteen years of overwork and no play, so she didn't beat herself up too hard.

"Now, you're next on the Makeover Hit List, Missy." Brandon started fussing with Suzanne's thick hair. "This is just crying out for modernization . . . And what can we do with these clothes?" He fluffed out her skirt. "They're very chic, but we could go for something more sleek and fitting, show off those legs and boobies. What do you think?"

"I totally agree," said Molly. "And what are we going to do about those *toenails*? You look like you haven't seen a pedicure this side of the millennium!"

Brandon and Molly gave each other a woeful look; it was clear that, in their eyes, lack of nail care was a crime that should be punishable by exile.

"*We're* going to keep our mitts off me." Suzanne ducked out from under his hands. "And since you're a gay guy, you can quit looking at my boobies. I'm perfectly happy in my vintage thrift store clothes, so you'll have to pry my granny dresses and sandals off my cold, dead body."

"Mom practically invented hippie mystic chic." Molly didn't sound particularly proud of this fact. "And I taught him all about fashion, Mom, so you can trust his judgment."

"Well, you and Anna Wintour," Brandon amended. "Don't get me wrong," he hastened to say, under the weight of Suzanne's scowl, "It's a great look for you."

"Screw how it looks," she informed him. "It's comfortable, I don't have to be skinny as a stick to look good in it, and it doesn't need ironing."

"Tell me honestly what you think," Ava commanded Suzanne. "You've yet to comment on my new appearance, and that's not like you, so I'm assuming the worst."

Suzanne pulled down her sunglasses, looking her mother up and down as Ava awaited the verdict nervously. Her only child was not known for pulling her punches, a quality that Ava usually found delightful and endearing . . . Just maybe not today.

"Too much, do you think? Or too little? Brandon wanted me to get a tattoo, a little rose right here," Ava pointed at her shoulder blade, "but Molly said I should sleep on it."

"A tattoo is permanent, Grandma," Molly stressed. "You don't want to make a snap decision that you have to live with the rest of your life."

"All ten minutes of it?"

"You'll outlive us all." Brandon stooped to kiss her on the cheek. "You're too fabulous to die."

Ava tapped her foot impatiently. "Well? Answer already, you're killing me here."

"I think you look great." Suzanne pulled her shades back up. She made a move as if to stand. "Now, if you'll excuse me, I'll just be packing up and getting off your corner."

Ava threw down her Kate Spade knockoff. "See!" she said indignantly. "I told you, I *do* look like an old hooker!"

"I'm kidding, I'm kidding!" Suzanne smiled playfully. "You look great. I'm so impressed I'm thinking of letting the Big Man over there do my makeover. *Maybe!*" she warned carefully, as Brandon started jumping for joy. "I said maybe, so don't get too excited." Turning back to her mother, she added,

"I just meant you might be a little overdressed for hanging out in Prescott Park on a Wednesday afternoon, but still beautiful. Really."

"She's right, Grandma." Molly sat up excitedly, swinging her legs over the side of the stone bench. "Let's find something fun to do this evening—we can't waste that hairdo here or at home in the courtyard."

Ava's face fell a little for a second. Suzanne wondered if Ava was hoping that maybe her new look wouldn't be wasted in the courtyard after all.

"Is there anyone in the village you want to make jealous?" Molly asked. "Like that woman with the oxygen tank who beat you for the lead in *Once on This All-Older-Female Island*?"

"Liz Isermann? I hate her—everyone does, I'm just sure of it," Ava agreed. "You're right! Let's all go out to a nice dinner, and then, maybe there's an outdoor concert, or we could take a small cruise, or . . ."

"Count me out." Suzanne picked up her purse in search of cigarettes; it would be her first of the day, and as it was after ten-thirty, she was terribly proud. "I shouldn't even be here. I'm meeting with your father's divorce lawyer, and I'm sure after four or five hours of arguing, I'll be in the mood for nothing but a hot bath and a Hugh Grant movie."

Molly stared at Suzanne for a moment, crestfallen. "Mom," she said slowly, "don't you think it would be nice if we all did something together? I mean, believe me, I know you have to get the settlement done so you can get your own place and start to enroll in school, but . . ."

"Do you have any idea how long we had to wait for both our lawyers to be free?" Suzanne puffed away on her cigarette. "Almost four months. I'm sorry, honey, but you'll just have to go without me this time. Next time, I promise, I'm there."

"But it's just, well, we're only here for two more days, and then we've got to take the bus up to Vassar. They like the freshmen to get there a couple of days early."

"And I'm a student advisor," Brandon said proudly. "Can you believe that? They actually trust me to guide these terrified, gullible little creatures."

"It just seems like since I've been here," Molly said, staring down at her toes, "everyone's been really busy. I was hoping we could all spend a little time together."

"And I promise you we will, sweetie." Suzanne rubbed her daughter's arm. "But I'm really and truly under the gun here, and I'm just nervous that if I don't get it all done now, then I'll lose my motivation and give up the money he owes me that I poured into the house he gets half of. Then I can forget college, because I'll wind up waitressing and doing retail sales jobs for the rest of my life."

"Your father was a salesman," Ava pointed out. "No shame in it, and a damn fine paycheck if you know what you're doing. And you certainly inherited your father's verbose charm."

"Why, thank you, Mother." Suzanne smiled again, this time a trifle ruefully. She fished around in her pocketbook till she found her billfold and plucked out the one credit card that she still held with Steve's name on it. "Have a good time, though, on me, and bring me back the doggie drinks."

Molly looked back at Brandon, officially surrendering, while Ava scowled at Suzanne. Drinking jokes didn't fit in with her program.

"Well," said Molly finally. "I guess I'll get back to the house, then."

"Honey, will you run with me to the drugstore before we go back?" Ava pointed to the Walgreen's on the corner. "I need some new nylons if we're getting all gussied up tonight. Do I need new earrings? I don't have anything long and dangly. Maybe I could borrow some of yours?" She stopped then, reaching out to touch Molly's hand disarmingly. "Oh, I hope I didn't offend you, sweetie. Do lesbians wear earrings?"

"Oh, sure," said Molly, "but they gotta be made out of flannel." She took a last look at her engrossed mother, then halfheartedly stepped over Suzanne's feet on the way to the sidewalk. "C'mon, Bran."

"I'll wait," he told her, leaning back to let the autumn sun splash on his face. "I'm enjoying the sunshine. I need a little color before I hole up in a classroom for the next nine months."

After basking in the sun for a few minutes, Suzanne suddenly felt the weight of a gaze upon her. The little hairs on her neck all stood up at attention. She opened her eyes and then gasped, startled at the cold expression in Brandon's eyes. "Jesus, God. What the hell are you looking at? What is it?" She twisted around, expecting to see a serial killer or a member of the Bush family behind her bench. "What the hell are you looking at like that?"

He shrugged, his eyes never leaving hers. "Nothing."

"*Nothing*?" She looked at him, aghast. "So, staring at me like I'm a piece of garbage, in your book, is nothing? Because to me, it's not nothing. In fact, to me, it sure looks like something."

"Wow." His expression never changed. "Wow, I sure didn't mean to stare at you like you were a piece of garbage. And, boy, if I did, I sure apologize."

"And you can cut the 'gee whiz' and 'golly' crap around me." She realized she was a bit over the top with the anger she was releasing on him, but venting felt so good she couldn't make herself stop. "Please remember you're dealing with Molly's mother, and she didn't exactly inherit her take-no-bullshit-and-give-no-bullshit attitude from her *constantly* bullshitting father."

"Okay, I'll remember that," he agreed, amiably enough. "Can I get a map?"

"A map?" she asked, baffled. "What do you mean, a map? A map of what?"

"Your mood swings," he said in that same calm voice. "I'd like to avoid the next land mine."

Oh, you arrogant little shit, she thought. "What in the hell is that supposed to mean?" She was on her feet now, bloodshed in her heart. "In case you haven't been paying attention, it's been rather a stressful summer; stressful *year*, stressful goddamn *two decades*, as a matter of fact. So, if my moods have been a little off while you've been a guest in my home, I'm so incredibly, deeply sorry." She realized, even as she said it, that technically, he wasn't staying in her home—he was staying in Buddy's. But when she was angry, she generally looked for the first guilt weapon in verbal reach. She gave a short scream of frustration; it scared her even more than it scared the other people enjoying the autumn weather. Several startled kite-flyers looked toward the sound of her screech; a few mommies with babies on blankets held their children close, for just a minute.

Before her humiliation had set upon her completely, Brandon leaped up onto the bench, holding his hands up in an "I surrender" gesture. Clearly, he understood that, whatever he'd said, he'd gone too far. After all, he was just a kid; kids were always running their mouths off about the wisdom of the world to those who knew better.

They stared at each other for a second before the ridiculousness of the situation completely overtook them, and then dissolved into giggles.

"I'm sorry," she said finally, holding up a hand, helping him down, and plopping down beside him. "I didn't mean to jump down your throat."

"You missed your calling, sister. You should be a collections agent for the local loan shark." He shook his head, half-admonishingly, half-admiringly. "Or a principal of a high school. You could have cut through that oak over there with the power of that nasty glare alone."

"I used to practice in the mirror when I was a little girl," she told him confidentially. "Back when I was going to be an actress and have three Academy Awards before I hit thirty."

"I didn't know you wanted to be an actress," he said, delighted. "That's terrific. What happened to that plan?"

"Um, let's see," she pretended to think. "Oh, that's right: I got knocked up before I graduated high school, third time in my life I'd ever been drunk. I didn't like it that much, because of my mother's, you know, *problem*. But I noticed it made some of the awkwardness around guys sort of float away, so I tossed a few beers back, maybe a couple of shots of tequila. In fact, I was so preoccupied with that all-important task—finding someone to buy booze for me—that I *completely* forgot to buy the condoms. That put the kibosh on my Academy Awards, college plans, and life in general."

"Well, clearly you had your priorities in order." He patted her on the back. "Were you madly in love with him, or was it just, you know, all those hormones and nowhere to go?"

She looked sideways at him through a pillar of smoke, exhaling. "I either love your brashness or I hate it. I haven't decided yet."

"Nice redirect, counselor." He applauded. "Compliments me to distract me, albeit backhandedly, and completely gets us off the question without benefit of an answer."

"If I didn't know better," Suzanne groaned, "I'd swear you and Molly were twins separated at birth. But so far as I know, only one gay child has come from this body." She sipped her coffee. "In answer to your question, at the time, I thought I loved him. He was a musician, and I've always loved people who could create music. Actually, we weren't going to let the fact we had a baby stop us. No, we were going to move to Manhattan and take turns taking care of the baby while the other one auditioned and worked. We were going to be the East Coast Kurt Cobain and Courtney Love."

"In case you didn't know, that didn't turn out so well."

"So I've heard." She smiled, thinking of that long-ago naiveté. "It was a heck of a plan . . . till the baby actually got here. We were going to save up a little every week until we had enough money to go. But somehow, nothing ever got saved up. After a while, it just became that thing we were going to do, when we talked about it at all. And awhile after that, we just stopped talking about it altogether."

"You could do it now that Molly's off doing her own thing," Brandon said excitedly. "Lop six, seven years off your age, and say you've been studying in London. Go live the crazy lifestyle: sleep on other actors' floors, clean theatres in exchange for acting classes, waitress till four in the morning. I grew up in summer stock, and the theatre is a drug like you can't imagine; besides, Estelle Getty didn't start out till she was in her fifties. Kathryn Joostyn was in her late fifties when she started auditioning, and BAM! she's on my hero Aaron Sorkin's first TV shows."

He was comparing her to a Golden Girl, and a sexagenarian, and this was supposed to encourage her? *Mama Mia*, as her dad would have said, *I'm old.* True, there was a lot of theatre in the Seacoast, and she supposed maybe one day she could drop in on an audition, just to see what it was like—if it looked like fun, or something she'd die of embarrassment while trying.

She shook her head. "No, I'm sure I'd become a Hollywood casualty without the benefit of actually seeing Hollywood."

"So get yourself a new dream." He patted her on the leg. "You're still young. Well, at least you've got a few good miles left in you."

"You are one wise eighteen-year-old," she marveled, looking at him with both amusement and amazement. "Or a hell of a kiss-ass. One of the two. Look, I'm really sorry about before. It's just . . ." She drew a deep breath, trying to find a Cliff's Notes version for all she was feeling. "Divorce sucks," she said at last. "Don't get me wrong, it's the right thing for me; hell, I'd have chewed my own arm off to get out of that trap if I'd had to, but we were married for eighteen years. That's literally half of my life—so, it's like saying that half my life has been a complete waste of time."

"Divorce didn't look like too much fun when my parents were doing it," he agreed. "Although, having a fantastic child like myself to tear apart during the process seemed to soften the blow for them somewhat."

Thank God Molly would be out of the state for the next round of fun; Suzanne was sure they hadn't fooled her much by not arguing directly in front of her. When things got heated—as they often did—both of their voices had carried all the way to the garage. They could always tell when Molly could hear them, because she'd turn her music up deafeningly loud. It was a point Suzanne got immediately, and it hit her like a stake through the heart.

She decided she did like Brandon, after all; it was kind of too bad he wasn't Molly's boyfriend. He had a way, this kid, of dropping little bundles of potent information about himself but in such a way that they were wrapped in self-deprecating humor. *And since they're not having sex,* she reasoned, *he's bound to be around longer.* There were only two cigarettes left in her pack before she was going to have to run across the street to Joe's Newsstands and replenish her supply.

"Can I offer you a slightly disabled American Spirit? It kind of got crushed in my coat pocket."

"Hard packs. Always ask for the hard packs," he scolded. He automatically reached out, but at the last minute reluctantly drew his hand back. "No, I can't. I finally quit smoking, and if I have so much as a puff, I'm back to a pack a day."

"Sure, I get you." Suzanne put the pack back in her pocket. "I'll smoke later, when you're not around to tempt."

"No, don't be silly—smoke all you want," he insisted. "Just don't let me have one, ever, even if I beg."

"You're sure?"

"I'm positive. Look, there's a grandmother, three college kids, and two nursing mothers smoking within a stone's throw, okay? I gotta get used to seeing it and not doing it."

"Okay." She scratched the match on the back of her Governor's Inn book of matches, watching the head burst into flame, smelling the brief whiff of sulphur. Then she touched the very top of the flame to the cigarette waiting patiently in her pursed lips. Waving out the match, she took a deep drag, held it for one second, then exhaled the smoke; it was almost a sexual experience.

"It is a satisfying little ritual, I'll give you that," Brandon said enviously. "I'd ask you if you wanted a cigarette, but you're already smoking one."

She cast her eyes sideways, wondering if she should ask him the question that had been on the tip of her tongue ever since he and Ava had been hitting the AA circuit like the Seacoast's weirdest couple. He and Molly were leaving in two days; this might be the last time she was alone with him.

"Listen," she asked hesitantly, "I know it's none of my business, but I've been been meaning to ask, aren't you just a tad young to be completely sober and all that stuff?"

Brandon smiled broadly, knowingly, as if he'd answered this question a hundred times or more. "Would you really want me spending so much time with your eighteen-year-old daughter if I wasn't?"

She laughed, wondering how that point could have slipped so easily by her. "I'll give you that one."

"I thought you might."

The next question she had for him was harder, and she struggled with herself, arguing both sides of the discussion. His private life was his private life, and she had no reason to ask him anything about it . . . Except that his private life might give her some insight to her daughter's private life, and it was this information she desperately needed. "Actually, I, um, I . . ."

". . . have another question for me," Brandon said in that damned likable tone of his. "Shoot."

"When did you," she groped for an appropriate way to phrase it, "*know?*" She rolled her hand in front of her, indicating a sensitive topic.

He frowned, not getting it. "When I did I *know?*" he repeated, mimicking the hand gesture.

"Yeah, you know," she repeated, "when did you *know* know?" A moment passed, Suzanne trying to convey the words with her eyes.

"Oh." He winked at her, suddenly understanding. "When did I *know* know?"

"Yeah, that's it, when did you *know* know?" She glanced at the drugstore, not wanting Molly to sneak up on this particular conversation.

"Well," he thought back, "let's see . . . back in grade school, I . . ."

"In *grade* school?" she cried, stunned. Had she been in the dark about Molly for over a decade?

"Sure. Think about it, Suzanne." He stopped himself. "Oops. Sorry, can I call you Suzanne?"

"Honey," she looked at him over the top of her sunglasses, "if you're giving me insights into my kid's sexuality, I think we're way past the first-name basis by now."

"Suzanne, then. See, the thing is, sexuality begins at a very young age. At an obscenely young age, in fact." He held his hands up. "Don't kill the messenger; it's just plain old biology. No one ever wants to talk about it, but it's true. Think *way* back to the very first time you felt that curiosity, that small little pull towards a boy."

Suzanne tried to remember.

She *thought* it might have been the time James LaPointe had given her a kiss on the cheek in the treehouse in second grade, and that funny tingle she'd felt every time she thought of it for weeks after. She'd been seven, and she could still remember how the light of the sun had glinted off James's hair through the tree house window.

She suddenly remembered how Steve used to tell the story, of how he was on the school bus and some little girl turned to him and said, 'Mom's having another baby, can you believe the stuff parents have to do to have a baby?' And Steve said, 'Yeah, it's weird all right . . . Wanna try it?' Suzanne thought he'd been eight or nine at the time; if he'd been older, it wasn't by much.

"I guess you're right," she lamented.

Brandon nodded. "So, think back on that time. When all the other boys were offering to catch the girls at the bottom of the slide to try to get a peek at their underwear, I, well, didn't. And then when all the little boys were chasing the little girls around the playground trying to get a kiss, I, well, didn't. Just no interest at all. For a long time, I thought I was sort of asexual. I kept to myself a lot, my best friend was Little Debbie, and my waistline showed it."

"*You?*" Suzanne stood up to look at him from several different angles. He was tall, maybe six one or six two, and if he tipped the scales at one seventy, she'd have been surprised. There was not one extra ounce of fat on him—anywhere that she had visual access to, that was. "You're so trim, I can't even *picture* you overweight."

"Oh, honey," he said wistfully, "I've got pictures, but if I showed them to you, I'd have to kill you. Anyway, when I wasn't gorging myself, I read a lot, kept to myself. And I started stealing from my dad's liquor cabinet. And my mother's secret stash. And, well, any cough syrup or vanilla flavoring that came into the house never lasted too long. Sometimes I'd have to have a sip of each one if there was just a little of each and there wasn't anything else in the house."

"Eww!"

"Eww, *exactly*. The taste would stay with you for hours, even if you brushed your teeth." He gazed off into space for a moment, thinking of those days. "But you know, that wasn't even the worst of it."

"I can't imagine what would be worse than vanilla flavoring and Nyquil." Suzanne shuddered.

"Oh, there's plenty worse," he assured her. "Remember high school, how much fun it was to go to school and see your favorite crush, to talk about boys with all your friends on the phone till the middle of the night, to dress just right just in case one of them might notice you? Remember how intoxicating that was?"

Suzanne smiled, nodding.

"I didn't have that—not once." He shook his head. "Since I hadn't let myself admit that I was drawn to guys, it was buried deep, deep down, let me tell you." Especially with an outdoorsman stepfather and two football player brothers . . . But he wasn't going to bring that up now. Some things were just too personal, and the way he hadn't fit into his family since the day he was born was one of them. Every day had been, well, okay. Just okay. Plain. Ordinary. He'd come to the conclusion that he was, in fact, the loser dweeb they'd dubbed him at school, and his life would never have any excitement or romance or passion. Just a long series of struggles, waiting for someone to pick on him for one of his many social flaws. He had protected himself with layers of snack cakes and a haze of alcohol.

Suzanne looked at him carefully. His eyes had gone far away for just a second, but she was curious about that second nonetheless. Much as she wanted to pry, she didn't—she might scare him off altogether, and then she wouldn't get the information she hoped would help her understand her Molly.

"Well," she said at last, "you seem pretty chipper to me."

"Oh, you bet I am," he grinned. "*Now* I am. But back *then*, it was a very different story. I was a different person. Believe me."

"So, how did you transform from the chubby boozer to the super-fit teetotaler I see here today?"

"Well, one day, I was sitting in the park, studying and drinking tequila mixed with grape soda to mask the smell."

"*Ewwww!*"

"You'd be amazed how well that works."

"I'll just have to take your word for it. Continue."

"Anyway, this guy—Jeff." Just saying his name brought a small smile to his lips even after all this time, she noticed. It was kind of cute, she thought. "Jeff came over, and he sat next to me. Just plopped himself down and started gabbing away, as if we'd already known each other for years. But he wasn't just talking, he was, you know. Dipping his head, tossing his hair, posing whenever he could."

He demonstrated, and Suzanne laughed delightedly. Steve had done that same dip back in the day. As Jacob Winter had, come to think of it.

"And then I realized: he was *flirting*. With me. A *guy.*"

"The very thought!" Suzanne cried, holding her hand to her forehead, palm up. "Hold me, I may faint."

"Exactly—this was eight years ago, but I remember it like it was yesterday," he nodded. "So, I'm not even sure what it was that kept me there. I kept thinking I should be uncomfortable. I kept thinking I should call him a faggot and take off, or even take a swing at him, right there in the park. I could even picture myself calling my super-macho stepfather and saying, 'Hey, I just smashed a fairy in the park when he put the moves on me,' if I got arrested for it. Boy, would that have made him proud."

"Your father," Suzanne lit up her second-to-last cigarette, "sounds like a true prince among men."

"Stepfather," he corrected her. "But, as big a voice as my stepfather was in those days, there was another voice too."

"Trust me," Suzanne tapped an ash into her empty coffee cup rather than defile the cobblestones, "I'm familiar with voices."

"Really?" He seemed pleased. "Do tell."

"Some other time. So, did you wind up belting the guy?"

"Nope. I didn't take a swing at Jeff. I didn't call him a faggot, and I didn't storm off. And I realized, I didn't do any of those things, because I didn't even want to. For the first time in my life, I had butterflies. Real, actual, all-out case of butterflies. I'd heard about them before, but I'd never had them—not the good kind, anyway."

Suzanne smiled faintly, remembering distantly what those were like. She wondered if Laura was right that she could have them again. But it seemed ridiculous; she was a thirty-six-year-old mother going back to school with no steady income. She was pretty sure that she wouldn't have men lining up at her door. Or that there wouldn't be a suitable suitor sitting next to her in English 101.

"So," Brandon continued dreamily, "when he asked me if I wanted to go for a walk, I said yes. When he asked me if I wanted to listen to some new CDs, I said yes. I'd never felt like that before in my whole life. Things were . . . tingling."

"I get the idea," Suzanne cut him off. "Look, if you're not comfortable giving me details then don't. But if you are, then don't leave anything out!!"

"Let me give you just one detail, then." He draped his arm around her shoulders.

She exhaled the lavender smoke and looked at him sideways, waiting.

"When we were back at Jeff's place, and he finally leaned over and kissed me," he said softly, "I *got* it."

"You got it." She repeated his words, but her eyes told him she didn't get what he meant at all.

"That's right," he said. "I got it."

She waited for a moment, hoping his meaning would suddenly become clear. "I'm sorry, hon," she said at last. "I'm just not following. Exactly what did you get?"

"What did I get? Everything." He jumped up on the bench and spun around. "I got the whole *world*. I was fifteen years old. I finally got every song ever written, every movie ever made. It all made sense now, and it was a relief." He pumped his fist in the air. "It was such a freakin' *relief*. And it changed everything. From the way I dressed to the way I formed my opinions, to . . ."

"Being gay," she interrupted him, "actually gave you that much identity?"

He looked at her for a long moment, and Suzanne had the strangest feeling—not for the first time—that he was the older, wiser one, and he was speaking gently down to her, who still remained an ignorant child. "No, being gay did not give me that much identity." He put his hand on her arm. "Being *me* did."

Suzanne let that sink in a moment. "Well, at least I don't have to worry about that with Molly. Molly's always had great self-esteem. How could she not? She's an amazing person, and everyone's told her so all her life." Laura's words suddenly filtered in her ears. *If you don't know what you're doing, fake it, and people can't tell the difference.* Had Molly been faking it? No, it just wasn't possible. She'd have noticed, she'd have seen, she'd have sensed something was off if Molly had been aware of this for years and just hiding it because she thought her mother couldn't handle it.

But Molly, since the second she was born, had been the most important thing in Suzanne's life, and whatever else she was doing should have taken second place. She had always thought she and Molly were buddies, that they were close, but as one of her friends had once told her, it was important to let your child know, 'I'm not your friend, I'm your mother. This is not a democracy, it's a dictatorship.' Suzanne had crossed that off a long time ago as being as ridiculous as the phrase 'Who needs a cow when the milk's free?' but now she wondered if she'd done Molly a real disservice. Maybe Molly didn't need someone who respected her privacy and treated her like an adult; maybe she'd needed someone who looked at her more closely, searched her room occasionally, and demanded to know what she was thinking when she locked herself in her room for hours at a time. She thought it was to get away from the invariable tension between Steve and her; it had never occurred to her that she was in there thinking of other things entirely. All alone.

She shook away the choking feeling of guilt. It couldn't be true.

"If there was one thing I did right in my life, it was to instill her with a sense of self-worth." She pointed a finger at him. "This is a patriarchal society, don't you forget, and it just hates confident women, so you'd better be pretty damn confident to deal with that . . . So thank goodness she is. That didn't come out of nowhere—I taught her that. And because of my telling her repeatedly and her own accomplishments, she knows how amazing she is."

"Sure. In a generic, academic sort of way, she knows she's a hot shit," Brandon acknowledged. "But she could still stand to hear it every now and then. Especially," he nudged her, "from her super-cool, finally-rid-of-the-loser-dad, trying-to-make-something-of-her-life mom."

"I told you." Suzanne laughed, but inside she was starting to feel a little impatient. "Molly already knows I think that."

Brandon didn't respond.

"I mean, she does know that, right? Doesn't she?"

He only looked at her with a soft, gentle gaze. It was absolutely unnerving.

She fastened her sandals and gathered her purse. Brandon had been spot-on about a lot of things, but that didn't mean he was right in this case. If nothing else, she had made sure that every single day of Molly's life, she'd told her how wonderful and amazing she was, how lucky she felt to be her mother. So, of course she knew how her mother felt about her. Or was this just something else Suzanne had screwed up?

It was too much, all at once, and she had to get away from here, away from him, and away from Molly, who'd be returning in just a minute. She gave him a kiss on the cheek, noting with relief that Laura was just entering her store, right up the block from the park.

"Can you tell them I had to get home to work on the divorce papers? If I don't get this done, I've got nothing." Before he could reply, she was off, heading in the direction of Goddess Treasures; she hoped Brandon didn't notice, because he'd probably deduce they didn't keep her divorce papers there. And then he'd probably tell Molly.

As Suzanne walked swiftly away, one thought, and one thought only pounded itself in her head. *Where did I go wrong? What did I do wrong? And whatever it is . . . why is Molly the one being punished for it?*

SEVENTEEN

An urgent pounding on the front door was damn near the only thing in the world that could have woken Buddy up from his Maggie Smith dream; she was wearing her costume from *The Prime of Miss Jean Brodie*.

Grumbling, he threw on a robe and made it to the hallway, past the computer room; he saw that the pounding hadn't roused his sleeping houseguest. *Another benefit of the young*, he noted. *The easy sleep that comes from not having made any life choices that you'd regret for the rest of your days.*

"Keep your pants on." He grumpily undid the chain. "For Pete's sake, it's only eight o'clock in the . . ." When the door was fully open, he froze. *Am I dreaming?* he asked himself wildly. *Or worse, have I died, and I get one last fool's fancy before I go up or down?*

"Hello," Ava greeted him, somewhat formally; she looked almost as nervous as he suddenly felt. She held a thermos and a Tupperware in her arms that looked full to bursting; he was surprised the top didn't pop right off. She wore a pale blue sundress and her most comfortable sneakers. She had made a firm compromise with Brandon. She would stick with the lipstick and eyeliner, but the heels were out, period.

"Brandon's still asleep," he said, cautiously. "I'll pass these along. Shouldn't be more than a couple more hours—he doesn't usually sleep past noon."

"I thought he might be still in bed." Ava clucked her tongue and shook her head. "Young people these days are unbearably lazy in the morning. In my day, we were up at the crack of dawn, doing chores and getting ready for school and . . . I'd hate to tell you just how long ago." She blushed then—he couldn't remember the last time he'd seen Ava blush. "Well, you remember what those days were like, I suppose."

"I sure do." He'd been the second son in a family of nine kids, and his family ran what was, at that time, the largest dairy farm in the southern part of the state. "Up with the chickens, down with the sunset: that was my old man's motto."

She laughed politely; her own giggles sounded ridiculous to her own ears, and she cut them off.

This is Buddy, for God's sake, she scolded herself. *I've never been nervous in front of him a day in my life, not even when we were dating.* But she *had* felt a deep connection, a level of instant comfort, like they'd grown up together, or at least known each other for much longer than they actually had. With Jimmy, there had been deep, exhilarating passion, and at nineteen, she supposed, it's easy to confuse that with love . . . But while she had loved Jimmy fiercely, she could, for the first time in decades, finally admit to herself she'd always held on to just a thread of her feelings for Buddy.

Jimmy was the life of the party, the guy with a joke or three on hand at any time, everyone's pal. Buddy was quieter, calmer, the guy who brought the snacks to the party while Jimmy was busy entertaining. And while she didn't regret a moment of her marriage, there had been times—oh yes, there had been many times—when she had wondered what it might be like to wake up next to Buddy. She had felt so guilty about these feelings that she had hastily tried to erase them by fixing him up with every woman she could find that she deemed even close to appropriate. If Buddy knew what she was up to, he hadn't let on; Jimmy had merely accused her of having a yenta complex.

But Jimmy had been gone a long time, and Buddy was right here, right now. And there were things to say that she could hold in no longer. If AA had taught her anything, it was that the truth set you free—corny as it was, it was also completely true.

Well, she thought, smiling again, *after* all this time, *here you go, Miss Ava . . . don't you dare shoot and miss.*

Buddy just stood there, so surprised to see her that he opened and closed his mouth several times, not sure of what to say. In the end, it seemed best to stay quiet.

"Oh!" she suddenly remembered. "Here." She thrust the Tupperware at him.

After a moment, he took them gingerly. "What's inside?"

"Well, they're muffins, you big dope." A soft smile took the bite from the words. "What do they look like?"

"All right, what's in them?" he asked suspiciously. "Did you coat the blueberries with arsenic? Mix powder laxative in with the flour?"

"They're not blueberry. See?" She tapped the cakes beneath the plastic wrap. "They're lemon poppy seed."

"*Lemon poppy seed?*"

"Lemon poppy seed," she repeated, amused at his expression. "I just, well . . . I remembered you always had a weakness for them."

He put the muffins down on the railing and crossed his arms firmly. "Okay, out with it."

"Out with it? I don't know what you mean," she said innocently.

"Am I dying?" he demanded. "Did Brandon take a message from my doctor, find out that I'm dying, and decide not to tell me? Is it your plan to be extra nice to me so I'll put in a good word for you with the Big Guy? Or am I getting completely senile and not recalling some big makeup session that we had earlier?"

"They're just *muffins*. You don't have to read that much into it, Mr. Conceited." She sniffed a little and primped her hair. The humidity always gave it a life of its own.

"It just seems," he said, still flummoxed, "like a strange thing for you to do. Even stranger that you'd remember that lemon poppy seed are my favorite muffins, after all these years."

"Yes," Ava agreed. "I suppose it is."

They stood there in the early morning light, Ava smiling so widely her face felt like it might break. She had to shake off this nervousness or she'd smile herself right into a stroke. Buddy, after years of being her whipping boy, stood there, waiting for the punch line.

"Well, we could do this awkward dance all day," Ava said finally, "or I could tell you that, last night, my daughter and I had a long, illuminating talk."

So *that* was it.

"I knew she couldn't keep quiet," he said, angrily. "Even when she was promising, I knew she'd . . . I knew it . . . I just knew it."

"I just have one thing to say to you, Buddy McKinley," Ava began primly.

"Ava, please." He laid his hand on her arm, and a spark of electricity went through his whole body, just like it had on their first date, during their first dance. "Believe me, the muffins are enough—plenty, in fact. I know how hard it is for you to say you're sorry. Or that you were wrong."

Ava looked at him for a moment, considering. Then she aimed, wound up, and cracked him across the face.

"Jesus Christ!" he cried, nearly dropping the Tupperware container. "Jesus Christ!"

She slapped him again. "That one was for taking my higher power's name in vain." She raised her arm warningly. "Want to try for number three?"

"Three?" he gasped, rubbing his cheek. Her blows weren't particularly hard, but getting hit in the face wasn't pleasant, no matter how soft. "I'm still wondering what the heck number *one* was for!"

"Oh, as if you don't know!" Ava daintily dusted off her hands. "Let me refresh your memory. Twenty-five years ago, my husband James was caught serving alcohol to kids—*curvy* ones only—who wore very short skirts and smelled really nice."

"Yes, I seem to remember something about that," he said drolly. "I seem to recall it disrupted my life for a bit of time as well."

"And then!" she cried. "Just as the boom was about to fall, just as the moment I'd been waiting for my entire marriage was about to happen, and he was finally going to get his knuckles rapped good and hard for it, right in public just like he deserved, what did you go and do?"

He saw then that her eyes, when she looked at him, had lost that hard edge he'd grown used to seeing there. Now they were once again limpid pools of startling, kaleidoscopic color.

"For reasons known only to yourself," she went on, "you stood up to the world, and you said *you'd* done it."

"I sort of thought," he was truly bewildered now, "that's the thing you just might be thanking me for."

"*Thanking* you?" she asked him incredulously. "Are you *insane*? You robbed me of perhaps the biggest and best upper hand in my entire marriage! Do you have any idea of the amount of nice vacations and jewelry your little act of bravery cost me?"

He pondered this. "I have to tell you, Ava, I never thought if it that way. And I wish to Goshen—Goshen! I said Goshen!" he cried, when her hand went up again warningly. "I wish to Goshen that you'd start making some bloody sense and quit hitting me. I mean, immediately. Talk fast—I gotta go hunt down some ice for this cheek."

"Fine, then." She deigned to sit down on one of his lawn chairs, and crossing her legs, she placed her hands primly on her knee. That was his Ava, all right: going from white hot rage to ladylike grace in under ten seconds. "Listen. I *know* that you were his friend. Probably the best friend he ever had, in fact. But I *lived* with the man for over forty years. Day in, day out. There wasn't anything about him I didn't know. What he didn't tell me, I learned from osmosis." She smiled then, her mind's eye seeing the comfort, the familiarity that all those years together had brought. "Let's just say, after nearly a half-century together, there are damn few surprises left. And there's something very . . . *sustaining* about that."

"I wouldn't know," Buddy conceded. "My longest relationship didn't break the six-month barrier."

"What I'm trying to say is," Ava looked down at her hands, "did you honestly, honestly and truly, think I didn't *know*?"

Buddy looked at her warily. *When in doubt*, he thought, *play dumb.*

"Know *what*?"

She sighed heavily. "Okay, if you're going to make me say it out loud. You honestly think I didn't know that my husband's eyes liked to feast on supple young flesh?"

"Ava!" It was true—every word of it—but it was also done and over with. The man was dead, for goodness' sake, and had been for a long, long time. "I have to tell you, I'm really not comfortable with . . ."

"But I finally had *proof.*" She cut him off smoothly. "I *finally* had something I could put my hands on and hold over his head for the rest of his life, but then . . ." She pointed at him, and despite himself, he took a step backward. "You!" she cried. "You had to go and take the blame for it, you . . . you . . ." She groped around for an accurate phrase and triumphantly came up with, "You big thunder-thief, you!"

She sat back with satisfaction; her brand-new, made-up word said it all.

"Ava, I'm telling you, I . . ."

"You have *no idea* how many plans I'd made," she interrupted. "How I was going to get him to apologize for all the glances down the shirts of waitresses or nurses. Hell, I was finally going to get a new dining room set. Not to mention a sizable upgrade on my engagement ring. And oh!" She clutched her hands to her bosom. "There was a gorgeous maple hutch in Boston I had my eye on for *years*! It was practically mine!" She dropped her hands with a doleful gaze. "But then you just had to go and be 'noble.'" She shuddered distastefully, as if the act he'd performed was a deed too dirty to soil her tongue.

"I still can't imagine what you're talking about," Buddy stalled, not ready to give up the ship just yet.

"You're really going to draw this out, aren't you?"

He shrugged. "My schedule this morning happens to be fairly open."

"Well, fine." She surrendered. "If you insist on playing as dumb as you look . . . As I told you before, I knew my Jimmy. There wasn't a thought that ran across that man's head I didn't know before it got from one end to the other." She cleared her throat then, surprised at how embarrassing this all was to admit. "And I know that Jimmy was a—what do you call it?" She tried to pluck the word out of the air with her new French tips. "A hot ticket, as my dad would have said. A ladies man. A *player*." She gave him a ghost of a smile that wasn't borne of amusement at all, and it tugged at his heartstrings in a way nothing had for a very long time.

"Are you sure?" he asked, wanting to defend Jimmy even now.

"Oh, please!" she cried. "There wasn't a woman that he didn't rubberneck. Discreetly, of course, but it was everywhere—on the street, in the movie theatre, at the mall. In the grocery aisle, for that matter. The rows at church . . ."

"He loved you, Ava." Buddy struggled to his feet. "I know it couldn't have been easy watching him eyeballing young girls the way he did, but no one— *no one*—ever meant anything to him besides you. You were his whole world. He used to say, 'There are women in this world, and then there's my Ava.'"

"And just what does that mean, exactly?"

"It means that, as far as Jimmy was concerned, there was the very highest class of woman," he used his hand to mark an invisible line right at eye level, "and you were right about here." He made another notch, just a few inches above it. "So don't you ever doubt—not for one minute, not for a millisecond of a minute—that man loved you."

"Oh, sweetie." She laughed heartily, patting his hand firmly. "I know *that*. What we had was . . . It was a marriage in every sense of the word. We were partners, right down the line. Oh, it wasn't all roses and violins, let me tell you . . . But we had our share of that. More than anything, we just fit well together. Even when we fought, we fit. So, don't get me wrong, I know what I was to him. And to tell you the truth, he more than loved me: he *liked* me." She smiled again, much more happily this time. "Do you have any idea how much more *important* that is? Liking, over loving?" she asked him wonderingly, tilting her head, looking out into the bright September morning at nothing in particular. "But, I'm a firm believer in being honest about your mate, and no matter how he felt about me, that simply doesn't change the fact that he liked to look at—and maybe a little more—a well-rounded tushie or a sweater that was filled out particularly well."

Suddenly Buddy felt sick to his stomach, just a little.

"You don't think . . . I mean, he couldn't have actually *cheated* on you, could he?"

He had expected her to deny it immediately, the way he would have done if she'd asked the question of him. Instead, she considered it for an awfully long time.

Oh, Ava, he thought with admiration. *Anyone else in the world would have just stuck his or her head in the sand, but not you. When you love someone, it's warts and all. You see everything, and you love that person anyway.*

For perhaps the millionth time in his life, he wondered if Jimmy had known just how good the steak was in his refrigerator while he was out leering at fast-food burgers. He shifted from foot to foot, wanting to say the right thing, say anything, but nothing came to mind. So he shifted again, stopping himself before she asked him if he had to use the bathroom.

"I don't know," she said at last, bringing her eyes back to meet his squarely. Leaning against the doorjamb, he could smell her perfume. White Shoulders. In all the years that had passed, she still wore the same scent. Every time a stranger who wore it walked by, his heart would beat a little faster. But there was no need to get all mushy with her just yet. For all he knew, she was setting him up to step on him later. But the way she smiled at him said differently. "But . . . let's just say that I didn't push the subject too hard when he was around."

Buddy raised an eyebrow; that didn't seem at all like the Ava he knew.

"I know, I know." She heard his unspoken words and waved them away. There were certain things in a marriage you just couldn't explain; it was only understood between the two of you. Buddy hadn't seen the loving, sweet Jimmy behind closed doors: the Jimmy that took care of her, that gently urged her to get help without making her feel like the burden she knew she'd become. How could she ask Jimmy if he'd cheated on her? And frankly, if he had, didn't she have that coming? In his place, would she have wanted to spend some time with someone who didn't suck the little energy out of her that her job didn't? She wasn't sure, but she knew enough to know she didn't want to think about it, now or ever. "But I didn't, because Jimmy was a proud, proud man. If he hadn't, and I asked him . . ." Her eyes glazed over for just a second, imagining. "You can never take back a blow like that. When you smack a man and question his unfaithfulness, that's when he might start thinking, 'If I'm already doing the time, I might as well go out and do the crime.'" She shrugged again; time had eased the wounds caused by these questions. "Plus, I figured if he ever had, there'd be, I don't know, some kind of *evidence*."

"No, he would've been too smart for evidence," Buddy mused. "He'd have dry-cleaned every bit of him that ever came into contact with her before he came within a ten-foot radius of you."

She raised an eyebrow. "Just what are you saying? That you think he . . ."

"No, no," he cut her off. "Here's the thing, here's how I just know he never cheated: it was the way you guys always talked. He loved talking with you, just telling you everything. I don't think he wouldn't have been able to stand not talking to you about it."

"You're right. In fact," she realized suddenly, "he probably could have resisted cheating more easily than he could resist *telling* me about it. But . . ." She hugged the thermos to her chest, her hands shaking ever so slightly; Buddy was again struck with how brutally honest she was with herself, even when it was so hard it made her hands shake. "If I'm going to be honest, I guess I'd have to say that I never knew because I didn't *want* to know."

"That's the easiest way not to know, I guess," Buddy conceded.

"There were times when I was sure of it, absolutely certain." Then she shook her head. "But, like I said, the other shoe never dropped. And frankly, in hindsight . . . I doubt it. For one thing, when would he have had the time? He was a workaholic, and then he would come home and take care of his drunken wife—and yes, I was drinking long before we opened the pub. Jimmy and I pretended that no one knew yet. It wasn't until after the pub . . . well, you know. As Molly would say, we've covered that."

She looked down at her lap then, not proud of what she must have been like to deal with in those days. There had been a time when Jimmy would come home from work, and for the next hour or so play 'Where's Ava?' It was a game without a bit of mirth, and it usually ended with him having to carry his unconscious wife home from the backyard, the playground across the street, the children's room at the library. She shuddered, hating to think of those days, but if she didn't . . . *Those who forget history are doomed to repeat it*, she reminded herself. "And let me tell you, if he had jumped the fence, I wouldn't have been exactly able to judge him on that one. No, frankly, I wouldn't have blamed him."

Buddy fought the urge to pull her into his arms. Instead, he said, "Alcoholism is a *disease*, honey."

Oops, that had just slipped out. They'd never openly discussed her problem, and now she was going to tell him it was none of his damn business and storm off toward her home. And who the hell was he to "honey" her? He gritted his teeth for the impending explosion.

Surprisingly, it didn't come.

"True, it is." She passed right over the term of endearment. "But that doesn't make it any easier to live with." She picked up a muffin and peeled back the cupcake wrapper, toying with the foil in her hands. It seemed she couldn't keep her fingers still for a minute.

Is it possible that Miss Ava is nervous? Buddy wondered. *Because of me?*

"No, I really don't think he did. I think he liked to look, not touch. Well," she corrected herself, "I'm sure he would have *liked* to touch, but he knew that if he ever reached out that hand, he'd pull back a bloody stump."

Buddy laughed aloud at that one, so hard he had to lean over, grabbing the rail for support. Ava had never been accused of being too soft on a man.

"I think it was all about him needing to know he was attractive, that he could still do that Jimmy thing, and that he could still draw women to him like a magnet. So I told myself that, and sometimes the flirting and the leering didn't matter." She looked at Buddy sideways, not sure why, but knowing she was going to confide in him now. "But other times . . . I didn't like it. There were other times, in fact, when it goddamn hurt so much it was hard to take a deep breath." She stopped then and did indeed take a deep breath. "It made me think, you know?" she asked softly. "Sometimes I'd wonder what they had that I didn't. Were they smarter, prettier, sexier, more ladylike, less of a handful? More . . . worth his time? After all," she sighed with just a trace of bitterness, "it was pretty clear he could have any woman he wanted. So, what did they have?"

There was no one more worth it, he almost blurted, but caught himself.

"I'm sure there was no one else," he said instead.

"Did he want more of a typical doting, adoring wife instead of a buddy who worked constantly alongside him, trading dirty jokes as fast as he could? Was I too little for him?"

"I can't imagine you being too little for anybody," Buddy said wryly.

"Well, then, was I too *much*? That feeling that deep down he might want someone else more than me, that he was stuck with me. That ugly kind of feeling is how it felt."

Buddy reached out to touch her knee this time; it was his turn to be the comforter, the consoler. And after all those broken affairs she'd nursed him through long ago, it felt damn nice.

"He should have had his eyes on you at every minute, Ava," he said tightly. "He just plain should've gotten over his insecurities and learned some damn manners. If you'd have been *my* wife, I would never, ever have looked anywhere else."

"I don't suppose you would have," she agreed. "After all, you did a pretty good job of looking only at me when I was someone *else's* wife, let alone yours."

And, bam! There she was, right back in the driver's seat of the conversation.

"Remind me to talk to your daughter," he sighed, "about knowing what is and isn't her business, and knowing when to shut the hell up."

"Oh, Suzanne didn't tell me that part," Ava told him, standing up, fluffing her hair, looking down on him with a bemused smile. "She didn't have to."

"She didn't?" Buddy found that hard to believe. "So, what did you do, call up one of those dial-a-psychics and . . ."

"You *men*," she sighed. "You all think you're so much more clever than you actually are. And, for the most part, stealth is something you're allergic to."

"What's that supposed to mean?"

"Buddy," she told him, "in case you've forgotten in your old age: for almost two decades, we worked in a restaurant that had mirrors on half the walls."

"Well, I . . ."

She giggled at his stunned expression. "Oh, Buddy McKinley, *please*! Don't bother denying it. I have *eyes*," she said gleefully. "And that creepy little tingling sensation on the back of my neck. You know, when all the hairs stand up? Of course I knew. Women almost always know."

"Oh, okay," he said, relieved. "For a minute there, I thought you were going to tell me that Jimmy was the one who told you, that he'd figured it out. It's a relief to know . . ."

"Oh, Jimmy knew too," she filled him in. "He wasn't stupid either. And he also had eyes."

Buddy covered his eyes in abject shame as her tinkly laugh washed over him once more. She certainly had a case of the giggles this morning, and it was nice to hear, even if it was at his expense.

"Hell," she went on, "some of the regulars had bets on whether I'd finally toss Jimmy over for all his looking and drooling and run off with you to Ireland once and for all."

"The *regulars* knew?" Buddy cried, dismayed. All those years of thinking he was playing everything so darn close to the vest. Turns out he might as well have had *I Heart Ava* shirts printed up. "They *talked* about it? They *knew*?"

Ava nodded, and he sat down again, dropping his head into his hands.

"I am a terrible man," he said mournfully. "I am a terrible, terrible best friend. I shouldn't be allowed to mingle with actual people. I should be put in a cage and studied to see if evil truly does live longer."

"Rest assured," she told him, "it does."

He finally pulled his head from his hands long enough to look up at her.

"What did he say? What names did he call me?"

"What do you mean?"

"I mean, if he knew, then he must have been . . ."

She laid her hand on his shoulder, stopping him; for another moment, their eyes met, and the sensation was both familiar and exhilarating.

"He felt guilty for a long time," Ava said gently. "After all, I was your girl first."

"Damn right," Buddy retorted, before he could stop himself, but he needn't have worried; Ava threw back her head, roaring with laughter.

"And every now and then, I think it got his goat a little to *know* that his best friend would always have—I don't know how you want to say it—a soft spot for me. And whenever that happened," she smiled again, her eyes dancing, "I'd usually get something pretty from Market Square Jewelers."

Buddy's woeful groan echoed throughout the courtyard, and could be heard, they later discovered, by two neighbors and a paperboy.

"My God, you must have just hated to see me coming; you must have been so uncomfortable every time I walked in the door. No wonder you hated me so much." He shook his head, still agonizing.

"Are you *kidding?*" She nudged his shoulder lightly. "Quite the opposite. First of all, you were our best friend, and we loved being around you, no matter what. And as for the other thing, the guilt of turning you down and then hooking up with your best friend finally went away—and that took a number of years, let me tell you." It was her turn to wince a little. "After that was over . . . Hell, you made me feel like a million bucks. And you made Jimmy realize every day that he was the luckiest man in the world—even if it didn't stop him from flirting with other women. It kept things fresh."

Buddy didn't know quite how to respond to that one. "You're . . . welcome?"

She clicked her tongue at him. "Goodness, Buddy, I'm not thanking you!" She admonished. "Maybe I *should* be, but, well, I gave you homemade muffins. That trumps a thank you." She waited a few minutes for him to pick up on the hint, and when he didn't, she exclaimed, "Why, yes, thank you, now that you mention it, a mug for my coffee would be perfection!"

"Sorry, sorry, it's early, and I haven't put on my manners yet." He reached for his cane, got to his feet, and went into the kitchen, coming back with a couple of mugs. He'd gotten used to the cane over the years, but Ava had never seen him with it; oddly, he didn't feel self-conscious about it—maybe because she hadn't seemed to notice it. When he poured the coffee from her thermos, he said, "I see you already put the cream and sugar in it, like I like it."

"Jimmy took it strong and black—ugh!" Ava made a face. "You and I, though, just enough coffee for coloring, and then the rest sugar and cream. Molly calls it a coffee-shake."

"The guy with the coffee and bagel cart," Buddy suddenly remembered. "You know, the one with the Golden Retriever named Fritz, in Market Square, what was his name again?"

"You remember the dog, but not the man?" Ava had to think on that one a moment herself. "Don, it was Don, or . . . no, wait!" She snapped her fingers. "Denny, that's it. Denny."

"The guy that dropped out of law school and sunk everything he owned into a coffee and bagel cart." It all came flooding back in a rush. "Still, without us, I'm telling you, he'd have gone under that first year."

"I don't know if we can take *all* the credit. He had the loveliest, lightest buttery muffins . . . I could eat three in one sitting if I wasn't careful." She rubbed her stomach happily. "In fact, I could have eaten myself into a fat, blubbery heart attack, but what a way to go!"

"I can only think of one better," he said, and then immediately bit his lip. *Okay, that was definitely too far. Now she's going to think you're a pig, and you deserve it,* he scolded himself.

It had been a nice conversation, for a while there.

But instead of getting upset, her laughter rang out, much to his relief.

"Oh, yes, I'd have to agree with you on that one." She dropped him a sly wink.

He'd forgotten that her sense of humor was comparable to a truck driver's. He ran his hand over his head, suddenly very aware that he was standing there in his robe and with what must be a good case of bed-head. He groaned inwardly, wondering why he never seemed properly groomed for the really important moments of life. In his senior yearbook, the picture was of a very young Buddy with a very distinct and noticeable case of conjunctivitis—or, as they called it, pink eye. He'd showed up at that dance at the Rochester Recreation Center in a rumpled shirt and dungarees. For his first job interview, he'd conducted himself professionally, intelligently, all without realizing that his fly was open. Later, he'd somehow managed to spill coffee on the perfect silk shirt he'd bought specifically for the opening of O'Shaughnessey's, and wound up smiling for the press wearing one of the extra staff polo shirts that was lying around—it had been two sizes too small, which emphasized his growing gut in black and white for all of the Seacoast to see. Bad luck, his mother had said, seemed to follow him around when it came to appropriate dress, and Buddy feared she was right.

Ava didn't seem to notice, however, and never had. Maybe for women it was enough for *them* to be gussied up in all that makeup and the perfect shoes and hairdo; maybe they didn't really care what anyone else looked like.

"So," she batted her eyes, trying to flirt her way out of twenty years of bad behavior. "You forgive me, then?"

"*Forgive* you? For what, exactly?" His eyes twinkled; it would be out of character for him to make this easy on her, and she'd expect nothing else.

"Well, I . . . I just . . ." she struggled. "I'm trying, here, to find the most elegant, feminine way to put the phrase, 'I've been such an asshole.' You see, it was just so . . . It was a difficult time, things were . . . they were . . ."

"Spit it out, for gosh sakes," he advised her. "You're going to sprain something."

She eyed him frostily. "If I didn't know better, I'd think you were enjoying this."

He looked at her innocently, but there was nothing he could do to smother the sparkle in his eyes.

"I shouldn't have blamed you, back then. And then, for all those years after, I shouldn't have held such a grudge," she said at last. "I think I knew all this time that it was James." She looked down at her hands, now completely bare of rings. "After all, he'd never have let you behind the bar. You couldn't mix a Tom Collins worth a damn, that's why he never made you get your TEAM license."

"Hey!" He put a hand on his heart, pretending to be wounded, but she looked at him firmly; no kidding around here.

"You just let me finish, or else I might not get this all out."

He gestured, showing her she still had the floor and that he was, indeed, listening with both ears and all his heart.

"When we lost the pub," she began, "it was as though the bottom just dropped out of our lives. Not only was that pub our means of making a living, it was twenty years of our creative sweat, blood, and tears. It was our family effort, our little family business. It was . . ." she sighed, thinking of the long, green stairway that lead up to the pub, the mahogany bar, the heavy wooden stools, the music, the crowds. "It was our very own little piece of the world."

"I remember that feeling, too," he told her.

"I know you do," she covered his hand gently with her own. "So, when it was gone, I was hurt, I was confused, and I was furious."

"*You?* Angry? I don't believe it!"

"You promised you'd let me just get it out!" she said indignantly, and for the second time, he was properly chastened, bowing his head; he'd gotten so used to batting away Ava's comments with a joke. Old habits were tough to break. "Anyway, I was so angry, and you know me, I can't hold onto my anger, it's got to go somewhere or I'll just . . ."

"Explode into little tiny bits?" he offered.

She nodded, surprised and delighted to be understood so well, even if she couldn't find ways to express it herself.

"Yes, that's it. That's it, *exactly*." She clapped her hands together. "So, there's all this anger, just looking for somewhere to land." She looked up at him shyly. "And there you were, insisting to everyone who would listen that it was all your fault . . . So, it was easy to do the math."

"So," he replied, lacing his hands behind his head and rocking back and forth in his chair. "You've known. Deep down, all this time you've known, and you just didn't have the guts to get in touch with me and tell me."

She squirmed in her chair. This was every bit as uncomfortable as she'd feared it would be. As she moved, he noticed how the sun hit the highlights in her auburn hair. They looked like glowing embers. "Okay, fine, you've got me." She smiled coyly. "But it's only because I'm so soft and vulnerable."

"Oh, you." It was his turn to laugh then. "You're trying to make me break a rib, and then you'll be good and rid of me."

"There was a time I would have," she agreed. Growing somber again, she added, "But I did miss you. I missed you terribly. Most of all, after James died . . . oh, my." She stopped to clear the catch in her throat. "They tell you you'll get over it in time, but that's just another lie, like, 'Once you see the baby, you forget how much the labor hurt.' I love my daughter more than my own life, but bringing her into this world hurt so damn much it kept me from ever having another. And insofar as forgetting the hurt of when your mate passes on . . ." She shook her head. "Well, it *doesn't* get easier. Oh, you get used to it, but it still hurts every bit as much as it did the day they buried him."

"I just bet it does."

Their eyes met then, in the cool morning air.

"Oh, Buddy." She looked down at her hands again, ashamed. "I'm so sorry."

"Oh, geez." He heaved a dramatic sigh. "What are you sorry for this time? What have you gone and done now?" But he couldn't tease her out of this one.

"I'm sorry I didn't let you come to the funeral," she whispered. Her eyes glistened with tears. Not having a napkin, he handed her the end of his bathrobe tie, which she took gratefully. Dabbing at her eyes, she added, "I'm so sorry for that—it was petty and mean, and I really regret it. I do."

He reached over and lifted her chin up so he could look at her lovely face. "My turn to confess." He winked. "I *was* there."

She sat up straight, astonished. "*What*? How?"

"Oh, it wasn't so hard." He smiled. "You were so distraught that you weren't looking around—just straight forward. I spotted you and Suzie with your red heads, right up at the front of the church, you were easy to keep track of. So, I just jumped in right as the service began, and bowed my head when you and Suzie and Molly went by on the way out. I didn't know that Molly belonged to Suzanne; she looked barely more than a kid herself."

"She *was* barely more than a kid when she had Molly," Ava told him. "I yelled and screamed at that girl like you wouldn't believe, called her every name you could imagine. Jimmy just sat there in his chair; I think he was in so much shock, he lost his voice for a day or so." She leaned forward, gesturing him to come closer. "I even told her not to have the baby, which to this day terrifies me." She clapped her hand over her mouth and shuddered, so horrifying was that thought now. "For years, I kept having these terrible dreams that it's 1994 and we're in that terrible argument, only this time she takes my advice; then, in the dream, we're swept right back here in the present, and we're having a lovely lunch, or Christmas, or walk in the park. Suddenly Molly is sucked away from us, up into the sky, so fast we can't grab her." She shivered, not even wanting to think about it.

"She's something special, all right," Buddy remarked, looking fondly toward Ava's house, where Molly lay sleeping. "No arguments there."

Ava sat for a moment, letting the relief sink in as she let the weight of the guilt she'd felt since the funeral go.

"You big jerk!" She grabbed the end of his bathrobe tie and flipped the end back at him teasingly. "You, you're just a big jerk, that's all. You could have let me know a long time ago and saved me all that agony."

"And waste all that good guilt?" he cried. "No, ma'am. If I had, you might not have brought me muffins."

"It was funny that you moved in next door," she said thoughtfully. "Assuming it really *was* a coincidence."

"I gotta tell you, honey," he said—and there it was again, that "h" word. "If I'd have known, I wouldn't have dared. You fucking hated me for *years* now."

She nodded. "Anyway, I was sure you'd be married with a handful of kids by now." She clucked her tongue, tsk, tsk, tsk. "I can't believe there hasn't been one female, in all the world, who could manage to wrestle you into settling down."

He looked at her for a long moment. "I got spoiled, early on." He fingered the edge of his robe a little too nervously. "It's not my fault you're such a damn hard act to follow."

Ava blushed, looking down at her lap. At that moment, she wasn't a grandmother of over sixty; she was a young girl who'd just told a young soldier to ask her to dance.

She's every bit as pretty as she was on that day, Buddy realized. *No, prettier, because I know what's inside now.*

"So," he cleared his throat. "Just to confirm . . . since we're forgiving each other, my tree-camouflage days are over? I can stop jumping behind the bushes every time I hear the squeak of your front door?"

"My front door does not squeak! I put WD-40 on it *myself*, thank you very much." She tapped her foot indignantly. "It's yours that sounds like a rabid bat every time you step outside for a smoke—which you seem to do a lot lately." She looked at him expectantly, clearly waiting to be told it had been her alluring presence that drew him.

"Well, it wasn't just for you," he had to admit. "You can be flattered without feeling stalked. It's Brandon. He kicks me out every time I light up."

"How in the world," she asked, bewildered, "does a young boy kick a grown man out of his own house?"

He opened his mouth to answer and then promptly snapped it shut.

"Now that you mention it, I'm not quite sure. He tells me what to do, and then I just find myself doing it." He leaned forward and whispered, "I think it's because he reminds me of my mother."

"Your secret's safe with me." She smiled at him. She felt . . . what was the word? Aflutter? That was it. Like she was walking on champagne bubbles, but without the booze. "By the way," she told him, "I've already put down your name for some of the activities at the rec center. I hope you like volleyball and the luge."

"The luge?" He hoped she was kidding, because the mental image on that one wasn't pretty. "At our age, that game should be called Pick-up Sticks. I think I'd rather join you in the chorus of *The Grandma of La Mancha* . . . I used to do shows in high school, you know."

She looked up at him hesitantly, almost nervously. "Do you think we could, Buddy?"

"Do I think we could what?"

She glanced down at the French tips she'd been picking at, and realized she'd completely ruined them, before looking back up at him.

"Have *fun* again. Together. You and I, that is." She covered her eyes. "I wouldn't blame you if you never wanted to talk to me again. There's so much water under the bridge, and it's all so polluted."

"And you're thinking you did most of the polluting?"

She shifted in her chair guiltily. "Well, if you have to spit the words right out . . ."

He laughed again, letting his eyes caress her face, suddenly wishing he could reach out and stroke her cheek the way he had a million times in his daydreams.

"Oh, my Ava," he said fondly, "when I heard from time to time that you were still cursing my name to the gods—people just love to be the bearer of crappy tidings, you ever notice that? Someone you barely know will call you up to tell you that someone said something just awful about you and then say something like, 'I just thought you should know.' Boy, does misery love company. Anyway, I'd remember all of our times together. Doing the books together. Going to flea markets, looking for stuff to decorate the restaurant. Taking you to plays, because Jimmy couldn't stand them. Those were some of the best summers of my life. I kept those memories right here." He tapped his forehead. "There was the time we went to see *A Funny Thing Happened on the Way to the Forum*, remember?"

She looked at him, startled. *A Funny Thing Happened on the Way to the Forum*? She hadn't seen that play in years, although she dearly loved the score and kept meaning to look for it online with Molly's help. *The last time I saw that*, she realized, *was probably when he took me.* For a woman who saw all the musicals she loved at least five times, this was a very big deal. Maybe in some way, buried in the back of her brain, she had been trying to keep that one experience singular, special. She uttered a small laugh—the secrets you could keep from yourself were truly mind-boggling.

"You sang along with the whole score," Buddy went on, "even though people around you offered you money to stop. I didn't watch the show, I watched *you*. Your face was so full of life, full of joy; that was better than any play could ever be. I kept that one right here." He tapped his chest. "So, to take a long way around to get to the point, yes. Yes, I certainly *do* think we could have fun again. If you just give me half a chance."

"Oh, my." Ava put her hands to her cheeks, which were completely flushed, and then cleared her throat. "Well, isn't that too bad, that all these years you've had nothing better to do than obsess about an old lady like me." She waited expectantly for a moment, then leaned forward to whisper, "Here's the part where you're supposed to tell me I'm not an old lady."

"I'll do no such thing," he countered. "Most women don't like to be told they're old, because to them, old are those who've had all the life sucked out of them. But you've logged the same sixty-plus years I have, and by our life-expectation grid, that makes you an old lady. But, looking at you," he gestured to her, "I see all the things that young girls have—the sparkle in their eyes, the color in their cheeks, the way they carry themselves, straight and proud. The so-called old ladies let that stuff go, so it shows. But you," he whistled, "it's a matter of how you think of yourself—probably a matter of what you think of life in general, if I can get a little corny about it. What can I say? The world will always have pretty young girls; it's easy to be pretty when you're young. But when those girls age up—*then* we'll see whether they're truly beautiful." He planted his cane on the step and struggled to his feet. "So, yes, my dear, you are, in fact, an old lady. But you're one of the few who makes 'old' look *smokin'* hot."

She stared at him, flabbergasted, wondering how in the world she could top such a comment, which was far and away the best compliment she'd ever heard in her life. *When in doubt*, she reasoned, *let your body do the talking*. She dipped her head down to her shoulder, smiling happily at him, letting her eyes shine at him. After a moment, she turned her smile coy, tossing her hair over her shoulder. After all these years, her flirting skills bubbled up naturally to the surface. If anyone had asked, she'd have assumed they were long gone, but apparently it was just like riding a bike.

"You're starting to talk like Brandon," she said, her breath catching slightly. "He sure has a way of making an impact, doesn't he?"

Buddy watched her and shifted his weight again. She caught it this time and knew what it meant: time to go. All this was a lot to absorb, so she should probably head home and let him get about doing so.

"Well, listen to you. You've made me all flustered." She fluffed her hair out, smiling at him. "But it's nearly nine, so I'd better get to my meeting."

"Oh, I'm sorry." He looked concerned. "I mean, did I say anything wrong? Something that makes you want a drink?"

"My wanting a drink is pretty much the norm," she said evenly. "I'm not going to have one today—and probably not tomorrow either. But being a drunk generally means that I always want one. So, no, it's not you at all. Some meetings are more fun than others. This is my morning ladies' group, and I hate to miss it, unless it's an emergency."

"So, those meetings." He spoke gingerly, not wanting to offend. "They work out for you, then?"

She laughed, and touched his arm. A spark of electricity charged from her hand to his, and she nearly gasped. *Oh, my.* She thought, well pleased and quite surprised. *Well, isn't that nice.*

Composing herself, she said, "They help. Oh, there are some wonderful people there, some people who are just like family, who are always there for you. And then there are some assholes who stand up week after week, whining about their lives because they've got a captive audience. But . . ."

She stopped, struggling to think how to describe the feeling to a non-drunk. "Just sitting there," she went on at last, "even if you're not talking, for some reason, this strength sort of washes over you. So then later on in the day, when you invariably *do* want a drink, you're strong enough to fend it off."

"I see." He nodded, and she thought he actually might, as much as any normy ever could.

"Well, thank you." She retreated a few steps toward the path to her house. "Thank you so much. For . . . for just, well, everything."

"You, ma'am," he assured her, "are more than welcome."

"I'll go inside and call Brandon on his cell phone, so he can come with me," she said. "Molly says he wakes up better to a ringing phone than to an alarm clock."

"Does he?" Buddy glanced toward the house, where the young man lay practically unconscious. "Well, that's the odd life of the young. I could pound on his door if you like. That'll get him up."

"Oh, no, that's okay. But thank you."

"You're quite welcome," he said evenly; his voice, a moment ago so soft and sincere, was back to the Buddy she knew. The Buddy she'd always known. There was something he wanted to say, she could practically feel it, but his mouth remained shut. *His mouth says no, but his eyes say yes*, she thought with dismay. She'd learned by watching her forensic shows that you couldn't count on the signals the eyes sent out. After all, the observation she'd just made was also the same phrase often invoked by date rapists. She took a few more steps, when an idea hit her, and then turned back again. "By the by," she said brightly, "I really hope you enjoy the muffins. I tried to make them as good as the ones we used to get from Denny."

"Oh, you've always been such a great cook, I'm sure they'll be just fine. Delicious." He looked down at the plate and then back up at her. He seemed about to say something, but in the end, he didn't.

C'mon, big guy, she thought, willing him to speak. *You can do it. Just go for it. I'm right here.*

She kept smiling again for a minute, standing there. He smiled back, until they both felt like a couple of idiots. It was official—time to let the moment go.

"So . . ." she trailed off. "Have a nice day!"

"I'll try," he called back, giving a little half wave. "You too."

She sighed and officially gave up. "Well," she said, dejectedly, turning toward her door, "bye."

She had just lifted her foot to climb the first step when Buddy called out, "Ava, wait."

She twirled around and strode back to him, exhilarated and exasperated all at once.

"*Well, it's about damn time!*" she retorted, eyes blazing. "Look at me, I got two thirds of the way there. I was practically over the threshold of my house, which was obviously the point of no return! I was about to be the girl that got away *twice!*"

"Twice?" Buddy asked, bewildered.

"But no matter," she beamed, taking his hand. "You finally stopped me; better early than late, but better late than never, so go ahead and ask me out." She patted his arm gently, but firmly. "Trust me. It'll be easy. I've got a yes all ready and waiting."

"Actually," said Buddy, trying to adjust to this new change in development, "I was just going to tell you to wait while I put the muffins in a basket, so I could give you back your container. But, well," he eyed her warily, "are you absolutely sure about this 'yes' you've got waiting?"

"I'm sure," she said firmly, "but the offer expires at midnight, so you'd better get cracking."

"Okay. Wow." He drew a deep breath and realized he was trembling, just a little. Silly, after all these years! "I didn't think this would be so hard. Look, my knees are knocking, and my armpits are all clammy."

"What an incredible turn-on," she deadpanned. "Clock's ticking, Buddy-boy."

"Buddy-boy." Why, he thought in wonder, *she hasn't called me that since . . . Gee, not since the night I was going to propose.* They say time always came back around to itself. *Well,* he thought happily. *What do you know about that?* "Okay, okay." He stood up straight and gave a slight bow. "Miss Ava, would you do me the honor of letting me escort you on an outing Friday night?"

"Friday night?" She frowned. "What's wrong with tomorrow? What are you, dating someone else and squeezing me in or something?"

"No, of course not, I . . .." he stammered, then saw that her eyes were twinkling up at him from under her mascaraed lashes. "Boy, you really love to knock a guy off his game, don't you? Okay, *fine.* Let's start this again." He stood up straight, offering his hand this time. "Miss Ava, would you do me the honor of letting me escort you on the outing *of your choice,*" he emphasized, "tomorrow evening?"

"Tomorrow evening?" She raised a hand to her breast with feigned surprise. "Oh, my, this catches me right off guard, Mr. McKinley. I'm just going to have to check my social calendar."

"I thought I had a yes I could take to the bank!" Buddy cried.

"Well," she conceded, "now that I think of it, I just might . . . yes, I do believe I'm free tomorrow evening."

"Well, fine then." He looked at her with a mixture of fondness and exasperation. Suddenly he was desperate to get inside, take some deep breaths, wash off all this nervous sweat. Then he'd get Brandon's opinion on what he should wear. He might have some shopping to do. He should probably get a haircut, and it had been a while since he'd gotten any new shoes. This could turn out to be quite a project. "I'll see you right here, right at the bottom of your steps, at sunset, then, all right? We'll have a twilight picnic, if that's okay by you."

"That's just fine by me," she agreed, and then turned to walk gaily to her house. This time her steps were light and giddy instead of hesitant. Halfway there, she turned back again, and for a moment his heart sank.

She's changed her mind, he thought sadly. *She thought about it, and it was just too weird for her, being that I was Jimmy's best friend and all.*

"Listen, Buddy," she began, and he winced. The last time she'd used that phrase, he'd gotten dumped. "I just think we ought to get something clear, right up front."

"Yeah?"

"I'm not trying to replace Jimmy in my life." She looked at him softly, but firmly. "I'll always love him."

"So, I guess that means you want to be friends?" He grinned, trying not to show how crestfallen he was. Friends, he supposed, was better than nothing . . . But just now it felt like freezing cold comfort on a bitter winter evening indeed.

But Ava surprised him yet again. "Just friends?" She gave her throaty laugh. This time, that laugh spelled relief for Buddy. "A life without romance is a life that's over. I like to think I've got a few more miles in me yet." She put her hands on her hips, posing haughtily for him, before growing serious again. "But, I didn't want you to think that I was using you to feel closer to him. You were his best friend, after all."

"Never, ever, would I try to fill that man's shoes," Buddy promised. "I know what you had will always be sort of . . . Well, it will always be." He smiled gently at her, wanting to take her in his arms right there, but still not quite daring to, not yet. "I can live with being second runner-up."

"And you know what?" She smiled as she walked up the path for the third and final time that morning. "I bet he's up there somewhere, looking down on us after all these years and getting a real kick out of this."

"I wouldn't be surprised," Buddy agreed. "No, that wouldn't surprise me in the least."

EIGHTEEN

Witches, witches, everywhere, and lots of brew to drink, Suzanne thought, amused, looking around at the women who filled the store. Some were dressed like they'd just come from work, some were more casual, and some looked like they were getting ready to star in a remake of *Hocus Pocus* or maybe *The Craft*.

"Officially, the store is closed and this is just a reading," Laura said, as she poured papaya juice over the dry ice in a huge wrought iron cauldron, "but there's no reason we can't sneak a little promotion in here as well, is there?"

Suzanne laughed. "You can take the girl out of Columbia Business School," she noted, "but you can't take Columbia Business School out of the girl."

"Law School," Laura corrected. "And yes, you can. It's called an exorcism."

Suzanne took in the animated scene before her. The bookstore was filled to nearly overflowing, and while some didn't dress to display their "religion" (Suzanne still found it hard to refer to witchcraft as a religion), there were also plenty dressed in garb that shrieked, "I'm a witch/ecogoth/pagan-at-large!" There seemed to be no happy medium. There were capes, long, flowing dresses cut so low you could actually see a navel ring or two, triple the amount of jewelry you'd see on any other person, hair glitter, overdone makeup. They wanted to stick out, and boy, did they.

"They really don't know how bad it makes us all look," Laura sighed. "They should be wearing T-shirts that say, 'Please, dear God, pay attention to me!'"

"We both wore combat boots and plastic barrettes well into our teens," Suzanne reminded her. "We need to let them have their expression, even if they look as horrible as we did back then."

"The thing is, that's just a phase, for most of us, and most of us never go to that extreme." Laura tipped her head toward the flamboyant attendees. "It's just like anything else . . . A lot of young people who are desperate for an identity—any identity—find out about us and plow through the books in record time. In a month, they've got seven pentagrams and three athames and likely the beginnings of an herbal garden at home, and their wardrobe has become a lot more flowing. They walk around in public, sticking out like sore thumbs, getting the attention they want, and they never actually sink themselves fully into the craft." She shook her head a little woefully. "Rather than using the things in the books to help find themselves, they focus on the veneer, because that's the immediate gratification. You can look like a real witch even if you ain't one yet. Then, in a year or two, all the books and clothes and seeds and crystals I sell them will be gathering dust at the back of a closet, and they'll refer to their time with the craft as a 'phase.'"

"The craft?" Suzanne asked doubtfully. "It's a craft now? As in arts and crafts?"

"Sort of." Laura poured Chex mix into a hollowed-out corn husk. "Think of it this way. We're such a get-up-and-go society that sitting still is tough for us. Wicca, or witchcraft, gives us rituals—things that we can do, and by actually doing something, even as little as chanting a prayer while lighting a candle, that makes us feel like we've accomplished something."

"So, they just forget about the readings and the spells and all that?"

"Most of them do, I'm afraid."

"Hmmm." Suzanne pretended to think it over. "Now what would someone who wasn't a witch do if she suddenly found herself in possession of a love spell tucked into some books given to her by a long-lost friend?"

Laura grinned impishly. "First of all, I would hope and pray to the Goddess that the person who found the potion would take a chance and just give it a try. If you believe in the potion, it'll work. If you don't believe in it, it won't work."

"So, it's all about what I believe?"

"Kind of, it's . . ." Laura stopped to think for a moment as she rearranged the snacks. "Let's just say, I'm a firm believer in belief." She giggled like the high school girl Suzanne had once known. "Many times in my life, I've seen someone decide, 'I'm going to do this. This is going to happen for me.' And good or bad, it always does."

"You're yanking my chain, right?" Suzanne asked warily.

"Nope." Laura looked right into Suzanne's dark eyes with her clear blue ones and laid a hand on her arm. "Look, honey, this isn't the time or the place . . . But you've had a tough time of it your whole life. You wouldn't believe anything that wasn't laid out before you because you've been taught the only thing you can count on is yourself."

Suzanne was startled. Had Laura read her tea leaves on their last visit? Or gotten that information from Ava as she searched for her beloved angel books (of which Suzanne had found a cache in her bedroom one day while Ava was at a meeting)? She didn't think Ava would describe her that way, and there hadn't been any leaves left from the tea, so the only answer left was that those clear, sweet blue eyes saw everything—on the surface and under. It was surprisingly refreshing, and more than just a little scary.

"Wow," she said finally. "I don't think anyone has ever gotten me this quickly in my whole life."

"Scary, huh?" Laura smiled. "A lot of it is basic psychology, the way people carry themselves, their body language, the way they conduct themselves. Just the structure of their lives in general."

"And the rest? You said a lot of it is psychology, but what's the rest of the secret to reading someone like a book?"

Laura stopped working entirely and looked at Suzanne, tucking an errant auburn lock behind her ear. "I trust my instincts," she admitted. "It's how I survive. That whole experience in New York, I didn't listen to anything my instincts told me—I didn't listen to any of the little voices inside of me. And look how that worked out."

Little voices? Inside her?

Suzanne took a deep breath, putting her hand on the table to steady herself. Short of Laura breaking into her house and reading her diary—which she hadn't updated since her second date with Steve—Laura knew things about her that she could only have seen with very, very perceptive eyes. And maybe a little gut feeling.

"So, I thought it was a good time for the love potion because even though you're just now getting divorced," Laura wrinkled her nose, "it's been a long time since you've had love—real, binding, passionate-but-full-of-friendship love."

It was Suzanne's turn to laugh. It didn't take any special insight to recognize that. In fact, it had been so long since she'd had sex that she wondered if she could be called a virgin all over again.

What if I'm not good at it anymore? she thought, desperately. *What if there's new stuff out there that I don't know how to do? What if . . .*

"You always find what you're looking for when you're not looking." Laura's voice cut into her thoughts. "Frankly, it almost always seems to happen at the most inconvenient times."

"Yeah." Suzanne could tell she wasn't going to be able to talk her out of it. After all, Laura was in love, and those hooked on the love drug almost always became pushers. Then again, Laura, who had always seemed to be at the top of her game, had never seemed more real, more alive, more at peace with herself than she had since they'd renewed their acquaintance. Maybe there was something to this witch stuff, after all.

"So, promise me you'll do the spell, and you'll try to believe in it?" Laura asked casually. "Just try?"

Suzanne looked down, toeing the carpet with her Converse high-tops. (Molly was mortified about this until someone told her how "cool" her mother was, and Molly then proudly agreed). "Well, I already, I sort of . . . it's . . ."

". . . on your bureau, or in your bathroom, or on the windowsill?" Laura said gravely. "Yeah, I kinda figured it would be."

Suzanne burst out laughing. "Okay, how did you know that? The other stuff, the psych and the gut feelings, I'll give you, but how did you . . ."

"Because you're a smart person," Laura smiled, "and a smart person's reasoning would go something like, 'Hmm, let me think about it for a few days . . . Well, it might not work, but it certainly couldn't hurt to give it a try, and *boy*,'" she inhaled deeply, "'it would be damn fine to get me some nice man action right about now.'"

Suzanne couldn't stop laughing. "That's pretty much how it went."

"That's pretty much how it always goes."

The bus stopped outside the store, and nearly two dozen people—some dressed in corporate clothing, some in track suits, some in Harry Potter garb—got out and filed inside.

"Are all of these people . . . witches?" The word, no matter how hard she tried, still felt awkward coming out of her mouth.

"No, some of them are just people who want to hear the readings of a strong female speaker. Remember, we also cater to the feminist crowd. Tonight, we've got Susan Poulin. She's a hoot."

"I think I've heard of her." Suzanne pondered for a moment. "What kinds of books does she write?"

"Oh, she doesn't write books; she impersonates women—types of women, I should say," Laura nodded. "She's a humorist, but then under the humor, you get to see the strength of the woman she's showing you. She's a friend of mine, I'm pleased to say. All of the writers, performers, and speakers I bring in celebrate the strength of women and the things we do to endure everyday challenges. Susan just happens to do it with laughter." Laura shook her head firmly. "There is no better teacher than laughter."

"That is true," Suzanne noted, "and that is *brilliant*. Did you make that up?"

"I'm quotin' my man," said Laura happily. She was so comfortable with herself, she didn't even notice the offended glares these words evoked from half the women in earshot. Obviously, some of the half just hated men, while the rest of the half just didn't want or need them.

With a jolt, she recalled that her daughter, her Molly, fell into that second category. Well, that was an exaggeration, she supposed. Look at her relationship with Brandon, who was the closest friend Suzanne had ever seen Molly invite into her life. But the information that her daughter was a lesbian, a gay, or whatever you wanted to call it, kept sneaking up on her like a cold splash in the face.

"Well, he's a smart one," Suzanne changed the subject before the glaring women could form a lynch mob. "So, how does a reading work?"

"It's all very casual. She'll get up, do her act, and then we'll all ask her questions that she answers in character and then as Susan. Afterwards, we'll try to get everyone to eat this snack mountain. Everyone always brings too much food, and there's nothing that bugs Billy more than food going to waste."

There were only a couple of cold stares at the mention of Laura's husband, but Suzanne ignored it this time. If they were going to be upset every time Laura mentioned she had a husband she was crazy about, then they deserved to be irritated.

"No booze?" Suzanne was pleased to note. Growing up in a drunken household had made her appreciate chemical-free events, even when her mother wasn't there to worry about.

"Oh, no, only dry readings here at Goddess Treasures," Laura told her, fanning out the napkins. "My mom is a huge drunk and druggie—has been her whole adult life, maybe even before—and Billy's dad came back from Vietnam with a pot habit he never shook. Since these things are genetic, we try to stay away from substances of all kinds."

Suzanne's jaw dropped. She would not have been more shocked if Laura, the prom queen, had told her that she was actually the mutant child of a space princess, abandoned here on earth because of her deformities.

While Laura, the perfect student, the girl everyone wanted to befriend or be like—while she was carving her place in Portsmouth High School history—she was also going home to a mother who was blitzed out of her gourd or passed out on the couch or, worst of all, out there somewhere in the world, waiting for some kind soul to deliver her home.

They had had the exact same secret, carried the exact same burden, hid the same shame as they sat next to each other in class day after day, year after year. Strangers within their little self-important world, with so much in common.

She wanted to crawl into Laura's lap and cry. She wanted to absorb Laura's serenity, to be so honest and open and brave and accepting of everything. To be able to just drop these things into a conversation so casually . . .

I will never be that brave. Her chest ached. *Oh, Laura, it's high school all over again; I want to be you.*

"God, I can't believe I didn't tell you that before." Laura put her hands on Suzanne's. "It took me such a long time to be able to say it out loud. You know, all during junior high and high school, I couldn't invite anyone over while she was there, because, well, they'd see how disgusting she was, and I couldn't tell a teacher or anyone, because . . ."

"Because they might have said it was your fault that she drank—that's what you were afraid of." Suzanne squeezed Laura's fingers. "You were too young to realize that they wouldn't. You were used to irrational adults at home—one parent always sauced, the other always defending the crazy behavior—so why not at school as well?"

Laura's eyes softened. "That's right. You know this path well, don't you?"

"That I do, my friend," Suzanne nodded. "That I do."

"Well, I consider Ava an inspiration." Laura went back to rearranging the snacks. "Maybe one day my mom will follow in her footsteps."

Suzanne's jaw dropped again, this time in dismay.

"You mean your mother still hasn't . . ."

"Hey, Mom!"

Suzanne turned to see Molly as she butted and excused herself past twenty or thirty people with no particular grace. She had an older man that Suzanne had never seen before in tow. A slightly embarrassed look was sprawled across his handsome face.

Molly, on the other hand, was simply beaming. "Hey, Mom. This is my friend Sean."

"Well, hi, Molly's friend Sean," said Suzanne, a little startled. "Who are you, and how do you know my very young female child?"

"Easy does it, Mama lion." Sean held his hands up. "Being old enough to be her father and then some, I can assure you that my friendship with Molly is brand-new. And not of the nature that you'd have to be concerned about."

"Oh, she's not worried about that," Molly interjected smoothly. "She knows I do chicks."

"*Molly!*" Suzanne glanced hastily around to see if anyone had heard. "For heaven's sake, you don't have to be so *loud!*"

Molly stared at her for an instant, the look in her eyes so full of disgust, Suzanne was jolted.

I know that look, Suzanne thought uncomfortably. *I know that look because I've done that look. That's the look that I used to give Mom back when I was peeling her off the kitchen floor, trying to get some coffee into her before Daddy got home.*

"Well, it was nice to meet you," offered Sean, clearly wanting to escape the suffocating tension. "Maybe I'll see you at intermission."

He disappeared into the crowd, and Suzanne touched Molly's hand, trying to diffuse the situation.

"I didn't mean it like that, honey, I just thought . . ."

"Hey, girl, I thought you weren't going to make it." A woman in a tight tank top, jeans, and very short hair approached Molly and put a hand on her shoulder, looking at Suzanne evenly. Suzanne desperately tried to keep her expression neutral. "Hi, I'm Sandy."

"Hi, Sandy," Suzanne said. To her own ears, her voice sounded a bit too hearty. Laura pressed a hand on her back, letting her know she was booming. Lowering her voice, she added, "I'm Suzanne. I'm Molly's mom."

Sandy's eyes widened, taking Suzanne in. "Sorry," she apologized. "You just don't look old enough to have a daughter as old as Molly."

"She's not," Molly said coldly. "Let's go."

Before Suzanne had a chance to ask, "What the hell was that supposed to mean?" Sandy had taken Molly's hand and was pointing toward a group of women. Mostly they were chatting amongst themselves, but a few of them were looking at Molly the way Suzanne had gotten used to construction workers looking at her when she walked down the street.

"You want to sit with the Dianas? We're all over there." Sandy pointed to them, and Suzanne felt her stomach tighten. She wanted to bat these women away, and she hated herself for it. She'd seen hundreds of programs on television in which lesbians were normal, often gorgeous women, but in her real-life experience, they all looked a little on the mannish side. She kicked herself for the generalization. After all, she'd marched a dozen or more times for the pride, twice in New York City, when they'd gone there to visit Steve's grandmother and his gay cousin Liam.

So why was it okay to be proud of Liam and not Molly? Damn it, where were these feelings coming from?

"Sure, let's," Molly nodded. "I mean, I'm only here with my mom . . ."

"Her very *proud* mom," Suzanne emphasized loudly, trying to make up for her initial reaction. She grabbed Sandy's hand and pumped it firmly, a huge smile plastered on her face. Molly looked like she wanted to fall through the cracks in the floor; Laura's pats on the back became more urgent.

"Well, Molly's very proud mom," Sandy said coolly. "You've raised up one fine girl."

Suzanne kept that grin plastered on her face as she let go of Sandy's hand, but she couldn't meet the girl's very direct gaze, so she pretended to look over the crowd.

"Laura, you really packed them in tonight. Great job with the marketing." She took a sip of the papaya juice, suddenly wishing there *was* a shot of something very strong available. "I've been thinking that might be something I'd be interested in going into."

"You'd be *great* at that!" Laura grabbed her hand, eyes shining. "For PR, you've got to be likeable, innovative, persistent, and not afraid to annoy people. In a word, it's you."

Suzanne raised an eyebrow at her new friend. "Try as I might, I'm not sure I can see that as a compliment."

"But I have to tell you," Laura smiled at the steady stream of women who were entering the room, "it's easy PR when you've got Susan on the bill. She's so amazing that people would line up and listen to her read the phone book."

"You bet they would," Sandy chimed in her husky voice. "I would, that's for damn sure."

"So, Mom, we'll see you later?" Molly was clearly ready for some space. "Have fun."

"See you," Suzanne called sadly, watching her only daughter take the hand of this stranger, this woman whose haircut was shorter than Brandon's, who wore men's jeans and a hoop in her nose. So this was her daughter's first romantic interest.

Are you really that naive? She kicked herself. *Come on, Denial Woman. She didn't discover this overnight. Chances are, she took a swim in the pool before buying a membership to the club.*

Then Sean came back out of the crowd, and Molly seemed to remember something. She whispered into Sandy's ear, and they both made their way back to the group of chairs Laura and Suzanne had staked out.

"We changed our minds," Molly announced. "We'll sit here with you guys."

"The Dianas won't like it," Sandy warned, but Molly didn't budge.

"If they don't like it, fuck 'em."

Suzanne was relieved beyond all measure to hear those words. Her Molly would always stick up for herself. Yes, at least she had made sure that was instilled in her. "What are the Dianas, anyway?" Suzanne asked Laura. "Are they a cult?"

"They're all right." Laura confided. "They're Wiccans who strongly identify with the goddess Diana. Diana wasn't big on men, so the Dianas are usually lesbians, but a lot of them are straight out-and-out man-haters. They've been really, really hurt, and they take it out on the entire gender." Laura sighed. "It gets weird sometimes. If you're speaking out against intolerance and are, in fact, intolerant yourself, it can get a little tricky." She watched Suzanne deliberately not watching Molly and Sandy, four rows ahead of them, for a moment. Laura dropped her voice to a whisper. "So, she told you this week, huh?"

"I'm still trying to take it in, I think. Not that I'm upset, or anything," she added hastily. "It's just . . . You know, for eighteen years, I thought my kid was a righty, and whaddya know, she's a lefty. I'm gonna need a few days on that one, is all I'm saying." She sipped her drink thoughtfully. "Can I ask you a question, Laura? And tell me the truth."

"When have I given you otherwise?" Laura asked haughtily. "Shoot."

"If you met Molly, just on the street or in the store, or something, would you have known?"

Laura considered this, watching Molly for a minute. Molly felt the weight of her stare and turned to find its source, but rather than looking hastily away, Laura blew her a big kiss. Molly stared at her, and to Suzanne's great relief, laughed.

Another one of your weird friends, she mouthed at her mother, and Suzanne shrugged her shoulders: Guilty.

"The answer doesn't matter either way, does it?" Laura asked.

"Just answer, you big jellyfish."

"Well, maybe," she said finally. "It wouldn't be my first thought, but by the end of the conversation, I think I'd have come to the conclusion."

"Oh." Suzanne tried to keep her voice neutral, but it didn't fool Laura at all.

"Is that such a bad thing?"

"I saw a play last year, at the West End Studio Theatre, called *Stopkiss,*" Suzanne said morosely. "In it, two girls were viciously beaten up by a guy who saw them kiss on the street."

"Oh, honey. . ."

Suddenly Molly was right in front of them, pulling along her new friend Sean by the hand. He looked both a little uncomfortable and a little curious.

"Hi, Sean!" Molly sang out, pulling out a chair next to Suzanne.

"Hi, Sean." Sandy's greeting was somewhat less enthusiastic.

"Sean's going to sit with us," Molly announced.

"I thought you were going to sit over there, with Sandy's . . . friends?" Suzanne asked, hoping she'd used the right word. If she offended Molly one more time, the kid might just go off to college and never come back.

"We were, but now we're sitting here," Molly said simply. "Better view."

Four rows back? Suzanne wondered. Clearly, something was up.

"He's a friend of Grandma's," Molly told her, all but shoving Sean into the chair she'd pulled out. She found two more in the row in front of them, and she and Sandy settled into them.

"I'm afraid that doesn't narrow it down," Suzanne told Sean. "My mother knows the *planet*. I can go into the drugstore to pick up some gum, and the cashier tells me to wish my mom a good day. Or a cop will follow me a few blocks, and I pull over to see what he wants, and he tells me he just wants to know if my mom's donating to the Policeman Safe Parks project." She shook her head, smiling a little. "She's like a movie star who never made a film. I call her The Mayor."

"She has—how can I say this?" He wrestled with it for a minute, then decided on "a presence, that's for sure. My dad would have called her a rig."

"What's a rig?" Suzanne asked, amused.

"You know, I'm not sure," Sean admitted. "But he always used it in terms of people who were really funny, or strong, or both. I think he meant people who were rigged up different, better than other people."

Satisfied, Molly sat back down in her seat in the row ahead and continued her conversation with Sandy, but she seemed to be keening her ears in their direction. Obviously there was some sort of plot afoot. Suzanne wondered what the hell it was, and if the plot included a need for bail money.

"Anyway," Sean continued, "it must be nice having her for a mother. I've only talked to her a few times myself, but the whole group is always going to her for a shoulder to cry on or to find that extra boost or to ask for gum and a Band-Aid. You name it, she's the girl."

Suzanne frowned. "I'm sorry, Sean, but exactly where do you know my mother from?"

"Shhh, shhh!" Sandy jumped up in her seat excitedly. "Here she comes! It's starting!"

And indeed, the beehive hairdo and the padded belly of Ida LeClair (the character portrayed by the writer in this one-woman performance piece) was indeed pushing her way to the podium. When she got there, she greeted the crowd with a "Howdy!"

"It's a retirement village!" Suzanne told her when Molly asked if it was okay to invite a few people over. "I'm not sure they're going to appreciate a late-night party on the lawn."

"Oh, we'll be quiet, Mom," Molly said, Sandy's hand resting lightly on Molly's hip. Suzanne hated how uncomfortable it made her and cursed herself when she had to flick her eyes away. *So apparently, after all my liberal preachings and live-and-let-live attitude, at the end of the day, I'm just a bigot. A bigot and a hypocrite.* No, she was in no mood for further socializing right now.

She pitched in with the cleanup, sweeping up the dirt the crowd had tracked in. Billy was making sure any uneaten food was distributed, while Laura collected the used napkins and cups. Sean had also stayed to give a hand to Molly, as she balanced on the front counter to take down the IDA'S HERE TONIGHT! sign.

"It's a weeknight, so if you guys don't feel like coming," Suzanne began weakly, "I wouldn't blame you all if you just wanted to go home and get some rest." But the Universe, or the Goddess (as Laura would say) had entirely different plans for her.

"We'd be glad to come," Sandy said drolly, lighting up a smoke. "Won't we, Sean?"

"Sure, if I'm welcome," he replied.

"Great!" Suzanne enthused. Turning to Laura, through her too-wide grin, she hissed, "You're coming, and don't even think otherwise."

"Oh, you think I'd miss this?" Laura shook her head. "Try and keep me away."

And this was how, after an evening with Susan Poulin in Goddess Treasures, the unlikely sextet wound their way together back to Ava's house.

"It's not even nine o'clock yet." Molly stopped and picked up a newspaper and empty cup on Daniel Street, on the way back to Ava's house. Suzanne recalled with a pang that when Molly turned four, she had declared that she hated litter worse than anything. She had carried plastic grocery bags around with her for several years, for just the purpose of public cleanup.

"Great idea to start these things early, Laura," Molly complimented her. "Is that a marketing ploy, to give the people time to hang out in the store and be inspired to buy stuff after the readings?"

"That sounds so smart—I should tell people that's how I planned it," Laura smiled. "But actually, I planned them to end early way back when my girl Hermione was little, so I could be home at a reasonable hour." She dug out her cell phone then, dialing the house where her daughter was staying for the evening. When Hermione asked to say hi to Daddy, Billy's face lit up like a jack-o'-lantern as he grabbed the phone to have a private daddy-chat. Laura watched him, her own face glowing.

"He was so nervous when we found out she was a girl," Laura explained. "He was all, 'What am I going to do with a girl? I've got three brothers and two uncles. What the heck do girls do?'" She laughed at the memory. "Now, they're the buds, the best of friends. He helps her make her soaps and lotions, they talk their money talk together, he's starting to teach her about welding for his artwork . . ."

"Wow," drawled Sandy. "My dad didn't stick around long enough to find out what my name was gonna be."

That drew an uncomfortable silence till Laura said, "I'm sorry to hear that."

"I'm not," she said. "Mom wasn't. Why should you be?" She and Molly lagged a few steps behind, talking softly.

"What were we talking about?" Suzanne asked finally. Sandy's words had stopped the warm conversation like a bucket of ice water.

"That's really something," Sean pointed to Billy, who was saying a prolonged good-bye to his daughter. "A guy teaching a little girl how to weld."

Suddenly the light feeling was back, and Laura smiled as Billy handed the phone back to her. "She's just gone for one night, you know," Laura chastised him. "She'll be back in twelve hours."

"Well, I was working all day, and she was at school all day, and I only saw her for dinner before she left, so that's practically two days. Plus, she's going shopping with your mother the day after tomorrow . . ."

"Just wait till she starts dating," Ava called out as she came down the steps. "Then, it's not only that you never see them but they act like they have no idea who you are, or why you're trying to take away all their fun, when you do happen to catch a glimpse of them in the hallway."

"We're here already?" Sean asked, surprised. "That was fast."

"It's a small seacoast," Suzanne groaned. "And Ma, no Suzanne-as-a-teenager stories."

"I told you before, if you ever called me 'Ma' again, all bets are off." Ava smiled primly. "I just thought I'd come meet your lovely friends, and God knows, with your hostessing skills, I'm going to have to make sure everyone has a drink, because you won't."

"Mother, I'd be happy to. I just . . ."

"Just what I thought. Well then, I'll just have to do it myself." Ava sighed wearily, and then she instantly brightened. "Tea, anyone? Iced? Herbal? Vanilla Chai? Lemonade? Shout out your poison, or go thirsty."

"When will you learn?" Laura chided Suzanne, who was holding her head in her hands. "Ava will never be happy unless she's serving people, and she can't be truly happy unless she makes those she's serving feel completely put-upon."

Suzanne grinned at her new friend. It was good to know she wasn't the only one Laura could read like a book. Apparently she'd pored over Ava's story a time or two as well.

Everyone found themselves a comfortable spot in the courtyard while Ava brought out the trays. One of the great things about having snacks at the ready, apparently, was being able to feed large numbers of unexpected visitors at all hours of the night.

"So, after my wife was gone, I decided we needed to move into a new house, get a fresh start," Sean was saying to Suzanne. He ran a hand through his hair, which was thick and slightly graying, with no signs of receding, Suzanne noticed. That was important—a full head of hair was on the make-or-break list in her mind, and always would be. "I don't know if it was such a good idea, hindsight being 20/20 and all. I think maybe it was too much change, all at once—not that it matters now, but there were some rough years," he explained. "I just worry that . . ."

"You can't start second-guessing yourself like that, or you'll go crazy," Suzanne told him. "You made a choice. It's not like you can change it."

"Yeah, you're right. I know you're right. My oldest two seem okay, but my youngest two . . . it's years later, and they still can't seem to get their feet beneath them." He sighed, lighting up a Marlboro. "I'm sorry," he gestured with the cigarette, "is this okay?"

"It's not only okay," Suzanne put a cigarette between her lips demurely. "It's encouraged."

"Hello, Sean." Ava planted a warm kiss on his cheek. Somehow, she managed to ignore Sean's cigarette while giving Suzanne's a disgusted glare. "How are you? The boys?"

"Just fine," Sean said in his easy manner. "My two youngest aren't thrilled about having to go back to college after a summer of lying around playing video games, but fine. They would have gotten jobs," he said hastily, "but neither of them fancy working for their dad for the summer, and that's about all that's out there these days."

"In my day, summer vacation meant doing things outside: beach days, bike rides, stick ball, tag in the park, tree climbing. But this one," she rapped the top of Suzanne's head, "I could barely pry the books out of her hand to get her off the couch, and her kid, well, just try to come between that one and a computer." She shrugged. "What are you going to do? Each generation is more sedentary than the last."

"That's why your tush is so much tighter than mine, Grandma," Molly called out cheerfully. "All those years at the swimming hole gave you a great start."

"I don't see anything wrong with your tush," Sandy said softly, though the comment somehow traveled across the yard to Suzanne's ears.

Is this fun for you? Suzanne asked Laura's so-called Goddess. *Are you trying to make me lose my shit in front of all these people? And it's not intolerance. I don't want to hear anyone, male or female, commenting on my daughter's "tush" right in front of me.*

"This is just unfair." Brandon came down the steps. "Here, I spend the past week being my loving, adorable self, and you reward me by throwing a party and not telling me."

"Hey, darlin'," Molly called happily. "I thought you were spending the night curled up with your sociology books. C'mere, I've got someone I want you to meet."

Suzanne watched Brandon join the couple—there was no denying that at least for the moment, Molly and this crude girl were indeed a couple—and she felt guilt and relief in equal parts. If Brandon was there, likely little more than conversation would go on.

"Suzanne?"

"Hmmm?"

"You seemed a million miles away—everything okay?" Sean asked.

"Oh." She kicked herself. Was she spying on her daughter that obviously? "Sure, I'm fine. It's just, you know. Tough summer."

"I know what you mean. I heard through the grapevine that you're in the middle of a divorce?"

"Did you, now? Well, as it happens, the grapevine," she said wryly, throwing a knowing glare at Ava, who pretended to be too busy with her cookies and drinks to meet her gaze, "would be right."

"I'm a widower, myself," he allowed, taking a sip of iced tea. Suzanne was struck with a wave of compassion so huge it filled her chest. When he was talking about getting over Margie and new houses before, her mind had immediately leapt to divorce. Death had never occurred to her.

"Oh, I'm so sorry," she stammered. "I . . . I mean, how . . ."

"Is it okay if we don't talk about it?" he asked. "Recently, I had to kind of go into detail about it, and for now, I'd just rather leave it alone. Plus, I get pretty nervous the first time I'm talking to a pretty lady, so if you don't mind, I'd rather sit back and listen to you talk. If you want to. About anything."

Suzanne stopped, mid-exhale, almost choking on the smoke. She turned and looked at him, really looked at him, for the first time. She'd already noticed he was good-looking, but that was just force of habit. Now, she was trying to see if her bullshit detector was in better shape than when Buddy conned her into the paternity confusion.

"You're willing to sit back and listen while I talk?" Suzanne asked warily. "About anything I want? Even stuff like tabloid fodder or soap operas?"

"Umm . . ." He looked a little disturbed at the prospect before him. "If that's what you got, then I'm here for you."

"You're willing to listen, and you'll let me pick the topic," Suzanne marveled. "Are you sure you're a guy?"

Sean's easy chuckle seemed to go with his perfect jeans, his casual smile. "Last I checked."

"You want the wide-screen version," she asked, "or the Cliff's Notes?"

"Hmmmm, that's a toughie," he contemplated. "Tell you what, let's start with the Cliff's Notes, and if I need clarification, we can always go back to the original author's work."

"Okay." She looked at him sideways, from up under her eyelashes, smiling. He was awfully charming. It had been such a long time since she had paid attention to any man romantically, even just to flirt. Too bad she was too exhausted from a pathetic excuse for a marriage and far overdue divorce, and too overwhelmed with the prospect of college, a newly gay daughter, and keeping a close eye on her mother to even think of letting anyone light her fire.

"Okay. Let's see. I was seventeen years old, and I had a crush on the coolest guy in class. Not the cutest," she stressed the point, "the *coolest*. The one who flipped off Mr. Knauer when he barked at him in class for lighting a joint in study hall. He wore a leather jacket and torn-up jeans, and he rode a motorcycle. Anyway, he wasn't my type. I'd always gone for the good boys, the college-bound guys—you showed me a guy with a straight-A average and a pocket protector, and I showed you a potential boyfriend. I just didn't . . . I mean, the idea of dating anyone without a future really scared me, you know? I had zero interest in anyone outside my academic circle."

"So, what kind of magic did Mr. Motorcycle conjure up to turn your head?"

It was a question Suzanne had asked herself over and over in recent years, always in vain. "It was one unimpressive spell in the end, I'm telling you," she sighed. "I think, at the time, he was sort of mysterious, and . . ."

"Don't let her kid you." Laura leaned into the conversation. "From the start, he brought out the Mommy in her."

"That's not true!" Suzanne cried. "It was all about the lust, if you have to know. He actually brought out this, well, this absolute animal in me that I just didn't know existed until then."

"Just the sort of table talk every mother enjoys," Ava remarked, setting down her ever-present tray of iced tea.

"I'm with you, Grandma." Molly shuddered, then brightened. "Cinnamon bread! Thanks, Grandma!"

Brandon helped himself to a huge chunk. Suzanne watched enviously, knowing that if she ate a piece even a third that size, she could kiss zipping up her size eight jeans goodbye. "I'm officially declaring you a goddess of the first realm," he enthused.

Suzanne turned to Laura. "Is there such a thing?"

Laura shook her head. "I think he invented it just for Ava—ten bucks says he's an online gamer. That sounds like something one of them would say."

"Well, if I'm a goddess, and everyone's full and happy, then my work here is done. Goodnight, all," Ava told them. "I'm going inside before the mosquitoes eat me alive. I've got an important date tomorrow, and I don't intend to be covered with little red marks." She disappeared inside quickly, leaving them all hanging.

"Date?" Molly repeated. When Suzanne glanced over, she tried not to react to the sight of Sandy's arms around her daughter, her multipierced head lying on Molly's shoulder. "Did Grandma say she had a date?"

"That's what it sounded like," Suzanne agreed, looking down at her lemonade. "But who . . ."

"Take a wild guess," Brandon called, from his position on the grass. "Go on, just one wild, crazy guess."

Well, Suzanne thought, *what do you know about that?* What a very little amount of grease it had taken to get those wheels turning.

Her first date since Daddy . . . well, since Daddy.

"Okay, back to Suzanne's shady past." Laura was more than happy to color in the details of her friend's teenaged sex life, seeing as she did once have a front-row seat. "You see, Steve, her ex, had this no-one-understands-me James Dean kind of thing going on." She nodded her head dreamily. "Let me tell you, he had half the seniors and all the juniors and sophomores just lusting after him. They were all aching to wrap their little arms around him and save him." She pointed at Suzanne. "No one more than *this* one, though."

"That's the second time this night I've been called 'this one,'" Suzanne protested. "When did I become 'this one'?"

"I remember that." Billy climbed up and sat behind Laura, taking her silky blond hair into his hands. She closed her eyes and enjoyed his touch.

It occurred to Suzanne that they didn't look like a married couple. Instead, they looked like a couple of high school kids who'd snuck out for a late night date. Their attraction to each other was so obvious, so honest and real.

I want that, she realized. *Just like Brandon says, I want to 'get it' again. Is 'he' out there for me? My Billy? My Buddy?*

Billy went on, "Suzanne would run out to the parking lot every day to climb on the back of that motorcycle, and they'd tear off like crazy. It was straight out of a John Hughes movie."

"See, that's the thing," Suzanne sighed. "I don't remember any of that stuff. It's like that was some other guy, and the Steven I know now is a totally different person. I look at him now, and I can't even imagine him making me go all gooey."

"'Go all gooey,'" Sean nodded. "Yes, siree, I believe I know exactly what you mean."

"So, anyway," Suzanne continued, "one day I took a history test, and then right after it I took a pregnancy test. Both times I saw a big ol' plus sign staring right back up at me. I took twelve more EPTs, praying I'd get at least one minus."

"Thanks, Mom." Molly blew her another kiss from across the lawn.

"You know how happy I am *now* that it was a plus," Suzanne scolded. "And you're eavesdropping on the grown-ups, dear."

Molly turned back to her conversation with—what was her name again? The lyrics to *Summer Lovin'* popped into Suzanne's head. Oh yes: Sandy. Lily-white, virginal Sandy. She looked at the girl, who oozed sexuality. Not so much, in this case.

"How'd Steven take it?" Billy asked. "I didn't know him that well."

"Neither did I," Suzanne said with a laugh. "But in the end, he just sprang into action, God love him. He had a plan all ready. We'd get married the day after graduation, even though the baby would be born by then. Neither of us was eighteen yet, and I think he knew my parents wouldn't approve. We'd both stay in school and graduate, he decided. And we made a zillion plans for the future."

"And what was Ava's take on it?" Sean asked. "I can just imagine her blowing, like, six gaskets."

"She actually guessed before I worked up the nerve to tell her," Suzanne admitted. "Overnight, my boobs exploded, and I was retaining so much water it looked like I was showing. I'd been on the skinny side before."

"Beanpole with boobs," Laura commented. "I've got the yearbook to show it."

"So, *anyway* . . ." Suzanne glared at Laura, who was laughing, well pleased with herself. "One day, I came home from school, and she had a bunch of bags of maternity clothes on the kitchen table and said, 'I think we need to talk about this before your father figures it out, don't you?'" She laughed at the memory. "Oh, was she *mad*! She was going to kill Steve, she was going to torch his parents' house, she was going to ground me until my fiftieth birthday . . ."

"Does that mean you still can't come out and play?" Laura cried, grabbing her hand. "I'll sneak over to your house when she's at work!"

"And we'll do each other's hair and talk about boys!" Suzanne chimed in excitedly.

"All right!" Brandon chimed in. "When do we start?"

The entire group was hit with the giggles then, and it took some time to calm down.

"Does anyone want a beer?" Sandy said suddenly. "I've got a twelve-pack in my car."

"Sorry, I don't drink," Sean said.

"I'll pass," said Suzanne out of habit; drinking while living in a recovering alocholic's house seemed unduly mean, although Ava had told her time and again that keeping Suzanne sober wasn't part of her program. "So, you're a non-drinker too?" Suzanne asked Sean. "By choice or by necessity?"

"We'll get to that later." Sean waved her question away. "I want to know how it ended with Motorcycle Boy."

"Motorcycle Boy! From *Rumble Fish*!!" Billy and Suzanne cried in unison, a little too loudly. Molly and company looked up the way kids do when the adults are talking about something before their time.

"Oh, my God," Laura breathed. "S. E. Hinton, the teen writer who gave us *That Was Then, This Is Now*, and *most* importantly . . ."

"*The Outsiders*!" Suzanne and Laura chimed in together, off in their remembered world of eighties romance. Billy and Sean laughed. Molly groaned and put a hand over half her face—the half facing her mother—in a gesture that Suzanne couldn't distinguish as sarcastic or comedic.

She grimly staved the feeling off—*I'm having a nice time*, she realized, *and I deserve it, dammit.*

"How many times did you see the movie?" Suzanne asked Laura. "Six times at the theatre, and if I'm not mistaken, it was the first videotape I bought. That's the movie where everyone fell in love with Ralph Macchio or Matt Dillion, but . . ."

"I hear you," Laura was once again reading her thoughts. "I was Ponyboy Girl myself."

"Aren't you glad you started this?" Billy asked as the women gushed about the sexual appeal of C. Thomas Howell—an actor who had long fallen into obscurity—and Sean held his hands up innocently.

"I was just trying to make a witty crack about her ex. I didn't mean to get them started down Teenaged Hunk Memory Lane," he apologized. He looked up to find Molly tearing her attention from her date—who was busy disputing the politics of the long-dead Clinton administration with Brandon—and for just a minute, their eyes locked. Molly gave him a smile, one of the smiles that made her look more like the happy five-or-six-year-old she'd once been rather than the I am Lesbian Woman, Hear Me Roar that she was now. Suzanne, still partly caught back in the life and times of Mr. Howell, caught the exchange out of the corner of her eye, wondering what the hell it was all about.

"In our world," Laura was explaining now, "S. E. Hinton's books were second only to, maybe, Judy Blume's." She patted Sean's arm admiringly. "Boy, did you say just the thing to secure yourself a spot on her good side."

"I've been known to crack a book or two now and again," he explained modestly. "Accidentally, of course, while looking for a centerfold."

"*Anyway*," Suzanne said in a tone that properly chastised Sean, although it did nothing to stifle Billy's laughter, "to get back on topic, the first year—or three—was great." Suzanne said simply. "We had each other, we had Molly, we had the world's shittiest apartment, but we didn't care. We stapled fabric onto packing crates for end tables, placed a couple of plants here and there, hung some decorative lighting, and put throw rugs and some of our friends' attempts at artwork on the walls." She shrugged, remembering those days more fondly than she wanted to; it was so much easier to out-and-out hate the bastard who'd sucked her life away for all those years. She stared off for a moment, remembering those nights. Remembering wanting to rush home from whatever restaurant or bar job she was holding at the time, to climb into Steve's arms and rouse him for a quick round or two of bed-shaking before sleep claimed them both. There had been the time that Molly cried for two days straight. They'd rushed her to the ER after the receptionist at Molly's pediatrician's office suggested she might have broken her leg kicking it against her crib, but several x-rays showed that the leg was fine. Her whole body was perfectly fine, in fact; she'd just overcharged her whole nervous system. The only thing to do was to wait and she'd eventually tire herself out, the doctor said and offered to give them a medicine that would help Molly sleep. To Steve's dismay, Suzanne adamantly refused, terrified of giving her baby *any* kind of narcotic; by then she'd read enough to know that addiction was a genetic trait. Suzanne came home from her second job so depleted that she wanted to cry but could barely muster the strength to push the tears out. When she'd stepped through the front door, the house was blissfully quiet; Molly had finally knocked herself out, just like the doctor predicted. Steve had been at the table, holding his head in his hands. An ashtray full of Newburyport butts covered with lipstick told her that his mother's help had been required, and for once she didn't blame him. Wordlessly, he'd stood up and took her in his arms, and they both just stood there, clutching each other, two survivors in the dangerous and energy-killing game of parenthood. He'd kissed her, and a spark of passion she didn't know she had left in her arose. Her waitressing outfit flew across the room, his dirty jeans dropped almost of their own accord, and right then and there, on the floor his mother had so recently washed, they fucked away all the stresses of the past few days.

Yes, indeed, she thought, some of the first years had not been bad at all.

"What happened?" Sean prodded gently.

"What? Oh, I'm sorry," Suzanne said, pulling herself back to the here and now. "What happened? *Time* happened," Suzanne lamented. "*Everything* happened—life happened. I blinked twice, and suddenly Molly wasn't a baby anymore. She was six and in school and coming home with a long, daily tally of all the things her friends had that we couldn't afford: dance classes, swim classes, karate classes. Though, when Molly really wanted to get involved in something, Steve's mom or mine stepped in to cover those expenses, thank goodness. Still, it was embarrassing to ask." She shivered, as much from the memory as from the cool night air. "So I took a few classes in office management and sales, and managed to get jobs that paid better. But it still seemed like everyone we knew was just sailing right by us, making so much more money, with such a strong idea of where they were headed."

"Or at least giving the illusion they did," Laura winked at her. "Stop knocking yourself, sister. You're not so far behind."

"Thanks," Suzanne said softly. "The same can't be said for young Mr. Lauder. The more money I managed to bring home, the more he took license to do *nothing*. It wouldn't even have been so bad if he'd just helped with the housework."

"Whoa, let me get this straight," Billy said, "He's not working, and he's not lifting a finger around the house? Changing a diaper? Mowing a lawn? Does the word 'leech' mean anything to you?"

"It does now," she replied, hiding her face in her hands ruefully.

"Live and learn," Laura consoled her, rubbing her back. "Honey, none of this makes you Idiot of the Millennium. There are so many strong, smart women with practically the same story."

"I know. So I took on a night job, and then I'd come home to a filthy house because Steve had been too busy meditating or practicing his synthesizer or smoking pot to lift a finger." She tried not to let the anger seep into her voice, but just remembering that she'd put up with that for one minute made her crazy. "And the best part was, his mother often told him I wasn't being supportive enough."

"Not *supportive enough*?" Billy cried.

"What did she expect you to do, shake his dick for him after a piss?" Laura wanted to know. "I'd like to meet this woman, I really would."

"Oh, you can con yourself into believing all sorts of ridiculous crap when it comes to your kid." Sean nodded knowingly, sparking another Marlboro. "For years, my mom thought I was just too high-strung and sensitive to deal with menial things, like paying the bills or raising my kids, which is why I *had* to drink. Not my fault at all—or, more importantly, hers."

"See?" Suzanne patted him on the knee. A little charge sparked between her hand and his leg, and she nearly gasped, she was so startled.

She didn't dare look up to see if he'd felt it too, but suddenly there was heat, a hotness that hadn't been there just a moment before. It had been so long since she'd felt this way—or any version of it—that for a moment, she replayed the touch over and over in her mind.

Is that *what it feels like?* She tried to remember.

It had been over a decade since she'd felt that for Steve, and because faithfulness seemed a trait she was stuck with (likely a side effect of working too hard to conjure up any sexual energy), whenever she needed that bit of "oomph" when Steve was on top of her or she was discreetly giving herself a moment of pleasure in the shower (the one place she had any privacy), she usually stuck to people like Hugh Jackman or Hugh Laurie or Hugh Grant (what was it with those Anglos and their Hughs?). But thoughts of celebrities ripping her clothes off in a moment of passion couldn't give her the jolt she'd just felt, the jolt she'd completely forgotten existed.

She tried to shake it off and found she couldn't. Apparently the spark had a lingering effect.

Clearing her throat, she said lightly, "Oh, you know. Mommies and their little boys."

"And if I had a son, I'd be worse than all of them," Laura moaned. Billy smiled and didn't disagree. It was another endearing moment between them.

"So what was the straw?" Billy reached for the Old Milwaukee Suzanne hadn't opened. "That one thing that made you say, 'I quit'?"

Suzanne grinned and pointed across the yard at her daughter.

"That's her, right there: the last straw." She looked at her daughter, realizing yet again that Molly was ten times the young lady she'd been. "For years, she'd seen me work my ass off while her father sat on his, doing nothing, and apparently she grew to resent the hell out of him for it—and to think of me as something like a doormat." She winced, recalling the look of disgust that haunted Molly's eyes for the last few months of her marriage. "The day after she graduated . . . she made it pretty clear what she'd think of me if I stayed with him."

"Good for her," Billy called to Molly, who gave him a thumb's up right back. Sandy was stroking Molly's back now, and there was a lot of giggling going on.

From this angle, Suzanne could see four tattoos on Sandy's back. *What is it with my kid and body art? Jesus.*

"Oh, yeah," Suzanne said sadly. "And it was too bad, really, because they were close, once upon a time. Not as close as we were, but he gave her regular piano and guitar lessons. They were some of the few things he was really consistent with—until she turned nine or ten."

Right around then, Molly had started getting more interested in the funkier fashions of her days. She began collecting music that had nothing to do with her father's tastes, to his great dismay, and having her own opinion over whether the lead singer for Rush was actually a belter, as Daddy called him, or just a plain old screamer. That alone, Suzanne often thought, could have been the severing point.

"By the time she was twelve and had gotten her period and developed breasts, the separation was complete. He'd pulled away from her completely; it was like he just didn't know what to do with her. Like he was afraid of her because she was so attractive. Afraid that men would be attracted to her, and he didn't know how he'd handle that. I think she was hurt, at first, but by the time she came to talk to me about it, she'd seen enough of his 'life's conspiring against me, I need special treatment' act to feel anything but disrespect for him."

She sat up suddenly.

Had Steve's pathetic lack of parental responsibility turned her child off men forever? Could that do it? She'd snuck down to the library and scanned on the Internet (in case Molly happened to check the history on the browser, and Suzanne for the life of her couldn't figure out how to clear it). What little she could find left a lot of big, fat blanks.

Having spent so much time doing theater as a child, Suzanne knew that despite many "studies" to the contrary, homosexuals are born, not made. *Reminds me of the old joke,* she thought. *Your mom made you a homosexual? If I buy her the wool, would she make me one too?* Just as Ava had been an alcoholic from the moment she'd first drawn breath, so had Molly been what she is. *Did I just compare alcoholism to homosexuality? What is wrong with me?*

Dear God, did something happen to my baby girl and I didn't see it? Couldn't see it?

Don't be ridiculous, another part of her brain—the less hysterical, more rational part—soothed her. *Molly tells you everything. She'd have told you.*

But Molly hadn't told her everything, after all, had she?

She shook off the horrible thought. She would force herself to ask Molly—before she left, maybe even tonight—but before that happened, she needed to take a few deep breaths and collect herself. She shook her head again, pretending to shoo away the mosquitoes and no-see-ums that were out in abundance tonight, even though the city of Portsmouth usually tried to spray such pests away.

Why the hell am I acting like being gay is some kind of disease? Like it's some horrible affliction? she asked herself, and to her relief, it sounded like her own voice—neither the hysterical nor the super rational one, but just plain old her. *I know lots of gay people, and they're just people like everyone else . . . Some are nice, some are great, and some are assholes, just like the rest of the human race. Hell, some of my best friends are lesbians, after all,* as the old saying went, although she couldn't think of any lesbians she was tight with, just now.

"So that's your story." Sean clapped politely, once again taking her attention away from her daughter's fondling session. "Not exactly a summary, but the salient points came across."

"We're so proud of her." Laura reached over to squeeze Suzanne's hands. "She could have left long before she did, but those vows, those weren't just words to our girl. No sir; lots of other people would have given up on the bum much sooner."

That was sort of true, Suzanne reflected, in spite of the hokey way Laura put it. She'd never thought of it quite like that. Maybe she hadn't so much as wasted half her life as really, really tried to make her choices work. She'd made a commitment, and she was the type of woman who honored her word.

Oh, yeah, I definitely belong in PR, she thought, *if I can actually make that bullshit stick.*

She'd stayed with Steve for the same reason a lot of people clung to crappy marriages—out of fear, out of apprehension. Her marriage was a joke, but it was familiar, it was what she was used to. After years of coming home to the sound of Steve's music in the studio, could she really handle a silent house, all by herself? Just her and Molly?

But when she could take it no longer, she had left. She sat up just a little straighter, feeling slightly proud of herself.

Suzanne lit up a cigarette and suddenly realized that, somewhere in the past forty-five minutes, she had stopped waiting anxiously for the first opportunity to get all her guests on their feet and moving toward their cars. At some point before her ice tea glass was empty, she realized she was having fun. Not only was the evening fun but it was a kind of fun she hadn't had in a long, long time. The kind of fun that her life hadn't had time for in . . . Her eyes misted up alarmingly quickly, and she blinked them clear, thinking, *Well, let's just say it's been a while.*

Suzanne glanced over and saw Molly and Sandy sitting as close as two people could without being in each other's laps. Sandy's arm was around Molly's shoulders, and she was toying with the strands of Molly's long, auburn hair. They'd shifted from the topic of Billary and were now deep in a discussion about the state of the pop scene today, especially the artists who were little more than tabloid fodder, the kind of conversation you had on a first or second date when you were still feeling each other out, taking baby steps toward getting closer. She was relieved to see Brandon was still there keeping things from getting too heated between Sandy and Molly, and hated herself for it.

"I personally blame that arrogant little shit from Youtube," Sandy insisted, clearly implying Justin Bieber. "He's not only a joke of a musician, he spits on people, and he's walking around free as a bird."

It was dark, and they were at least twenty feet away, but there was a smile on Molly's face and a blush on her cheeks that Suzanne hadn't seen since—actually, she realized, this was a Molly she had never seen, a Molly that very few people had probably ever seen. She knew Molly despised Justin Bieber, but suspected that had very little to do with her daughter's smile.

"It just doesn't look like what you expected, huh?" Laura tilted her head toward the girls.

Suzanne lowered her voice to the barest whisper possible. On the Seacoast, a voice traveled easily, and Molly had ears like a bat, just like her grandmother.

"I keep trying to tell myself I'd be this uncomfortable if it were a guy hanging all over her," Suzanne admitted, breaking a cookie in half and crumbling chunks of it with her fingers. She'd just put out a cigarette and needed something to do with her hands in the twenty minutes before she had decided she'd allow herself another one. Watching Sean out of the corner of her eye, she had realized that was about the same allotment he allowed himself.

"You probably would," Laura said calmly. "This part, the actually seeing someone lustfully touching your daughter . . ."

"Keep your voice down!" Suzanne hissed.

"Sorry." Laura lowered her voice. "But the fact of the matter is, this means No More Little Girl. And looking at it—even though it might be a little different from what you had in mind—hurts. You're thinking all kinds of things—that now that she's seeing people, she won't need you as much, that she'll spend her free weekends with her dates instead of coming home to visit, but more than anything," she leaned forward and tapped Suzanne's hands lightly, "you're thinking that even though things might be a lot better than they once were, this still isn't an ideal society to be a gay chick in."

Suzanne glanced quickly at Billy and Sean, wondering what they had heard, if anything, but Sean had flown past high school tales to AA war stories.

That's where Mom knows him from, Suzanne thought, and oddly felt a wave of relief.

She supposed after watching her mother dive into gin and tonics and her husband light a bong the second he awoke, it probably wasn't such a wonder. She glanced at her cigarettes, which Steve had always claimed were much worse than any habit he might have.

But for the moment, Sean was in full storyteller mode, in the same hypnotic voice that had so charmed Molly, and Billy, an avid talker, was apparently also a rapt listener. From her experience with Ava, Suzanne knew that they could be awhile, and she was grateful.

"Can I ask you a question, Laura?"

"Anything but my weight—that info goes with me to the grave."

"How the hell do you always know exactly, to the letter, what to say?" Suzanne shook her head. "I've got to tell you, since you were once a self-centered, smug asshole, it's disturbingly unsettling."

Laura tossed her hair back, and there was that easy, happy laugh. Her hair, Suzanne noticed, wasn't too thin or too thick, but just right. It floated back down to her shoulders in loose waves. Yet another trait to envy about her, and Suzanne did.

"Yes, I was a smug, self-centered asshole in high school. I had all the right answers, but I had no idea what the real questions were." She nudged Suzanne's shoulder. "Besides, you were a spazmoid drama queen in school, bouncing off the walls so hard it made a thud each time you hit the floor, which was, quite frankly, often."

"Do you hear me denying a thing?" Suzanne asked. "I ate five candy bars a day and still wore a size four, that's how much I burned off in a day. And that was back in the day when they hadn't made zero a size yet, so in today's terms, I'd have been a two."

"Yeah, well, now we both know what we were doing—distracting ourselves from the drunks waiting for us at home." Once again, Laura got to the heart of the matter in a matter of moments, while Suzanne would have stumbled and stuttered over the topic for ten minutes before broaching it. "But, to answer your question, no." She shook that enviable hair again. "No to the supernatural. I *wish*—can you imagine how much dough I'd rake in if I could add a psychic to the regular staff?"

Suzanne laughed. With Laura, everything invariably went back to business, and that *was* just like high school. Some things never changed, as they say, and it was a comfort in her recently-turned-upside-down life.

"But it's easy to know *you*," Laura went on, "because I know me. I spent a long time getting to know *me*." She was smiling at her new friend, happily, without an ounce of reservation; her whole personality shone through in that smile. "And since we've, what do you want to call it, renewed our acquaintance . . ."

"That's implying we had one before," Suzanne interjected. "I think the extent of it was that we could probably pick each other out of a lineup and had just enough surface info to come up with a zinger or two when the situation called for it."

"If you have to get graphic, I suppose that's true." Laura pretended to look down her nose at Suzanne. In that moment, she looked like the prom queen about to stomp on the pregnant drama queen with her sharp wit. After all these years, it was still unnerving. "I've come to realize that you're not unlike me, well, apart from a law degree and a professional witch's license, that is."

"That must be true," Suzanne conceded, sipping her iced tea, wondering at the fact that there was actually such a thing as a professional witch's license. Or maybe Laura was pulling her leg. Hard to tell. To her intense relief, it was time to light up again. As soon as she put the cigarette in her mouth, Sean leaned forward and sparked his old-fashioned Zippo, touching the tip of the flame to her American Spirit. Their eyes met, there was an almost audible sizzle, and then he smiled, winked, and turned back to listen to Billy, whose turn it was to speak, apparently.

Okay, he's hot. I admit it, no question, she thought. *But don't, I repeat, do not mistake sexual attraction for anything other than what it is. Of course it feels intense—anything would after all these years.*

She couldn't remember the last time she'd had sex with Steve, but it had been sometime before the new millennium. He'd complained and pushed and begged for a while, then discovered all kinds of ways to deal with his needs on the Internet. Suzanne, thoroughly relieved, made sure he had his own Hewlett-Packard in the basement.

"It's funny," she said to Laura, sneaking one last peek at Sean. "At the reading, that's what I thought to myself. That back in high school, we had so much in common, but no one, least of all us, ever guessed it. We could have been a real comfort to each other."

"Coulda, shoulda, woulda." Laura waved it off, biting into a cookie she held in one hand and running the other through her husband's paint-flecked hair.

"But," Suzanne lowered her voice to a decibel only the poodle next door might hear, "the things you've said about Molly, they've all been spot on. It helps, you know? To hear this stuff out loud, to have someone actually say it."

"Corny, but true," Laura admitted. "Now, I don't have a gay child— that I know of," Laura corrected herself. "After all, Hermione's young still, although she's had 'boyfriends' every school year, starting with a kid with black hair named Angus." She nodded at Suzanne's aghast expression at the boy's unfortunate name. "The big attraction to him, she said, was that his teeth were so white they burned her eyes."

"And that's a good thing?" Suzanne asked doubtfully.

Laura shrugged, giggling. "To Hermione, it was. She's also been moon-eyed over more boy band members than I care to think of."

Suzanne snorted, remembering the walls of Molly's room. "Molly used to have posters of One Direction up on her wall," Suzanne realized. "But, now that I think of it, she never begged and pleaded for tickets to their concerts, even though her friends were all going. I thought she was old enough to be aware of our budget situation and didn't want us to feel bad by asking for something she knew we couldn't give her."

"Yeah," Laura marveled, "kids are usually real considerate about that sort of thing."

Suzanne laughed, taking a fake swat in her friend's direction. "Thinking about it now . . . she was probably doing what the other kids were doing. Just because they were doing it." Suddenly her heart ached for that long ago-Molly, thinking she was different and desperately trying to fit in by pinning up posters that had no meaning for her. Had she been scared? Had she thought there was something wrong with her? Had she thought pretending to swoon over Justin and Lance would make these strange feelings go away? And why hadn't she told her mother what she was feeling? Why hadn't she come to her?

Maybe because she saw me getting treated like a doormat all those years, and she didn't respect me, Suzanne realized, a lump forming in her throat that she tried to politely cough away. *Maybe something did happen to her, and I was too busy or too tired to notice, and I didn't help her. Maybe she didn't like me any more than she liked her father. I can't think about that now.*

She glanced over just in time to see Sandy nibbling on Molly's earlobe, while Molly stroked her hair as she casually spoke to Brandon.

She hastily pulled her eyes away, but the image was burned into her brain. She felt as if she'd invaded Molly's privacy, but then again, Molly wasn't going out of her way to be private.

I really need a break from thinking of my child's sexuality. Or seeing it.

"So, while I don't *know* what it's like to have a child come out to me," Laura was saying as if she could read her thoughts, "I can imagine what it would be like. This is a patriarchal society, no matter who says different. I worry about all women and the things they face. Men don't have to freak out about walking to their cars at night, for example, or getting told that their body is an asset to a white-collar job. But to be a gay woman?" Laura shook her head. "God love her for accepting herself, but I'm sure she knows she's got a hard row to hoe ahead of her. She'll hear ten zillion jokes from assholes asking if they can watch, asking if she's sure she's gay or maybe it's because she's never been with a 'real' man before. Like I said, it's better than it used to be," she sighed, "but it still ain't easy. I see enough of them at my store every day to tell you that. The only thing worse would be if she were fat."

"If she were fat?" That came completely out of left field. "What does that have to do with it?"

Dear God, maybe because Suzanne's size-eight jeans weren't zipping up so well and she'd had to discreetly buy a pair of size tens from Déjà Vu, the chicest second-hand store on the Seacoast. Maybe Laura was hinting that fatness was coming, and she should try to get Molly to do something about it.

Laura, once again utilizing the near-psychic powers Suzanne was sure she possessed, read her thoughts and kicked her ankle.

"The average size for an American woman is five-foot-four, one hundred forty-four pounds, and size twelve. Both you and Molly are much taller than five four, and you both have a ways to go before you're there."

"Not that far," Suzanne mumbled, but Laura ignored her.

"I'm just saying," Laura sighed, "that this country will forgive anything—alcoholics, drug users, wife beaters, people who cheat on their income taxes—they'll come to terms with all that crap. But there's nothing in this world that they hate more than a fat chick. How pathetic is that? But we can't fix it unless we say it out loud. And that sick POV really, *really* needs fixing."

Suzanne closed her eyes, knowing Laura was right, and hating it. Hadn't she herself, at the reading, noticed distastefully that there were a number of women there who could use a little exercise, to put a polite spin on it?

I'm no better than they are, she thought despairingly. The realization that she had been conditioned by her society to be this way was a cold comfort.

In addition to the possible prejudice she'll face, now I have to worry that one day she'll eat too many Klondike bars and get crapped on even more.

"Speaking of alcoholism, insofar as being a survivor of someone bitten by the bottle," Laura steered the topic to another topic, and Suzanne was desperately grateful, "I didn't figure that out until Ava first came into the store. But once I did, it was like all these puzzle pieces fit into place. All the things I thought I knew about you in school . . . I suddenly felt like I knew you."

She reached over with such a comically sudden fierce hug, it made Suzanne burst out laughing.

"That's why I was so glad to see you—I felt like we were alike enough to be sisters, sitting three desks apart, and never knew it." She smiled and touched Suzanne's hand again, a gesture she performed often and one that Suzanne felt profoundly comforting, "But then, I knew it, so I figured when we bumped into each other again, well, we'd have a lot to talk about."

"That's how I feel, too. Exactly how I feel—like, we could have been together talking about our problems rather than competing with each other."

"Yeah, but again, hindsight is a beautiful thing." Laura sneaked a drag off Suzanne's cigarette, careful that Billy didn't see it. "How long has she been sober?"

"A long time, about seventeen years." Suzanne smiled. "She said she realized she was going to miss out on Molly's upbringing if she didn't clean up her act. So, she cleaned up her act."

"Must be nice," Laura's blue eyes clouded. "My mom can't seem to choose Hermione over the rum or the Valium."

"I'm so sorry, sweetie." Suzanne didn't know what to day. She tried to imagine what it would be like to have a mother who'd never stopped boozing, and, thankfully, she couldn't. She wanted to reach into her mind and find comforting words, the way Laura had done for her, but there was nothing there except another "I'm so sorry."

"I know. But it's like they say: That's who she is; it doesn't have to change who I am. It *does* mean that Hermione has absolutely no contact with her grandmother, but that's just the way it is." She brooded a few minutes, sneaking another drag. "It's just that when she's sober, she's . . ."

"The coolest, smartest, sweetest person you could ever want to meet," Suzanne finished for her. She squeezed Laura's hand. "Trust me, these alchies, they are likeable, clever, adorable creatures; that's how they get away with so much crap."

"You know, you're right—you're exactly right," Laura marveled, and Suzanne was proud to have found an insight to offer after all. "You're so fucking smart. UNH is lucky to get you."

"I always said that about you," Billy chimed in affectionately. "After high school, after you nearly gave birth in the cafegymatorium, I still always said, 'that Suzie girl, she might dress like she's stuck in the nineties . . .'"

"Hey!"

"And she might have a voice like a eunuch with the croup, if you have trig with her first thing in the AM . . . But," he added sagely, "in spite of all these flaws, and the many others that we haven't discovered yet, I always said that Suzie girl was *smart*. And fertile."

"Fertile?" Sean asked. "You could tell that back in high school?"

Oh, Lord, Suzanne groaned. *Here it comes.*

"Her water broke at graduation," Billy informed Sean cheerily, and the expression on Sean's face was such that they all burst out laughing; so hard, in fact, that Suzanne wasn't sure, but she thought a little pee might have leaked out.

"I can't believe I used to have a crush on you," Suzanne sighed. "What wasted daydreams."

"You used to have a crush on me?" Billy brightened.

It was Laura's turn to groan. "Okay, you've made not only his day but his year, and I'm going to have to hear about it until the end of time. Haven't you heard of the chick rule, Thou Shall Not Covet the Ass of Thy Girlfriend's Future Mate?"

A real live girlfriend. Well, it's about damn time.

Suzanne tried to remember the last time she'd had a really close girlfriend, and couldn't. There hadn't been time to bond with anyone, with two jobs and a full-time child to look after. Two, if you counted her husband.

She glanced over to see how Molly's "date" was going. To her dismay, the kids had taken off at some point in the past few minutes.

"Did anyone see where they went?"

All shook their heads, and Suzanne tried to shrug casually and push her anxiety away. After all, Molly was eighteen. She didn't need to be policed twenty-four-seven anymore. And she would surely resent any attempt Suzanne made toward that end.

There are things I don't need to see and things I don't need to know, she reasoned. It assuaged her somewhat to realize she would feel this way if Molly just disappeared with a guy.

Molly can take care of herself, she realized. *She really and truly can. I can still care about her, but I don't have to worry about her every second of the day anymore.*

No Ava, no Steve, no Molly to look after.

For the first time in *eighteen years*, this was a night to herself, with a handsome and interesting man at her side. Placed there by her daughter, she discerned with amusement.

Suddenly the cool evening seemed less a night to load herself down with guilt than a night of tingling possibilities.

"So, Sean," Suzanne asked, "what do you think my daughter had in mind when she corralled you to the bookstore and then dropped you off in my lap?"

"That it's time to get Mommy laid?" Billy guessed. "You see, this is why you have kids."

"That's just it," Suzanne pointed out. "I'm not sure how comfortable I am having my daughter go trolling for men for me."

"Well, actually, I'd like to think," Sean said drolly, "that she saw something in me and thought, 'Hey, he might just get along with my mom.' You know, maybe it had a little do with me and my enormous . . . charisma, rather than just my stud services."

"She's trying to take care of you," Laura whispered. "She's watched you take care of everyone else your whole life; now it's your turn."

That's sweet, that's thoughtful. That's pure, one hundred percent Molly . . . But I'm not ready for her to be doing that. No, not yet.

But it looked like the time was here, and there was nothing she could do about it. This was a graduation of a whole other kind.

To stave off the feeling of loss, Suzanne took out another Spirit and dipped her head into Sean's flame. For the first time since the spark of his touch, her full attention was focused on the man beside her. She was pretty sure Dr. Phil—or any other shrink of the moment—would advise against jumping into any sort of comingling with another member of the sex that she was currently divorcing.

But hey, I don't have to marry the guy, she thought. *In fact, chances are huge he won't propose before the evening's out. So maybe it's okay to enjoy just a nice conversation or two with a man my daughter thought was good enough for me to go out with.*

"Okay, Sean, your turn." She gave her full and complete attention, for the first time, to the handsome man before her. "Give me your Cliff's Notes, starting with where you know my mother from." No need to let him know he'd already tipped his hand.

Sean looked at her gravely for a moment and then smiled, bracing himself for the story. "Well, let's see, just so's you know where I'm coming from, I should probably tell you, I never met a beer I wasn't best friends with . . ."

NINETEEN

$\mathcal{U}$t was sixteen hours later, and Suzanne was feeling particularly pleased with herself. She had dreaded the meeting with the lawyers—after all, Steve's mommy's money brought in a much better lawyer than what little savings she'd had. But Suzanne wanted what was coming to her—which would have been the entire house, since Steve's mother paid for the occasional dryer or lamp or tank of oil, but the mortgage each month came out of her salary.

On the Seacoast, you didn't get a $300,000 house without a hefty down payment. She'd used the money her dad's life insurance left her, determined not to ask Steve's Mommy for a dime, although Steve had begged her to. (Try as she might, she had never been able to think of Steve's mommy by her name, or as Mrs. Lauder or Mom L. Aloud, and in her mind, she'd been Steve's Mommy, period.) After all, he'd argued, a hundred thousand dollars could buy him a lot of newer musical equipment, a van to carry around all this equipment to his nonexistent gigs, and a stageworthy wardrobe for these nonexistent gigs.

"It could be just the break we've been waiting for," he'd argued. "I'll use your dad's life insurance money for new equipment, and my mom will take care of the down payment on the new house. You know we won't have to pay her back."

But Suzanne wasn't a starry-eyed eighteen-year-old anymore. After a decade of being bought and sold with Steve's Mommy's money, she was very jaded twenty-eight-year-old. She wasn't about to give that woman one more thing to hold over their heads, one more thing to beat into Steve's head that he owed her and therefore she owned him.

Furthermore, she saw no reason to invest in equipment and a van when, in the ten years since their marriage, he'd never played out a single time. He insisted he was getting his album ready, but she figured that if he was truly the genius he and his family claimed he was, ten years would have been more than enough time to record an album in his little home studio and start promoting it in some of the local pubs to try to get the attention of a booking agent.

But Steve didn't do that, had never done *any* of that. Steve would work and work and work on a song until it was finished, then decide it wasn't his "vision" and put it away to work and work and work on the next song. A full bong, of course, was always by his side. The only concerts Steve would ever play, she'd realized long ago, were the ones in his head when he was stoned off his ass.

So, her father's insurance firmly in hand, she'd flatly refused to buy more equipment for Steve's studio. Steve had had a tantrum that lasted for months. He actually threatened to leave, but when she started packing his bags for him, he'd panicked and dropped that strategy pretty damn fast—it was almost a record.

She put twenty thousand in a trust for Molly's education—which, it turned out, was totally unnecessary, but it would make a nice nest egg for when she graduated, and that was good to know. The rest, every penny, went for the down payment on the house. She'd thought of it as her house only twice—when she signed the papers and the first day they moved in.

But the only part about the house that was hers was the money that went to sustain it. While she was at work, Steve decorated it with his usual brass Buddhist figurines, loads of plants, and pictures of musicians he admired. She made double mortgage payments whenever she could—she'd read somewhere that would lop years off the time it took to pay it off—but it wasn't often she could manage that.

Considering all this, she expected the fight to be long and weary, but surprisingly, Steve's lawyer had made an offer that wasn't ridiculous. In fact, it was downright generous.

"The value of the house has increased, since you purchased it, from $300,000 to nearly $420,000," Steve's lawyer intoned. Portsmouth had developed like mad in the late eighties and nineties, so she'd expected as much. "Mr. Lauder feels," Steve's lawyer continued, "that since you provided the down payment on the house, plus all of the mortgage payments, you deserve the entirety of the house's value, plus equity."

Suzanne looked at her lawyer, shocked. "This is a trick, right?" she whispered to her counselor fervently. "He's just going to give me $420,000? Not the Steve I know."

Her lawyer silenced her. "We haven't heard what he wants yet. That could make a lot of things clear."

So she'd sat back, waiting.

"In return, Mr. Lauder asks that since you paid for a great deal of his musical equipment, worth nearly $40,000, that he be allowed to keep said instruments."

She and her lawyer waited. But apparently, that was it.

"So, he's going to give me all the money for the house," Suzanne finally managed to say, "and all he wants is to keep his equipment? What the heck would I do with it?"

Steve's lawyer shrugged. "He's trying to be generous," he explained gently, "as he truly doesn't want this divorce to go through."

"So he's hoping that you'll melt at the mere mention that he'd be willing to do such a thing," her lawyer finished.

She was stunned, to say the least. She hadn't thought—or cared—if Steve still loved her in years. But that kind of money was an awful lot of love, no matter how you sliced it.

I suppose now is the part where I'm supposed to crumble and start crying, call Steve and tell him we can work it out.

It made her sad that he thought such an offer was even possible. Steve was a child, but granted, it wasn't entirely his fault. First Mommy had catered to his every whim, and after years of trying to get him to grow up, she'd taken over the job. She also supposed she should feel guilty about all of these things. But she didn't—try as she might, she couldn't. Steve had sucked so much out of her over the years that there just wasn't anything at all left to give him. *And if that's a bad thing, I can't worry about that. Not while I'm looking at a half-million dollar check with my name on it.*

"I'll take the offer," she said firmly, before Steve or his lawyer or, more likely, his mother could run in and change his or her mind. She signed where they told her to sign, and to her surprise, Steve's lawyer handed her a check right then and there. Including equity, the amount Steve was paying her was just over half a million dollars.

Suddenly she felt dizzy and leaned over to whisper, "Please get me to my bank. Right now."

Her lawyer smiled, reading her thoughts. "He's already signed the papers—he can't cancel it."

"I don't care," she whispered ferociously. "Take me to my bank. Now." Then she turned to Steve's lawyer. "Where did Steve get this kind of money, anyway?"

"He found a buyer for the house," The lawyer answered smoothly. Suzanne's heart dropped, just a little. Maybe she had paid for it, but it had been Steve's house, down to every last throw rug and decoration, not to mention the herbal garden in the well-groomed backyard (it was the one chore he took on without an argument). He was almost always there. It was his little corner of the world where no one could bother him.

"Well," she said finally, "tell him I'm sorry he's going to have to move, but . . ."

"Oh, he doesn't have to move," Steve's lawyer said smoothly, and suddenly Suzanne felt like an idiot.

Of course.

Mommy had bought the house, Mommy had coughed up the extra equity, and Mommy was paying for this lawyer. Now that Suzanne was out of the picture, Mommy was probably having to do a lot more attending to her demanding son. Maybe this was her way of telling Suzanne she understood.

Or maybe it's kiss-off money, making me promise to stay away from him.

She wouldn't have minded that, and for a moment wondered if she could get it in writing that they would no longer speak to each other. A glance down at the check, however, got her up and moving, and she stood in line at the bank impatiently, waiting her turn to deposit the money. The cashier's face had gone white at the amount, and Suzanne laughed.

Since Steve's mom shared the same bank, the transaction would go through immediately. Suddenly her battered bank card, which usually caused her so much stress when she looked at it (wondering if there was enough for a pack of cigarettes before her next shift) suddenly looked like freedom.

This would definitely take a while to sink in.

She floated home in a daze, stopping at a couple of stores, looking at some clothes she would have considered way too expensive. The thought that she could buy them, if she wanted to, made her burst into giggles, right in the middle of the boutique. The salesgirls looked at her warily, and she looked at them apologetically, unable to stop the giggling, and fled the store in search of a latte and muffin at Breaking New Grounds.

She ate while she walked home, sipping slowly, eating in small bites, so when the giggles invariably returned (which they did, a couple of times) she wouldn't choke to death. A check for over half a million dollars. The thought made her double over with laughter. A concerned mother with two kids in car seats pulled over to ask her if she was okay, if she needed any help.

"I'm fine," Suzanne said happily. "Better than I've been in a long, long time."

Watching the mom drive away, she realized she truly was better than she'd ever been. Her daughter wasn't pregnant, her divorce was finally complete, her college years were just about to begin, she had a nest egg to fall back on, and last night she'd had a pseudo-date with a very cute man.

She barely knew what to make of it all.

Could it be that that my life is really working out? Is it? Don't even think it! she scolded herself. *You'll jinx it! Now, knock wood, turn around three times and spit!* She giggled. After all this time, it felt damn nice to be silly again.

As she was thinking these happy thoughts, her nonpregnant daughter and Brandon came up the walk.

"So, what's up, my darlings?"

She gestured to give each of them a hug and a kiss, but Molly gave her the half-hearted, perfunctory pat on the shoulder. Suzanne didn't mind; she knew that "hugs from your mom" could be a drag. Nothing, absolutely nothing could dampen her spirits today. She sat back down again, reaching for her cigarettes.

"Where have you guys been?"

"Brandon had never been on the *Thomas Leighton.*" Molly looked down the road, obviously bored beyond belief. "So we did that, then we had coffee in Market Square and people-watched."

"You've got a huge mix of people in the Seacoast. I used to spend the summers in Maine. It's so predominantly white there." Brandon showed Suzanne his sketchbook. "But here you've got all kinds. I got some great sketches, I think. Tell me what you think."

"I didn't know you drew." Suzanne flipped through the pages, impressed. "Wow, these are really, really good, Brandon. You even got the guy who drives the horse and buggy. Chris, I think his name is—isn't it, Molly?"

"Yeah," Molly answered listlessly. "It's Chris. Chris, the Buggy Driver."

"You even got the tiny scar on his cheek down pat," Suzanne said approvingly. She studied the drawing for a few more moments, then handed it back. "Are you going to be a, what do you call it, graphic artist?"

"Actually, I'm . . ."

"He's going to be a psychologist, Mother," Molly snapped. "I told you that on the very first day you met him."

Suzanne stared at her daughter, startled and a little hurt.

"You'll have to forgive me, sweetie," she said calmly, "if I haven't troubled myself to commit his entire life story to memory."

An icy tension settled like a fog between the two women.

"Hey," Brandon said suddenly, "you're in a really good mood. Does this mean your meeting . . . ?"

"Yes!" Suzanne took Brandon's distraction gratefully. "Yes, it went well. So much better than well, I can't even tell you. And it's over, done, finito!!!" She offered Brandon a high-five, which he matched so hard her hand stung a little. "Wow, you got game for a gay guy."

"So they tell me," he said smugly. Molly sighed harshly and rolled her eyes.

"So, now all I have to do is sit back and wait for my information about the January semester to come in the mail and figure out how to spend the next three months."

"I wish my mom would go back to school," Brandon said. "She works in the principal's office at the high school. It doesn't take as much skill as it does patience, and she comes home completely fried."

"Yay, Mommy. Good for you," Molly said. Her tone was blasé.

Suzanne forgot about her sudden windfall. She felt the last of her ebullient mood slip away as she looked at Molly, whose eyes were blazing with things she'd been thinking and was now going to say.

Maybe that's a good thing, she tried to convince herself. *Maybe this is the way we need to do this, to get everything out in the open.*

"Molly, love," she carefully put her latte down and folded her arms, "is there something you'd like to say to me?"

"There is." Molly folded her arms right back and looked squarely at her mother. Steam was practically rolling out of her nostrils. "As a matter of fact, there really, really is."

"Well," Suzanne asked, "what's stopping you?"

"Okay, girls, let's just . . ." Brandon tried to interject.

"You want to know what my problem is?" Molly fired at her mother. "I'll freakin' tell you what my problem is. You're a hypocrite, Mother."

"What?!" Suzanne gasped even before the full slap of the word had impacted her.

After a moment of tension so thick it threatened to bend the branches of Ava's maple tree, Brandon asked helpfully, "Does anyone want a Coke?"

"No thank you, Brandon. I'd like my daughter to repeat what she just said," Suzanne said, as she tried to hide the fact that her breath was coming in heaves. She would not let Molly see how deeply she'd stung her; that was another lesson she'd learned from Steve.

"Oh, I could repeat myself," Molly replied icily, "but I think you heard me."

"Yes, I heard you," Suzanne replied, still stunned, "but I'm having just a little trouble believing what I'm hearing. Have you *met* me?"

"Because," Brandon went on, "if anyone wanted Cokes, I could run to the store and get some."

"You need to explain yourself, lady," Suzanne spat out, really angry now. She hadn't called Molly "lady" since she'd stolen the family car in the middle of the night and driven it to a friend's house at the age of thirteen. Worrying about the possibility of car accidents and abduction had nearly driven Suzanne insane.

But this definitely felt like a "lady" moment, if ever there was one.

"Explain myself?" Molly wasn't backing down, not an inch. "You see, the thing is, Mother, you *lied* to me. My entire fucking life, you lied to me."

"I don't drink sodas myself—I'm a vegan," Brandon interjected, "but I'd be happy to go get them. I could use a good walk. Walks are good," he finished lamely. It didn't matter. He could have recited the entire Bhagavad Gita and his words would have made no impact.

"When?" Suzanne demanded. She reached for her cigarettes and noticed her hand was shaking—just a little, but shaking nonetheless. *Dammit!* She cleared her throat, sparked the lighter, and pulled a cigarette out of the pack, trying to buy a moment to get herself back together. After a few drags, she spoke again, this time in a tone much closer to her normal voice—albeit slightly louder than usual. "When the hell have I ever lied? In your whole entire life, when the hell have I ever lied to you?"

"You *did!*" Molly fired back. "You did when you said that all you ever wanted was for me to be happy. That was a lie."

"Of course I said all I wanted was for you to be happy. That's what I want more than anything in this world! I want you to be happy more than I want *me* to be happy! In fact I couldn't *be* happy unless *you* were happier than I am!" Suzanne raged.

"Oh, that is *crap!*" Molly screamed back. "That is crap, and you know it, Mother!"

"How *dare* you say that to me?" Now it wasn't just her voice that was shaking; her hands, her shoulders, everything seemed to be twanging like a violin string, but there was no music coming out of anywhere.

"Calling all hypocritical mothers!" Molly shouted at the top of her lungs. Suzanne looked up and down the street, and sure enough, the Schwartzes and the DeCaturs were both idling about in their yards. Mrs. Steinmann was walking extra slowly to her car, but Suzanne knew from Ava that this was probably due to hemorrhoids.

"Molly, just lower your . . ."

"I'm a lesbian!! A *dyke*!!" Molly shouted, and Suzanne sighed and waved politely to their elderly audience. Pointing out the listening neighbors to Molly would only fuel her fire now. She'd just have to send them each a hanging plant later. Or a bottle of Hermione's foot-soaking cream from Goddess Treasures.

"I'm aware of that." Suzanne smiled broadly as she waved, trying to diffuse the traveling sideshow aspect of this scene. "In fact, I'm so aware of it, I watched a girl named Sandy practically maul you right in front of me, and even though watching my child in any kind of romantic act makes me incredibly uncomfortable, I sat there, and I dealt with my discomfort."

"Wow." Molly was aghast and then began clapping. "Good for you, Mom! I didn't realize how hard this had been on *you*! But to hear that you *dealt with your discomfort*—that's tremendous. In fact, that's really, really big of you, Mom." Molly clasped her hands and bowed. There was no way the neighbors were going anywhere now. Molly dropped the act, and a sneer crossed her pretty features. "But it doesn't change the fact that ever since I told you I was a lesbian, you've been treating me like I have the plague."

"I have *not*!" But something in Molly's words tugged at her. She'd been uncomfortable with her daughter for the first time ever, hadn't she? But not because she was ashamed of her but because . . .

"Gays are great, gays are fun, some of your best friends are gays, but it's different when it's your own daughter, isn't it, Mother? Then it's arm's length all the way!"

The trembling threatened to get worse, so Suzanne crossed her arms, putting her shaking hands under each armpit.

"Did it ever occur to you I had some things that were weighing on my mind—things that were causing me a boatload of stress, wondering how the rest of my damn life was going to play out? Things that your friend here was considerate enough to ask about, but which seemed to completely slip your mind?" Suzanne swallowed, trying to get the sandpaper out of her throat. "You are way out of line, little girl. *Way* out of line."

"Getting called on your bullshit hurts," Molly ignored everything her mother said—she was finally acting like a typical teenager, Suzanne thought—and tilted her head to the side, looking at her mother knowingly, "when you constantly preach love and tolerance, doesn't it?"

"Moll," Brandon said softly, putting a cool hand on her overheated shoulder. "Come on, be fair. You've had years to work this out; she's had a couple of days."

Years? Suzanne thought in dismay. *She's known for years?*

"Take it easy?" Molly barked at him furiously. "Damn it, Brandon, whose hag are you, anyway?"

"I like to think of myself as the Universal Hag," he said sagely. It was a funny line, but Suzanne didn't have a laugh to give up just now.

"And anyway," Molly went on, turning some of the heated anger to her friend, "it's so easy for you to say. It must be nice sitting on your side of the fence, Bran—your family practically threw you a party when you came out."

And that was when Suzanne decided she'd had enough. She may not have been the perfect mother, but she was a good one, and she had tried every step of the way. Every decision she made had been with Molly's best interest, not her own, at heart. Every extra job she took, every night she spent poring over the Internet, trying to learn calculus so she could help her daughter with it at the table after dinner. Whatever else she was, she realized, she did not deserve this tirade.

"Yes, Molly." Suzanne suddenly stopped shaking and dropped her hands from their defensive posture. She looked at her daughter and spoke in a voice both calm and clear. "You're absolutely right. They *did* just about throw him a party. And why do you think that was?"

For a second, the furious arrogance that had been smeared across Molly's face faltered, just a little. "What?"

"Why is it, do you think, that Brandon's parents were so damn happy," Suzanne repeated, in an equally calm voice, "when he finally came out to them?"

Molly looked at her mother for a long moment, through a thick sheen of tears and betrayal. "Because they love him, and they accept him," she breathed. "No matter who or what he is. Crazy me, I thought you felt that way about me too." She stormed off, leaving her mother and the Universal Hag staring after her.

It was maybe an hour and a half later. They were back in the courtyard, and Suzanne was on her seventh cigarette.

"Now," Brandon puffed out his chest in his self-designated role as mediator. "Let's try this again. Only this time, no one's allowed to yell—to raise their voices at all, in fact."

"But she . . ." Molly began, but Brandon immediately cut her off.

"Bup, bup, bup." He wagged a finger. "Our control over our speech is what separates us from the animals. Well, the fact that we talk at all separates us even more, I suspect. Anyway, this time, we're going to try the fine art of really listening. Capisce?"

"Capisce?" Suzanne groaned. "Oh, yeah, Buddy mentioned you'd been watching a lot of *The Sopranos* on On Demand."

"Are we all agreeing to the rules?" Brandon inquired. Molly and Suzanne shrugged, then crossed their legs and their arms in unison. It took all of Brandon's willpower—and an oft-employed mental image of his nanna in a teddy—not to laugh.

"Suits me." Molly was aiming for an I'm-too-cool-to-give-a-shit tone, but her incessantly bouncing leg belied her blasé attitude.

"The rules will do just fine, Brandon," Suzanne coolly agreed.

"So," he clapped his hands together before him, "who wants to go first?"

The bitter silence stretched out and threatened to blow up the courtyard, then the street, then the world at large.

"Come on, someone's got to go first," Brandon urged. "Anyone? Anyone? Bueller? Bueller? Okay." Suzanne couldn't help but think that she could see the counselor he was studying to be in him already. "It needs to be totally fair; should we draw straws? No, wait. I've got a coin, we could . . ."

"Excuse me." Suzanne raised her hand slightly and spoke in the clipped, polished voice she reserved for customers at restaurants who had really bad attitudes, or in general when she was really pissed off. "Before we begin, my daughter made some pretty serious accusations of me, and I really feel like she owes me an apology. What she said," she pointed at her daughter, "I did not deserve, and I want that acknowledged immediately."

"Tell that woman," Molly replied, equally polished, "that I'm not going to apologize for holding the mirror up to her face."

"Well, this has been fun, Brandon, but," Suzanne started to lift herself out of her chair, but Brandon gently pushed her back down.

"Come on, come on, this is crazy," he implored. "Do you think it was easy for me to come out to my family? And we all worked it out. And if we, the dysfunctional yet loving family that we are, can do it, so can you."

"Clearly," Molly said frostily, "your family is different than ours, I'm sad to say."

"Me too." Suzanne nodded.

"No—not so different. Look, Suze." He sat down next to her on the bench. "You should hear the way Molly talks about you. She talks about you *all* the time."

"She does?" Suzanne was surprised but wary. After eighteen years of being manipulated with false compliments by her husband, she wasn't about to fall for anything now, at least not without cold, hard proof. "Really?"

"Oh, yeah," Brandon went on, ignoring Molly's burning looks. "And it's like you're not only her mom but you're, like, this person that she really gets, who really gets her, who's her best, best friend . . . maybe even, you know, sort of a role model."

Suzanne looked away at his last statement as she ground out the hastily smoked cigarette. What Brandon just said—no, it couldn't be true. Her chain was definitely being yanked, for sure, in the name of family harmony. A role model—*her*? Now there was a laugh. Not just a laugh, it was an annoying, high-pitched *chortle*. A girl who had thrown away her childhood, gotten pregnant, married the wrong guy, cashiered and/or waitressed her way through her baby's earliest years, and chain-smoked her way through life. Her daughter thought of her as a *role model*? Suzanne dealt with her raging emotions the way she always did: with a lighter and some well-packed tobacco. She breathed deeply, evenly, trying to regain control of the cyclone inside her chest.

"Isn't this true, Molly?" Brandon asked pointedly.

Molly didn't say anything for a minute, but she didn't, Suzanne couldn't help but notice, deny it.

"It still doesn't change the fact," Molly finally pointed out, "that *your* family was so happy, they were practically dancing in the streets when you came out. Whereas, mine . . . Look at her, over there. She can't even look at me."

"Actually, Molly," Brandon interjected, "that's not why they were so happy."

"Brandon, I was *there*." She glared at him for stepping on her perfectly made point. "Don't try to rewrite history that I personally witnessed."

"Okay, then. Tell me." He leaned toward her. "What *exactly* did my brother say?"

"He said . . . well, he . . ." Molly frowned. She'd been so caught up in the moment, the specifics were hard to recall. "Give me a minute; I didn't memorize it." She sighed impatiently, and her leg, always the betrayer of her innermost feelings, started bouncing again. "It doesn't matter, okay? It doesn't matter *what* he said, what matters is how he felt. He was really happy, and *that's* what matters."

"I wasn't even there," Suzanne lit another cigarette, noting that her throat was starting to scratch, "and I remember what he said. They were so thrilled, so incredibly happy that he'd come out to them, because they already knew and were just *waiting* for him to tell them. And when he finally did, it was a *relief*. They felt like he finally *trusted* them."

"*So?*"

"So?" Suzanne looked at her, aghast. "So? *So?*" She leaped to her feet before she spat out, "So, Patty has been divorced for five years, and she has four kids!" She began pacing back and forth rapidly, like a hungry lion in a traveling circus, huffing and puffing all the while.

Brandon looked at Molly. "I'm sorry," he admitted, "but I'm going to need a translation for that one."

"Patty's one of her friends—she was one of the other moms in the drama club car pool," Molly told him. "She moved to Boston last year."

"And she has four kids. *Four.*" Suzanne repeated, holding up four fingers. "One, two, three, *four.* Anyway, Patty and I used to go grocery shopping together. With four kids, that can take quite a while, you know? And she homeschooled all of them, do you remember that?"

Brandon nodded, even though Suzanne's questions were directed at Molly. *At least he's listening*, Suzanne thought remorsefully. Molly's gaze was fixed firmly far off into the distance, down the street.

"So, she knew who was good at English and who needed special help with math and who wanted to take more years of a foreign language," Suzanne went on, her voice rising toward a fever pitch. "She knew which of her kids wouldn't eat mushrooms and that Andrew was allergic to onions and that Sarah's favorite jam was raspberry. And she was a single mom, so she did this all by herself . . ." Suzanne paused, trying to catch her breath.

Molly threw her hand in the air and waved desperately.

"Please the court," she cried, "is there a question or statement of pertinent fact anywhere in our future?"

"Molly, willya just . . ." Brandon began, but Suzanne cut him off.

"Don't you get it?" she asked, almost pleadingly. "Don't you? Think about it. Patty knew everything her kids wanted or needed, before they even had to ask it. Still does."

Molly was still not looking at her, but the sight of her beautiful profile in the sunlight brought back a thousand memories in one huge, bursting rush. Molly, her daughter, her baby, the little bundle they'd handed to her after two hours of labor, who had turned into the intelligent, confident, accomplished young woman sitting here before her.

"Patty's got four, but I've got *one*," Suzanne said, her throat so tight that speech was painful. She plowed on. "*One* kid. One beautiful, amazing, brilliant daughter. You. I always thought, no matter what else, you and I had this connection, this bond that nothing could touch. I thought we were strong and solid. I thought we were 'tight.'"

"I did too," Molly agreed icily. "Until recently, I really, really did."

"And I had no idea," Suzanne could hold it back no longer, and finally burst into tears, "none whatsoever, that you were a lesbian until you told me last week. *I didn't know!*"

And there it was. The sobs were coming hard and fast now, great gulping sobs of air. It was a relief to let it out, finally. Her bomb. Her big failure. Her lack of perception and her amazing blinders. Now the world would know.

"Ohh . . ." Brandon breathed, the light dawning on him. He put his much-inked arms around Suzanne and rocked her like a small child, as Molly looked from one of them to the other, still bewildered.

"Ooohhh?" she asked. "You don't get to do the understanding 'Ooohhh' to my mother while I still don't know what the fuck is going on. And I don't understand *at all* how my coming out leads you to feel all depressed and comparing yourself to Patty, who, by all accounts, is the perpetual motion machine."

After a few minutes, the worst of Suzanne's sob storm had passed. "I thought I knew you." Suzanne's words were muffled in the fabric of Brandon's shirt. He was still patting her comfortingly on the back, and frankly, it felt damn good. It had been a while since she'd let herself go to pieces and had someone there to put her back together. "I thought I knew you every bit as well as Patty knows her kids."

"Why do you keep bringing her up?" Molly demanded. "How well Patty knows her kids has nothing to do with us."

"Doesn't it?" Suzanne asked. "Because when push came to shove, I *didn't* know you, did I?"

"Mom, I . . ."

"And do you know what the first thing I thought of was, when you told us? Do you?"

"Do tell," Molly said in that same bored voice, but she was at least looking at her now, and that was something.

"The first thought I had was," Suzanne asked softly, "what else don't I know?"

Molly's arrogant, angry expression faded away. Now she looked confused.

"I mean, clearly we're not nearly as close as I thought," she rubbed her hands on her face, trying to stave off even more tears, "and that *hurts*, Molly. That really, really hurts. But you know what really kills me about all this?"

"No." Molly's tone was now genuinely curious.

Suzanne stopped pacing and looked directly into the face of her child.

"You went through it all alone," she whispered. "All by yourself. I had no idea. I just didn't know. And because I didn't know, I wasn't there."

"Mom . . ."

"I'll never forgive myself for that," Suzanne pressed on. "In fact, I *hate* myself for that. I could have been there. I *should* have been there." By force of habit, she tried to explain. "But there was so much going on—my jobs, all the stuff to do around the house. Then this year, I was so wrapped up in the idea of finally getting rid your dad and so terrified by the idea of being free of him. And damn it, I didn't see a thing. I should have, I should have. You were so independent, I thought." She paused to scrub away her tears, knowing her mascara was probably down to her collarbone by now. "I should have been paying more attention. I should have known something was . . ."

"I *wanted* you to be thinking about those things!" Molly suddenly erupted. "I was the one who *told* you to get rid of that asshole. From the time I was ten years old, I wanted you to divorce him. He was right there ignoring me and mooching off my time as much as he was yours, you know. Any chores he was supposed to be doing invariably got pawned off on me, unless I wanted to see you work another eight hours at home once you got home from a double shift. So, I mean, I know you didn't know, but how could you when . . ."

Suzanne was already shaking her head.

"Because you're my *daughter*, that's why! *My little girl!!* The most important thing in my life! I should have sensed something; I should have confronted you. Instead, you must have just . . . You were all alone. I didn't help you."

The image of Molly sitting alone in her room, lonely, scared, feeling like a freak, feeling like an outcast, considering all of the scary punishments for lesbians in the world, rose to her mind unbidden. Then came another image of herself netsurfing or reading or doing the dishes outside Molly's room, oblivious to the pain that was only a few feet away, and her nearly spent sobs were renewed. It was time to ask her the biggest question, the hardest question, the question that had choked her ever since she'd read about it.

"Did something happen to you to make you like this?" she managed to ask.

"Like this?" Molly asked, raising an eyebrow. Brandon gave her a look, and she let it go. "What do you mean, like this?"

"I read this article that said victims of sexual abuse sometimes . . ."

"Oh, my God, no." Molly immediately put a stop to that horrible thought. "No, Mom, *of course* not. If something like that had ever happened, I'd have told you. But no, nothing like that."

"Then how did it happen?" Suzanne asked.

"It doesn't really work on a 'how did it happen' kind of basis," Brandon began, but Molly interrupted yet again.

"*That's* why you've been so upset these past couple of days?" Molly asked incredulously.

Suzanne nodded, her face still buried in Brandon's flamboyant flame-colored shirt.

"Really? You're sure? Not even a little bit that you're disappointed that I'm . . ."

"A lesbian?" Suzanne pulled away from Brandon and rummaged through her pocketbook for a Kleenex. "Oh, for God's sake, Molly. I practically grew up in the theatre. There was a time, when I knew more gay couples than straight ones." She blew her nose good and hard. "I'm not going to lie to you, it was a shock at first, and it took me a day or so to get used to the idea."

"Really?"

"Well, sure." Suzanne blew her nose again for good measure. "It takes a little time to make a radical adjustment, you know? So now, instead of asking after boyfriends, I'll be asking after girlfriends, that sort of thing." She looked down; no use holding anything back now. "But, I'd be lying if I didn't say that I'm not worried. This isn't exactly an easy society to be gay in . . . for either gender."

"I know all that." Molly looked hard at her mother. "But if this was so easy for you to accept," she asked, and the hurt little girl inside her peeped out with these words, "then why have you been avoiding me?"

Suzanne touched Molly's hair, tucking it behind her ears. "I told you why, sweetie. Between marrying too young and missing college and job-hopping for the past eighteen years, there wasn't a whole lot I was proud of in my life," Suzanne admitted. "But I was proud of my relationship with *you*. My friendship with my only child. And it seemed like even *that* wasn't as good as I'd thought. I just can't believe that I had no idea whatsoever."

"None? None at all?" Brandon asked skeptically.

Suzanne elbowed him in the ribs. "None at all." She continued to stroke her daughter's hair. "Oh, honey, I'm so proud of who you are. Look at you, Molly. You're so . . . You're such a complete person. Far more so than I ever was, especially at your age. And even better, you're so comfortable with who you are, with where you're going. And I had nothing to do with that. I don't deserve a daughter like you."

A moment passed as Suzanne, struggling with her tears, gave into the desire for her tenth cigarette of the afternoon. Counting them up like they suggested online could cause depression, she'd read. But maybe that was the point.

"Well, that takes some of the wind out of my argument, Mom," Molly finally admitted. She took her mother's hands in her own. "Mom, you *did* help, you did. Whenever I was in one of my funks, you'd make me laugh or take me shopping. You always asked me what was wrong if I was grouchy, and you always laughed with me when I was goofy. But no offense, Mom, sometimes . . . How can I put this?"

"Sometimes, there's stuff you just aren't comfortable talking to Mommy about?" Brandon chimed in helpfully.

"Yeah, but see," Suzanne stammered, tears threatening to come again, "I always wished I had a mom I could talk to about that stuff. I told her the first time I slept with Steve, but that was it."

"Maybe deep down, you were hoping she'd have a stroke," Brandon guessed. It earned him a ghost of a smile from the two women, but it was the first smile he'd seen in a while, so he'd take whatever he could get.

"I always thought we were best friends, you know?" Suzanne said, her voice finally starting to return somewhat to normal. "At least, you were mine."

"We were, Mom!" Molly insisted. "I mean, we *are*! It wasn't like I woke up one morning and suddenly had it figured out. It took a long time before I could admit it to myself, even."

"Did you think I'd judge you?" Suzanne clutched Molly's hand tightly to her breast. "Did you think I'd try to deny it, or try to convince you it was some kind of crazy phase?" She paused for a second. "Hey, honey, it's not some kind of crazy phase, is it?"

Brandon burst out laughing, and Molly groaned.

"Just when I think you're the coolest mom of all time, you gotta throw a little bit of old-time, geeky fifties housewife in there," Molly sighed.

"Geez, Suze, up till then, you were doing so well," Brandon complained. "This is definitely going to affect your overall score by the judges' ruling."

"Hey!" she replied warningly. "I haven't said or done anything to embarrass my kid yet. I'm allowed a few dumb-assed remarks, aren't I? It's practically a parental prerequisite."

"Well, let's dial down the embarrassment factor on the Moll-ster just a little," Molly squeezed Suzanne's hands tightly, "and let me cut to the chase on a few major points. I've known I was attracted to girls—no, wait—I've *admitted* to myself that I was attracted to girls for about a year."

"How did you—I mean, what was it like for you before that? I always knew you weren't as into boys as other girls are, but I thought . . . well, you were so serious about your studies, and I thought you were just trying to avoid getting pregnant in high school like I did."

"Mom, not every single thing I do is a direct reflection of you." Molly rolled her eyes, exasperated.

"Stay on point, Molly," Brandon advised.

"Right, right." Molly was properly chastised. "Okay. Well, when all my girlfriends were gushing about cute boys, I sort of just went along for the ride. You know, pretended to have a crush on Matt Gruber because everyone else did."

Suzanne wrinkled her nose. Matt Gruber had been thrown out of high school amidst accusations of date rape and a proven case of prescription medication theft. Basically, he'd been the new millennium's equivalent of her ex-husband. Ex-husband, she thought. Wow, did that phrase feel good.

Time to revel later, she reminded herself. *Now it's time to listen . . . Listen like you've never listened before.*

"Yeah, yeah, I know. But it was sixth grade, who knew? I figured I was a late bloomer and sooner or later it would kick in for me." Molly shrugged. "But, then it never did. I thought I was sort of, I don't know, asexual. Like it just wasn't as important to me as other things were."

Suzanne nodded, relieved to hear that at least she had understood that part without being told anything.

"And this past year, you know, senior year, the big one, when three different guys asked me to the prom and everyone else was talking about what party or hotel room they'd get laid at after. The thought of getting intimate with any of those guys . . ." She shuddered. "And then I had to admit, the thought of being with any guy at all made me feel the same way. So, I finally had to admit to myself that boys just didn't do anything for me."

Suzanne nodded. "Well, with your father as an example, I could see why," she said sympathetically. Brandon winked.

"And," Molly squeezed her hands and looked deep into her mother's eyes, "before you ask yet *again*, I want you to know, it was nothing you did."

"Really?" Suzanne looked back into her daughter's eyes and saw nothing but sincerity reflected there. "Really? I didn't fail you in some way and turn you into a lesbian?"

Brandon groaned, but Molly's laughter rang throughout the courtyard. "It doesn't really work that way, Mom. And you didn't fail me."

"You promise?" Suzanne asked fervently. "You're not just saying that so I'll look better when I tell this story to my court-ordered shrink?"

"I swear, I'm not just saying it," Molly insisted. "I promise."

"Suze, trust me on this one," Brandon reassured her. "She's not just saying it."

"Thank God." Suzanne sighed, picking up her cigarettes and lighting one up. For once, Molly didn't make a face or feign a coughing fit. "Because, frankly, I thought if there was a Mother of the Year Award, I'd get the gold."

Molly smiled, then pretended to consider. "Maybe the silver," she said. "You'd have gotten the gold if you'd kicked Dad out sooner."

They smiled at each other then happily, both relieved, both with a new respect for the other, but knowing they didn't need to say it, in words.

"So, everything's cool?" Brandon asked softly.

"Almost. I just need an answer to the most important question," Suzanne began.

"Yes, Mom," Molly smiled. "I'm happy."

"Not that, silly." She looked at Molly expectantly. "Am I *ever* going to become a grandmother?"

"She's *gay!*" Brandon cried indignantly. Shocked, Suzanne pointed an accusing finger at him.

"Don't enforce your sexual roles and expectations on my child, thank you very much," she said haughtily.

"Geez, Mom, I don't know," Molly said, squirming a bit. "I'm only eighteen. I haven't even thought about it. Kids are quite a ways away for me, if at all, you know?"

"Well, you think about it." Suzanne cupped Molly's chin in her palm. "You're my only child, so you're my only chance at having grandchildren and therefore achieving total happiness in life . . . But no pressure."

"You're only thirty-six," Molly retorted. "You've got some time before that uterus stops ticking."

Suzanne started to groan but then remembered her date with Sean the previous night.

"You know, I guess that's not completely out of the question. Babies are so much fun," she added, sounding like Ava to her own ears. "Your grandmother was somewhat disappointed when she found out you weren't pregnant. Maybe I can make it up to her."

"Wow, Suze," Brandon howled. "You don't just land on your feet, you bounce back with a vengeance, don't you?"

"Well, I was mostly kidding, and what's with this 'Suze'?" Suzanne demanded. "I said you could call me Suzanne. I didn't say you could get cute with it."

He shook his head, smiling. "Sorry, Suze, it's stuck to you like gum to a bedpost."

Suzanne turned back to her daughter. "All that matters to me is that Molly Juliet Lauder is happy. And I can't be happy, ever, until I know that."

"I am happy, Mom," Molly told her. "But I'm not a Lauder."

"I hate to tell you, dear, but it's truly impossible for you to be anyone's but Steve's . . ."

"No, you goofball," Molly admonished. "I'm giving up the name Lauder. I've got no emotional connection to it whatsoever."

"What are you changing your name to?" Brandon asked.

Molly looked at her mother for a moment, her eyes dancing. "I was going to tell you and Grandma together, but . . . the thing is, I'm changing my name to Applebaum," she said proudly. "I want to be like you and Grandma, and I want the world to know it."

Suzanne hugged Molly tightly again. It had been such a relief to go back to her maiden name; it almost felt like reclaiming herself again. For her daughter to want to join her, it was a gesture so sweet that it was beyond tears.

"Wait a minute," she paused, suspicious, "Grandma didn't offer you money to do it, did she?"

"Nope." Molly shook her head proudly. "I thought of it all on my own. After all, I'm just as much Applebaum as I am Lauder, and frankly, I'd like to fumigate the Lauder part of my genes. This is a good start."

"You *are* happy," Suzanne said, and it wasn't a question. "And if you're happy, then I'm happy. That's all that matters to me."

Molly's own tears started now, trickling black eye makeup all the way down her cheek. In Suzanne's mind, it did nothing to make her look less lovely. "You're the best, Mom," she said tearfully, throwing herself into her mother's arms.

"No," Suzanne corrected her, "you're the best!"

Brandon couldn't stand it anymore, and he burst out crying. "I promised myself I wasn't going to do this!" He threw his long arms around both of them.

Suzanne and Molly laughed, and for the next few minutes, the three of them rocked in one long, crazy hug, laughing, squeezing, and crying. It was crazy, dopey, and very, very good.

TWENTY

"Are you sure this dressy is a good idea?" Buddy asked doubtfully as he fiddled with his tie. "This seems awfully fancy for a date in the front yard."

"See, the chinos balance out the dress shirt and the silk tie." Brandon straightened it for him, leaning back with a critical eye. "I wish you'd have let me talk you into a pair of distressed jeans. Now that's a look."

"I'm sorry, I don't do jeans," Buddy said firmly. "Reminds me of all those peacenik bums who were throwing shit at the buses and calling me a 'baby killer' when I got home from the war."

"No war talk tonight." Brandon firmly tapped Buddy's shoulder. "The ladies find it a turnoff."

"How the hell would you know?" Buddy asked.

The man had a point.

"Okay, *I'd* find it a turnoff," Brandon admitted, "and I'm not a girl, but I have opinions just as strong as one." He picked a brush and went to work on Buddy's hair. "There's this one cowlick that doesn't want to lie down, no matter what I do."

"That's been there since the day I was born," Buddy said cheerfully. "It was the bane of my mother's existence."

Finally Brandon stepped back, finished with his transformation.

"Okay," he said proudly. "You look great."

"Great?" Buddy asked in dismay. "*Great* is all I get? I thought you fellas were supposed to be all up on sensitivity and stuff. Look at me. I'm practically shitting my pants here. You're gonna have to do a lot better than a one-word compliment, even if the word is 'great.'"

"You're right, I'm sorry. My bad." Brandon clasped his hands together and clicked his heels, ever the good servant. "You're regal, you're elegant, you're the man. You're a tiger. A tiger trapped in the body of a man with the legs of a stallion."

"Okay, you've officially made me nervous," Buddy said flatly. "But that's better. So, I'm ready?"

"You're ready," Brandon pronounced him. "You've been ready for this for several decades now, and you damn well know it."

"And then some," Buddy told him, glancing out the window. His beaming face fell just a bit. "She's not out there."

"She's waiting for you to be out there first," Brandon informed him, standing. "That's a lady's game. Come on, let's go out and get the table all set up."

"You sure?" Buddy worried that maybe she'd changed her mind. The last thing he wanted to be was the schmuck standing in front of her picnic table in chinos and a silk tie while the moon shone brightly overhead, mocking him.

"I'm *sure*. You know how they like to make the big entrances," Brandon said. "Trust me, I know this one."

"For someone who's not attracted to women, you sure seem to know an awful lot about them," Buddy commented.

"Maybe because we think alike," Brandon guessed, opening the door for him and bowing low. "Up, up, and away!"

Buddy shuffled out the door, thinking of his little secret, the bottle he'd picked up and stashed in his bedside table, where even in the mightiest of cleaning fits Brandon wouldn't look. Ava was a lady, but there was no sense in not being prepared, not living up to the Boy Scout code. The name on the label might be Viagra, but it was really a bottle of hope for men of all ages.

Up, up, and away, indeed.

"Laura wants to know if you went with the white suit," Suzanne called from the kitchen, the portable phone pressed to her ear. "She thinks that would be great with your coral-colored shell."

"She did. She's just putting on the last touches of makeup," Molly called back.

"What did she do for a necklace?" Laura asked, her tone suggesting that this was a matter of incredible importance rather than a simple accessory.

Maybe witches have a thing about jewelry, Suzanne thought. *They sure as hell wear enough of it.*

"Mom!" Suzanne called. "Laura wants to know what necklace!"

"Tell her the pearls," Ava bellowed back.

"She went with pearls," Suzanne informed her. "The ones Grandpa gave her when she graduated."

"Single strand or double?"

"Single."

"Good." Laura nodded on her end. "Classic, elegant, never goes out of style. Perfect. Earrings to match?"

"My mother wouldn't leave the house without earrings to match," Suzanne said wryly. "But they're dainty pearls, not those god-awful great big fake monstrosities you see on little old ladies at the mall."

Molly rushed out of the bathroom beaming, clasping her hands in excitement. "Wait till you see her," she gushed. "She's a *vision*. She looks like a *model*."

"For cream for mature skin or for adult diapers?" Ava asked airily, floating out into the kitchen and twirling slowly. "Do I have anything stuck to my ass? And while we're at it, does my ass look like a buffalo's in these slacks?"

"Grandma!" Molly said, swatting at her. "You look fabulous, and you know it. You do yoga at least once a week, and you walk half an hour a day, and that pays off. I'd kill for your glutes."

"Me too," Laura shouted over the phone.

"Okay, Laura, I've gotta hang up now. We're about to put the *HMS Ava* out to sea," Suzanne said happily.

"You call me the *second* she gets back with all the details," Laura warned, "or there will be swift and terrible retribution."

"I promise! I said I promise three times! Geez, trust a girlfriend, wouldja?"

Laura lowered her voice to a whisper, so only Suzanne would hear it. "And we can also talk about what you're going to wear to the dinner you're having with Mr. Sean next week."

"Shh!" Suzanne glanced over at Molly and Ava, who were looking at her eyelashes in a hand mirror, trying to decide if Ava should use fake eyelashes or not. She lowered her voice. "I haven't told them yet. I didn't want anything to distract them from this evening. I'll tell them tomorrow, I promise."

"If you don't, I will!" Laura sang happily before hanging up.

Molly placed her hand on Suzanne's shoulder, heaving a mock sigh. "You think you're prepared for it, you spend years telling yourself it's only a matter of time, but then, it finally happens . . ." She paused to wipe a fake tear away. "Your Grandma finally starts dating."

"Oh, hush, you," Ava scolded, but she was obviously pleased.

Suzanne whistled. "I don't know how to tell you this, Mom," she sighed, "but you look absolutely, completely, drop-dead gorgeous."

Ava looked in the mirror. "I do, don't I?" she said proudly. "Not bad for a broad on the farther reach of sixty-ish." She closed her compact and slipped it into her purse. "Okay, here I go."

"Mom?" Suzanne called out warningly. "Don't be late. If you're going to be late, call. And just because he buys you dinner doesn't mean you owe him anything."

"Boys like it when you play hard to get," Molly offered.

Ava turned to her, exasperated. "The man has been lusting after me secretly since we were teenagers," she reminded her granddaughter. "How much harder could I be to get than that?"

Molly smiled impishly. "Then don't forget to bring protection."

"What for?" Ava wanted to know. "Neither one of us has had sex since you'd have to worry about such things . . . And I'm pretty sure I won't get pregnant."

"Buddy's been on the sex wagon?" Molly's eyes widened. "Wow, from the stories Mom's told me . . ."

"Yeah, but in my experience, the more you brag, the less you do it," Ava said loftily. "Besides, I asked him."

"You did *what?*"

"I asked him."

Molly was laughing so hard her stomach hurt. "You mean, you called him up and said, 'Hey, how's it going? And by the way, when was the last time you got down and dirty?'"

"No." Ava looked down her nose at her granddaughter. "I did no such thing. I called him to ask if he liked the muffins, and then I asked him—discreetly—when the date of his last, shall we say, intimate contact was."

"Tell us!" Molly demanded, and Suzanne nodded. "No fair dropping a bomb and then not giving us the details!"

But Ava was shaking her head.

"Let's just say," she allowed, "that it couldn't be safer sex if we were both wearing full body rubber suits."

"You know what?" Suzanne said suddenly, "I think that Daddy would really, really have liked this."

Ava turned to her, her eyes both fearful and hopeful. "Do you really think so, dear?"

"I do," Suzanne nodded. "I think he'd have hated for any other man to have you, but if he couldn't be with you, I think he'd pick Buddy to be next in line, every time."

"So do I, Grandma," Molly echoed enthusiastically. "Buddy's just . . . well, he *rocks.* He's good people."

"I'll have to tell him you said so," Ava said wryly. "Okay." She drew a deep breath, checked her lipstick one last time in the hall mirror, and squared her shoulders. "Okay, girls, off I go."

"Ladies don't do it on the first date!" Suzanne and Molly called in unison and then dissolved into giggles. Ava rolled her eyes. Sometimes, those two, when they got the giggles, there was no stopping them. Now that the tension was gone around the house, all she had to worry about was Suzanne and her disgusting devotion to tobacco.

"None of that tonight," she told herself aloud. "No worrying tonight. Tonight's for me. For me and Buddy."

And from far, far away, she could have sworn she heard Jimmy say, *You go get him, kid . . . You're too great a treasure to stay buried forever.*

She opened the door and started down the stairs.

"You're sure I can't talk you into a little foundation?" Brandon asked. He was setting up the final touches of the picnic table: two glasses, a bottle of sparkling cider on ice, a boom box quietly playing romantic music. He lit the candles, and the spread was perfect.

"Yes, I'm sure," Buddy replied. "I'm as modern as any man my age would be, but I draw the line at makeup."

"Okay." Brandon took a quick inventory. "Got the candles, got the drinks, got the music, got the citronella candles so you won't get eaten alive by no-see-ums . . . All we need now is the girl!" he sang, gleefully quoting Gilbert and Sullivan.

"I think that must be my cue." They heard Ava's voice cut through the dusk. "Although, I must admit, it's been a while—several months at least—since anyone's called me a girl."

Buddy then saw Ava come down the stairs, her fingertips daintily trailing the handrail.

"Wow, Ava," Brandon marveled. "You make me think that the straight guys might know what they're talking about, after all."

"Do you think?" She turned her eyes to Buddy. "What do you think, Mr. McKinley?"

It took a moment for Buddy to answer, and when it did, he breathed, "Wow."

"Okay, I'm going to take a powder," Brandon announced, clapping Buddy on the shoulder. Buddy reached for him, suddenly nervous at the thought of being alone with her. "Hold up a sec," he said, fumbling. "I think the CD player is . . ."

"Fine." Brandon leaned in close to Buddy, whispering, "The CD player is fine, and so are you. You've got this one covered, Superstud. And to give you privacy, I'm going to hang over at Molly and Suzanne's tonight."

"Don't you mean Ava's?" Ava complained, pouting her lower lip out seductively. "I'm the one paying the mortgage; I should at least get first dibs on the title."

"Fine, I'll be at Ava's, doing my nails, just a screech away." Brandon bowed low to the lady—his big move of the night—and leapt up the stairs.

"Make sure you open the windows first this time!" Buddy called after him. "Trust me," he told Ava, "last time he did that, it took three days to get rid of the smell."

"I'm used to it," she told him. "Been sniffing the fumes since I was twelve. Whatever brain cells the booze didn't get, I lost to acetone."

Buddy chuckled and then stepped back to get the full view of Ava in her outfit, bathed in candlelight. "You look lovely," he said simply.

"Thank you for saying it." She touched her hand to her pearls, then patted her hair, shaking it a little so the back flowed over her shoulders in auburn waves. It made Buddy's mouth go dry. "When Brandon decided to give me a makeover, and then tonight when the girls were fussing over me, telling me what to wear, I was afraid I would look a little silly."

"No, you don't look silly." He couldn't stop looking at her, couldn't really believe she was here, with him. "Silly is definitely not the word that leaps to mind."

Ava gazed at him then, in the soft light.

"You look just the same," she said tenderly. "Minus the dimmed lights of the Rochester Community Center, of course." They shared a laugh about that, and Ava realized suddenly that she already shared a lifetime of memories with this man.

"I have to tell you," Buddy confided, "I've replayed this moment over and over again in my mind for quite some time now. Not that I thought it would ever happen, outside my dreams, that is."

"I did too," she admitted. "Couple of times, anyway."

"You *did*?"

She smiled. "Don't sound so surprised; you're not an easy man to forget, Buddy McKinley. Certainly several dozen of the ladies in your life have told you *that*."

"Yeah. But it didn't mean a damn thing, coming from any of them."

"Why?"

"Because," he shrugged, "they weren't you."

Ava heard his words and let them sink in for a moment. "For a while," she recalled, "I just felt so guilty. I hated leading you on, I hated hurting you, I hated breaking up with you at all. But I just couldn't get that telegram. Two of my girlfriends got that telegram, and they were never the same. You were so upset, I thought you probably hated me, and then when Jimmy started writing . . ."

Buddy held up his hand; no need to go on. It was water that had long since passed under the bridge.

"And then," she continued, "you were our best friend. Part of the damn family, even. You were the first person to hold Suzanne after she was born. Every Christmas, every Thanksgiving, every Fourth of July, there you were, with your flavor of the moment . . . Every one of them gorgeous, and most of them even able to carry on a conversation with words that were multisyllabic."

"Dumb women never did much for me," he agreed.

"And then, after the restaurant business," she clapped her hands over her eyes, shaking her head, "I hated you. Oh, how I hated you!" She giggled again, the moonlight shining in her hair. "But in all that, I *never* forgot you. Not ever."

Buddy tried to think of something witty to say; nothing came to mind.

"Hey, do you want some champagne?" he asked, fishing the bottle out of the ice bucket. When he saw her doubtful gaze, he hastily added, "Well, you know, not champagne, but that stuff that looks like champagne."

"That would be delightful." Her ladylike grace was on full tilt that night.

"Here you are." He carefully handed her a champagne glass not quite filled to the rim. "To . . ." He searched his mind, but he didn't want to come on too strong too fast. Brandon had warned him that too much gushy right up front could be a turn-off. "Your hair," he said at last. "I always loved your hair."

"Really?" She shook it out again so the light from the candles danced in her golden highlights. Buddy wanted to plunge his hands into it, but he managed to control himself. "I always loved your eyes," she continued. "Not just blue. Dark, dark blue. That's rare."

"Oh, sure, as if you could see them," he tapped his frames, "behind these lenses."

"Sure you could," she softly contradicted. "All you had to do was look hard enough."

Out of the corner of his eye, Buddy could see the kids and Suzanne peering at them through the window. They were having a merry old time spying, then shoving each other out of the way for a better look.

So this is what it would have been like to have children and grandchildren.

He supposed it was the closest he'd ever get, but he didn't mind that. No, those kids (he still thought of Suzanne as a kid, thirty-six years old or not) were pretty damn special, and he wouldn't trade a single one of them, even if they weren't actually flesh and blood.

"I can't believe this." He gestured around, his faux champagne sloshing just a little in his cup. "See? Look at my hand. See how nervous you make me?"

"Blame me, will you?" She turned on the boom box. Brandon and Molly had been in charge of the music, and they'd assured Buddy that he'd be pleased. After a moment, the Byrds's "Turn, Turn, Turn" came flowing from the speakers. "Ah, real music!" Ava cried happily. "Never has there been any decade that could touch the music of the sixties. *Ever.*"

"I agree with you completely."

"Care to ask a girl to dance?" Ava batted her eyelashes coyly, just like Brandon had taught her.

For a startling second, Buddy was catapulted right back to that dance, all those years ago, when Ava had uttered those exact words to him.

"Sure," he said. "But I'm warning you: I've got two left feet. You'll be the one needing a cane by the time we're done." He tentatively put his arms around her. She responded by putting hers around him, firmly.

"See? You're doing fine," she chided him. "In fact, I feel like I'm walking on air."

"Yeah, whaddya know?" Buddy asked, pleased with himself. That afternoon's worth of dance lessons with Brandon and Molly was really paying off. "I guess I'm not so bad, after all."

"I appreciate you letting me lead with grace and dignity," she told him.

"Considering the option was falling flat on my ass," he admitted, "it wasn't a difficult decision."

They danced in silence for a moment, drinking in the night.

"You know, on the day I first saw you here, I wouldn't have believed I'd ever be saying this, but . . . I'm so glad you moved in next door, you big jerk."

"I wish I could say I planned it," Buddy said wistfully. "That would be romantic as hell—would make a good story. I can see the headline: OLD BACHELOR CAN'T LIVE WITHOUT HIS FIRST LOVE, SO TRACKS HER DOWN IN THEIR TWILIGHT YEARS." Oh, now he'd gone and mentioned love. He hoped it wasn't too soon, but Ava didn't seem to notice.

"Sure. And if you look in the dictionary, you won't find the world gullible," Ava scoffed.

Buddy shrugged, and Ava stopped the dance dead in its tracks.

"You can't tell me, oh, my goodness, you honest-to-Goshen didn't know?" she asked suspiciously. "It's okay. You can tell me if you did. I won't be mad. I'll be flattered. Can you imagine how jealous Liz Isermann will be? I'm actually surprised she hasn't made a move for you already."

"What would be an example of one of Liz's moves?"

"Oh, she's got a bagful," Ava snorted. "But her classic is knocking on the door and telling you she's got car trouble. Then she'll ask you to pop her hood and help get her running."

"Oh, Lord" Buddy winced. "I like direct, but that's a bit on the too-easy side."

"Or, she'd drop off a casserole that she made, insist on heating it up for you, and drop enough hints until you couldn't help but invite her to eat it with you."

"Ah," he nodded. "Okay, if she comes over, I'll just sic Brandon on her."

"Anyway," Ava demanded, "don't think you're getting out of answering the question. You really, honestly, swear-on-your-life didn't know I lived here?"

"I'm telling you: I really, really didn't know." He shook his head. "Frankly, my dear, if I *had* known, I don't think I'd have dared. You, ahem, f-ing hated me for years, you know."

"Sssshhhh!" She covered his mouth gently with her hand. "I just hate that word, Buddy. Even if you only say 'f-ing.' What can we say? What is it that they do on television when something's live, they . . ."

"They bleep it?" Buddy offered.

"That's it! *Bleeping.* That's it, we'll call it bleeping. I bleeping hated you." She grinned at him with satisfaction, then she ducked her head and looked up at him, shyly. "And I didn't hate you, Buddy. Not really. You know that. I hated what happened." Ava looking up at him with those big dark eyes was almost too much to bear.

"Me too." Then he brightened. "Hey, maybe Jimmy talked to some guys up in heaven, and it appealed to their sense of irony."

Ava laughed, "Suzanne said something really similar right before I left."

"Did she, now?" His smile broadened. "Well, you know what they say about great minds thinking alike, and all that sh . . . jazz." He corrected himself at the last minute, and the effort was not lost on Ava.

"Stranger things have happened. I can't think of any just now, but I'm sure they have." She gazed into his eyes, giddy with happiness. "I feel like I know you so well in some ways—I mean, all that time together, all those long talks after your dates never worked out. But it's still been a long time. Things to learn." She laid her head on his shoulder, leaning on him a bit.

"I like that," he told her.

"You like what?"

"When you . . . when you leaned on my shoulder, just now." He cleared his throat. "It's really, well, it's nice."

"It is, isn't it?" she sighed. "It's been such a long time since we last spoke."

"Well, civilly, that is," he pointed out.

She wrinkled her nose, nodding. "And it's all my fault."

"It's no one's fault, or it's everyone's." He stroked her hair softly, and her knees went rubbery. "So let's just get over that. What matters is now. We've got time. Well, some, anyway."

"Time," mused Ava. "It goes by so fast, doesn't it? It truly seems like just a few months ago Suzanne was telling me that she wasn't going to college because she was going to have a baby. And then Molly was *walking* and off to school herself. Then, of course, our Jimmy was getting sick." She stopped herself. It was okay to talk about him, but she didn't want to cry for him, not tonight. Tonight was for something altogether different.

Buddy glanced up to see the peepers, still fighting over the front spot in the window. There were at least three other windows they'd be visible from, Buddy figured, but the Three Stooges apparently hadn't thought of that.

"We've got an audience, you know. Don't look now."

"Do we?" She caught them out of the corner of her eye as Buddy spun her around slowly, in time to the music. Now it was "Mr. Tambourine Man," another one of her favorites. "Well, will you just look at those little busy-bodies? We should really give them something to look at, as long as they're going to watch, don't you think?"

"Sure." Buddy peeked again at the crew at the window. "What did you have in . . ."

He never got to finish the sentence, because Ava grabbed his face with both hands and planted her soft lips on his.

He forgot their audience. He forgot every other woman that he'd ever kissed. He forgot the smell of the citronella candle. He forgot his own name. It was, by far, the sweetest, most meaningful kiss of his life.

"There!" Ava batted her eyelashes prettily again. Brandon was right. This flirting thing was just like riding a bike, something you never really forgot. "That should keep them busy for a while."

"Uh, I guess," Buddy said shakily, trying to compose himself. It seemed he might not need that Viagra, after all. "Well. So. What do we do now?"

"In a little while," she told him sweetly, "I want to go into your house. Tie a kerchief on the knob—Brandon'll know what it means. We'll be all alone."

"All alone? You mean," he innocently raised an eyebrow, "you mean that we'll . . ."

"I mean," she smiled coyly, "we'll have a little privacy."

"We will?" He couldn't resist asking. "Like what?"

"Well, we can talk," she shrugged casually. "We can watch a movie, we can look through photo albums, drink tea, laugh, cry. Or maybe we could just go into the bedroom and see if we both remember what it's for. Away from the peanut gallery."

He cleared his throat. "That would be nice."

"Sorry to be so bold," she apologized, "but dancing with you, well, it's nice. It got me to thinking that maybe other things might be fun too."

"They just might, at that," he admitted. "So, Miss Ava, sky's the limit. Just what do you want to do till it's time to go in?"

She looked up at him, and he thought that he'd never seen such a happy look on her pretty face.

"I suppose," she raised herself to her tiptoes and kissed him again, this time softly, "we just keep dancing."